HORN OF WINTER

A RELIC HUNTERS NOVEL

KERI ARTHUR

With thanks to:

The Lulus
Indigo Chick Designs
Hot Tree Editing
Dominic Wakeford Editorial
Robyn E.
The lovely ladies from Indie Gals
Julie from Cover Craft/ Covers by Julie

CHAPTER
ONE

THE GENTLE RUMBLE OF TRAFFIC RAN ACROSS THE CHILLY NIGHT
air, breathing a sense of life into an otherwise dead area.
The night was clear but bitterly cold; frost danced across
the neatly cut grass and gave the nearby gravestones a
luster age otherwise denied them.

Cemeteries were not one of my favorite places to be. I
simply couldn't understand the human need to commemo-
rate the dead by raising often elaborate tombs over their
loved ones' bones, especially when those same tombs were
left to decay as the years went on and visiting the dead
became less of a priority or even slipped from memory.

Pixies spread the ashes of our dead in the ancient
forests of our homelands—although technically, we
Aodhán pixies no longer had a homeland. We maintained a
connection to the ancient Ysbryd forests, but most of us had
lived in cities ever since we'd lost the job of guarding the
relics of the old gods eons ago.

I was only here tonight because I'd learned this cemetery was inhabited by a ghul, and I was hoping it might be
able to provide some much-needed information. While

ghuls did like to feed on flesh, their preference was for decaying, not fresh. They were for the most part insubstantial but fearsome-looking beings who held a very deep fascination for the living. It wasn't unknown for them to choose a "target" to follow through the night, listening to their conversations and watching their movements. Which, according to my mother, made them the ultimate gossip gathers with eons of information behind them. As far as I was aware, she'd never used this particular ghul, but she had regularly talked to one up in the Peak District. I have no idea why she'd travel that far, but if there was one thing I'd learned over the last few months, it was how much I *didn't* know about my mother and what she did beyond the realms of running the family's tavern.

And now she was dead—murdered.

I sucked in a deep breath and resolutely pushed away the grief that automatically rose. I hadn't yet allowed myself to properly grieve for her—even after we'd found her body—and I remained utterly determined not to do so until I found her killers and brought them to justice.

Or killed them.

I frowned at the dark ferocity rumbling through that thought. Revenge never went well for us pixies. In fact, killing in general—unless in self-defense—was generally very bad news. Both the Aodhán and Tàileach pixies— who'd co-guarded the relics with us before a light-fingered ancestor of mine had spoiled the gig for everyone, and who were the only other human-sized pixies of the five branches here in the UK—were notoriously hard to kill, but like every gift a god gave, there was a flip side.

In this case, it was the blood curse.

Basically, if you shed blood without just cause, you doomed your offspring to a miserable existence or faced servitude to the dead person's family until the debt was paid off—and the length of time spent in said servitude was decided by the old gods, not the relatives. Given the predilection of those gods for causing chaos in the lives of humans, and the likelihood of the punishment extending centuries rather than years, few of us ever dared put the curse to the test.

I certainly didn't want to be the first in my family to do so, especially when there were already too many old gods interfering in my life.

The barely audible whisper of steps had me looking around. Mathi Dhār-Val—who was not only a former lover but also the liaison between me and Deva's Fae Council, who I now worked for—strolled casually toward me, snappily dressed in a long blue trench, crisp black trousers, and shiny black boots. Like all Ljósálfar elves, he was lean in build but absolutely divine to look at—golden skin and hair, angelic features, and eyes the color of summer skies. We'd been together for nearly ten years before splitting eight or so months ago, and although I'd always known he was not my one true love—and could never be, in fact, given he was a highborn light elf, and they only married their own kind *and* rank—I'd always enjoyed his company. I still did, although we would never again be bed buddies.

I pointedly glanced at my watch and said, "And what time do you call this?"

"An inconvenient and ungodly time, that's what." Though his tone was cool, amusement danced through his eyes. "There are few people I'd get out of bed for at three in the morning, dear Bethany—"

"But plenty you'd get *into* bed with at three in the morning," I cut in, amused.

"Well, yes, that goes without saying." He stopped

beside me and stared at the old wrought iron gates. "Why, exactly, are we here? I wasn't really listening when you rang. I was in the midst of fornicating with a delicious prospect."

Amusement twitched my lips. "A future-wife-type prospect?"

"Yes, although in all honesty, I doubt I'll be making any sort of offer. She's perfect in the bedroom but somewhat tedious outside of it."

My amusement grew. "I can't imagine she reacted all that well to proceedings being so rudely interrupted by a former lover."

"I am not a man to leave things unfinished and that is, of course, the reason I am late."

"Your dedication to satisfactory endings is something I always appreciated during our time together." My voice was dry. "But why—given highborn marriages are considered little more than business and breeding transactions—does it matter if she's boring beyond the bedroom? It's not like you'll be faithful to her. That's not the Ljósálfar way."

"We may not believe in love or indeed fidelity, but divorce is not usually an option thanks to the contracts signed. I find myself needing at least some degree of compatibility in *all* matters, not just sexual, with the woman I'm going to spend the rest of my life with." His glance was somewhat pointed. "We do have very long lives, remember."

I laughed. "I *have* spoiled you for other women, haven't I?"

"Quite possibly so." He motioned to the gate. "What lies beyond them that is so important you drag me out of not only a warm bed, but the arms of an even warmer woman?"

"A ghul."

"Of course." There was an odd sort of resignation in his voice. "Why else does one come to a cemetery at three in the morning if not to talk to a ghul or a ghost?"

"This particular ghul has apparently been haunting the area for as long as there has been a cemetery here, and may or may not know what guards the old scrolls that were part of the Éadrom Hoard."

Though those scrolls remained safely tucked away in the Ljósálfar's vaults, the hoard had been stolen the same day Mom had been killed. We now knew Mom had probably been trying to stop the theft and had been betrayed and murdered by someone she trusted. We had no idea who that person was.

Yet.

"And why am I here? It's not like you need to be guarded, given you're no doubt wearing your knives." He paused, and his gaze skimmed my length. "By the way, that has to be the ugliest coat I have ever seen. It hides your luscious curves and makes you look like a pale green marshmallow."

"But I'm a very warm marshmallow."

"Who cannot easily access her knives."

"You forget they're not ordinary knives and I don't actually have to physically draw them. I just have to imagine them in my hand, and voilà, there they are."

In truth, I hadn't actually done that very often, mainly because it tended to wreck whatever coat I was wearing, and that was a problem if said coat was expensive or a favorite. I was only wearing the knives tonight out of habit more than any real concern that we'd be in danger, but given how wrong even the simplest of tasks had gone of late, I wasn't about to take any chances, either. These knives—which weren't only goddess-blessed but also immune to magic—had saved my life more than once.

He pushed open the wrought iron gate and ushered me through. "That still does not explain why I am here."

"This particular ghul apparently has a liking for gorgeous, golden-haired men, and if they're elves, all the better."

"I'm *bait?*"

My grin broke free again. "And very natty-looking bait you are too."

He shut the gate with a soft clang, and the noise echoed across a darkness inhabited by forgotten tombs, gorgeous old trees, and the occasional wisp of a ghost. The latter kept well away from us; as a general rule, the ghosts found in cemeteries tended to be rather elusive, even with those they'd called family. Gran had once told me it was because they feared acknowledging their death or even their kin would force them on to whatever fate awaited—and most of them feared *that* would be hell rather than heaven.

I'd never actually known how much of Gran's stories to believe—I'm sure most of them had a large kernel of truth, but she'd had the gift of the gab and always tended to embellish a story.

"If she tries to nibble my neck," he said, as we followed the path that swept gently to the right, "I will not react well."

"She won't nibble. She may run her fingers through your hair and demand a lock of it in payment for answering questions, however."

He stared at me for a second. "Next time you want someone to play bait, invite your brother. Or better yet, Eljin."

"Eljin definitely fits the sexy bill, but he's a Tàileach

pixie, not an elf." As for Lugh, well, he was a six-foot-six giant of a man, and his sheer size tended to intimidate more fragile creatures such as ghosts or ghuls. Or so he claimed. In very many ways he took after Gran and definitely wasn't above embellishing a story. "A lock of hair is a small price to pay if we get an answer."

Mathi's sniff was a disbelieving sound if ever I heard one. "Knowing what guards the scrolls isn't likely to help, given no one on the council actually knows the location of them."

"Someone on the council must know something." I motioned him toward the smaller path that led down into a dell and the oldest part of the cemetery. "Carla apparently got the contact details of one of the bibliothecaries from someone there, remember."

That bibliothecary was now dead, of course, so we couldn't exactly get any answers out of him, and Carla Wilson had not been sighted since murdering some of her "clients" in jail. The woman *behind* the Carla Wilson identity remained very much alive, however. As a multi-shifter, she was able to assume the form of anyone she touched for a reasonable length of time, and we now suspected she had a swath of different personas she could slip into.

Unfortunately, none of us had any idea which one she was currently using. She had appeared in a number of my visions, but I'd only ever heard her Carla identity, and given different forms would have different speech patterns, that probably meant it was her original. Every time I'd visioned her, she'd been speaking to the man we suspected was the key behind the hoard's theft *and* my mother's murder, which made it doubly frustrating that they'd been voice only, rather than a mix of sight and sound like most of the others.

While *that* might be due to my inexperience with second sight—the gift did run through our family, but mine had only appeared very recently—it could also be due to the fact that the man appeared to not only be using a voice modulator, but also some type of invisibility shield. They were expensive, and illegal, but very readily available on the black market if you had the right contacts.

Or so Cynwrig had told me....

A swift stab of longing rose, and I grimly pushed it away. He and I were likely over, and there was nothing I could do about it, not even call or text. I knew better than to even try. His father—who was the king of the Myrkálfar elves—had died five days ago, leaving him and his twin sister to jointly rule. Three-month mourning period aside, he'd have no time for casual dalliances, no matter how incandescent the attraction between the two of us might be. I'd known going in that ours was a relationship destined to burn bright then flame out, and I'd willingly accepted it. I'd just never expected the deep and intense connection that had so quickly developed. It was something I'd never experienced with a man of my own race, let alone one outside of it. I didn't even have that type of connection with Eljin, though I enjoyed his company immensely, and he was certainly the only real long-term prospect currently in my life. Granted, our relationship was still very new, and a deeper connection might well develop given time, but I rather suspected part of me would always yearn for the man I could never have.

"Even if you do manage to uncover what guards the scrolls," Mathi was saying, "I can't see how it's going to help, given the council has already said you will not be able to view them."

"No, they said they were dangerous to the mortal eye,

but I'm the daughter of a minor god of storms. That might just give me a pass into places others cannot go."

A smile tugged his lovely lips. "Be that as it may, it does not negate the fact the council will never give us the location. We're better off trying to find the scrolls your mother took from Loudon. They, at least, might provide information on who is behind the Ninkilim."

The Ninkilim were a secret society dedicated to bringing Ninkil—a god who reveled in destruction—back from his earthly banishment. Loudon Fitzgerald was an elven dealer of antiquities who'd at one point been Mom's lover, but over the course of the last sixty years or so had become a trusted source of information. He also happened to be the secretary for the Ninkilim—the organization behind the theft of the hoard. Someone had recently tried to kill him—and almost taken me out in the process—so he obviously could name names. As far as I knew, he hadn't yet, but he was being protected by the Interspecies Investigation Team, and I had no doubt they'd eventually get him talking. Mathi's father—who ran the IIT's daytime division—certainly had a reputation for cracking the most difficult nut.

"It's on my to-do list," I replied, "but there's only so many things I can tackle at the one time."

He gave me a shocked look, though mirth danced through his blue eyes. "What is this? Bethany Aodhán finally admitting she cannot do it all?" He lightly touched my forehead. "I'm not feeling a temperature...."

I laughed and knocked his hand away. "Idiot."

Up ahead, a wisp of fog briefly stirred, though elsewhere the cold night remained free of its presence. No surprise there, given this wasn't actually fog but rather our ghul giving notice that she'd seen us but hadn't yet decided whether to reveal herself or not. We continued on down the sloping path, past tombstones that were no longer legible and graves so old only a few stone markers or rusted ironwork hinted at their location, eventually reaching the small bowl-shaped seating area. Grand old oaks ringed the area, their gentle song of contentment filling the air, and the golden rivers of energy that pulsed through their limbs and leaves were so bright it was almost blinding. Humans tended to believe it was only light elves who could manipulate trees, but both the Aodhán and Tàileach pixies had that skill. The difference between us and elves was our ability to manipulate *all* wood—not just trees, but anything made from them. Time, usage, and even the thickness of paint or stain could curtail that ability, but healing and rebuilding wooden structures remained a booming business for many in either line.

Just not mine or indeed Eljin's. Like my brother, he was a relic hunter, and in fact now worked with Lugh at the Fae Museum.

I let myself drown in the beauty of the trees' song for a couple of seconds, then sighed and said, "We wish to speak to she who is the mistress of this necropolis."

The tendril of filmy gray stirred briefly to our left, then a surprisingly cultured, if whispery, voice said, "And what might you seek from said mistress?"

"Information."

"Few know of my existence. Fewer still come here to ask questions." She moved closer, remaining indistinct except for the long, clawed fingers forming at the very end of her incorporeal being. "I find it intriguing it's a pixie whose line has fallen out of favor with the old gods and a golden elf belonging to a family with a reputation for brutality who do so."

"Not all that was, is," I replied. "The old gods are once again active, and they again seek the help of those who once served."

"That is information I had not known, and I thank you for sharing."

The ghul moved around us, her long claws gently brushing up Mathi's right arm and across the back of his neck. He didn't move or react, but the look he cast me was less than impressed. I somehow restrained my grin.

She appeared to my left and slid her fingers down my arm, her nails gently scraping the pale puffer sleeve. "You have an energy that is not of this world, young pixie. It tastes of storms and violence."

"My father is a minor storm god. His energy—"

"Is not the violence I sense. It is far more personal than that. Explain."

I hesitated, though in truth, if I wanted answers I really had no choice but to comply. She felt even older than what I'd been told, and that meant it was entirely possible she had the capacity to interact with the living in an unpleasant manner. Just because we believed ghuls were harmless didn't mean all of them were. There were always outliers, no matter what the race.

"My mother was murdered. I seek those who are responsible."

"As I said in conversation with another seeker only a week ago, revenge is a dish best served cold. Remember that going forward."

"It sounds as if you've some experience with revenge," Mathi said, keeping his tone carefully neutral.

A smile flashed—a brief reveal of sharp black teeth in a sea of gray. "Nowhere near as much as you, Mathi Dhār-Val."

He raised a pale eyebrow. "You know who I am?"

"Oh, I know many things." Her attention flicked to me, something I knew through the sudden shift in the weight of the air. "Is that not why you seek me, Bethany Aodhán?"

Instinct stirred uneasily. While I'd like to think it was nothing more than a coincidence that we weren't the only ones who'd come here asking questions, it was odd that she knew both Mathi's and my names. Perhaps Fate—who, like many other old gods and goddesses, liked tossing grenades humanity's way occasionally—had decided our lives had been entirely too comfortable over the last forty-eight hours.

"Was the other person someone you've talked to before?" I asked. "Or someone new?"

Again, her gruesome smile flashed. "New."

I scanned the deeper shadows, though I wasn't entirely sure why. If this person had visited last week, it was unlikely they'd be back again so soon. Unless, of course, the information provided wasn't adequate. "What did he or she want?"

"Such conversations are my business, not yours, though I will say your motive stems from the same source as hers." She paused. "I will also note she was not as polite as you. In fact, I would go so far as saying that of the many unhinged minds I've come across in the eons I've spent on this land, hers might be one of the finest."

Oh, great, another nutter wandering around Deva. Just what we needed. Hopefully, she wasn't armed with a dangerous relic like the most recent ones had been. I shared a glance with Mathi, who said, "If you cannot tell us what your conversation was, can you at least give us some clue as to her identity?"

Her filmy presence briefly sharpened, revealing a

hunched, skeletal figure with long bony arms attached to those murderous claws. "No, I don't believe I can at this moment. Few are those who come here to talk directly, and I treat such moments as rare and precious jewels. I will not abuse their memory by sharing our conversation, even with those as delicious to the eye as you."

"But will you share information gleaned from those you follow?" I asked, more to draw her attention away from Mathi than anything else.

"Of course. What is it you wish to know?"

I hesitated. "What knowledge have you of the scrolls the Ljósálfar hold in their vaults alongside the Éadrom Hoard?"

"Little enough. They were created eons ago by the ancient ones, and this place did not exist at that time."

"But you did?"

"I am old, but I am not ancient. They roamed the earth at a time when humanity was a bare glint in their eyes, and left when the old gods arrived to play their games."

"Then who placed the scrolls in the vaults? And do you know what guards them?"

"What guards is beyond your understanding, young pixie. It is of a time that no longer exists."

"Dangerous?"

"Perhaps. Its reaction would depend on intent and, for the most part, humanity's intentions are rarely pure."

Was that why the council believed no mortal beings could view the scrolls? Because those in the past had gone in with the wrong objectives and been punished for them?

Would it consider mine any different to theirs?

"What of the scrolls—have you any idea what information they hold?"

She studied me for a second, something I felt via a

thickening in the weight of the air more than saw. Her eyes, like her form, remained shrouded in fog. "Why do you wish to know this?"

"Because Ninkil's followers seek the Harpē to call him back into this world. The wind whispers of its malevolence but holds no answers as to where it lies. I'm hoping the ancient scrolls that remain in the vault might provide some clues as to where it was hidden."

"His rising would indeed be unfortunate," she agreed. "But as I have said, I have no knowledge of the scrolls."

"Then I am sorry to have bothered—"

"You give up too easily, young Aodhán, and ask the wrong question."

My eyebrows rose. "What question should I have asked?"

"Would it by chance be the location of the vault?" Mathi said.

Her shroud shimmered as her gaze shifted from me to him. "Pretty and clever—a rare combination. Perhaps I should take a token to remember this event."

Mathi gave me a deadpan look that was somehow filled with annoyance, and it was all I could do not to laugh.

"A lock of hair, I'm presuming?" he said in a flat tone.

"That would indeed be perfect."

"Fine, but do try not to scalp me."

Her laugh was a low, somewhat unpleasant scratch of sound. "Indeed, it would not do to in any way damage your divineness."

He raised an eyebrow again but otherwise didn't reply. She slipped between us, her filmy gowns brushing my hand. Energy prickled across my skin, and my second sight briefly flared, revealing in quick succession a woman cloaked in black, the hood pulled over features hidden by a ski mask. Pale hands that were almost skeletal offering a bag containing locks of reddish hair. Her strange, almost lurching gait as she walked away. Then the energy—and the images—faded as the ghul raised her hand and, with a quick snip of her claws, took a small lock of hair before retreating.

Was the woman in the images the one who'd come here last week? If so, why in the gods' name was she so tightly wrapped up? Granted, it was winter, and the nights hellish cold, but that amount of coverage implied she didn't want anyone to see who she was, not even a ghul.

It was tempting to question our ghul further, but given she'd said she wouldn't share confidences, it would not only be pointless, but could also risk annoying her. The last thing I wanted to do right now was to cut off a useful line of future information.

I switched my gaze to Mathi and studied his hairline. "You can barely even see where she's taken the lock from."

"Good," he murmured, then in a louder voice added, "Thank you for that, madam."

She laughed again. "A thank you from a Dhār-Val? That, perhaps, is an even greater prize than a lock of golden hair." Said hair quickly disappeared into the shrouds of gray. "As to your question—much has changed since I walked the lands beyond old Deva, but the entrance to the ancient vaults lay in a place I knew as Pwll Dwfn. I stayed awhile in the nearby encampment, but highborn Ljósálfar do not bury their dead in a manner conducive to the presence of one such as I."

Because they buried the ashes of their loved ones under a newly planted tree, in a ritual that somehow transferred that person's ability to enhance and strengthen the growth of trees to the sapling, ensuring a strong, vibrant, and living memorial.

I glanced at Mathi, eyebrows raised, silently asking if he knew that name. He shook his head and then asked, "The name suggests it's located in Wales—is that true?"

Movement rippled across her form; I suspected she'd shrugged. "Back in my day, the area was known as Cymru. More than that, I cannot say."

"It at least gives us somewhere to start."

"Indeed." She paused for a long moment, her gaze heavy on me once again. "Should you wish it, I am willing to listen for any information about Ninkil. He is a god who should never be allowed to walk this world again, and it behooves all of us who exist here to do what we can to prevent such happening."

Surprise ran through me, but I covered it with a slight bow. "Any assistance you could give us in that regard would be greatly appreciated."

"That is as it should be." There was amusement in her tone. "The price, of course, will be a lock of hair."

"If you keep shearing me, I won't have much hair left to give," Mathi commented.

Her scratchy laugh echoed again. "Indeed, which is why in future I will settle for the hair of a woman born of Ambis-agrus's loins."

A comment had me suspecting the brief caress of her energy across my skin had not been accidental. While I'd been gathering snippets of her memories, she'd been gathering information about me. There was no other way she could have known my father's name—not given the number of minor storm gods that abounded. Hell, Mom hadn't even told *me* anything more than his name. And while ghuls could roam the streets at will, they could not enter buildings unbidden. Which, according to Gran, was where the human legend of vampires had come.

"That was very well played, madam," I said, amused. "But I will be aware of your trick next time."

"That, also, is as it should be." Her form began to fade. "Be wary when you leave, young Aodhán. Ill intent roams this night, and I fear it has you in its sights."

And with that, she disappeared.

"Well, that's a cheery thought to leave us with," Mathi said. "Perhaps we should depart before the aforementioned ill intent finds us?"

"Indeed." I hooked my arm through his. "What time is the council meeting tomorrow?"

He gave me a sideways glance, something I felt rather than saw. "Nine. Did you not read the text I sent?"

"Read, yes. Remember what it said? Obviously not." I paused. "That's an indecently early hour for the council, is it not?"

"If it had been a full meeting called, yes, but this is little more than a brief for your next assignment. I doubt more than a half dozen representatives will be there."

And Cynwrig wouldn't be one of them.... I sucked in a breath and released it slowly. This instant stream of longing that rose every time I thought of the damn man was ridiculous. I hadn't even known him for very long, for gods' sake.

"I already know my next assignment."

"Not officially. They'll give you what information they have on Borrhás's Horn tomorrow."

"I'd rather they just give me access to their records so I can look these things up myself."

He laughed softly. "You lie, Bethany Aodhán. You want access to hunt down your mother's killer."

"Well, yeah, that too, but it's not like they need to know that."

Movement stirred briefly to our left, and my gaze shot that way. It was only a ghost fleeing our presence, but my unease nevertheless ramped up. The night no longer felt right....

In that moment, Mathi cannoned into me, knocking me sideways, his arms slipping around my waist as he twisted in midair to take the brunt of our fall. We hit hard, and a grunt escaped both our lips, the sound sharp in the quiet night. Then something pinged past my ear and thudded into a nearby gravestone, sending stone splinters flying.

A bullet.

A goddamn *bullet.*

The ghul's ill intent had found us.

TWO

Mathi rolled me off him and said, "Move, move."

I scrambled upright and dove toward a nearby larger tomb, hunkering behind it as I scanned the night. I couldn't see the shooter and there was no sense of movement on the still air, but he was out there. I could feel it. Feel his tension and desperation.

That latter emotion was definitely odd.

Mathi knelt beside me. "You okay?"

I nodded. "You?"

"I'm fine, but my coat is utterly ruined." His tone suggested the shooter would pay for *that* thoughtlessness.

"Have you any idea where the shot came from?"

While I could feel his presence, the stillness of the night and the lack of wind was making it difficult to sense a direction. I could gather the air and send it on a quest, of course, but that might well take more time than we had.

"From the highest point of the tree line near Grosvenor's Road," he replied.

I carefully peered past the edge of the tomb and scanned that area, though I was unlikely to see anything when it was so far away. My night sight was pretty good—and well beyond that of a human—but it wasn't as sharp as Mathi's. He might not be Myrkálfar—who could see in the darkness as easily as they did daylight—but a light elf's night sight remained far sharper than most other fae.

Air stirred briefly, and I jerked back sharply. A second later, something hit the edge of the tomb, and stone chips flew. "Well, he's definitely still there. How do you want to play this?"

"I don't suppose you can call down a bolt of lightning or two, can you?"

I half smiled. "If there was a cloud in the sky, maybe, but there's not even a scrap of wind."

"What about gathering the air and using it as a weapon? You've done that before."

"Yes, but I need to at least *see* the person I'm attacking. It'd take too long to gather enough air for a broad blanket attack."

"Then we do it the hard way."

I raised an eyebrow. "I'm not liking the note of anticipation in your voice."

He smiled. "I'm a Dhār-val. We do relish the odd bit of danger. Gets the blood moving."

I snorted softly. "What's odd about *that* statement is the fact I never sensed that predilection in all the years we were together."

"That's because you got my blood moving in other ways." He motioned to my left. "It's pretty simple—you run out and head into the trees, drawing his attention from me."

"I'm bait, in other words."

"As the old saying goes, what is good for the gander is good for the goose."

I half smiled. "That's presuming I *am* the target. There's no certainty—"

"Yeah, there is." He lightly touched my right arm, and it was only then I noticed the hole in my jacket's sleeve. "If not for me seeing the brief flash of movement *and* the puffiness of this godawful jacket, you'd now be dead."

I leaned forward and kissed his cheek. "Thank you for saving my life."

"I haven't very many close friends, Bethany, and I'm not about to let one of those few be taken from me. Not if I can at all help it." His hand slid down to mine, squeezing lightly before releasing. "So, we get this bastard, and we squeeze every little bit of information from him. Agreed?"

"Agreed."

"Then go. But please, keep in mind that whole 'me not losing a friend' comment, and don't get shot."

I smiled and kissed his cheek again. "Promise."

"Then I shall meet you at the top of that hill."

I nodded, took a deep breath, then thrust upright and charged out, running hell for leather across the path and up the hill. A bullet pinged into the ground beside me, spraying dirt across the side of my calves; a heartbeat later, grass and dirt flew up from the ground inches from my toes.

Either our shooter was a very bad marksman, or he was trying to maim rather than kill me.

I had no idea which was true, and no intention of finding out. Aside from the whole "I like life too much" aspect, there was my promise to Mathi to consider. I started to zigzag, although I wasn't entirely sure how much it would actually help.

I hit the treed area, but their cover was sparse and didn't alleviate the overall danger, given I was still below the shooter and most of the trees here were winter bare. For several heartbeats, the barrage fell silent, then air stirred sharply to my left. I went right, ducking behind a lovely old oak. Her gentle song turned to one of pain as three bullets thudded into her trunk.

I dragged up the bottom of my coat and drew the two knives. Dark purplish light flickered down their fullers, an indication someone was spelling close by. Unfortunately, the knives weren't capable of telling me where, and *that* meant I had better move before that spell had a chance to find me. I thrust to my feet and ran on, weaving through the trees, the ground gently rising as I drew closer to the cemetery's boundary. Bullets continued to thud into the ground inches from my feet, which only strengthened my suspicion that the shooter was deliberately missing.

I scanned the rise above me but couldn't see him, despite the sparsity of the trees and the fact I was now close enough to hear the snick of bullets being fired. Which meant the spell the knives had reacted to—were still reacting to—was most likely a shadow shield. They were the next best thing to an invisibility shield, and far cheaper to purchase.

From up ahead came a flurry of noise—wood splintering, cloth tearing—followed by a venomous and yet oddly desperate curse. Then, a heartbeat later, another sharp snick.

No metal speared into the ground near my feet. That last bullet had not been aimed at me.

Several yards farther on, I saw the body.

He lay at the base of the scrubby embankment that separated the cemetery from the road, the bottom half of his leg bent back against his thigh at an unnatural angle. There was a small handgun loosely clutched in his left hand that, given the length of the barrel, obviously had some sort of silencer attached.

He wasn't moving, wasn't breathing, and after a moment, I saw why.

On the left side of his head, just behind his ear, was a small scorch mark and a slightly rimmed, neat round hole from which blood trickled. He'd been shot—killed—though whether it was by his own hand or another's, I couldn't say.

Another shot rang out, the sound muted by distance but coming from the general direction of the very first shot.

Fuck, *Mathi*.

I spun and ran as fast as I could back through the trees, my grip on the knives so fierce that my knuckles practically glowed. I wasn't quiet and wasn't attempting to be.

Then in a voice that was clear but filled with an odd sort of annoyance, he said, "You can ease off, Beth. I'm not hurt."

I came out of the trees into the top row of several lines of old graves. Mathi was standing close to an old grave marker, and at his feet lay another man. I slowed and, after a quick look around, sheathed the knives and walked toward him.

"What happened? Did you deck him after he shot at you?"

"That last shot wasn't at me. He killed himself." The annoyance remained in his voice, though little crossed his expression. "I tried to stop him, but wasn't fast enough."

I halted beside him and rubbed my arms. "There's another man in the trees back there, and he also appears to have killed himself."

"It's rather odd behavior for hitmen."

It was indeed. "Have you looked for an ID?"

Mathi nodded. "Nothing on him."

"I guess that isn't surprising if he was a professional."

"No professional would ever miss as badly as this man did—or indeed, make a stupid move when their target is in clear view, thereby giving that target a chance to escape."

"Unless, of course, killing wasn't what they'd intended." My gaze jumped to the gun lying on the ground. "Would nonprofessionals have access to silencers? They're both using them."

A smile tugged at his lips. "There is such a thing as the black market, remember, and it is rather active here in Deva."

And anyone wanting to purchase a firearm in the UK had to be registered and have an owner's certificate with the caliber approved by the police. If these two *were* hitmen, then a legal purchase was certainly unlikely, but it never hurt to check. "You know, there's something very odd about this whole situation."

"In what way? The ghul warned us of danger, and a few minutes later, someone attempted to kill us. The only thing odd about the whole thing is the fact they took their own lives rather than simply disappearing."

"Were they really attempting to kill us, though?" I glanced at him. "Even if they weren't professionals, surely not even amateur shooters could miss us so badly. It seems to me they were deliberately doing so."

"To what possible purpose?" He waved a hand to the dead man at our feet. "If it was simply a warning of some kind, why off themselves?"

"I don't know, but there was an odd sort of desperation emanating from the other shooter. There was also a spell-caster in his vicinity, though I had no real sense of him or her."

"Where's your shooter?"

I motioned toward the trees. "It sounded like he fell down the embankment and then, rather than being caught, blew his own brains out."

"Which implies they were ordered to avoid capture at any cost." His expression was grim. "And that sort of compliance is generally only brought about by some sort of leverage or pixie magic."

Said magic was a so-called blessing given to pixie women by an ancient goddess who had given us the so-called six gifts of womanhood—beauty, a gentle voice, sweet words, wisdom, needlework, and chastity. The women in my line somehow managed to avoid most of those—thank the gods—but we did have a variation on the gentle voice and sweet words theme and could either calm people down or control them with voice and touch. It worked on humans, shifters, and most fae, but not elves. Maybe if it *had*, I wouldn't have wasted so many years with Mathi.

Though, in truth, it probably wouldn't have mattered, because our split was the result of him breaking his promise to *tell* me if he took other lovers rather than the fact he actually *had* other lovers. Honesty was the key, not monogamy.

"It would certainly explain why our shooters appeared to be deliberately missing, as ordering someone to kill in a situation like this risks evoking the blood curse, and that's something sane pixies avoid." Though that did lead to the possibility we were dealing with an *insane* mind. "But I'm currently the only Aodhán woman in Deva, and there's very few Tàileach."

"That's presuming it's a Tàileach or Aodhán woman

involved—are no other branches of pixies capable of mind enforcement?"

"It can technically be found in the other lines, but it's mostly the two taller branches that have the variation."

"But there's also no indication the person behind this attack or indeed these two men come from around these parts." He paused. "What about your aunt? It's certainly possible she holds you responsible for her daughter's death."

"Vincentia's dead because she ignored my warnings and worked for the wrong people." I rubbed my arms lightly. "And it can't be Riayn. She's also dead."

"No, she's presumed dead," he replied. "They never actually found a body, did they?"

"No, but it's not like she could have left the property, given she was under the red knife."

The red knife was the most serious of all punishments given out by the pixie council, and only applied for the most grievous of offenses. It was both a symbolic *and* physical cutting of ties, meaning not only were you excommunicated from pixie society and bound in one place for a period of ten years, but your ability to hear and use the song and power of trees was ripped from you. I'd feared a similar punishment after I'd deep mind read—and controlled—Vincentia, but had instead been tasked with working for Deva's council for a period of two years.

As much as I hated being bound to them, it was certainly a far better option than the red knife.

"Dead doesn't always mean dead," he said, rather darkly. "There are ways and means of faking it."

"Not when it comes to the red knife."

His soft "hmmm" was loaded with disbelief, and in many respects, I couldn't say I blamed him. If the gods were intent on causing chaos, then throwing my aunt into the mix would certainly be an excellent option.

"Did you have a chance to pat down the other man?" he added.

I shook my head. "You go do that; I'd better ring Sgott."

Sgott Bruhn wasn't only the head of the IIT's night division, but had also been my mom's lover for nigh on sixty years, and the only real father I'd ever known. He'd always treated me as one of his own, though I suspected I'd caused him far more grief than any of those born from his loins ever had, especially of late.

I dragged out my phone, noticed I had a message, but ignored it and made the call. As the phone rang, I trailed after Mathi, my gaze scanning the night. I couldn't sense anything untoward, but that didn't mean we were entirely safe, given the soft pulse still emanating from the knives. Our spellcaster was still out there somewhere.

Sgott answered after a couple of rings. "And what has happened now for you to be ringing so early in the morning?"

There was a decided edge of resignation running through his Scottish brogue, and I couldn't help smiling. "I'm afraid someone decided I was the perfect subject for a little target prac—"

"You've not been hurt?" he cut in sharply.

"No, thanks mainly to Mathi knocking me out of the way in time."

"Given the Dhār-Val line has more lives than cats, I take it he's also okay?"

"Yes, and before you ask, I haven't questioned either shooter. They topped themselves before either of us could get to them."

"That is rather unusual behavior for a professional. Or indeed, anyone I would judge as sane. Where are you?"

"The old Deva cemetery, up near the Grosvenor's Road embankment, several hundred yards past the gate on that side."

"It'll take us about ten to get there."

"See you soon." I tucked the phone away and stopped a few feet away from the dead man Mathi was patting down. "Sgott and his people are on the way. You find anything?"

"No phone, no wallet, and no car keys. He's not even wearing a watch." He motioned toward the body. "And the fact he came out on an evening like this without a coat suggests he was likely driven here, either via a cab, Uber, or whoever told him to shoot himself."

"We're only presuming the latter." I scanned the area again. "The frost is light on the ground here, but it's possible our spellcaster left some prints further along."

"Unless he went up the embankment and over the fence."

"Even if he did, there'd be some evidence of it. We should look." I glanced at him. "It's better than standing around doing nothing but freezing our butts."

"Oh, I can think of one or two ways we could keep the chill at bay, but sadly, you refuse to even entertain the prospect."

"Because you're past entertainment, not current or future. Shall we move?"

His sigh was a dramatic thing, though amusement danced through his bright eyes. "I guess if I have no other option—"

"Well, you could stand here and stare at a dead man."

"Not something I've ever been prone to do, even when responsible for said death."

"You know, there's a part of me horrified by that comment, and yet, also intrigued."

"As our ghul noted, the Dhār-Val line does have something of a reputation." He carefully stepped around the body and fell in step beside me. "Two shooters and a spell-caster is certainly what most in the business would consider overkill, and suggests once again we're not dealing with professionals."

We came out of the trees, but there was no sign of disturbance on the frost-kissed grass or indeed the embankment. Either our caster walked more lightly than elves, or they had wings.

As the faint sound of approaching sirens began to bite the air, I shoved my cold hands into my pockets and said, "This is useless."

"I would have to agree," Mathi said. "But hopefully, there'll be a tracker amongst Sgott's people, and they'll have a little more luck."

"I wouldn't be putting money on it. If you ask me, this has all the hallmarks of a carefully planned, even if not perfectly executed, event."

"Which brings to mind a question—how did you learn about the ghul's presence? I had no idea one existed here, and I've been living in Deva far longer than you."

I wrinkled my nose. "Overheard a conversation between a couple of customers and asked them about it."

His eyebrows rose. "New customers, by chance?"

"Tourists, so yes." I glanced at him. "You're thinking it was a setup?"

"Well, you have to admit it's likely."

"The ghul wouldn't be party to such a thing. They are honest folk."

"But, as she said, two visits in under a week is rather

unusual. It's a shame she wouldn't tell us what that other person wanted. I suspect it might provide some clue as to her identity."

The wail of sirens ended abruptly, but blue and red light washed across the darkness. The silence briefly felt heavier, but the sound of approaching voices soon changed that. I didn't hear Sgott's voice amongst them, but maybe he was still on the way or had simply sent the investigative team that was closest.

"You head up there and meet Sgott's people," I said. "I've got a tree I need to heal first."

He raised an eyebrow but kept on walking. I moved back down the slope, following the song of pain until I found the bullet-ridden old oak. I brushed my fingers down her trunk, then gently connected to the golden rivers of her energy, following the network of fibers until I found the deeply embedded bullets. One by one, I gently eased the metal back up the tunnel it had gouged, healing the wound behind it as I went. As the bullets neared the surface of the trunk, I tugged a sleeve over my hand to catch them, then reconnected the torn fibers over each entry point, allowing the river of light and the tree's song to once again run rich and unimpeded.

But as I stepped back, the faintest glimmer of red caught my eye. It was hanging from the very tip of a low-hanging branch of a nearby tree, and very much looked like several strands of fiery red hair.

My heart leapt in hope. The woman I'd briefly glimpsed in the ghul's memories had traded strands of red hair, so there was every chance that these strands belonged to our caster. And if we could find her, then maybe she could lead us to the pixie who'd magicked our dead men.

I walked over to untangle the strands from the limb, but

the minute my fingers touched the hair, my second sight leapt into action.

In quick succession, I saw a thin woman with a nest of wiry red hair and, on a silver chain around her neck, a pendant in the shape of a half circle with two uneven lines underneath it. While I'd never seen the latter before, I certainly knew the woman.

It was none other than Maran Gordon, the caster who'd firebombed the tavern and aided the two shifter thieves who'd stolen the moonstone from me.

Except, it couldn't be—I'd killed her when she'd claimed the sword of darkness and attacked me and Vincentia.

Did Maran have a twin? A sister? I had no idea, but maybe Sgott would.

It was also possible we were dealing with the multi-shifter we only knew as Carla Wilson—the woman who was second-in-command to the hereto unknown man in control of the Ninkilim—but as far as any of us were aware, she was not also a mage.

I scanned the area yet again, but there was—unsurprisingly—little evidence or clue as to the direction the woman had gone. If we were dealing with a sister, then it was likely she had similar talents and was at least somewhat adept at concealment and body-morphing spells. Even if she was using some sort of magical shield, she was also smart enough to remain under the tree line, where the frost hadn't ventured and prints wouldn't show. A tracker would undoubtedly find her scent, but that was unlikely to end in a result given that, by the time they arrived, she'd have had more than enough time to jump into a vehicle and disappear.

The bigger question right now was, if this wasn't a

random attack and someone had placed another contract on me, who'd brokered it?

It surely wouldn't be Kaitlyn Avery. While she was Deva's—and maybe even England's—largest broker of illegal services, she knew far better than to get involved in *any* way with another contract on me. She was already walking a fine line with Sgott, and one more transgression would see her thrown in jail. And no matter how much goodwill she'd built with Ruadhán—Mathi's father—by supplying him various bits of information, she knew well enough even he could not help her if Sgott pressed forward with charges.

However, she wasn't the only broker in town, even if she was the largest, and any one of the minor players could have accepted the commission. I had no idea how many we had here in Deva, but I suspected there'd be quite a few given this was basically a black-market hotspot. Sgott would no doubt be aware of them all and task his people with interviewing them, but it just wasn't in my nature to sit back and let others sort out my problems. I was just like my mother in that respect.

Of course, Mom had also ended up dead...

I shoved the thought away and resolutely made my way back to the body of the man who'd broken his leg. Mathi wasn't there, but two others were—a man taping off the area and a woman taking photos. The latter was the fox shifter who'd attended the fire-bombing at the tavern.

I gave her a nod and asked, "Is Sgott here yet?"

"He's up with Dhār-Val at the first body."

"Thanks," I said, and continued on.

Sgott had his phone in his hand, obviously taking a statement from Mathi, but turned as I came out of the trees.

"You canna stay out of trouble for very long, can you?"

The amusement in his voice echoed through me. He was a big bear of a man—quite literally, given he was a bear shifter—broad of shoulders and chest; thick, wiry brown hair; brown skin; and a fierce, untamable beard. He also had a heart as big as his body, at least when it came to those he considered family, anyway. "Yeah, sorry, but that was Mom's lot in life, and it appears to be mine now. You got any evidence bags?"

"Indeed." He dragged a couple from his pocket. "What have you found?"

I carefully dropped the bullets into the first bag. "Dug them out of a tree—they're from the second shooter's gun, and I haven't physically touched them. The other is several strands of hair from a woman the spitting image of Maran Gordan."

"Maran's dead," Mathi said. "No matter how powerful the magic, there's no coming back from cleaved in two."

"I know, but when I touched the hair, I saw Maran."

"It was more than likely Keeryn rather than Maran," Sgott growled. "They're basically two chips off the same block, and there's only a year between them."

"Maran has a sister?"

He nodded. "Has similar talents, too, though we've no evidence Keeryn followed the same dark path as her sister."

"Well, that has obviously changed given the attempt on our lives here," Mathi said.

I glanced at him. "If she's kept her nose clean up until now, her taking a kill contract on me makes no sense."

"Well, that very much depends on just how annoyed she is that you killed her sister," Mathi noted dryly.

"How would she even know something like that? All the main players are either dead or in jail."

"Maybe she found someone who could raise and talk to the dead."

I guessed that was possible. Unlikely, but possible. "Even if someone has placed another contract on me, Kaitlyn is unlikely to be involved."

"Indeed, because she's well aware operating her business inside a prison cell would be nigh on impossible. And yes," Sgott added, before I could say anything, "I'll still talk to her."

He wouldn't be the only one talking to her, but I wisely kept that to myself. "Given both men shot themselves rather than be caught and questioned, it'd be wise to have a sniffer and a pixie present to make the relevant checks at the autopsy."

"And now you're telling me how to do my job?"

I grinned and held up my hands. "Wouldn't dream of it."

"Then you'd best be giving me your statement and go home. And don't forget, we've the commemoration at one."

Mathi's gaze shot to mine, his eyebrows rising. "You got an invite?"

I shook my head. "I'm Sgott's plus-one."

"Interesting."

I frowned. "Why?"

"Because as far as I'm aware, they weren't including partners on any invitations because of the sheer number of people who'd dealt with Gethen over the centuries wishing to pay their respects."

My frown grew. "Then perhaps it was a mistake."

"And perhaps it was Cynwrig's way of getting around formalities."

"Why would he do that for someone like me?" Someone who was a good time, not a long time.

"Why indeed?" His expression was speculative, but he didn't elaborate. "Either way, if the invitation is for two, it would be considered rude if Sgott did not bring a companion."

"Which is why I invited you, Beth," Sgott commented. "Cynwrig knows well enough that Lugh is the only other person I'd consider bringing, and I wouldn't call he and Cynwrig close."

"Not in the same manner as he and I are, at least," I said, with a twitch of my lips.

"Indeed. Now, best be giving me your statement."

Once I had, Mathi and I left, walking silently through the many gravestones and tombstones, the occasional ghost our only companions.

"Do you want a lift home?" Mathi said, as we once again reached the old metal gate.

"No, but I would like a lift to Kaitlyn's."

"Sgott will not be pleased."

"Sgott no doubt has every expectation that I'll be doing this very thing."

"Which doesn't negate my statement at all. The car is this way."

"You drove?" I said, surprised.

"Of course not."

I laughed and slipped my arm through his arm. "So, you admonish me for dragging you out of a warm bed, but you do the very same thing to your poor chauffeur."

"Henrick is very well paid to cater to out-of-hours avocations."

"And, of course, sworn to secrecy."

"No need, given he is well aware of what happens to those who tattle on a Dhār-Val."

"There you go, horrifying and intriguing me all at once."

"But not enough to intrigue you back to my bed, I'd wager."

"No. And you know that."

"Yes, but accepting the utter lack of hope given the centuries of living that remain ahead for us both is an entirely different matter."

I laughed. "Hopefully, I'll be spending those centuries with someone who loves me."

"I do wish that for you, but it will never negate the optimism that burns within."

Up ahead, a dark-haired man in his mid-fifties climbed out of the driver's side of a silver Mercedes and walked around to the rear passenger door, opening it once we drew closer. "Where to, sir?"

"Kaitlyn's, thank you, Henrick."

The driver closed the rear door, then returned to the driver's seat. As he drove off, a privacy screen slid up between him and us.

"She's not going to be pleased at being woken at an ungodly hour," Mathi commented.

"Do I look as if I care?"

He smiled. "No, but she's definitely more taciturn when she's had less sleep."

Suggesting he had personal experience. I frowned. "Surely even a broker of her stature would be working mostly at night."

"Surprisingly, only the lower rung operators do so at night. The higher up the brokerage tree you get, the less likely it is. I think they believe it adds an air of legitimacy if they work standard hours, though it does also make good business sense, as most of their higher-paying clientele would be keeping regular hours."

"The Myrkálfar don't."

"Elves, be they Myrkálfar or Ljósálfar, have no need for her services."

And yet, his statement about her crankiness suggested that wasn't *always* the case. "Even if the contract was brokered by a lower rung operator, she'd still be aware of its circulation."

"Yes, because the wise man—or woman in this case—always keeps a close eye on the market *and* the competition."

Something in the way he said the latter had me glancing at him. "You and Eljin are not in competition. You left the race eight months ago."

"I wasn't talking about me. I meant Cynwrig."

"Then Eljin has nothing to worry about. In fact, he's the only horse in the running right now."

"Oh, I wouldn't be putting money on that."

"Mathi, Cynwrig's highborn, and they, like your lot, do not get serious about anyone outside their own race."

"While highborns don't *often* marry outside their own race, it has happened. It's certainly not unknown for them to become serious about a partner not of their own kind."

"You never did."

A smile tugged at his lips. "*I* am a Ljósálfar, and a very different proposition to Cynwrig. Besides, I was monogamous for nearly eight years, dear Bethany, and that is very much a record for me."

Or indeed for *any* light elf. Myrkálfar elves were almost the exact opposite; not only were they far more emotionally connected than their Ljósálfar counterparts, but they also married for love, not profit or standing. Once their heart was committed, it never strayed.

Or so said the myths. Who actually knew if that remained true in this day and age?

"Does that mean there was someone else before Gilda?"

"A couple of someones. Occasional dalliances; nothing more."

I harrumphed and glanced at the window, watching the steady procession of bright street lights sweep by for a second. "The thing is, Cynwrig is not only highborn, but heir to the Myrkálfar throne. He wouldn't jeopardize that position for someone like me. Why would you even think that?"

"Sgott's plus-one invitation is an interesting deviation to normal practice, as I said."

"Well, it's not like he's personally sending out the invitations, so maybe, as *I* said, it's just a mistake." I half shrugged. "I guess we'll find out this afternoon—if I get turned away, well, we'll know who's right."

There was a small, weird part of me hoping that I *was* turned away, because that would mean he hadn't bent the rules, that I wasn't special, and therefore had no reason to hold on to the sliver of hope that Mathi's comments had raised.

"They are unlikely to turn you away. They could not afford the affront to Sgott."

I didn't reply. There was little point. We'd know the truth soon enough.

We continued on through the silent night, eventually turning into Kaitlyn's street. Unlike all the other times we'd paid her a visit, this time we parked right out the front. Mathi told his driver to remain in the car, then climbed out, offering me a hand as I slid across the seat.

The night seemed even colder than it had been earlier, and fingers of frost climbed up the nearby streetlight. Even the footpath bore a silvery sheen that weirdly did not seem to extend to the buildings either side of Kaitlyn's. I glanced up; tiny icicles gathered along the edge of the building's guttering.

Mathi stopped beside me and looked up. "That guttering looks new, so why are icicles forming?"

"Question of the morning, right along with, why the hell is the chill apparently confined to this one section of the street?" I glanced back to his car. Frost ran like water across the Merc's roof. "You might want to get Henrick to shift the car further down, just in case this cold isn't natural."

His gaze snapped to mine. "Are you sensing anything untoward?"

I hesitated, studying the silent buildings either side of the road. The wind remained quiet, and I had no sense of any sort of weather magic happening, but still... "It just feels wrong."

"Then move the car we most certainly will."

As he leaned in to speak to Henrick, I walked across to the bright blue door. The small brass sign in the middle said, "Kaitlyn's Kurios," and there was an intercom and small camera on the wall to the right.

I leaned heavily on the buzzer and smiled up at the camera. After several long seconds, a sultry but very annoyed voice said, "Go away. I have no desire to talk to you, especially at this hour of the morning."

"Sentiments I wholeheartedly agree with, but I have no choice and now neither do you. Get up, or I shall make you do so."

"My bed is metal, so your threat is an empty one."

I splayed my fingers across the bright blue door, feeling the chill in the wood even as I listened to the song of the inner fabric. It was faint, mainly because a good portion of the building was brick and concrete, but what remained nevertheless told me the location of her bedroom—top floor, to the right of the living area we'd previously confronted her in.

"Yes, but it sits on floorboards," I replied evenly, "and I do not have to be within a building to alter or destroy it. Would you like a little demonstration?"

Her answering sigh was a sharp, put-upon sound. "Fine. Come on up."

There was a soft buzz, and the door clicked open. Mathi reached past me to push the door all the way open. "Seriously, your threats are worthy of a Dhār-Val."

My fingers had left a watery imprint on the wood and that only had trepidation stirring harder. "I'll take that as a compliment."

"You should." He closed the door behind us and then followed me across to the stairs. I gripped the banister as I walked up, listening to the soft song and hearing the echo of Kaitlyn's movements as she climbed out of bed and went into the living area. I hoped she was lighting the fire rather than grabbing a gun, because the latter would be inconvenient and probably result in me having to tear up the lovely old floorboards again.

Thankfully, when we arrived upstairs, Kaitlyn was kneeling in front of the large fireplace, stacking kindling on top of several firelighters rather than pointing a weapon our way. She was a dark-skinned, sharp-faced woman whose long black hair was currently contained within a green silk sleeping cap. She looked to be in her mid-forties, but the age spots on her hands suggested she was much older. How much older, it was hard to say, as she was part elf and had obviously inherited at least some of their slow aging genes.

She struck a match and lit the fire, then rose to face us,

wrapping her loose, fluffy dressing gown more tightly around her body. "I will be putting in a formal complaint about this harassment."

"Feel free. Sgott or one of his people will be here to interview you later this morning, so you can do it then."

She frowned. "Why? I've done nothing to warrant his attention. Not recently, anyway."

I stopped behind the well-padded armchair directly in front of the fire, keeping it between me and her. It probably wouldn't offer all that much protection if she had a gun hidden in the voluminous depths of her dressing gown, but it was better than nothing. Mathi moved to my left and stopped next to the old sofa. If she did make an untoward move, he was within launching distance.

"Oh, you've done *plenty*," Mathi said, voice dry. "In fact, I know of a number of contracts you've placed in the last few days that are... shall we say, unsavory? My father isn't the only one who has receipts, dear Kaitlyn."

She studied him for a moment then lazily raised an eyebrow—a pretense at nonchalance countered by the quick flick of fear in her eyes. "And is it one of these contracts you—and Sgott—wish to speak about?"

"No," I said. "I'm more interested in the one that's been placed on me."

"Not by me it hasn't." There was dry amusement in her sultry tone. "I am not foolish enough to go down *that* path a second time."

"Someone has, and it would appear that Maran Gordan's sister has taken up the option."

"Keeryn has spent half her life refusing to join the family business. I doubt that has changed." She threw some more wood on the fire and cast me a wry smile. "Although the gossipmongers whisper of Maran's death and a certain

Aodhán pixie being responsible. Revenge can be a mighty motivator."

And if Keeryn had heard those rumors, it would certainly explain her accepting a kill contract on me. Why not profit while gaining revenge?

"Have you any idea who might have brokered the contract on Bethany?" Mathi asked.

Kaitlyn glanced at him. "I do not."

"But you could find out, could you not?"

Though it was formed as a question, it definitely wasn't. Kaitlyn stared at Mathi for several seconds, her expression a mix of amusement and wariness. I watched the silent battle and lightly rubbed my arms. Despite the fire, it seemed to be getting colder in here. Even the song of the building's wood was beginning to slow as the chill increased.

Eventually, Kaitlyn said, "A favor given is a favor owed."

"Or perhaps, a favor given is one receipt lost. The Oldaker incident, perhaps."

That faint flicker ran through her eyes again but all she said was, "That would be ideal."

"Good. You'll contact me with the details the minute you uncover anything?"

"I will." Her gaze returned to mine. "Is that all?"

I hesitated. "I don't suppose you know if Keeryn Gordan is staying in town?"

"If she has accepted the contract on you, then she would have gone to ground. Just because she didn't join the family business doesn't mean she hasn't the family talents. And, of course, that also means it's unlikely she used her true persona to accept the commission. Maran never did."

I raised my eyebrows. "I would have thought that would make contract breaches a trifle harder to deal with."

"Aside from the fact few would dare breach any contract I broker, I *always* have a no-fault clause inserted to ensure problems do not rebound back on me."

In other words, as long as she got her money, she really didn't care. "Well, if you do happen to hear anything about her, could you pass it on?"

"It would be my utter pleasure."

The insincerity positively dripped off every word. I smiled and stepped back, then hesitated, gaze scanning the shimmer creeping across the ceiling. "You haven't annoyed a weather mage of late, have you? Because the chill in this place is invasive to the point of being unnatural."

She waved the comment away. "The heating system broke down last night, and I'm awaiting the arrival of a plumber. They are rarer than hens' teeth of late, apparently."

"Which explains the chill inside, but not the concentration of ice that is happening on the exterior. It looks and feels targeted, Kaitlyn."

Her gaze narrowed. "What is your second sight saying about the matter?"

"Absolutely nothing, but that doesn't negate the fact that this just doesn't feel right. It might be wise if you pack some things and spend a few days at a—"

"I will never get a plumber here if I'm staying elsewhere," she said crossly. "I'll be fine."

Famous last words, but it wasn't like I could force her out. As a half elf, she was immune to pixie obedience magic. I waved a hand. "Fine. Your choice."

"Indeed. Now please, do leave. I'd like to get a few more hours' sleep before the day's work begins."

We headed out, the gently fading song of the building's fabric sounding very much like a final goodbye. There was absolutely nothing I could do about that except hope that I was wrong, that it was nothing more than the lack of heating in an old and very likely insufficiently insulated building.

The front door's locks slid firmly back in place as we left, the sound echoing in the cold stillness of the night. The ice on the pavement was thicker, the icicles longer. I studied the nearby buildings but once again had no sense that a weather witch or even a storm mage was near—though surely a storm mage would be more thunder and lightning than ice and a bone-deep chill.

And really, why would either be targeting Kaitlyn? If someone was after revenge for a contract she'd arranged, surely they'd go after the person who *placed* the contract or even the person who fulfilled it, rather than the intermediary between the two.

"So, what was the Oldaker incident?" I asked as we walked down to the car.

"An incident you're better off knowing nothing about."

"A statement guaranteed to fuel my curiosity."

"Said curiosity will not be fulfilled."

"Was it a hit? A theft? A deal gone wrong?"

He rolled his eyes. "Two of those three are correct. More than that, I cannot say."

"Frustrating."

"And I'm always willing to help ease said frustrations, but that is not possible in this case."

He opened the car door, ushered me in, and then directed Henrick to the lane behind my tavern. It didn't take us all that long to get there, and Mathi insisted on walking me down to the door. Thankfully, nothing untoward happened.

"Thanks," I said, punching in the code, then holding the

door open with my fingertips. "I'm guessing I'll see you in a couple of hours?"

He nodded. "I'll pick you up at eight forty-five. It shouldn't take us all that long to get around to the council's offices."

I resisted the urge to kiss him goodbye—old habits continued to die hard—then headed in. Ye Olde Pixie Boots —the name Mom had given the tavern when she'd taken over its running after Gran retired—had now been home to three extremely long-lived generations of Aodhán pixies. It was a listed building that stood in the middle of Deva's famous rows, and consisted of a small bar in the undercroft at street level, another at Row level, and our living area on the top floor. Aside from a few changes here and there, it was basically the same late medieval building that had been rebuilt on this spot after the fires that had destroyed most of the old city in the late 1400s. I loved the place and really couldn't imagine living anywhere else. Which was going to be a problem if I happened to fall in love with any of the men currently—I determinedly cut the rest of that thought off. As I'd said to Mathi earlier, there was now only *one* man I dared gift my heart to, and our relationship was still too new to know if that was wise.

I took off my coat and hung it on the nearby hook, then headed down the long, rather narrow hall, moving past the various rear storage and cold store areas. But as I reached the door that separated that area from the small ground-floor bar, a sudden realization hit.

I wasn't alone in the building.

CHAPTER

THREE

I STOPPED, MY HEART HAMMERING AND MY HAND AUTOMATICALLY reaching for one of my sheathed knives. I might not be formally trained in hand-to-hand knife combat, but I'd been getting plenty of practice in recent times, and I definitely felt safer with the weight of them in my hand. Still, in this case, it might be a tad overkill because, despite sensing the presence of others, there was no immediate suggestion of danger.

I pressed a hand against the door between this rear area and the main room instead, mentally slipping past its song and sliding deeper into the building's interconnected network of power. To someone like me, it was a roadmap of golden arteries that gave me a deeper understanding—and ultimately control—of not only the building's fabric but also, more importantly, the location of my two intruders.

The first was upstairs, in my bed, which meant it had to be Eljin. The only other person—aside from Lugh, Sgott, and Darby, of course—who had the code for the electronic lock on the door leading up to the accommodation section was Cynwrig, and the wood song would have told me if he were here. The old building did seem to like him. A lot. Of course, it also appeared to like Mathi, so it obviously wasn't too discerning.

Why Eljin would be here, I had no idea. He knew Mathi and I were going to the cemetery this evening to talk to the ghul, and he certainly hadn't called or sent a text saying he was on his way. Of course, it was also totally possible that the still-unread message sitting on my phone *was* from him.

The second person was seated at the table sitting next to the largest of the three oak beams supporting the upper floor in the bar beyond the door. The wood song couldn't "show" me that person; it could only speak of the weight resting on its fibers.

Whoever it was sat very lightly, and it wasn't someone the wood recognized.

So how did they get inside? Aside from the fact I'd bolted the medieval front door before I'd left tonight and the rear door was keypad controlled, this entire building was ringed by protection spells. Anyone intending mischief could not have gotten in. Well, a gifted enough witch could—and in the past, certainly had—but the spells remained intact, suggesting whoever it was out there, they weren't a mage. Unless, of course, he or she had taken the time to repair the damage they'd caused after breaking in, and why in the hell would they bother doing that?

I drew in a deeper breath and released it slowly. It didn't help ease the rising tension. Still, the knives weren't reacting, so that at least confirmed there was no immediate magical threat within that room.

A physical threat remained a possibility, however.

I warily opened the door. The room lay in semi-darkness, lit only by a couple of softly golden lights—one near the bar, the other near the steps leading up to the old door.

The stranger didn't move, and wasn't immediately visible, thanks to the big old beam they sat behind.

"Whoever you are, I know you're here. What do you want?"

"I would be disappointed if a pixie of your caliber did *not* know I was here." Her voice was warm and sultry, with intonations that reminded me a little of Cynwrig's. "As to why I'm here, I believe it is beyond time we finally met."

Realization leapt, and something within me stilled. This had to be Treasa, Cynwrig's twin sister. There could be no other explanation for the similarity of her voice to his or the fact that she'd gotten in here without setting off alarms, physical or magical. Either he'd given her the rear door code, or the magic protecting this place had registered her "feel" as his and hadn't reacted when she'd used the Lùtair ability to manipulate metal and slid open the front door's medieval iron locks.

I walked past the bar, my gaze on the table slowly becoming visible, wariness front and center despite the fact I doubted she meant me any immediate harm.

"And why would an heir to the Myrkálfar throne want to meet one of her brother's lovers, especially when that lover is not, and never could be, anything more than a temporary liaison?"

"When you live as long as we elves—or indeed, even as long as the Aodhán and Tàileach pixies—temporary can take on very different connotations."

I stopped a few feet away from the table. She was—not unexpectedly, given the magnificence of her brother and dark elves in general—a stunningly beautiful woman with sultry silver eyes several shades lighter than Cynwrig's and long dark hair that glimmered with bluish highlights. It had been casually swept up into a ponytail, revealing more of her lovely features while emphasizing her chiseled cheekbones and full lips. She was sitting sideways on the chair, her back against the beam, her long legs crossed casually at the ankle. Her knee-high boots, I couldn't help but notice, were the most glorious shade of cobalt blue and looked absolutely divine.

"Did he send you here?"

"No. In fact, he'll undoubtedly be quite cross to discover I came."

"Then why did you?"

"Because I wish to meet the person rules were broken for."

Well, fuck. The stupid part of me that had clung to hope beyond all good reason might well be dancing in joy at this news, but the saner sections were wondering why he'd risk something like that before the official coronation had even happened.

Or was it as Mathi theorized—he simply wasn't ready to let me go just yet?

And yet, if that *were* the case, why wouldn't he have come here himself? Or hell, simply picked up the phone and called me?

It made no sense.

"I have no desire to have rules broken on my behalf," I said. "I'll not attend—"

"That is not what I came here for, or indeed, what I want." She motioned to the chair opposite. "Please, sit. My neck grows tired of looking up at you."

I pulled out the chair and sat. For several seconds, she didn't speak. She just studied me in an intense manner, her eyes luminescent in the semi-darkness. It almost felt as if she were digging inside my very being, gaining a deep sense of the inner me even though that was not a talent the Myrkálfar had. Not as far as I was aware, anyway.

But then, Cynwrig had commented several times that his sister was far better at dealing with the day-to-day running of their kingdom than he ever could be. Perhaps this ability—whatever the hell it truly was—had something to do with that.

"Isn't your coming here to see me also breaking the rules? It's not like it could be considered business, given who I am."

Her smile held so many echoes of Cynwrig's that my stomach twisted. "Oh, this is most certainly a business meeting, even if I'm using it as an excuse to finally meet you."

"Why now, though? What is so urgent that it could not wait until after your father's commemoration?"

"That is something neither my brother, nor indeed I, are heavily involved in—other than his insistence on making that exception—"

"Technically," I cut in, "he didn't. The only reason I'm going is because Sgott was given a plus-one. I'm not even mentioned."

"Yes, but anyone who knows Sgott is aware of his attachment to you. It was my brother's way of inviting without doing so directly." She eyed me for a second. "As you have no doubt guessed, so please, let's do move on to the matter at hand."

"And that is?"

"A curious note I found when I was going through my father's files."

I frowned. "About me?"

"No. About your mother."

"Your father knew my mother?"

"She was the preeminent finder of relics in all of England, so it does make sense that he'd have used her services on certain occasions."

A comment that was just another reminder of how much I didn't know about Mom. Sure, I'd known she was a hunter, I'd known she'd occasionally worked for the fae council, but the preeminent finder in all of England, even above Lugh?

Certainly not. But I guess I shouldn't feel too bad, because even my brother hadn't known just how deeply involved in relic hunting Mom had been.

"I'm not aware of any specific time she worked with the Myrkálfar," I said. "Though she certainly undertook hunts for the fae council quite a few times."

"If my father hired her services, he would not have done it through the council. It would have been more personal in nature."

An interesting comment, given just how deeply Myrkálfar fingers were in the black-market pie. They certainly had more hope than the average human or even Ljósálfar elf of finding missing goods. "Was the note you found about one of those tasks?"

"It is more a task in waiting, and simply said, 'Contact Meabh Aodhán and ask her to find Geitha. You will need it for the coronation to keep the Dorcha Dearg throne safe from challengers.'"

Dorcha Dearg, the main Myrkálfar encampment in this area, and situated on—and under—the Peckfort Ridges to the west of Deva. I'd never been there, of course, but I'd seen plenty of photos of the weighty but wondrously exotic buildings that ran the length of the ridge. Over the centuries it had become something of a tourist attraction, forcing the Myrkálfar to not only patrol the area, but construct viewing platforms at a "safe" distance. Of course, ninety percent of the main encampment remained underground; the visible buildings housed those dealing with day-to-day administration tasks and meeting rooms for interactions with outside officialdom, including Deva's fae council.

"Who or what is Geitha, and why would it be needed to keep the throne safe from challengers? Both you and your brother are uncontested heirs, aren't you?"

"Yes, we are, but that doesn't mean there aren't those who would challenge given the opportunity. As to Geitha, there is a Myrkálfar goddess of destiny who bears that name, but it is unlikely my father wanted your mother to seek her. Not even a seeress with her capabilities could successfully undertake such a quest."

Maybe, maybe not. It would depend on what Beira—the goddess of winter and storms who'd been condemned to spend her time here on Earth in hag form, and who'd assigned Mom multiple relic hunts to undertake for the gods themselves—knew about Geitha, and whether in fact she remained one of the few gods who still interacted with their worshippers.

"There is no further mention of it in his personal files," she continued, "and there is also nothing to be found in the greater records. I have, of course, requested a review of all the old scrolls, but that will take some time." She paused. "However, my mother did have a necklace she called Geitha's Tears, and that is perhaps what he was referring to. It did go missing on my mother's death some two hundred years ago."

"It never resurfaced on the black market?"

A smile tugged at her lips. "You could be sure that if it had, we would have taken swift action to reclaim it."

And no doubt would have buried—quite literally, given the main talent of the Myrkálfar was the control of earth and stone—anyone involved in the theft.

"Your mother never spoke about it?"

"She once said it was gifted by the goddess to her at my father's coronation, and that one day, if we were blessed, the goddess's eye would turn to me and Cynwrig."

"That would suggest it has some sort of ceremonial place within the coronation."

"Yes, indeed. We have, of course, already started arrangements for the coronation, but the only time Geitha is mentioned during the formalities is after the crowns are placed; the goddess is called upon to give her blessing and her guidance to the new ruler. There is no mention as to how this should happen, which is damnably annoying." She studied me for a heartbeat. "I take it you have found nothing in your mother's files mentioning such a meeting with my father or indeed the commitment to undertake such a task?"

"No, but I haven't actually gone through my mother's files."

Or indeed, anything of hers. I might have moved into her bedroom in the months after her disappearance, but I certainly hadn't emptied her wardrobe or her drawers in the bathroom, or hell, gone through any of the boxes of old records she kept in the office. To do any of that would have meant accepting the fact she really wasn't coming back, and I hadn't wanted to take that final step.

There was a part of me that *still* didn't, even though we'd now found her body.

Grief surged with that thought and I pushed to my feet. "Would you like a cup of tea?"

"No, but thank you."

I strode over to the bar and dragged out the old kettle we kept underneath it for emergencies—such as the coffee machine breaking down and staff needing to make coffee the old-fashioned way—then filled it up and flicked it on. By which time, I had my emotions back under control and could face her again. "If Geitha's Tears do play a part in the coronation, however minor, why wouldn't your father have undertaken its finding earlier?"

Her hesitation was brief but nevertheless there. "You are aware my father was ill for some time?"

I nodded. There'd been various rumors about his illness, of course, but nothing had ever been confirmed. Even the official press statement released when he'd stepped back from physical duties had simply said the move was designed to ease the eventual succession of his heirs.

The intensity of her gaze increased, and that translucent glow appeared once more. Just for an instant, the knives flickered—a warning that something unusual rather than threatening was happening, and that basically clinched my suspicions that she was psychically "reading" me.

I obviously passed, because she continued softly, "For the few elves who live beyond a millennium, there is always a price to be paid. For my father, it was his mental faculties. By the time we realized it was happening, it was already too late, and it progressed rapidly once my mother died. Fae healers can work miracles, but diseases of the brain are beyond their ken."

"I'm sorry. That must have been hard to watch."

"Indeed." Her eyes gleamed briefly again, but this time, its cause was the sheen of tears. "The difficulty is, of course, that we believe the note was written in a moment of lucidity and then forgotten."

"There must be some sort of record explaining its importance, though, surely."

"Of course there should be, but remember, there hasn't been a coronation for a thousand years, and, for whatever reason, the scrolls detailing the minutiae were not fully transcribed when the digital age came. Then add the fact that many records and scrolls were lost in the fires that swept Dorcha Dearg back in the late 1400s, and you can see the problem."

I frowned. "I take it, then, with my mom no longer around, you want me to undertake the search for this item?"

"That would be ideal, yes."

"I can certainly try, but I am not my mother, and I generally need something more than a mere name to search out an item."

Which wasn't exactly true given I'd certainly searched the codex—which was basically a godly library I now had access to—with nothing more than a simple name before now.

"All I ask is that you try. Usual terms?"

I smiled. "I have no idea what the usual terms might be."

She laughed. "An admission that would have a less scrupulous person taking full advantage."

"Cynwrig wouldn't."

"Oh, my brother would, if it suited his purposes. He is no angel."

The kettle boiled, so I made my mug of tea and then walked back over and sat down. "How long have I got to find Geitha?"

"The coronation will be held at the end of the three-month mourning period."

"Which at least gives me a decent amount of time." I took a sip of tea. "I take it you'll pass on any information you might find in the scroll search?"

A smile tugged at her lips. "Which I suspect is a round-about way of asking if my brother will be in contact with you on this matter, and the answer is no. The rules of mourning forbid physical interaction with lovers who are not of Myrkálfar origins."

Meaning they *didn't* forbid "interaction" with their own kind. The lovely Orlah—the tall, dark-skinned elf with long, curly black hair and to-die-for figure who'd briefly interrupted our dinner at an upmarket and very expensive restaurant recently—would no doubt take full advantage of *that* situation. She'd certainly made it abundantly clear that she had her sights set on marriage *and* him.

"Unless on a matter of business," I added, somewhat uselessly, given I already knew what her reply would be.

"Yes, but this is not a matter he can deal with, because of your position in his life."

I half smiled. "I have no position, remember?"

Her cheeks dimpled. "Oh, I heard you and he had plenty of positions."

I just about choked on my tea. Talk about getting some of my own medicine back. Darby—my best friend since forever and the light elf who was now dating my brother—and I always shared sexual gossip, but I just hadn't expected Cynwrig to be doing the same with his sister.

Although maybe he hadn't; if she was a reader, she could have easily skimmed that bit of information.

"Well," I managed, when I could speak again, "he is a dark elf and you lot are very imaginative."

"Indeed, we are." She reached into her pocket, drew out three pieces of paper, and handed the first to me. It was a simple black business card. "That is my private number and not to be shared elsewhere. Call me when you find anything, and we can arrange a meeting. It is best not to talk over the phone—the palace has ears, and not all of them are friendly."

I raised my eyebrows but dragged out my phone, added her name and number to my contacts list, then gave the card back. She nodded and slid the other two pieces of paper across the table to me. The first was an intricately drawn picture of a gorgeous-looking silver pendant that contained two tear-drop-shaped deep red stones— Geitha's Tears, obviously. I tapped the image. "Are they rubies?"

"No, painite, which is far rarer. It's a pleochroic stone that emits different hues depending on the angle you're viewing them from, and has a strong green fluorescence under certain lights."

Maybe their rarity was why the necklace had gone missing. If the palace had ears then it undoubtedly also had light-fingered thieves—though it'd be a risky business at the best of times stealing from a Myrkálfar, let alone from the Lùtairs.

She motioned to the larger, folded piece of paper. "I debated whether to give that one to you, but given the search for the hoard and the rise of certain darker elements, it's better that you have it. Make of it what you will."

She rose, gave me a nod, and left, unlocking the front door with a flick of her hand, then relocking it once she was through.

I picked up the larger piece of paper and unfolded it. It appeared to be an old newspaper article on what looked to be some sort of archeology dig. Before I could read it, wood song whispered of movement. Eljin was awake and up.

I quickly downed the rest of my tea, then rose and tucked the two pieces of paper into the front pocket of my jeans. Instinct was suggesting I keep them to myself for the time being, and I wasn't about to gainsay her. Not when she'd saved my life multiple times over the last few weeks.

I ran lightly up the stairs to the second floor, punched in the code for the lock, then headed up to my living quarters. The smell of bacon teased my nostrils and my stomach rumbled.

"I heard you moving around downstairs," he said, the faintest hint of French accenting his warm tones, "and figured you might like a bite to eat."

"You figured right." I stepped onto the landing and immediately tugged off my sweater. The room was warm, the fire still bright, suggesting he hadn't arrived all that long ago. "To what do I owe the honor of this visit, though? I thought you were meeting some friends this evening for a boys' night out."

He glanced around, the burnished gold flecks in his buttery brown eyes gleaming brightly in the fire's light. He was a typical Talien pixie in looks, with wide shoulders, slim hips, and thick mahogany hair. Though his face was probably a little too sharp to be called handsome, his lips were full and definitely made to give pleasure, be it as a kiss or in more intimate explorations. I knew that from experience.

Right now, he was wearing my ratty old green dressing gown, which should have made him look ridiculous, but somehow succeeded in doing the exact opposite.

"I was, but it ended far too early. I thought I might as

well come here and surprise you with breakfast." He paused briefly. "Who was with you? It sounded like a woman rather than Mathi."

"It was just someone wanting me to find something."

"At this hour?"

"Most night folk don't keep the same hours as the rest of us." I slid my hands around his waist and kissed the back of his neck. "So, breakfast. Why? Or is the answer to that one obvious?"

He chuckled softly. "It's been two days since I had you in my bed, and I ache. Badly."

I laughed. "Then you shouldn't have started cooking the bacon. Now we are fated to eat it before we can do anything else."

"The pan is barely even hot. It can certainly be taken off the heat for the necessary amount of time."

"If the necessary amount of time is anything less than an hour, I'll be severely disappointed."

He chuckled again. "I am certainly not one to disappoint a lady."

He definitely hadn't so far. I undid the dressing gown's sash, then slid my hands down the chiseled length of his body and lightly ran my fingers across his erection. He made a low sound deep in his throat, then flicked off the gas and spun around, sweeping me up and off my feet in one smooth movement. I laughed and snuggled against his chest, even though the bedroom wasn't all that far away. Nothing really was up here—the word bijou had definitely been developed with this place in mind, even if we had far more space on this floor than many of our neighbors, thanks to Gran illegally raising the roof line and creating a usable loft.

Once we reached my bedroom, he placed me on my feet and began to undress me, taking his time to explore the flesh revealed with teeth and tongue before removing the next layer. By the time I was naked, I was aching with desire and needing him so badly I could barely think.

I slid my hands up his taut body and slipped the gown from his shoulders, then pushed him backward, onto the bed. I climbed up after him, straddling but not immediately sheathing him.

"There is a vital question you've yet to answer," I murmured, my lips so close to his, I could taste the desire raging through him.

"You," he whispered huskily, "are an evil woman, asking questions at a moment like this."

"Ah, but it's a question vital to my future happiness."

I lowered myself just a fraction, and he groaned, his hands sliding to my hips but holding no force. "And what might that question be?"

"Are we having eggs with the bacon, or will it be a simple butty?"

He laughed and kissed me hard, thrusting upward even as I went down, until he was completely and utterly sheathed.

We moved as one, slowly at first but with increasing urgency, until all I felt, all I wanted, was him coming deep inside. Need and desire combined, a force so fierce it was nigh on explosive. My orgasm hit, and I gasped, shuddering and shaking, unable to breathe or think as the deep, unde-niable pleasure consumed me. He came a heartbeat later, his body stiffening underneath mine, his deep groan echoing.

For the longest time after, neither of us moved. When I could finally breathe again, I rolled to one side and tucked myself close. He traced a finger lightly down my cheek and my neck and stopped at the stone pendant sitting just above my breasts.

"You're always wearing this, and I have to say, it's an extremely unusual piece of jewelry. The casing looks hand-made, and the stone has an odd resonance."

"We call it the Eye, and it's basically a focus stone. It used to be Mom's, and now it's mine. Lugh made the cage so I could keep it close to my heart and not risk losing it."

None of which was a lie, even if it wasn't exactly the whole truth. The Eye was in fact the actual eye of the goddess Ethine, who'd been turned to stone long ago and who'd gifted her eyes in the form of these black seeing stones to both an ancestor of mine and the hags. Mom had indeed used it to amplify her second sight when relic hunt-ing, and to keep in contact with Beira and the other hags when she was undertaking tasks for them, but it was in truth far more than that. It was one third of a triune—the knives and the codex being the other two—that had been designed to gift the women of my line with foresight, knowledge, and protection, supposedly providing all the tools we needed to fight those seeking the rebirth of the dark gods in the tangible world.

Or so Beira had informed me recently.

Of course, the Myrkálfar weren't the only ones who'd forgotten or lost items vital to their futures, and until I'd come into possession of all three items, the true power of the triune had not been used or even remembered for centuries. Which meant that between the lack of directions and my own inexperience when it came to my recently emerged talents, my ability to use the triune to its full capacity was currently somewhat limited.

"It sometimes glows when you sleep," he commented.

"Probably when I'm dreaming." I shrugged. "Not that I get prophetic dreams all that often, thankfully."

He ran a finger across the cage, his skin briefly caressing the stone. The Eye flared to life, its heat burning against my skin while the lightning that sat deep within its dark heart flashed violently, spinning purple light through the shadows haunting the room.

It had never reacted that way before—not to someone else's touch, anyway. I wasn't entirely sure what it meant, especially given the odd edge of violence that seemed to accompany the flash.

"Is that supposed to happen?" he asked.

"The lightning often appears when I'm attempting to do a seer search, but generally, no." I paused, then added with a grin, "Maybe it simply doesn't like you."

"Maybe you should take it off when we're together, then," he said, amused. "Getting burned by all that energy at the wrong moment could definitely be deflating."

"And here I was thinking there is very little in this world that can put a man off his game when they're close to the summit."

"Depends on the man and the distraction." He kissed my forehead, his lips warm on my skin. "What time do you have to get up in the morning?"

"Mathi's picking me up at eight forty-five."

"Then shall I wake you at eight with bacon and eggs? That should give you time for breakfast and a shower."

"Seven thirty would give us time for all that *and* sex."

"But only a couple of hours of sleep for you."

I grinned. "I'll survive."

"If you fall asleep in the middle of that council meeting, do not blame me."

I laughed and kissed him goodnight. The Eye's heat chased me into sleep, and though no dreams disturbed my slumber, the thick sense of approaching danger nevertheless settled deep within.

As usual, though, there was very little explanation as to exactly what form that danger came in. As Treasa had noted, it was damnably annoying.

The fae council building was located next to the Deva City Council offices and was an uninspiring red-brick and concrete construction. Mathi's driver parked illegally out front, then jumped out and ran around to the rear passenger door, holding an umbrella above the two of us so we didn't get soaked walking to the entrance. I was wearing a long woolen coat with a hood, and thick, wool-lined, waterproof boots, but given it was bucketing down, the umbrella was nevertheless appreciated.

The guard opened the door with a perfunctory nod at Mathi, and we headed up the bland but functional concrete stairs to the second-floor meeting hall. The double doors were metal, and led into an antechamber that was protected by spells designed to detect both regular and magically enhanced weapons. Which meant, of course, that alarms went off the minute I strode in, thanks to the fact I was wearing my knives.

Mathi rolled his eyes and switched the sound off, then motioned me on through the next set of doors. The meeting chamber was the size of a grand hall, but without any of the usual decorations generally found in them—no wall hangings, no crests, no paintings. Basically, there was nothing here that could be manipulated in any way by the elves or pixies present. Even the furniture was plastic, which would have normally given the shifters a serious advantage thanks to their greater strength, but aside from the chambers being an electronically null zone to prevent the use of listening devices being deployed and conversations recorded, it was also wrapped in magic so strong it actually prevented shapeshifting.

Unlike the other two times I'd faced the council in here in this room, the table was less than half occupied. There were three light elves, four shifters—including the rat shifter who'd been the convener at the previous meeting—and the blue-haired pixie who seemed to be a fixture at these things. But then, she was a Malloyei, and they'd always been more political than any other branch of pixies.

My gaze was drawn to the far end of the table, where Cynwrig usually sat. His seat was empty, of course, but I was rather surprised to see there were no other Myrkálfar here. I could understand the Lùtairs undertaking a three-month morning period, but I couldn't imagine it extending out to all Myrkálfar.

But maybe the Myrkálfar just didn't think the allocation of the relic for my first official hunt to be of any sort of importance, and I couldn't say I blamed them. In all honesty, I was surprised they'd called a meeting at all—surely they could have just passed whatever information they had on to me via Mathi.

Or they simply wanted to remind me I now worked for them, and had best start taking things seriously. Which I most certainly was, but more because this council represented a means of finding Mom's killer and uncovering the Ninkil who infested their ranks rather than any real need to find the hoard.

Mathi pulled out the plastic chair at the head of the table and seated me, then moved around to sit next to a gray-haired elf with heavily lined features and pale blue, somewhat rheumy eyes. In elf terms, he was an elder statesman—an elf who'd moved past breeding age and slipped into his twilight years. I didn't know his name, but from the little I'd seen of him, his mind remained as sharp as a tack. I couldn't help but wonder if that would change the closer he got to his millennium year, or whether he'd be far luckier than Cynwrig's father.

"It is a pleasure to see you again, Ms. Aodhán," he said, in his cool, somewhat whispery tone.

I smiled. "I'd wager there's a few here who'd disagree with that statement, given they think my brother is a thief and I'm a necessary evil."

A smile tugged very, *very* briefly at his lips, which was probably as close to a laugh as I was ever likely to get from someone of his vintage. "I daresay you could be right, but that is neither here nor there. You were called here to receive your first assignment."

Mathi had already told me what my first assignment was, but given he shouldn't have, I wasn't about to out him. "And how are we tackling these things—in order of danger-ousness, or via a simpler method, such as alphabetically?"

"We do this alphabetically, for the most part."

I raised my eyebrows. "Why 'for the most part'?"

Though the elder elf's expression remained benign, I'd been around them long enough now to sense the quick flash of his irritation.

"Borrhás's Horn is your first target. Borrhás was a god of the cold north wind and the bringer of winter. In times past, he was also known as the North Wind or the Devouring One."

The latter no doubt being the reason he'd leapt ahead in the finding order. "There were no relics starting with *A*?"

"There are indeed a couple," a shifter to my left replied.

I waited for a second, but when nothing else was forthcoming, I glanced at Mathi. He was lounging back in his chair with an amused sort of expression, and simply raised an eyebrow. Which, in this case, was Mathi shorthand for "keep on questioning them."

I flicked my gaze back to the elder elf. "So why has the horn hit the top of the find list? Was there an incident or something that prompted it?"

"There was indeed," the rat shifter said. His nose was twitching slightly, though whether it was in distaste at my presence or something else, I couldn't say. "We were notified of an unusual occurrence a few weeks ago, and a subsequent investigation led us to believe the horn might be the cause."

"Meaning we have someone running around armed with a dangerous relic, but if I had not asked the question, you would not have informed me—have I got that right?"

"You will be told exactly what you need to be told," another elf said, in a condescending manner. "Besides, there are few relics that are not dangerous in the hands of the wrong person."

"Though we do hope," my pixie counterpart added, "that finding one to two might indeed lead us to the hoard itself."

"It's been over six months since the hoard disappeared," the youngest-looking elf said, glancing her way. "It's unlikely the hoard remains intact, even if, as far as we can ascertain, no items have as yet hit the market."

The urge to say it most certainly hadn't been dismantled as yet rose, but I resisted. It was unlikely Carla Wilson was physically in this room—surely the spells that prevented the various animal shifters from taking their alternate form would also prevent a face shifter from doing it—but even so, I couldn't risk mentioning my visions of her tete-a-tete with her boss. She might not be here personally, but she most certainly had her claws in at least one of the councilors, and I had to presume that person or persons were in this room. One mention would give them warning, and I couldn't risk the man in charge extending his shield to prevent me even hearing their conversations.

"With the hold the Myrkálfar have on the black market, anyone with any sort of sense wouldn't risk selling or even moving any item from the hoard this soon." The speaker this time was a woman with a sharp face and wiry red hair —a fox shifter, obviously, though not the same one I'd seen previously.

"Six months is hardly what most would consider soon," the rat shifter commented. "But I do agree that, for whatever reason, it is likely the hoard remains intact."

And the main reason it remained that way wasn't so much the Myrkálfar, but rather the fact Carla and her boss wanted to find Ninkil's Harpē—a relic that was both a sword and sickle, and the only means by which Ninkil could be called back into the world—first. Why they'd stolen the hoard *before* they'd found it, I couldn't say; maybe the perfect opportunity had presented itself and they'd simply taken the risk. Or maybe they hadn't expected the Harpē to be so hard to find.

And maybe if they'd used Mom's finding skills rather than murdering her, they might have had it in their hands by now.

Although, given Mom had, according to Beira, been having worrying visions about Ninkil's rise and wouldn't have willingly gone along with such a search, the latter was unlikely.

The elderly elf banged the gavel, drawing attention back to him. "Conjecture over what is and isn't happening with the hoard is pointless. Our objective is to find it, and if we have to do that one item at a time, then we shall."

"Just how many items were in the hoard to start with?" I said. "Because you only have my services for two years, remember. After that, it'll cost you."

"There are twenty-three items in the main hoard," the blue-haired pixie said. "But several other chests were taken. We suspect the thieves were uncertain as to what, exactly, they were meant to take."

I frowned. "They had the help of the bibliothecary, be it willingly or not, so that really isn't likely."

"That may well be true, but given the bibliothecary is dead, it is also a statement that can never be confirmed."

And that was the precise reason Carla and her boss killed off their employees once they'd outlived their usefulness. The dead could wag no tongues. "What else do we know of the horn?"

"Not a lot, aside from the fact we believe it was cleaved in two at some point. It is made from the horn of an auroch —a breed of cattle that no longer exists—and has an intricate sleeve of carved gold around the rim and a similarly intricate stopper," the old elf said. "We're unsure whether it comes with fitted rings through which legs could be attached to allow it to stand, or if indeed it could be strung with rope and slung around the shoulder and be carried."

"That's not much to go on."

"It is all the information the recent archives have."

"And the older archives? Or even the council records?"

"You forget that the council was not responsible for

guarding the hoard, nor did we know where it was located," the rat shifter replied. "It is also fair to say the Ljósálfar would never share such information willingly."

"But surely you must have records somewhere—maybe some old scrolls listing all items when the hoard first came into Ljósálfar hands for safekeeping?"

"While it is true we were the guards and did undertake the necessary inventory," the older elf said, "we were not responsible for the safety of those records. That has always been the council's purview. At least, it has been since the great war and Liadon was installed as keeper and recorder."

In other words, no one was about to claim responsibility for any records that were missing. Nothing worked quite like officialdom.

"Speaking of Liadon," I said, "has my request to access said records been granted? Because if you want results, you cannot keep hamstringing me—unless, of course, one of you fine people is happy to undertake the odious task of going through eons of records yourself."

"That was certainly an option put forward," Mathi said, amusement evident. "But it was in the end decided that the council's time was better spent elsewhere. Of course, Liadon's presence was also a factor."

I raised my eyebrows. The fact the councilors were wary of her had trepidation stirring, but at least I had two advantages over them—my knives were not affected by the restricting magic of this building, nor was my ability to use the air as a protective or aggressive force.

"Does that mean I've been given unqualified approval to search the records?"

"Yes, indeed, although Liadon will always be present to keep an eye on everything that you do," the older elf said. "Abuse our trust, and access will be revoked."

I nodded. That was not unexpected, and simply meant I'd have to take more time—and perhaps win the trust of this Liadon, whoever or whatever she might be—before I began the search for any mention of Mom.

The older elf studied me for a second and then said, "You have been given access to both the building and Liadon 24-7. Mathi will take you there now and give you entry into Liadon's domain."

"Good luck," someone muttered farther down the table.

I raised my eyebrows but didn't reply. Mathi rose and motioned me to the door ahead of him. I waited until we were out of the antechamber and moving toward a much smaller set of stairs to the left of the doors before asking, "So who or what is Liadon?"

The stairs were concrete, like everything else in this place, but barely wide enough for one person. Mathi stepped ahead of me and began the climb. "No one is really sure what she is, other than the fact she is not, and never was, human."

"Is she dangerous?"

"Again, unknown."

"Then why are councilors scared of her?"

He glanced over his shoulder, expression amused. "They would strenuously object to the word scared. Wary is their preferred term."

I rolled my eyes. "Then why are the councilors so *wary* of her?"

"You'll see soon enough."

I scowled at him. He was well aware of it, too, because his amusement seemed to drift past me. The stairs wound around to the right, and an odd scent touched the air—a scent that was musky and unpleasant, reminding me vaguely of either rotten eggs or produce.

"Next time I'll be bringing nose plugs," I muttered, switching to breathing through my mouth. It didn't help. The scent just coated my throat and made me want to dry retch.

"Oh, it gets better."

"Are you being sarcastic?"

"You're well aware that there's not a sarcastic bone in my body."

I snorted and did my best to ignore the increasing toxicity of the scent as we continued to climb. After what seemed like forever, we reached a large, intricately carved iron door. One that was layered with magic that felt old but neither foul nor good.

"What is this place?" I murmured.

"The council calls it the cavern of the gods."

"It's hardly a cavern when it's sitting in the roof of the building."

"The magic encasing the door isn't protective, and the door isn't really a door. It's one part of a portal—one that allows Liadon access to this world and us to interact directly with her. But only when necessary, which for most is never."

"I'm not liking the sound of all this."

"It is definitely a case of being careful what you wish for." He glanced at me, amusement twitching his lips. "You ready to enter?"

"Well, I didn't climb all those stairs and endure that gods-awful smell just to back away at the end goal."

"Then press your hand against the door. The magic has been set to register your imprint and your access will start immediately."

I glanced at him. "I take it you've already got access?"

He shook his head. "I wasn't given clearance."

I frowned. "Why not?"

"Because Liadon has final say over who does and does not enter her domain. You were approved. I was not."

"To repeat, why not?"

He shrugged. "One of the conditions under which she agreed to become keeper of the records was having the final say over access. We cannot gainsay her without risking the destruction of said records."

"This Liadon becomes more and more intriguing."

"And if you stop delaying the inevitable with your questions, you'll have the answers to them and all the others undoubtedly rolling through your brain."

I reached past him and pressed my hand against the door. It was weirdly warm to my touch and a little bit oily—not enough to be repulsive but still unpleasant. Then the symbols on the door came to life, glowing with an odd green luminosity, and heat rolled across my palm and fingers. It reminded me a little of a scanner's light, and made me wonder if the magic was taking a record of my handprint.

Then the light died and the door slid silently open. Darkness lay beyond. Darkness and that thick, musty, and very off scent. I warily stepped over the threshold. Prickly energy washed against my face and hands, and I stopped, even though the knives weren't reacting. I glanced at Mathi. "Are you waiting here or leaving?"

"Leaving, as I have a meeting I must attend before the commemoration." He paused. "Do not fall down the rabbit hole of information, and remember to keep your wits about you at all times. She'll be watching everything you do closely, and she does not like others taking liberties with her information."

It was hardly hers, but I knew what he meant. I nodded

and impulsively touched his arm. "Thank you. I'll see you this afternoon."

"With an official and unofficial report."

"Indeed." I smiled but it faded quickly as I stepped fully into the gloom. There was a soft "swish" as the door slid shut behind me, and the gloom deepened. I didn't move, waiting for my eyes to adjust, aware of movement somewhere in the distance but unable to see a damn thing.

After a few tense seconds, a pale green light flared to life a couple of feet above my head, and a soft but strangely remote voice said, "Welcome, Bethany Aodhán. The orb will lead you down to my vaults. Please do not stray from the path it takes, as this world of mine is vast, and dangers lurk in her deeper depths."

I didn't immediately reply, because the little light took off with surprising speed, and it was all I could do to catch up with it. Liadon must have seen my struggle, because it slowed, allowing me to catch up, and then proceeded at an easier pace.

"Am I allowed to ask you questions?"

"You can always ask. Whether I reply is a different matter."

A smile tugged at my lips. "That very much sounds like something Beira would say. She's—"

"I'm well aware who Beira is" came the reply. "She and I had dealings in far earlier times."

"Good dealings or bad?"

"When dealing with old goddesses, they are often one and the same."

There was amusement in her otherworldly voice, which went some way to easing my immediate tension. The existence of a sense of humor didn't mean she wouldn't kill me, of course, but it did at least mean there was far more to her than just the soulless guardian the council's warnings and my own imagination had suggested.

The orb continued to bob along, washing its strange green luminance across walls that were glass smooth and black. As Dorothy had been known to say, "I've a feeling we're not in Kansas anymore."

Down and down we went, the path never altering its steepness. The deep sense of distance between me and the "upper" world increased, as did the growing awareness of the vastness of this place, though I could see little more than vague shapes beyond the gloss of the sheer walls surrounding me. The stench, I noticed, didn't appear to be as bad down here, although it was always possible my nose was simply adjusting to it.

The little light finally led me into a circular cavern that was as high as it was wide. There were no computers, no shelves full of books, no scrolls of any kind, and little in the way of furniture other than the solitary, comfortable-looking chair sitting in the center of the room. I glanced behind me. There was also no sign of the tunnel I'd come through. Nothing but smooth rock.

I was trapped here until Liadon decided to let me go.

I flexed my fingers and tried to relax. I had no reason to fear Liadon unless I did something stupid, and I wasn't about to do *that* on our first meeting.

The little green light was hovering over the chair, meaning I was probably meant to go sit. I hesitated, briefly imagining all sorts of scenarios where chains or arms whipped up from the plush sides and trapped me. Sleep, or lack thereof, had definitely supercharged my imagination.

With a slight shake of my head at my own errant thoughts, I walked over and sat down. It felt like I was sinking into a supportive cloud. A bell chimed, and I had a sense of movement, though the cavern and the light looked unchanged.

The only thing that had changed was the presence now standing in front of me. Although standing was something of a misnomer given she didn't actually have any legs.

Liadon, the keeper of the records, was a goddamn Nagi.

FOUR

"Welcome to my world, Bethany Aodhán," she said, drawing my gaze up her long, snake-like lower body, past her naked human torso and full, round breasts, to her face.

A face that was both angelic and demonic all at the same time, and surrounded by a cobra-like hood.

Nagi, according to Lugh, were semi-divine—though in their case, "spirit" replaced "human" in the "more than a human but not quite a god" definition. He'd apparently come across one in a hunt that had taken him to an old underground palace deep within a South Asian rainforest. He hadn't stolen anything from her but had instead engaged in a conversation and gotten the location of the relic he was actually looking for. From what he'd said, they were capable of attaining either full snake or spirit form, and their venom could kill in an instant, though under the gods' decree, they could not attack without reason, or risk losing their divinity and be cast out into the fold of neverness forever.

Neverness, apparently, was the spirit world version of hell.

Stealing treasure from them was the surest way of getting dead, though, so if Liadon considered these records her "treasure," then I sure as hell needed to ask for permission before I tried undertaking any search for information about Mom.

"I see very little fear in your eyes, young Aodhán."

"I must be hiding it extremely well, then."

She laughed, a soft and surprisingly warm sound. "I have known your line before. Fear might rise, but it is often overridden by stubbornness or even incaution."

"I'd love to say I have none of those traits, but that would be a lie."

She smiled, her golden gaze sweeping my length, only to still when she saw the knives. "Ethine's Claws. I take it you also have the Eye and the codex?"

"Yes." I hesitated. "Did you know her when she lived?"

"Indeed, I did. Can you use her gift to its full capacity?"

"I'm still learning but basically, yes."

"Then why have you asked for access to my records?" Her gaze hardened just a little. "The codex can give you far more than all the words I protect ever could."

I hesitated. The truth wasn't something I wanted to reveal this early, but it wasn't like I had a choice. Nagi abhorred dishonesty almost as much as they did theft.

"There are several reasons, the first and main one being the fact the codex holds no records of the modern world or indeed, human interaction."

"And your other reason?"

"Has nothing to do with the codex, but rather the fact that the council has been infiltrated by the Ninkilim, which is how we believe the hoard was stolen."

"We?"

"Beira has asked me to help stop their rise."

"Knowing Beira, she would have demanded rather than asked. Anything else?"

I drew in a deeper breath and released it slowly. "The people behind the theft killed my mother. I believe there might be information within the council records that could lead me to find them."

"Theft and murder? Now there is a quest I can get behind."

"Then you'll help me?"

She didn't immediately answer, instead sliding around me, her body coiling and uncoiling almost languidly as she moved, her black scales possessing a vibrant green and gold sheen under the pale light still hovering above my head. "I can see no lies in you, but caution is nevertheless warranted on my part, given the records I protect hold an importance beyond the ken of many."

I frowned. "Don't take offense, but why would council records—"

"It is not just council records I guard, young Aodhán. It is the records of races, *all* races, for all the eons they have existed."

I stared at her for a moment. "Meaning this place is basically the earthly equivalent of the codex library?"

"In some respects, yes, though I would imagine their surrounds are far more beauteous than mine."

"It's certainly far airier, but I would think there's far more to your domain than what you're currently allowing me to see."

"Perhaps." She stopped in front of me again, her long body coiling close to her torso. She crossed her arms over her breasts and leaned back against those coils, studying me some more. "What information do you wish to find for your current quest?"

Current quest—a deliberate choice of words, no doubt, given her earlier statement of caution. Perhaps she intended to judge the merits of my overall quest on how I handled the official one. "What are the boundaries of my searches? Am I just restricted to council records?"

She smiled. "You were given all access, though I do not believe the councilors understand the entirety of my records or the freedom that allows you."

"That is excellent news."

Her smile increased, revealing the tops of two large fangs rather than human teeth. It was a somewhat ghastly sight, but I somehow managed to curb my instinctive gasp.

"For one such as you, seeking revenge through the texts of time, I would imagine it is."

"Then, for this first search, I would like all the information you have on the god Borrhás, anything you might have on his Horn, including how and why it became part of the hoard, and any mention there might be of it within the council records, for as far back as they go."

She raised a pale eyebrow. "That is indeed a large request."

"Go big or go home, as the saying goes."

"A saying I am not familiar with, even if the intent is obvious. The scope of the search means it will take some time. I would suggest you start by cross-checking with your godly library."

"I will." I paused. "How long will your search take?"

"It will take as long as it takes, but I will send my orb to fetch you when I have the information ready. It will now guide you back to your world."

The chair tilted forward a little, politely dumping me onto my feet. The green light darted forward toward the wall behind the Nagi. As its light caressed the black stone, a small section slid to one side, revealing the dark corridor once again. The light shot inside as I cautiously made my way around Liadon to follow.

But as I stepped into the corridor, she said, "You are very much your mother's daughter, Bethany, but your father's blood runs strong in you, and darkness flows deep in the master of storms and lightning's line. Be wary of falling too far into the tempest."

Then the door closed on her words, leaving me with her orb and a shit ton of questions.

The first thing I did when I reached the "real" world again was drag out my phone and check the time. It was close to twelve, meaning I'd been down there for a whole lot longer than it had seemed.

I swore and ran down the stairs, my footsteps echoing into the emptiness. As I reached the first floor and regained cell service, I called an Uber; five minutes, they said.

I hoped they broke the land speed record because even though the traffic at midday wasn't anywhere near as bad as it was in peak hours, the shitty weather would still slow things down. And with my clothes stinking of the Nagi, I desperately needed all the time I could get to scrub my skin before Sgott picked me up for the commemoration.

The Uber hadn't arrived by the time I got down to the main road, so I dug out some old spray-on deodorant from my purse and tried to at least mute the fouler scent. I wasn't sure it worked, but the Uber driver didn't say anything. Maybe he was simply being polite.

For once, the traffic was on our side, and it only took ten minutes to arrive at the rear lane. I ran through the still-heavy rain to the rear door and punched in the code. The building's song was alive with movement and weight, suggesting we had a good crowd in today, which was surprising considering the weather. I shucked off my wet coat, slinging it over my arm as I made my way down the hall. Ingrid—the green-haired pixie who was now the full-time manager—was behind the bar serving customers, but glanced up as I walked in.

"Jonnie rang in sick, so I had to call in Kitty."

Jonnie was one of our full-timers who worked as a waiter on the first floor. Kitty was currently a temp, but likely to go full time come tourist season. "You're running the show now, Ingrid. You don't need my approval for that sort of thing."

Her cheeks dimpled. "Old habits die hard. I also put a list of the stock needing reordering today on your desk, or do you want me to run with that as well?"

I hesitated. I'd already done the week's payroll and payments, but orders were an almost daily task. "It might be safer if you do it for the time being. I have no idea how long this commemoration is going to run for, and I have the council business to attend to on top of that."

"I'll do it after the midday rush is over with, then."

"Don't be afraid to do it after hours and claim overtime."

Her cheeks dimpled again. "Since when have I ever been afraid to claim overtime?"

I laughed and headed on up. After relocking the door to my quarters, I ran up the remaining stairs, chucking my purse onto the sofa, then stripping off my clothes and dumping them all into the washing machine. I set it on the longest cycle possible, then headed into the bathroom for a shower. Sgott arrived just as I was standing in front of my wardrobe in my knickers and bra, deciding what to wear because I had absolutely no idea what the traditional mourning color was for the Myrkálfar. Humanity favored black, but something within suspected the dark elves would not.

"Bethany?" he called out as he reached the top of the stairs.

"In the bedroom trying to pick an outfit. Any suggestion, color-wise?"

"White. They believe it signifies purity and rebirth."

"Huh."

I glared at my wardrobe a few seconds longer, then dug out a knitted, slim-fitting, long-sleeved dress with a subtle gathered detail on the side and a small V-neckline. It was simple and elegant and, most importantly, warm. Or as warm as any dress was likely to be in winter. I paired it with knee-high nude-colored boots and a camel-colored woolen jacket. Once dressed, I grabbed a matching purse and tucked my knives into it. While I definitely wouldn't need them anytime soon and could technically call them to me from any location if a situation did happen to arise, I still felt safer with them close. That might change as time passed and I grew used to the foibles and powers of the triune, but for now, I was playing it safe.

Sgott waited near the stairs, wearing a neatly creased white suit and black-and-white wingtips. I rose onto my toes and kissed his cheek. "I had no idea you could still buy shoes like that. They're pretty impressive-looking, especially when you've feet as big as yours."

"They're golfing shoes. Had them for ages."

"Since when did you play golf?"

"Not since becoming head of the night division, but

they're the only shoes I have that are anywhere close to white. You ready?"

I quickly snagged my phone and wallet from my other purse, then nodded, even though my insides quivered at the thought of seeing Cynwrig again. Or worse, the thought of *not* seeing him, or talking to him, one last time.

I followed him down to the ground floor, then out the rear door. It was still pouring outside, although I could feel a lessening of its ferocity around the more distant reaches of the storm cell, suggesting it was likely to clear by nightfall.

And the fact that I knew all that without deliberately connecting to or reaching for the storm's power was yet another indicator of how much stronger that part of me had become in such a short amount of time.

Sgott had driven his car all the way down the lane and parked it next to the rear veranda, basically blocking the lane for any delivery vans needing to use it but ensuring neither of us got saturated while we got into the car.

The commemoration was being held in the Pavilion Suite at the racecourse, which was apparently one of their larger rooms, capable of holding over five hundred people. Ushers with big umbrellas met us as we parked in the flagged-off area and guided us in the right direction. It was a massive operation, and there was literally a sea of white umbrellas moving back and forth from the parking area to the main building's entrance, but everything flowed without any problems that I could see.

The long hallway down to the Pavilion Suite was hushed, the gloom of the day barely lifted by intermittent downlights. There was an usher at the door to take our names, and another to take our coats, then we were waved inside.

The quiet murmur of conversation ran across my senses as we entered the room. Sgott caught my elbow and guided me right, toward a quieter corner in this vast open space.

"How does this sort of thing work?" I asked softly, my gaze scanning the room, looking for someone familiar. I couldn't see Mathi or even Ruadhán, let alone Cynwrig or Treasa.

"We drink and mingle, but because of your unique situation, I would suggest waiting until he approaches us." He paused. "It's likely he won't, though, so don't be getting your hopes up."

"If he doesn't come talk to us, what was the whole point of breaking the rules and inviting me here?"

"That is a question I cannot answer, lass."

I waved a hand. "I know. I was just thinking out loud." I snagged a sparkling water from the tray of a passing waiter. "Will there be much in the way of official speeches? Or is it basically just a wake and we're here to do nothing more than pay our respects to the family, and to reminisce about the glorious life of the deceased?"

"There will be a couple of speeches, likely one from Gethen's long-term business partner, and one from both Treasa and Cynwrig. They probably won't mingle until after that duty is done."

"Then expect me to haunt your heels, because I know very few people here." I paused. "Though if Ruadhán wanders by for a chat, expect me to abandon you."

A smile tugged at his lips, though it was barely visible through the—admittedly much tamer than usual—beard. "Whatever opinion Ruadhán may have of you, he's unlikely to be anything but cordial while you're in my presence."

"He's nothing but cordial when I'm not," I replied. "It's

just that his distaste practically oozes from his skin, and that makes him rather uncomfortable to be around."

"Understandable, given the man sometimes makes my skin itch." He shrugged. "Though that's due more to his oft-deliberate stretching of the law while remaining within its broader terms. Shall we brave the tempest of small talk?"

I slipped my arm through the hook of his and forced a smile. "Let's do it."

In the end, it wasn't as bad as I'd thought it would be. Sgott's presence by my side definitely eased the coldness I'd have otherwise gotten from many of those in the room. Inevitably, we did come across Ruadhán.

He gave me a stiff, somewhat perfunctory nod. "Bethany, it is a pleasure to see you again, even if the circumstances are less than ideal."

A comment that made me wonder what he would consider ideal. A dark alley where a body could be disposed of easily, perhaps? Which was a totally inappropriate and unwarranted thought, but still...

I replied politely, then touched Sgott's arm. "I'm going to get a refill. Would you like something?"

"No, I'm right thanks, lass."

I glanced at Ruadhán and raised my glass in silent question. He shook his head and, as I left, began talking shop with Sgott. There were a number of white-clad waiters circulating around the room with drink trays and nibbles, but I made a beeline for the bar, wanting to avoid being in the same airspace as Ruadhán for as long as possible. Which was something of a new development. Granted, I'd never liked the man, but I'd always been able to at least tolerate him, if only for Mathi's sake. Was the fact I no longer *had* to a contributing factor to the increasing intensity of my dislike? Possibly.

A tall pale woman with short bright yellow hair took my order and empty glass, then filled another and slid it across to me. As she did so, a small bell chimed, and silence instantly descended.

I swung around, the drink forgotten behind me. At the far end of the room, on a small stage sitting in front of white curtains on which the Lùtair family crest—a hammer and anvil—was emblazoned, three people appeared. The first was a man I didn't know, but likely the long-term business partner Sgott had mentioned. The second was Treasa, looking stunning in a white pantsuit, her long dark hair curled on the top of her head like a crown. The third…

My breath caught in my throat, and my heart ached.

Cynwrig.

Looking divine in a white suit that emphasized his wide shoulders and classic V-shaped torso that tapered down to legs that were long and perfectly muscled. His chiseled features, so achingly familiar, were set into hardness, and though I couldn't see his eyes from this far back, I knew his gaze was withdrawn and unseeing. Knew, because that indefinable connection between us flared briefly to life, a wash of awareness and heat that only made the ache in my heart that much fiercer.

The unknown man stepped forward to the single mic standing at the front of the stage, and without preamble, began speaking about Gethen Lùtair, listing his contributions to Deva and the arts, the differences he'd made to the lives of so many within the business world. When he finished, there was a small spattering of applause before silence fell again. Treasa stepped up. Her speech was more personal, a remembrance of family life, and while there were no images shown, she crafted them with her words, leaving no one in the room any doubt that their father had been an active part of their lives, and a man who had loved and been loved.

Then it was Cynwrig's turn. He spoke more to the official side and his father's life of duty as king, his deep, velvety tones clear and concise, showing little of the emotion I could feel bubbling underneath that calm, beautiful exterior. He finished with assurances that he and his sister would follow in their father's footsteps, strengthening existing connections and contracts while enacting their father's plans for new operational ties going forward. Then he bowed lightly and stepped back.

But as he did so, his gaze rose and, with unerring accuracy, hit mine.

The world stilled and faded away. There were who knew how many too-rapid beats of my heart where nothing and nobody existed but me and this man. The emotions that swirled between us were thick, strong, and all-encompassing, filled with desire and need even if nothing showed in the smokey silver depths of his eyes.

I was suddenly glad we weren't close, that I was tucked at the back, well away from any sort of scrutiny, because I rather suspected my gaze would reveal all the things his did not.

Then the first man stepped up to the microphone again, blocking our line of sight and severing the connection, enabling me to breathe again. I turned, picked up my water, and gulped it down. It didn't ease the tumbling in my stomach or the deeper down ache. The waitress behind the bar refilled my glass without being asked, and I picked it up, holding it with a too-tense grip as I turned around again.

The speeches had ended, and the stage was empty. I scanned the room but couldn't see either Cynwrig or his sister. I made my way back to Sgott, spotting Mathi closer to the stage, talking to his father and a tall, statuesque woman with glorious golden hair, a somewhat pert nose, and large breasts. Or at least, large when it came to Ljósálfar elves. I didn't go over. As much as I would have liked to talk to Mathi about what I'd discovered this afternoon, I wasn't up to confronting Ruadhán again, for however brief a period that might be. Besides, I could hardly talk about the hoard, given Ruadhán was not privy to council information in that regard. Even Mathi couldn't talk to his father about it—all councilors had undertaken a blood oath not to talk to anyone outside the limited circle who were already aware of it.

Sgott *did* know, because no one had forced a blood oath on me, and it was far too late to do so now, given I'd already blabbed to everyone I trusted.

I found Sgott talking to the tall, elderly elf who'd been the convenor at the meeting this morning.

"Bethany," Sgott said. "I take it you haven't been formally introduced to Dhruv Eadevane?"

"Formally, no, though we have met." I inclined my head. "A pleasure to see you again, Mr. Eadevane."

"I wager *that* is something of a lie," he said, in a soft echo of the statement I'd made earlier. "Tell me, how did your meeting with Liadon go?"

"It was... interesting."

"Interesting is such a non-informative word."

I smiled. "I requested any and all information she might have on the horn. She replied that it would take some time to go through all the records. That was about it, really."

"And you weren't... startled by her appearance?"

"Well, it's not every day you come across a demigod, but I've certainly confronted worse over the last couple of weeks." I hesitated. "Tell me, is a Nagi also what guards the scrolls that were kept near the hoard? Because if that were the case, I'm surprised the thieves were able to steal anything."

"They were in the company of a bibliothecary, remember, so that likely explains it. As to the other part of your question…" He paused, expression contemplative. "I have not personally seen the scroll guardian—there would be few alive today who have—but I cannot remember her being described as a Nagi."

"Which doesn't mean it isn't some other kind of demigod."

"No." He eyed me speculatively for a second. "This line of questioning is troublesome, given you were expressly forbidden to seek out those scrolls."

I couldn't help the smile that twitched my lips. "Given the council's belief about thievery and my family, are you really all that surprised I seek to view the forbidden?"

Again, that wisp of a smile tugged his lips. I actually found myself warming to this old highborn elf in a way I never had with Ruadhán. "To be honest, no, but I would not mention it to the council, or they may enforce a blood oath on you."

"They could try. They won't succeed."

"Oh, I wouldn't be too sure of that, young woman. The council has ways of ensuring obedience, and your knives cannot protect you 24-7."

Before I could reply to either the threat or the more surprising suggestion he was going to keep my comment to himself, the soft bell chimed again. Dhruv glanced around. "Ah, the family leaves. I am not surprised—the Lùtairs did not want this commemoration in the first place."

I did my best to ignore the disappointment that surged

at them leaving without being able to speak to Cynwrig, and resisted the urge to stand on my toes to look one last time at him. They were the actions of a desperate woman, and I wasn't desperate. Really, I wasn't.

And if I repeated it often enough, I might just well believe it.

"Then why did they accede to it happening at all?" I asked.

"Both the fae and business councils were planning a memorial with or without Lùtair involvement, so I daresay they thought it was better to control proceedings than not." He bowed lightly. "It was a pleasure catching up with you again, Sgott. Young lady, I await your next update with anticipation."

And with that, he wandered away. I turned to Sgott, my eyebrows raised. "You know, for a highborn and very ancient elf, he's turning out to be pretty decent."

"Always was once you got him outside more formal settings. You ready to go?"

I nodded. Despite those silent few seconds filled with nebulous promises that could never be, I couldn't help but wonder why Cynwrig had broken all the rules to invite me here if he'd never intended to even approach me.

We made our way toward the exit. Our coats reappeared and, after a slender young man had politely helped me into mine, I followed Sgott down the long hallway. The day was probably darker than before, the storm I'd sensed earlier rippling across the sky in sheets of lightning. A shower of tiny stars danced across my fingertips in response, forcing me to shove them into my coat's pockets to hide the energy show.

That's when I felt the velvet box.

I stopped abruptly, exploring the size of the thing

without taking it out of my pocket. It wasn't a ring box—it was far too wide—but there was a definite possibility of it containing a necklace or bracelet. And there was a small piece of paper tucked lightly into one edge of the box.

Sgott paused and glanced over his shoulder. "Everything all right?"

I jumped slightly and hastily caught up to him. "Sorry, it appears I've been left a message."

"I would have been disappointed with the lad if he hadn't done something like that. Best read it in the car, though, where there's less watchful eyes."

I resisted the urge to look around and wondered what Sgott was seeing that I wasn't. I hurried after him again, my fingers clenched around the soft box and my heart tripping along at a million miles an hour. The white umbrellas appeared again as we left the building, though in truth I barely noticed the thunder and the sharp snap of rain as it bounced off the pavement as we were escorted over to the car. Once Sgott had informed Dispatch he was available—technically he wasn't on duty until the evening, but that had never stopped him answering callouts if he deemed them relevant to cases he was investigating—he reversed out and we were on our way. I tugged the box from my coat pocket.

It was roughly five inches square and a rich black velvet with the Lùtair shield emblazoned in silver on the top. If the box looked this expensive, its contents had to be pretty special. But I resisted the urge to immediately open it, and slid the note free instead.

It said, in sweeping, decorative strokes, *The restrictions of the mourning period mean I cannot see or contact you by any physical means for the next three months. And while I'm well aware it is inappropriate and unreasonable of me to ask you to wait for at least that long before your heart makes any decision in regard to your other suitor, that is exactly what I am now doing. The bracelet within this box is a Bruadar—a dreaming bracelet. Wear it if you wish a continuation of what we share in a non-physical manner.*

It was simply signed, *Cyn.*

"Well?" Sgott said. "Is it a goodbye or something else?"

"Something else." And wondered what the hell a dreaming bracelet was. "He's asked me to wait until the mourning period is over before I make any decision about a full-time relationship with Eljin."

Sgott glanced at me, eyebrows raised. "Has that lad even mentioned the possibility of becoming exclusive?"

I hesitated. "He's skirted around the edges of it a few times, but never come out and directly asked."

"And do you want that?"

My hesitation was longer this time. "Eventually? Maybe? We're really still in the 'getting-to-know-you' stage, and I don't want to be rushing things. That's never led to good situations in the past, at least not romantically."

Sgott snorted. "You do indeed have a horrible history of picking the absolute worst men."

As demonstrated by the now-incarcerated former teenage boyfriend who'd very recently popped back into my life. He'd not only made the very bad mistake of misjudging the adult me, but had also been stupid enough to threaten my brother's life. He was damnably lucky I hadn't killed him as the hazy cloud of inner darkness had wanted.

I safely tucked the note and the box into my purse. "I'm pretty sure Eljin can't be counted as one of them."

Even if the Eye seemed to dislike him.

Sgott smiled. "Yes, but if you're wanting any sort of

advice from a fatherly figure, I vote for the wait-and-see approach. It'll give you time to shake out any secrets or bugs the lad might be keeping."

I laughed. "I can totally assure you the lad hasn't got any bugs, but I'm sure there's a secret or two still lurking."

And considering how early into our relationship we were, that was to be expected. Hell, I certainly hadn't been upfront about everything, so there was no reason to presume he was.

Sgott chuckled softly, then reached for the radio as it squawked. "Bruhn here. Go ahead."

"Chief, we've just received an urgent call from Kaitlyn Avery."

I remembered the chill invading her place and my certainty that it was due to more than just a lack of heating, and instantly knew my trepidation had been right. That cold *hadn't* been natural.

"What did she want?" Sgott replied evenly.

"Bethany Aodhán," Dispatch said. "She said she tried to contact Bethany directly, but her phone is off."

And it was. I hastily dug it out of my purse's side pocket and switched it back on. The phone began pinging as multiple messages came in—one from Lugh, one from Eljin, and five from an unknown number that had to be Kaitlyn's.

"And why is she requesting Bethany?"

"She said Bethany was the only one who could save her."

"From what?" Sgott said, exasperation creeping into his tone.

"From the ice," the dispatcher said. "Her entire building is encased in it."

"It's not cold enough—" I stopped. It might not be cold

enough for ice under normal circumstances, but whatever was happening to Kaitlyn's place wasn't normal. It was magic. Perhaps even godly relic-type magic.

"Tell her we'll be there in ten," Sgott said, then flicked on the lights and sirens. As the car surged forward, he cast a brief but confused glance my way. "Why on earth would her building be encased in ice? My men made no mention of it, and they arrived not long after you'd left, apparently."

"There were a few icicles hanging off the guttering when we were there, but no obvious signs of magic. My instincts twitched, though the knives didn't." I gripped the edge of the door as we slid way too fast around a corner. The car fishtailed for a couple of seconds, but Sgott quickly brought it under control. "But I think Fate might be having a good old laugh at my expense right now, because just this morning the council asked me to find a relic known as the Horn of Winter."

"And it's capable of encasing a building in ice?"

"The council were light on details, but given the god who wielded it was known as the devouring one, it's probably wise to presume it can. Question is, who would want to set such a thing against Kaitlyn?"

"Lass, there's a queue several miles long of people wanting—but not daring—to take revenge against our queen of dubious contracts. The better question is, why do it like this? It's not exactly a quick or easy death—though maybe *that* may might be the whole point."

"Isn't freezing to death supposedly a peaceful death?"

"Only to the degree that once you're unconscious, you can't feel your body shutting down." Sgott's voice was grim. "But I can't imagine frostbite, loss of coordination, and the extreme shivering that comes before unconscious-ness would be in any way pleasant."

I clutched the edge of the door again as we spun around another corner and hurtled toward Kaitlyn's building. Up ahead, two regular police cars were sitting across the road, each a good distance away from Kaitlyn's. A third sat directly out front with its tires encased in ice, though the bulk of the vehicle only had a small smattering of frost across its front and along its roof line, the crystals gleaming with a bluish fire in the storm-spun gloom.

The building itself was fully encased, and somewhat reminded me of a big blue ice block. But, just like the police car sitting directly in front, that ice only extended small slivers onto the buildings on either side. Either the person behind the freezing was being careful not to take out innocents or the horn's powers were not as all-encompassing as the God of Winter and Destruction wanted everyone to believe.

It wasn't like we could ask him, though I would certainly ask both the codex library and Beira.

"Are your knives capable of acting against that sort of magic?" Sgott asked as he came to a halt beside the blue and fluorescent green police car blocking this side of the road.

"I honestly don't know." I climbed out and slung my purse over my shoulder. "If the ice threatens me directly, then yes, they will, but whether they can counteract what is happening to that building, I can't say. They didn't react when I was here this morning, but the building wasn't encased like it is now."

A policewoman lifted the tape so we could approach the building. The chill in the air grew noticeably sharper. Two plainclothes officers stood in the middle of the street directly in front of the building, one of them on the phone. The other glanced at us as we drew nearer, and I recognized him. Harry Preston, a wolf shifter who worked for Sgott. His pale yellow eyes scanned me briefly, then he cast a nod my way and returned his attention to Sgott.

"Bec's on the phone to Kaitlyn. Apparently she's holed up in the basement and, given the increasing vagueness of her replies, is not doing too good. We've tried breaking in through the windows, but barely even scratched the ice. It's rock solid."

"Have you managed to track down a fire mage?" Sgott said.

"There's no one close. We've a spellcaster on the way, but she's still five minutes out. Not sure if Kaitlyn will last that long."

"If we are dealing with a relic, then a spellcaster probably won't help." I suspected a fire witch might not, either, if only because few humans had the power to counteract godly energies.

"It's still worth having them on hand in case your knives fail to have any impact." He glanced at me. "How do you want to work this?"

"I get closer to the building and see if the knives react."

"And if they don't?" Sgott asked.

"I'll stab one into the ice and see what happens, but given we have no idea what we're currently dealing with, that might well cause more problems than not."

"Well, if we don't do *something* soon," the woman on the phone to Kaitlyn said, "it'll be too late. She's no longer responding."

"There are ambulances on the way," Harry added.

Sgott nodded and returned his attention to me. "The show is yours."

I dug my knives out, drew the blades, then handed him my purse and the sheaths. The softly gleaming ice covered the entire building; there were no features visible. No doors or windows. Harry and his companion might have tried breaking in through the latter earlier, but there was no evidence of their efforts or indeed the windows. It was as if the ice had thickened to protect itself. Or perhaps whoever was wielding the horn—if that was indeed what we were dealing with here—was close enough to see what was happening.

I jerked a look over my shoulder, quickly scanning the rooftops on the buildings opposite. There was no immediate sign of anyone, but that didn't mean anything.

"Has a search been done of the area?" I asked. "Because if we're dealing with a relic, the wielder might well be close."

"Harry?" Sgott immediately said.

He shook his head. "We concentrated on evacuating the nearby buildings."

Sgott nodded. "Then you and Bec get onto that, starting with the building opposite. But be wary—if we are dealing with someone using a relic, they might well turn it on you."

"I'd like to say we'll stay frosty," Bec murmured, "but that would be a bad pun considering the situation."

It was also a variation of a line in one of Sgott's favorite old movies. I watched them leave, then flexed my fingers against the knife hilts and said, more to myself than Sgott, "Let's get this show on the road."

"Be careful."

"That's become my new motto when dealing with oddities and relics."

Sgott snorted. "I believe that as much as I believed your mother every time she said it was a simple hunt and nothing could go wrong."

And it didn't. Not until the very last hunt, anyway.

Overhead, thunder rumbled and, a heartbeat later, lightning forked across the sky, a deep, dark, dangerous tree of power that echoed briefly in the two blades. Rivers of electric energy briefly ran across my vision—a rainbow network I could perhaps call on if the knives had little impact?

While I now knew to ground myself when I was channeling lightning through the blades, thereby lessening the risk of it boiling me alive, I wasn't immortal. I'd come close to dying the first time I called down the lightning, and had only been saved by the song and power of an old forest the second time.

Did I really want to risk a third time?

Especially for someone like Kaitlyn?

All life was important, I knew that, but that kernel of deeper darkness whispered not all lives were the same.

I shoved it aside and forced my feet forward. The closer I got to the building, the colder it got. I stepped past the front of the police car onto the pavement, sliding a little on the ice before my boots caught traction. The wall of blue ice loomed above me, the lightning spearing the clouds above mirrored on its surface.

The knives weren't reacting to the ice, although they seemed to be pulsing in time to the fury overhead.

"Anything?" Sgott asked.

"Not at the moment." I moved forward slowly, wary of slipping on the sheeted pavement. My fingers began to ache, though it was more from the sheer intensity of the cold this close to the building than the force of my grip on the hilts.

I stopped several feet away from where the door should have been. The small alcove was completely filled in and there was no sound coming from the building's interior.

The wood song had died, just as Kaitlyn was dying. I guess it was unsurprising that, given what I was, the former made me angrier than the latter.

I raised the knife in my right hand and lightly pressed its tip against the ice. For several seconds, nothing happened. Then lightning flashed overhead, and the blade responded, its dark inner lightning rolling down the fuller and sparking brightly when it hit the ice. Fine cracks slithered away from the knife's tip and water pooled around the point before dribbling down to the pavement where it froze again.

I wasn't calling to the storm, so why did its intensity echo through the knives?

I didn't know—a somewhat common refrain when it came to the triune and what it was actually capable of— but I had nothing to lose by following through with my earlier threat. Kaitlyn certainly did have something to lose, but if we didn't break the lock of this ice, she'd soon be as dead as the wood song anyway.

I glanced around and met Sgott's gaze. "I'm going to try stabbing the knives into the ice and see what happens. If I shout, run."

"As long as you do the same."

I smiled, though it was filled with tension. "Trust me, being buried under a mountain of ice is not on my to-do list today."

"I would hope it's not on your to-do list *any* day."

I snorted, but my amusement slithered away as I returned my attention to the wall in front of me. Giving myself little time to think or worry, I raised both knives and thrust them, with as much force as I could muster, deep into the cold blue depths. The blades slid in smoothly, only stopping when the hilts hit the surface. Once again, nothing immediately happened, then thunder rumbled so damn loudly, I'd have sworn the pavement quaked under my feet. Lightning flashed, rolling across the groaning skies in fierce, bright waves.

Light pulsed around the hilts, as if in response to the light show happening overhead. Though their fiery touch didn't hurt or burn my fingers, I nevertheless released the knives and stepped back.

Tiny cracks began to appear in the ice, spreading out from the two hilts in uneven lines, spiderweb-fine at first and then increasing in size and shape. The old building shuddered, and a sharp snapping sound echoed, reminding me somewhat of the noise a tree limb made when torn from the trunk.

I took another step back. The fierce glow coming from the knives was now so bright it washed across the ice, turning the blue purple. The shuddering increased, the snapping sound grew louder, deepening the cracks that swept over the ice. On the roof, a tile exploded, sending sharp shards into the air.

Then, with a groan not unlike that of a dying beast, the whole building began to crumble.

CHAPTER

FIVE

I TURNED AND RAN. THICK SLABS OF ICE SHATTERED ON THE pavement behind me, sending dagger-like shards spearing through the air, pockmarking the police car and thudding into my back. Pain rippled down my spine, but my coat appeared to be protecting me from the worst of the barrage.

As I slid around the end of the car, a huge chunk of ice-wrapped brick hit its roof, collapsing it inward. The rumbling behind me grew louder, the sound of falling ice sharper. The entire building was going to come down before I could reach safety....

Movement caught my eye, coming in from the left. Sgott, barreling toward me. I didn't slow down and neither did he; he simply swooped in, swept me up into his arms without breaking stride, and then ran on down the street, heading for the police car blocking the other end of the road from where we'd parked.

I looked over his shoulder, and shock hit. A strangely glowing vortex swept around what remained of the building, disintegrating some sections of ice while jettisoning others. The police car continued to take multiple hits and was now all but flattened. Though the buildings on either side of Kaitlyn's—or indeed those opposite—basically remained unscathed, the portion of the street directly in front of the collapsing building was littered with rapidly melting chunks of ice, revealing a broken mass of bricks, timber, and metal, though which part of the building the latter had come from was hard to say, given how badly it had been twisted. By the time we'd reached the safety of the patrol car, the only thing that remained of the building *or* the ice was the debris covering the patrol car and the street.

What the vortex *hadn't* taken out was the flooring at ground level, which meant either the person behind the attack hadn't been aware of the existence of the basement, or the destruction of everything above it was all that he or she had intended. But it also meant there was at least a chance—a very slim chance, granted—we could rescue Kaitlyn before she died from exposure.

Sgott put me down, then held me still as he brushed the few remaining shards from the back of my coat. "Any of those things break your skin?"

"I think one sliced the back of my knee, but it doesn't feel bad."

"Hitch up your coat so I can check." I did so and, after a moment, he grunted. "There's a wee cut, but as you said, it's not deep. You were lucky."

"Again." I dropped my coat then held out my hands, silently calling to my knives. Energy pulsed deep within me and, a heartbeat later, they came spinning through the air and thudded into my hands. Neither of them was damaged in any way, despite being trapped within the havoc they'd unleashed.

"That," Sgott said, handing me back my purse and knife

sheaths, "is a very neat trick, and not one I ever saw your mom use."

"My connection to the knives is very different to Mom's."

"Obviously." His gaze returned to Kaitlyn's. "Is the building safe to approach?"

I sheathed my knives, then glanced over again. "I'm still not sensing anything, but that doesn't really mean much given some sort of magic was very obviously used."

"You'll be needing to come with us, then, just in case."

He didn't sound happy about that, but then, he was probably still in fatherly mode rather than police chief. I nodded and followed him back down the road. The knives remained inert, and the storm that had raged overhead only a few minutes ago was already dissipating. I suspected that was *not* a coincidence. Suspected that the connection between me, the triune, and storms was strengthening—mutating—in as yet undefined ways.

And the only person I could ask about it tended not to be too forthcoming when it came to information. But maybe, given Beira's liking for whiskey, I could ply her with a bottle or three of the top-shelf stuff and see if the alcohol loosened her tongue.

Was it even possible to get an old goddess tipsy, let alone drunk?

Sgott stopped in front of the building, where the door had once been. The floorboards were unscarred aside from the odd puddle of water, but the wood was silent, its song gone forever. The hush made my heart ache.

"I've called emergency services to come check the gas and electricity lines," Harry said as he and Bec stopped either side of us. "That floor looks surprisingly solid."

"Looks are often deceiving when it comes to the aftereffects of magic," Sgott said. "Bec, the basement stairs are in the back corner—if they're accessible, sweep down and check what the situation is with Kaitlyn and the joists. But be careful."

She nodded, her gaze narrow and unfocused, an indication she was reaching for her alternate form. Energy flooded the air, prickling across my fingers and face, and her body rippled, becoming ghost-like as genetics and magic made the necessary adjustments.

Then, with a quick flick of brown-gold wings, she swept upward and arrowed toward the rear of the building. After briefly circling, she swooped down the stairs and disappeared. I waited tensely, but for several minutes there was little sound beyond the steady drip of water coming from the guttering of the building on the right side and the distant rumble of traffic and incoming sirens.

Then Sgott's phone rang sharply, making me jump a little. He answered with a quick, "Anything?" After a few seconds, he added, "Stay with her. I'll send in the medics now."

"Kaitlyn's alive?" I said once he'd hung up.

He nodded. "But unconscious, with a very slow heart rate and frostbite on her nose and cheeks. No guarantee she'll fully recover."

"But?" Because there was one. I could hear it in his voice.

"Someone left a message in the basement—it was written in ice across a wall."

I raised my eyebrows. "A message or a threat? What did it say?"

"Revenge might be a dish best served cold, but mine rages beyond control. It will find all who deserve it."

I stared at him for a second, a thick knot of fear

clutching my stomach. The first part of that message was an echo of what the ghul had said to both me *and* the woman who'd questioned her a week ago. And while it might be nothing more than a coincidence that revenge was also the motive behind the destruction here, I seriously doubted it. The old gods did like their games and Fate was a dab hand at unleashing chaos in subtle ways.

"Why do you suddenly look like you've seen a ghost?" Sgott said, gaze sweeping me with concern.

"Maybe because I did?" I held up a hand to cut off the inevitable next question. "The ghul said something very similar to me last night *and* to a woman who'd been seeking her the week before."

"Did the ghul mention anything else about this woman?"

"No, and she won't, given how highly they prize such conversations."

"That is unfortunate." He paused. "I might attempt to talk to her tonight. Most ghuls are law abiding and tend to cooperate more often than not."

"Fingers crossed our ghul is one of them." I studied the empty expanse of flooring again. "Do you know if there's any ice witches here in Deva?"

"I'd have to look at the council's business register to find out, but it's unlikely anyone registered would be responsible for this sort of destruction. All magic leaves a tell, and it's a fairly easy process to track it back to a practitioner."

"Really? I had no idea."

He half smiled. "It's not something we advertise, though I daresay it's something most practitioners are aware of. It's also the reason why so few witches working the black market accept contracts in their own backyard. Records are regional, *not* national."

"That makes no sense."

"No, but the spellcaster's guild is extremely strong and has very deep pockets. I can't see any national system being introduced as long as Marjorlaine Blackguard and her elk remain in control." He looked around. "Ah good, the medics are here. Do you want to head back to the car to wait? Or do you want me to arrange a car to take you home?"

"I'll just catch an Uber."

He nodded then stepped through the nonexistent doorway and led the medics down into the basement.

I walked down to the café at the far end of the street, then dragged out my phone, first calling an Uber and then my brother.

He answered on the second ring. "I take it the commemoration is over and you survived emotionally unscathed?"

I smiled. "Only because we didn't talk, but that's not what I called for—you home?"

"Will be in about an hour. Darby's there though—she's got the day off. Why?"

"I've a couple of things I need to ask you about, one of them being an old archeological dig."

"Has the dig got a name?"

"I haven't got the article discussing it on me right now, but I am on the way home."

"Why don't you come over for dinner, then? Darby usually cooks enough to feed an army, so one more at the table won't make an impact."

I smiled. Darby was currently working on the "the way to a man's heart was via his stomach" theory with added spice in the bedroom... and wherever else they happened to be. "Just make sure you let her know. I'd hate to spoil things if she has something special planned."

"I doubt she has, but I'll send her a text."

"Thanks. I'll see you in an hour or so."

As I hung up, the Uber arrived. I jumped in the back and, as the driver took off, pulled the velvet box from my purse. I didn't immediately open it, mainly because I was more than a little scared of what I might find. Which was ridiculous, really, but still...

I ran my finger lightly over the crest, then, after a steadying breath, pressed the small button on the side of the box. The lid sprang open, and a soft gasp escaped me. Sitting in a bed of black silk was a smooth stone bracelet the color of midnight and alive with tiny stars that shone like jewels. I hesitated, then carefully ran a finger across its surface. The stone was warm against my skin, and the stars pulsed as if in recognition of my touch. The urge to slide it over my wrist was so strong I'd lifted the bracelet from the silk before caution reasserted itself. There was magic in this thing. I was certain of that, even if my knives weren't reacting and no awareness prickled my senses. Cynwrig's note had implied the bracelet would somehow facilitate us meeting in a nonphysical manner, either telepathically or even on what some called the dreaming field, but until I knew for certain what accepting this gift meant, I really shouldn't. At the very least, I owed it to myself and to Eljin to understand what it fully entailed before making any decision.

I placed the bracelet back in its bed of silk, snapped the lid closed, then returned it to my purse. While I had no true idea what a Bruadar bracelet might be, surely Darby would. And if she didn't, then she'd probably be able to point me in the direction of someone who did.

It was just after five by the time I arrived back at the tavern, which was not a busy hour for us—in the off-peak seasons, that tended to be after six and generally consisted of locals enjoying the quieter times—so after checking in with Ingrid again, I bounded up the stairs and quickly changed into more sensible, warmer clothes—jeans, ankle boots, and a thick wooly sweater. After dragging the two pieces of paper out of the front pocket of the jeans I'd discarded last night, I made myself a cuppa, then sat down and read the newspaper article.

It was a story about an archeological site in Portugal and the unusual number of accidents that had occurred during the dig, which had eventually led to the site being closed and subsequent rumors that the area was cursed. There was a somewhat grainy picture of the dig team standing in the middle of what looked to be an Iron Age hill fort, but there were no names listed. It shouldn't be all that hard for Lugh to track down who'd been involved given museums—or at the very least, all the fae museums —generally kept track of what the "competition" was doing.

I squinted at the picture for several seconds, trying to spot a familiar face without success, then dragged out my phone, took a photo, and did a reverse image search. Google came up with similar images, most of them from foreign reports, and none of them providing any additional information. Hopefully, Lugh might be able to shed some light on the matter, because right now, I was confused as to why Treasa thought this might be of interest. And, in fact, why she'd hesitated about giving it to me.

I picked up the other bit of paper and studied the drawing of the necklace for several seconds. It really was a glorious piece, but I wasn't sure why Treasa expected me—

or even Mom—to succeed where her family had not. Especially when, as I'd already said, I was not my mother.

I finished my tea, then, with a quick glance at the phone to check the time, grabbed my knives from my purse then walked down to the far end of the room. After pressing the button to release the loft ladder, I waited for it to unfold, then scooted up.

After Gran had handed over the tavern's reins and moved out, Mom had converted this area into a chill-out zone where she and I could escape the noise of the lower floors and read our books or listen to music in peace. Lugh had found a place of his own by then, but even if he had still been living here, he wouldn't have been able to use the area. Not without some serious modifications to both the hatch *and* the loft, and given the council still griped about Gran raising the roof height eons ago, they weren't likely to grant us permission to lift it any further.

Though night was setting in, enough light filtered in through the three skylights to see. Down the far end of the long room, two bookcases stood on either side of a wood fire, their dusty shelves lined with a mix of old leather-bound classics, Mom's romances, and the various trinkets and statuettes she'd picked up over the decades. Some of those had been destroyed in the break-in that had ultimately led to Vincentia's death, but I'd cleaned all that up, along with her blood, which had stained the floorboards and briefly added a note of sadness to their song. Mom's chair—which, like most of the furniture up here, was secondhand but gloriously comfortable—remained where it had always been, complete with the badly crocheted rug I'd made to warm her knees covering the back of her chair, and her to-be-read pile neatly stacked on the nearby coffee table. I didn't intend to change that area anytime soon, if only because it somehow made me feel closer to her. Yes, there were still too many memories up here for me to linger too long, but on the other hand, the peace and contentment she'd always found up here also remained, and that was ultimately comforting.

I blinked back the threat of tears, placed the knives and the drawing on the small table beside the cushion-adorned sofa, then walked toward the wood heater. Gran had created a small storage pocket in the back of the mesh to hold her smaller valuables, but I'd needed somewhere larger to not only store the codex, but also the Eye and my knives when I wasn't wearing them. Cynwrig had reworked the entire flue and its surrounding mesh for me, ensuring the hidden compartment remained unseen and inaccessible unless you knew where the catch was.

I hooked a finger into the small hole that served as a handle, opened the door, and reached down for the codex. As my fingers brushed its glassy surface, energy stirred, a sharp electricity that echoed deep within the stone sitting between my breasts.

The triune was eager to be used.

I drew out the codex and closed the door. When I'd first found this book, it had been nothing more than a worn and very plain-looking leatherbound notebook, but the blood ceremony that had bound me to all three items had changed that, turning the old leather a glassy black. The light that rolled across its surface at my touch echoed the light found deep in the heart of the Eye and the knives, but it held none of their dangerous electricity. Which was something of an illusion, given all godly items had a cost and stepping into the library's godly realm was no different. If you lingered too long there, you could die, as its price for usage was strength.

I walked back to the old sofa, reorganized a couple of cushions to make myself more comfortable, then grabbed the knives and sat down. Once I'd unclipped the Eye from my neck, I placed it and the knives on top of the codex then pressed a hand against all three, ensuring they all touched, and said, "What can you tell me about Geitha's Tears?"

Light erupted from the triune, surrounding me in a dizzying whirlpool that swept me up and then swept me away. But it wasn't a physical departure so much as a mental—or perhaps even spiritual—one. I could still feel the cushions pressed against my spine, could still hear the building's gentle song, though the latter was decidedly muffled against the sheer wall of noise being generated by the colorful maelstrom I now arrowed through.

I came to a halt in a bright, open space filled with a multitude of different shapes. Long and tall, thin, or thick, some round, but most square or rectangular. Not shelves. Books.

Books that hovered in orderly rows in the nothingness of this place and glowed with an unearthly energy.

It is such a pleasure to see you again so soon, young Aodhán. What do you wish to know about Geitha's Tears?

The voice was neither male nor female and exuded not only wisdom and knowledge, but also a little more warmth than on previous occasions—though that could undoubtedly change in the blink of an eye. Gods—and the beings who bore no flesh and who served as their gatekeepers—had a long history of smiting first and asking questions later, so it paid to be cautious.

Anything you can tell me, really.

They are the tears of the goddess Geitha, it replied, *who is beholden to destiny, happiness, and ruling.*

Those last two don't often go together, I commented.

Indeed, which is why the goddess often cries.

I suspected it was said in amusement, although there was no hint of it in the guardian's voice. *Why are the tears important to Myrkálfar accession to the throne?*

The goddess gifted her tears to the Myrkálfar eons ago. More than that, I cannot say.

There's no book on it in this library?

If those who attained her gift could not be bothered to record its meaning, why should such records be kept here?

I frowned. *You keep plenty of records about artifacts humanity and fae have forgotten.*

True, but Geitha was not the most verbose of goddesses and never acquiesced to giving this library information.

I blinked. That almost sounded like a criticism. *Did that often happen? Gods not giving information, I mean.*

No. It behooves those who play in humanity's timeline to keep the information options open.

Meaning I'm not the only one with the means of accessing this library?

You are not, but you are the only one who has done so for eons.

I guess it wasn't too surprising that there'd be others with access, given it made absolutely no sense to have a resource like this tied to one person or bloodline.

What about Borrhás's Horn?

The librarian didn't answer, but the books around me spun with dizzying speed for a couple of seconds before one popped out of rotation and floated toward me, hovering in the air while the pages flipped open.

As before, there were no words, only images. I suspected my godly librarian feared I wouldn't understand anything written—and rightly so, given I couldn't even read Latin, let alone a language as old as the gods themselves.

The images showed an old man in white with a fierce-looking mop of white hair holding what looked to be a fancy drinking horn to his lips. Ice spun out from the opposite end, coating the nearby trees and people. The page flipped over; the trees and the people were nothing more than blocks of ice.

I glanced up. *Borrhás controls the cold north wind and is supposedly the bringer of winter—is his destruction via ice his only vice?*

He has other gifts, but the horn is the caller of winds that destroy and ice that coats and fractures.

And can anyone use it? Or does one have to possess magic?

It was designed as a lover's gift to a queen who wished to bring winter down on all her enemies. When she achieved her goal, she forsook Borrhás, to her endless regret.

Really? What happened?

The book flipped several more pages then stopped, revealing images of a castle wrapped in ice, and a woman asleep in a bed of ice. Only she wasn't asleep. She was frozen. The final image was of the horn cleaved in two.

When did her kingdom fall?

It didn't. It remains, forever locked under ice that will never melt until the earth itself no longer exists.

Under one of the ice caps, then, perhaps?

Did Borrhás only have the one horn? The one I'd been shown earlier didn't really match what I'd heard, but that didn't mean it wasn't the same one.

The gods rarely duplicate their artifacts.

Then he was the one who split it in two? And if that were the case, were we dealing with his horn rejoined or some sort of godly copy?

He was mortified that his weapon was used in such a manner, and determined it should not be so used again.

Then why didn't he simply destroy it?

That is rarely the first choice of the gods.

And we were currently paying the price for that reluctance. *Any idea how I might find it, then?*

This is a library, not a lost and found, came the somewhat severe reply, though once again I detected the hint of amusement running through it. *And surely the daughter of a storm god, however minor, could set the winds to such a task.*

I suppose she could certainly try. I smiled, but it faded quickly under the sudden pulse of aching tiredness. Time to go. I hesitated, then said, *Tell me, do you have a name?*

Surprise shivered briefly through the expanse of endless books. *Why would you wish to know such a thing?*

Because a name would be better than simply calling you "the librarian" or even "it."

There was a long pause, and the agitation in the books briefly increased, though it was more surprise than any form of discomfort or annoyance. *I was... am Aasym.*

And may I use your name?

That would be... pleasant.

Good. And you may call me Bethany, or Beth; whatever you're comfortable with.

Thank you, Bethany.

I smiled, though in this space it was more a gentle song of joy. *Thank you for your help, Aasym, and I'll see you next time.*

And with that, I stepped back into the maelstrom, and then into my body. My heart raced, my breathing was rapid and shallow, and my chest on fire. I released the triune and dropped my head into my hands, rocking back and forth for several minutes, trying to take deeper breaths in an effort to control the fierce ache in brain and body.

It took close to ten minutes before I approached anything close to normality. I carefully pushed upright, my knees shaking a little as weariness washed through my limbs. I glanced at my watch and saw that close to an hour had passed. Way past time for me to get moving.

I secured the codex behind the flue, then rang for an Uber as I headed back down the ladder. After shoving my knives into my purse—while I could basically auto-call them into my hands any time I wanted, it still felt safer to keep them close—I grabbed a coat and the two pieces of paper Treasa had handed me, then collected two bottles of Bordeaux to have with our meal before heading out to wait for my ride. Traffic was slow, so it took close to half an hour before I made it over to Lugh's.

He lived in a decommissioned power substation that was the ugliest building on the street. It was a single story, constructed with brown bricks that were now black and grimy with age, and the black wooden door that sat at its midpoint still had all the rusty old electrical warning signs on it. Of course, it also had two things the surrounding buildings did not—plenty of ceiling height, which for a man of Lugh's size was important, and a ton of floor space, which came in handy for a man with a ton of archeological "trinkets" to store.

I tapped the code into the lock to the left of the door, then turned the handle and cracked it open. "Hello? Anyone home? It's me. I arrive with booze."

"Is that a polite way of giving us a five-second warning in case we're doing anything nasty?" Darby said as she all but bounced into the wide hallway. She was a typical light elf in looks—tall and slender, with long pale gold hair currently swept back into a ponytail that brushed her butt, and eyes the color of summer skies. Her features were sharp but ethereally beautiful, and she moved with lightness and grace I would never achieve, no matter how long I lived. "Because you should know better. Your brother never does the nasty on an empty stomach."

I stepped inside, kissed her cheek, and handed her the Bordeaux. "Given no splutter of outrage comes from the living area, I take it he's not home yet?"

"No. Caught in traffic." Her cheeks dimpled. "Which is probably just as well, because the casserole is taking longer to cook than the recipe suggests."

"It's more likely that Lugh's oven is not up to the task. He's never used it, and it was secondhand when he installed it. You should replace it."

"I should, but I can't make too many alterations too soon without making him run to the hills in fear of domestication."

I laughed and followed her into the kitchen, pulling out one of the stools in front of the counter and sitting down. The room was comfortably large, and combined a kitchen and living area. There were two good-sized bedrooms and a bathroom to the right, and on the other side of the hallway, Lugh's large office and storage area. He'd recently completed a proper, climate-controlled basement for his more precious artifacts, but the entrance was hidden—and fingerprint coded—so wasn't outwardly visible unless you knew where to look.

"How come you've got the day off?" I asked. "I thought you were doing a training course this week?"

She worked at the fae hospital as a poisons specialist, with a secondary specialization in wound repairs. The new course—which she was doing in monthly, week-long slots over the course of several years—would add pediatrics to her poisons and wound repair bows. Handy given how often she had to deal with kids in Emergency.

"The instructor got snowed in, so they've pushed it back a week. They asked if I wanted to pick up additional shifts, and I wisely said no. An unexpected week off is always to be enjoyed."

"Won't it cause problems for next week's shifts?"

"We're not in peak period, so they should be all right." She opened one of the bottles of Bordeaux and poured two glasses, sliding one across to me. "How did the commemoration go? Did you speak to him?"

"No." I slung my purse onto the next stool and dug out the velvet box. "He did, however, arrange to have this left in my coat pocket."

She sucked in a soft breath. "That looks expensive. Too big to be a ring of any kind, though."

I half smiled. "I think we can both be certain that the one thing I will never be getting from Cynwrig is a ring."

"He's Myrkálfar," she said. "They oft times do the very unexpected. Can I look?"

"Well, I didn't bring it over here for you to simply stare at the box."

She grinned and slid the box closer. After a few moments of simply admiring the box, she pressed the button and opened it. Her gaze widened in surprise, and she sucked in a breath. "Holy fuck, a *Bruadar* bracelet."

"Which answers my initial question—do you know what it is?" I said with a smile.

"I do, though I've never seen one. I'd actually thought them more myth than reality."

I took a sip of the wine and raised an eyebrow. "Why?"

"Because they're Myrkálfar specific and rarely seen. As far as I'm aware, you can't even find one in a museum."

I frowned, an odd mix of uncertainty, trepidation, and delight running through me. I mean, to be given something so rare had to mean he cared, if only a little, didn't it? "What were they used for?"

"They're dreaming bracelets."

I nodded. "Cynwrig said as much in the note he left with it."

Her gaze jumped to mine. "What else did the note say?"

"Basically, he asked me to wait out the mourning period before I made any decision in regard to Eljin, and said I should wear the bracelet if I wished a continuation of what we share in a non-physical manner. Which I take it means the bracelet allows some form of telepathic communication."

A smile twitched her lips. "Telepathic, and a whole lot more, by all accounts."

My eyebrows shot up again. "Meaning? I mean, seriously, stop with the riddles and just spit it out."

She laughed and pointed to the bracelet. "The Myrkálfar have a second, less than polite term for this thing."

I gave her an impatient look, and she laughed again.

"Okay, fine. It's a fucking bracelet."

"I know it's a fucking bracelet—" I stopped, my eyes widening in realization. "*Oh.*"

"Yes, indeed," she said, blue eyes shining with mirth. "It allows two people to actually *fuck* on the dreaming plane."

SIX

"But... how?"

I certainly wasn't averse to the thought—far from it, especially if it meant I kept getting a little Cynwrig action— but surely if something like that was possible, someone, somewhere, would have put it into wide production and made a mint off it. The market for such a thing would be *huge*.

As would be the abuses.

"I don't know the physics behind it," she said, "so I've only got rumor and speculation to run with. But apparently, the bracelets are created as a pair, via Myrkálfar magic and a dreaming specialist—"

"Specialist as in an oneirologist?" A term I knew only because she'd briefly dated one once.

She shook her head. "Oneirology is the scientific study of dreams. A dreaming specialist is a witch of sorts, generally employed to seek out and erase the spirits and demons that sometimes target dreamers. They're more commonly known as dream hunters."

"Not a term I'm familiar with."

"Few would be outside hospitals and sleep clinics. Anyway, the Myrkálfar created the bracelets so that the highborn—be they man or woman—could remain in contact with a loved one while traveling distant lands."

"*Sexual* contact."

She nodded. "Remember, the Myrkálfar tend to gift their hearts for life and do not stray, so these bracelets enabled couples to, well, couple, no matter how far or how long away their partner was."

"Cynwrig and I aren't married. We will *never* be married."

"Nowhere in any of the rumors was there any mention of a requirement to be married. As far as I'm aware, the only requirement is emotional compatibility." She motioned to the bracelet again. "For whatever reason, Cynwrig obviously believes you two are that, even if that compatibility can never go anywhere. He's obviously intent on making damn sure he doesn't lose that *or* you until he's good and ready."

I took another drink and stared at the bracelet for a few moments. "So how does it work? Do I just wear it, and whenever I'm asleep and horny, he can sweep in and ease things? Because *that* might get embarrassing."

Especially if I happened to be sleeping with Eljin.

She laughed again. "I would imagine there'd be some sort of gateway or means of signaling readiness, especially considering these things were often used when the two people involved were in other time zones. More than that, I can't say. Maybe you should just wear the thing and find out. Have you even touched it?"

I nodded. "There's definitely magic within it, and it did react to my touch. Which is why I'm wary."

Her phone pinged. She glanced down briefly, a smile tugging at her lips. "Lugh is five minutes away."

"You want me to set the table?"

She nodded and grabbed the oven mitts to get the casserole out. "I'm guessing Eljin is part of the reason you're wary?"

I tucked the bracelet back into my purse, then collected the plates and cutlery. "Some. I like him, but there's a part of me that remains unconvinced."

"The same part lusting after Cynwrig, perhaps?"

"No." I laughed at her disbelieving look. "Well, only partially."

"It's natural to be wary, given how new the relationship still is and how horrid your history with men has been."

"I keep telling myself that exact thing, but I have yet to convince myself." I walked back over to the bench to get the heat-resistant placemat for the casserole. "You know, it's situations like this I wish I could talk to Mom about. She was a really good judge of character."

Which is probably why, as a teenager, I'd never introduced her to either Mkalkee or Halak. Somewhere deep down I'd known they were very bad news and had feared her reaction, with good reason. She did *not* take *anyone* messing with her family lightly. It was a trait that had carried onto Lugh, though he tended to be a bit more evenly tempered when it came to retaliation. Hell, he'd warned both Mkalkee and Halak to walk away when I was a late teen, and they actually had—though not without fucking around with my memories first, of course.

The pixie curse might prevent us from killing unless in self-defense, but it did *not* prevent us harming others in order to protect ourselves or those we loved.

"Surely if Lugh had any doubts about Eljin, he would

have said something. He does work with him on a daily basis." She paused and cocked her head. "Speaking of Lugh, a car has just pulled up."

"Meaning this conversation is temporarily shelved."

She frowned at me. "If you have doubts about Eljin, Lugh is the best person to ask."

"Yes, but I don't want to risk their relationship if my doubts are based on nothing more than emotional fear. Besides, we've more important things to discuss once dinner has been had."

Lugh came through the front door with a loud, "I'm home," and Darby once again bounced out to greet him. I grabbed the crusty bread, a knife, and a board, then picked up the butter dish and took everything over to the table.

By which time, Lugh and Darby had finished their "hellos" and walked back in.

"Smells delicious." Lugh stripped off his coat and slung it over the back of the chair. "How are you, Beth?"

"Hungry, so sit your butt down so we can get started."

He laughed and obeyed, and the next hour was filled with general catch-up chatter and much laughter.

Once the table was cleared and coffee was served, Lugh said, "So, what are the two things you need to discuss?"

I rose to retrieve the two bits of paper, then slid the article across the table to him. He crossed his arms on the table and studied it for a few seconds. "I recognize a couple of the people in the photo—I've worked a number of times with both Frank and Gena." He pointed to a lighter-haired man and a small, dark woman. "But the rest don't look familiar."

"And the dig site?"

"It says Portugal, but it has to be from at least fifty years ago given the gear that's behind them. More than that, I can't say. Why?"

"Someone implied that it would be in my best interests to find out more about that dig."

"Does this someone have a name?" he asked. "And do we trust them?"

"We do."

He sniffed. "I believe Gena died a few years ago, but Frank is still alive and kicking. I'll see if the museum has his contact details and give him a call. No promises though. And the other thing?"

"What do you know about Geitha's Tears?"

"Geitha, as in the Myrkálfar goddess?" Darby asked.

I nodded and pushed the drawing across. "I've been asked to find it."

Lugh picked up the drawing and studied it. "Who by? Cynwrig?"

"Treasa. He's not allowed any physical contact, remember."

"But he's definitely planning nonphysical," Darby murmured.

Lugh glanced at her. "Meaning?"

"Meaning, that lad has no intention of allowing Beth's heart to be captured anytime soon by Eljin."

His gaze went from her to me and back again. "I feel like I'm missing vital information in this discussion."

Darby patted his hand. "I'll fill you in later."

He rolled his eyes and returned his attention to the drawing. "It's not something I can remember seeing, but I'll search the archives and see if there's any mention. Is it a relic?"

"No, though it is goddess-gifted, as the name implies. It was stolen a few centuries ago, and now they need to find it. Apparently they've discovered it has a part to play in the coronation."

"So of course they leave tracking it down until the last possible moment." Darby shook her head. "Honestly, officialdom never changes, does it, no matter what the race. They're all fucking useless."

"Why don't you tell us how you really feel?" I said with a laugh.

Her smile flashed. "It's a motto I definitely try to live by."

"And one I'm still getting used to," Lugh muttered. "It's bad enough having a sister who holds little back, but having both of the two most important people in my life swearing by that code?" He shook his head, his sorrowful expression countered by the amusement creasing the corners of his green eyes. "I'm obviously a glutton for punishment."

I glanced at Darby at *that* little statement. Her eyes shone with happiness, though neither she nor I pointed out he'd just admitted how important she now was to him. "So," she said, taking a drink and leaning back in her chair, "Tell us what happened with the council this morning."

I quickly updated them, both on my mission for the council and the attack on Kaitlyn, then asked him, "I think you mentioned not so long again that you'd found some notes Nialle had made about the horn?"

"I did, though I haven't had time to check them. I'll gather them all for you tomorrow."

"Thanks." I paused. "Just in case the attack on Kaitlyn isn't related to the horn, however unlikely that might be, where's the best place to find a listing of local ice witches?"

"They'd probably fall under the umbrella of the spell-casters guild," Darby said.

"Yeah, but from the little I've heard about *that* mob, they're notoriously hard to get information out of."

"Which is why you're better off leaving it to Sgott," Lugh commented. "But of course, you won't."

I grinned and raised a glass. "To a brother who understands the workings of his sister's mind."

He rolled his eyes, but before he could reply, Darby said, "I can suggest a different information avenue, depending on what you wanted to know, of course."

"Oh? Do tell," I said.

"A few years ago, I treated a retired ice witch for exhaustion and heart problems. He was a lovely, somewhat lonely old fellow, and I still see him once a month, not to check on him but just to chat."

"Would it be possible for you to ring him up tomorrow and arrange a meeting?"

"Sure. I'd ring tonight but he's probably already in bed. He tends to do that rather than turn the heating on."

"An ice witch affected by the cold? That's rather unusual, isn't it?"

She shrugged. "It happens as they get older—as their ability to manipulate the weather wanes, so does their immunity to the forces they used to raise."

"Huh." I wondered if that would happen to me. My father wasn't mortal, so possibly not, but it wasn't like I could ask him. Besides, I wasn't even very *good* at raising the forces I could apparently manipulate. Not yet anyway.

We moved on to discussing non-work stuff again, and I left at ten, walking home rather than catching an Uber, enjoying the crispness of the night and the distant electricity of a storm while I thought about options. About what I *wanted* to do and what I *should* do.

By the time I arrived back at the tavern, I was no closer to an answer. But I didn't put the bracelet on. I didn't dare.

Coward, thy name is Bethany, I thought, and fell asleep with a wry smile on my lips.

After working on the tavern's accounts for a couple of hours the following morning, I grabbed my purse, my knives, and my long, waterproof trench coat, then shoved on my wellies and headed out into the miserable day. Though I'd managed to direct the wind and even storms a number of times now—be it for attack, defense, or even the protection of certain relics—it had mostly been in an ad hoc manner. But I had a feeling that if I wanted any real hope of setting the wind a more complicated task, I'd need to be more fully immersed in the weather—a fact backed up by the vague whisperings riding the breeze. Whisperings that sounded an awful lot like Beira.

She was not a happy goddess, if they were anything to go by.

I shoved my gloved hands into my pockets and quickly made my way through the rain-washed, surprisingly empty streets. It was just after midday, so there should have been at least *some* people out and about seeking something to eat. It was a weekday after all, and it wasn't as if storms like this were unknown in Deva, especially during the winter months.

Up ahead, the eastern wing of the lovely old red sandstone cathedral loomed, ghostly in the gray. The gardens that surrounded it weren't visible thanks to the gloom, but as I crossed the street and headed into the memorial section, the freestanding bell tower came into view. It was much younger than the cathedral, having been commissioned in the early seventies after the original tower was deemed no longer safe to house the bells. This one was a modern interpretation of the old Roman watchtowers that had once guarded Deva's walls, and while its base was the same rose-red sandstone as the cathedral, the tower itself was reinforced concrete hung with gray slate. Directly in front of it was my destination—a circular garden bed, in the center of which was a round seating platform. In the summer months it was usually claimed by parents resting up while their kids ran wild through the lovely gardens, but right now the whole area was empty.

If the storm *did* demand full immersion, then this was probably the safest place for me to attempt it. While there were few races beyond humans who considered church grounds sacrosanct—except, rather weirdly, the Annwfyn, who tended to avoid them—there weren't many who'd consider spilling blood a viable option here either.

And I did *not* want to think about why I was suddenly worried about blood spillage.

I sat cross-legged on the wooden platform, arranged the trench around my jeans so they didn't get soaked, then drew in a deep breath and reached for the power that rumbled above me.

And found Beira.

Well, she said, her terse manner briefly echoed in the increase of ferocity whipping around me, *it's about fucking time.*

You know, I replied, in much the same manner, *if you want me to instantly reply to the messages you send on the wind, you might want to teach me how to actually do that rather than letting me muddle along on my own.*

She harrumphed, though her amusement briefly spun

around me. If there was one thing I'd learned over the brief time I'd known her, it was that she preferred bite over meekness.

You may have a point, young Bethany, but given what rises, it is not something I dare risk too often.

I frowned. *Surely the Ninkilim haven't the capacity to sense your presence within the wind, though.*

That would depend on who exactly they have in their ranks. A weather mage could, even if they can't fully understand what the wind carries.

And are they the reason why you risked speaking to me now?

No. In fact, they have been worryingly quiet over the last few days. I fear they plan something big.

If you're keeping such a close eye on their movement, why not just tell me who they are so I can get Sgott and his people onto them?

Because the law does not work that way. Just cause, and all that rubbish.

The Ninkilim murdered my mother.

You have no direct proof of that as yet.

True, but I suspected all Sgott would need was a name to at least haul the ring leaders in and question them. *That still doesn't tell me why you can't just reveal their identities.*

Because the wind also does not work that way. She is a weapon, and a gatherer of locations and intent, but she cannot reveal deeper information such as identity. She cannot even whisper a description, because wind and storms are of land and tree, cities, and seas; they have no care for those who dwell within them.

Does that mean I can't send the wind on a mission to track down a particular person?

In normal circumstances, I would say yes, but in your case, that is a great unknown.

I frowned. *Why?*

Because you were born of both an Aodhán line given a triune blessed by multiple goddesses and the loins of a minor storm god. No one truly knows how your genetics will combine, and what might come of it. Expectation does ride high among those gods who remain that splendid chaos will be forthcoming.

You gods and your chaos, I muttered.

Her laughter spun around me, as sharp as it was warm. *It is the spice of godly life.*

Why were you attempting to contact me if not about the Ninkilim?

There has been an unsettling energy asserting itself on the storms.

Is it a relic-type energy? Or human? Because the council has tasked me with finding Borrhás's horn, and there was a recent ice attack where the entire building was encased.

The horn's ability to encase would depend on who, exactly, wields it.

Does that mean a regular storm witch could still use it even if he or she wasn't an ice witch?

Possibly. I would have to ask.

My eyebrows shot up again. *Borrhás is still hanging around? He hasn't moved on?*

He is one of the inconsistents.

Meaning what?

He hasn't fully committed and has a godly foot in both worlds, so to speak.

Then you'll ask him?

I will, but he may choose not to answer, particularly if he's the reason the horn has fallen into human hands. As I have mentioned previously, chaos is a drug few can resist for very long, and he has not partaken of that well for a while. She paused. *He also has little liking for me.*

I frowned. *And that impacts the situation how?*

If the freezing is a result of his horn, it's likely not a coincidence it's made an appearance here, in a city I often frequent, and a place that holds a godly seedling.

A godly seedling was certainly a new way to describe my origins. I wrinkled my nose. *If you are going to speak to him, can you also ask him if the two halves can be made whole and how I can rid the world of it? The council wants it back, but I'm not sure that is ever going to be a good option for any of the relics. Destruction or at least removing them from this world would be the optimum, wouldn't it?*

For the relics of those who have moved on, yes. For the inconsistents, or for those who remain attached to this world but are neither hag nor curmudgeon, I would think they'd prefer their relics remain.

Because of the chaos thing?

Indeed.

Well, fuck.

She laughed. *My sentiments exactly. Especially given I do not trust the elves to learn much from this mishap.*

Surely even they will be more cautious about security for at least a few decades.

What are decades when you deal with centuries or even millenniums?

I guess that was true. *If I want to use the wind to find the horn, or whoever might be using it to ice buildings over, how do I do that?*

You cannot be precise, but it is pointless being obtuse.

Well, that makes everything perfectly clear.

You simply have to define your parameters, such as an intense and sudden increase of ice in the air or a surge within a storm related to such an event. Her amusement spun around me again. *I will walk you through this first inquiry, but I will impress once again the need for you to learn via trial and error. As I have already said, your bloodlines mean what you can and cannot do remains unpredictable.*

Which is no doubt why my father begat me. Chaos and all that.

Ambisagrus was never a god who played such games. While none of us are privy to his current plans, he would still have seduced your mother with an end goal in mind—and that goal would not have been chaos.

I hesitated, but couldn't resist asking, *Has he had other children with mortal women, be they human or fae?*

One, a long time ago.

And?

It did not go as he planned.

Why not? What did he plan?

That is a question I cannot answer, because it is not my story to tell.

Well, that's fucking frustrating.

No doubt, but we hags had certain boundaries placed on us when we were given these meat suits and, even now, we cannot step beyond them. Are you ready?

I shifted a little on the wooden seat, then nodded. She quickly guided me through the steps of creating a simple inquiry stream, then added, *Once you cast it free, you'll need to be available to the wind at all hours, so sleep with at least one window open.*

I nodded and made a mental note to add another comforter on the bed. Her presence within the storm faded, and I climbed off the platform, tugging my trench back down before shoving my hands into my pockets and heading for the exit gate. The phone rang just as I reached it, the tone telling me it was Darby.

"You free right now?" she said as soon as I answered.

"Sure am."

"Then I'll swing by and pick you up. We've been invited for afternoon tea."

"By your lonely old ice witch, I gather?"

"Yes, and he was rather excited to be meeting someone new."

"You know, if he wasn't coping so poorly with the cold, I'd suggest he catch a cab over to the tavern at night and hang out with Jack and Phil."

Jack and Phil were a couple of old pixies who were evening fixtures at the tavern. Like many of our elders living permanently here in Deva rather than one of the widely scattered enclaves, they basically treated the Boot as a second home. The fierce joy that radiated off the old oak beams was part of the reason, but the main one was the fact that we supported our elderly with deep discounts on meals—more to ensure they had at least one decent meal a day in a city that didn't do all that much for its elderly fae, whose needs were often very different to those of humans.

"I might bring him along one night when winter is over, just to introduce him, but I do think he'd really enjoy it. I take it you're at the tavern?"

"No, just leaving the cathedral."

"What the hell are you doing there?"

"Communing with the weather."

"You can take two steps out the back door and do that."

"I definitely could, but I needed to be somewhere where I wasn't likely to be disturbed."

"Fair enough, I guess. Do you want to walk back to Watergate Street near the corner of Bridge Street, and I'll pick you up? It'll take me about fifteen to get there."

"I'll grab us coffee from Panna's if they're not too busy." I paused. "Would your witch like one?"

"His name is Winter Frost—"

"You're kidding me."

"Apparently it's a tradition—a rather mean one if you ask me—that the firstborn son every generation gets that name."

"And I bet they all got a lot of ribbing from their peers growing up, him being an ice witch and all."

"No doubt, and yes, he undoubtedly would love a cappuccino, as he doesn't treat himself too often. See you soon."

I hung up, but before I could tuck the phone away, it pinged. It was a text from Eljin, asking if I wanted to go out for dinner that evening. I smiled and sent back, *Feeling horny again, are we?*

Insatiable.

So, we're eating at your place?

I am not *a heathen. There will be a divine restaurant experience at Viridis before we indulge in sex.*

Viridis was one of the five supposed "dining sensations" within Deva, and one of only twenty-three restaurants in the UK to be given a Michelin green star for high levels of gastronomy and sustainability. When it had initially opened, the waitlist had been at least eight months long, but there were always a few daily cancelations to be snared if you rang early enough. I'd been there once before, and it had indeed been a divine experience.

What time?

I'll pick you up at eight.

Perfect. See you then.

I tucked the phone back into my purse, then made my way across to Bridge Street, enjoying the music of the storm and the dance of rain across the pavement. Thankfully, Panna's wasn't busy, so I ordered two cappuccinos and a latte for Darby, grabbed a half-dozen sticky buns, and then headed out to wait under the awning. She arrived a few minutes later, and leaned across the mini's front seats to open the passenger door for me.

I handed her the drinks then climbed in. She drew in a deep breath and sighed in delight. "Sticky buns. You'll be Winter's best friend from now on."

"Thought he might appreciate them given what you said, and besides, they just smelled too good to ignore."

"That they certainly do."

Once I'd buckled up, she gave me back the tray and drove off. Winter lived in Hoole, which was beyond the walls of old Deva, in a two-up, two-down red-brick terrace that was close to both the train station and Hoole's Community Center. Darby found a parking spot a few doors down and we walked back to his bright blue door.

Darby rang the bell then stepped back a little. A surprisingly robust voice called out, "Coming," but we were huddled in the confines of the small awning that covered the top step for quite a few minutes before the door opened.

Winter Frost was tallish, thinnish, with silvery white hair that hung in clumps that somewhat resembled icicles, and pale, almost parchment-like skin. He was stooped over and using two walking sticks that again looked like ice, though the gentle humming coming from each told me it was just a paint effect over wood.

He greeted Darby with a smile and a quick hello, then his strange, silvery-blue gaze swept me and what I was holding, and his smile grew even wider. "Ah lass, you know the way to an old man's heart. Come in, come in, before you and the goodies get soaked."

I smiled and followed Darby inside. It was a pretty standard layout for a house of this age—stairs directly ahead, a reception room to the left, through which was a combined kitchen-dining room. The kitchen was basic, but had all the usual appliances—a four-burner stovetop, underbench oven and, in the corner, a front-loading washing machine. The fridge was tucked between the dining room window and the glass door that opened out into a small patio yard.

"Please sit," he said. "I'll get some plates and cutlery."

I glanced at Darby and raised an eyebrow, silently asking if we should offer to help. She shook her head and sat down. I handed out the coffee, placing his and the buns in the middle of the well-maintained, white particleboard table.

I sat down next to her and watched as the elderly man gathered the plates, knives, and the butter dish, balancing them all in the crook of one arm while he used one stick to steady himself and walk back. After carefully depositing them on the table, he shuffled back and retrieved a cake tray. Once he'd displayed the buns and given us each a plate and a knife, he finally sat down.

"Now that we've got that done with," he said, sliding the tray toward us. "Why don't we start with the official introductions. I'm Winter Frost, Win to my friends, and I was adjutant to Halston Moore, who ran the guild before Marjorlaine took over."

Adjutant meant he'd been second-in-charge, I think. I reached across the table and shook his offered hand. His fingers were crepey against mine, but not as gnarled as I'd expected. "I'm Bethany Aodhán. I own a tavern over on Eastgate, but I'm currently working for the council hunting down some missing relics."

He sniffed. Loudly. "Why on earth would you be willingly working for them bastards?"

"Long story, but it was that or jail."

"I believe there are many within the guild who'd think jail might be the better option, but that is a tale for another time." His eyes glittered with ice, and though I wasn't sure if it was distaste or amusement, mirth twitched his thin lips. He made an "eat, eat" motion toward the buns, then added, "Darby tells me you're here to pick my poor old brain."

I plucked a bun from the cake tray, then reached for the butter. "Yes, I am, though I suspect there is nothing poor about your brain."

He laughed. "You could be right in that. What do you want to know?"

As he sliced open and buttered a bun, I quickly told him what I'd seen at Kaitlyn's. "I was just wondering if you knew of any active ice witches in Deva."

He took a bite rather than answer, then briefly closed his eyes. "Damn, these are good."

"Made fresh this morning."

"Do they deliver?"

"No, I don't think they do," Darby said, "but I can alternate between these and eclairs on my visits, if you'd like."

"That would be fabulous, young lady, but only if it's not too much of a problem. Wouldn't want you going out of your way for an old fool like me."

"I wouldn't for an old fool, but for a friend, it's no problem."

A smile creased the corners of his eyes. "You do say the nicest things. To answer the question on the table, though, there's quite a number of storm witches in the guild these days, but as far as I'm aware only one ice witch. But he's unlikely to be active within Deva. It goes against guild rules."

"Why is that?"

"Because, if you'll excuse the crudity, it's never wise to shit on your own back door."

I laughed. "Are you able to give me the contact details of this ice witch? Even if he's not responsible for the attack, he might be able to give some pointers on who was. I mean, there can't be too many ice witches in the UK, can there?"

"There were five registered during my time at the guild, but there could be more now, with the next generation filling the ranks." He frowned. "I will say, however, that the strangely glowing vortex you mentioned is generally *not* something that happens in either the creation or destruction of ice formations. We use what already exists in the air —the chill and the moisture—to build walls or to sheet items. I've certainly never seen or heard of an ice witch who can deconstruct a building in such a manner. Usually, if we're intent on destruction, we freeze and shatter."

I hesitated, wondering how much I should tell him given the council's edict the general public couldn't know about the missing hoard. But I couldn't *not* tell him, either. While it was possible he still had friends within the guild, the slight emphasis he'd put on Marjorlaine's name when he said it suggested he was no fan of hers, and might have left on a bitter note. After all, there had to be some reason he got so few visits from the organization he'd spent a lifetime serving.

"We think the witch behind the attack might be using a relic to enhance his powers."

Win wrinkled his nose. "If that is the case, I'm surprised the guild hasn't already reacted. The last thing they need is a rogue operator in the city."

"They might well have," I said. "It's not like I've been in contact with them."

"No." He picked up his cup and took a careful sip. Pleasure briefly lit his expression. "I would have thought, though, that you'd have felt the formation of the ice vortex given the electricity of storms all but surrounds you."

"It does?" Darby said and scanned me critically.

"You have to be a witch to sense another," he said with a sharp laugh.

"And I'm not a witch. At least, not a trained one. I've only recently started developing the skill."

"Then you should contact the guild. They'll be able to get you up to speed in a few years."

Except we didn't have years and I was not inclined to undertake any sort of official training, especially given Beira's recent comment about storm witches listening into her conversations. The last thing I wanted was to give the Ninkilim any sort of heads-up as to the true depth of my abilities.

"I'll think about it."

"Which is a female's way of saying 'not on your Nelly.'"

I laughed and lightly touched my cup against his. "Have you got the contact details for this ice witch?"

"His name is Harold Gould, but he's not likely to talk to someone like yourself."

I frowned. "Why not?"

"Guild edict. No talking to anyone about guild business without guild permission."

I sighed. "Then we go through the guild."

"Or I could talk to him," he said. "The cost will be another morning tea, complete with coffee and sticky buns."

I laughed. "Deal. Thank you, Win."

He nodded, and the conversation moved on. He regaled us with stories of past exploits, and Darby and I returned in kind, telling tales of the strange things that had happened at both the hospital and the tavern. We left on a promise to visit the next week.

The rain had eased by the time we got back outside, though the wind promised more would be unleashed in an hour or so. Once we were back in Darby's mini, I dragged out my phone and googled the guild's webpage. Once there, I flipped over to their listings page and scrolled down the list. "Well, Winter's right. There's no other ice witches listed, and only one storm witch—a man by the name of Harper Jones. There's no contact details, though. If Win can't convince Gould to talk to us, we'll have to go through the guild itself."

"Might be better to get Sgott onto it."

"Except he has to follow the rules and can't use pixie magic to make them talk."

"Yeah, but he has a database that can get phone numbers and addresses. You don't."

I grinned. "Which is where Mathi comes into it. He has full access to his father's computer."

She glanced at me. "Seriously? Why on earth has Sgott allowed that to continue?"

"Because he and Ruadhán are equal counterparts, and until Mathi steps out of line with the access, he can't really override Ruadhán's authority. He is keeping a close eye on things, and has restricted access to the night division files and cases."

"Makes sense, though given Mathi's father would still have that access, it's also pretty pointless."

"Ruadhán won't do or allow anything that'll set Sgott off. He very carefully walks the gray area between legal and not. Mathi is well aware of that."

"I'm still surprised Sgott puts up with it. He's generally a straight-down-the-line man."

"He's also very careful, and certainly wouldn't risk jeop-ardizing an entire department without just cause and lots of evidence."

Darby nodded. "You want to be—"

Before she could finish, my phone rang, the noise so sharp and unexpected it made me jump slightly. I glanced down at the screen, saw it was Sgott, and hit the answer button. "Were your ears burning or something?"

"Burning ears would be welcome, given the situation right now."

Alarm leapt through me. "What situation? What's happened?"

"It's the Lùtair Enterprises building—they've just come under an ice attack."

"Cynwrig's building?"

"Aye, though none of the immediate family are likely to be there. Where are you?"

"With Darby, just heading onto Hoole Way." I glanced at her. "Do you know where Lùtair Enterprises is?"

"Yes—I'll get you there as fast as I can." She paused. "Tell Sgott to warn his people and the cops there's a bright red mini coming in hot."

"I'll send a car to meet and escort you." He paused and quickly spoke to someone, though the conversation was muffled, suggesting he was holding the phone close to his chest. The seconds seemed to tick by extremely slowly. "I'll have two cars waiting for you at the Fountains Roundabout. They'll run lights and sirens front and behind, and get you here faster."

"Awesome," Darby said with a wide grin. "Always wanted to truly test the handling and speed of this little beastie."

"I take comfort in the fact that you have, at least, done an advanced driving course." His voice was a gravelly mix of amusement and concern. "But please do try not to bend my girl or your good self."

"Not to mention the mini." She swung around the first roundabout adeptly at speed then flattened her foot again as we barreled toward Fountains Roundabout. The mini hugged the ground as well as any rat. A speedy red rat.

"How bad is the ice encasement?" I asked Sgott.

"The ground floor exits and windows are iced over, but the rest of the building remains free, though frost is starting to creep slowly up the stonework."

I frowned. "That's a different approach to the attack on Kaitlyn's—and a whole lot faster."

"Different building could explain it."

Maybe. I'd imagine any Lùtair building would have been constructed with a means of countering magic, given they were capable of it themselves. But it could also be a matter of this attack happening too close to the other. It was an undisputed fact that all magic had its cost, and I certainly knew from experience that the rule also applied to the use of godly relics. "Are you able to evacuate?"

"Yes, because nearly all the buildings in the business park are two story, and they all have external fire stairs. We're just moving people up to the first floor and getting them out via the stairs and fire ladders to the windows."

At least that was something. Up ahead, blue-and-red lights spun brightness through the gloom. "I can see our escort, so we'll see you soon."

As we pulled into the roundabout, the first cop car took off. The second fell in behind us, and we were quickly whisked through the various other roundabouts until we reached the A483 and then the business park. The area did actually look like a park rather than the usual concrete and brick expanse of most business hubs, and was filled with lots of green space and a variety of gorgeous trees, both old and new. The cops up front slowed, forcing Darby to do the same, and we all turned right into a parking area that was filled with cars and emergency services.

A policewoman directed us to a parking spot and, once we'd stopped, Darby and I climbed out and were escorted through the mess of vehicles and into a small, grassed area filled with the vibrant song of youngish oaks. It wasn't hard to spot the building under attack—it was a black, almost monolithic structure in a sea of red-brick modernism with mirrored windows and a towering front entrance. In the face of all that darkness, the ice stood out starkly. It covered all the ground floor windows and the main entrance area, a thick barrier that gleamed with blue-white intensity in the gloom of the day. Sharp fingers of ice were extending toward the first-floor windows but seemed to be moving very slowly. I would have thought that, given whoever was behind this attack had to be close enough to see both the building *and* the ongoing evacuation, they'd have sped things up a little. But maybe death wasn't their intent. Maybe they were simply after destruction. *Material* destruction.

But what in the hell was the connection between Kaitlyn and the Lùtair building?

As Mathi had noted earlier, the Lùtairs did *not* need her help when it came to acquiring black market services. They dominated the damn thing, for fuck's sake.

Sgott glanced around as we approached. "We're just evacuating the final few people now. We've also done an aerial search of the entire area. We're not finding anyone even remotely suspicious. No drones, and no person or persons perched high on a rooftop."

"That makes no sense," Darby said. "No matter what

the kind, witches generally have to see the person or item they're working on for the spell to work."

I wrinkled my nose. "Perhaps they scouted the location at an earlier date, or are familiar enough with the area to direct their attack from afar."

"It's also possible they're using one of the many vids available on YouTube that go into great detail discussing this place," Sgott commented. "They do hold great fascination to both architects and aesthetes."

I frowned at him. "What the hell is an aesthete?"

"Someone who has an eye for design and appreciates works of art and fine things," Sgott replied, his gaze meeting mine. "Do you think your knives can counter the ice here without destroying the building?"

"I have no fucking idea at this point, but there is at least one thing in our favor this time—the entire building isn't as yet encased."

And while the glittering fingers continued to creep toward the first floor, the building's roofline remained relatively clear. Which, again, differed from Kaitlyn's, but until we discovered who was behind these attacks, we really wouldn't have any true understanding of his or her motives.

"You might want to evacuate the rest of the area though," I added. "Especially given what happened last time."

He nodded and began speaking into his phone again. As people began moving away from the building, I scanned the sky, extending my senses enough to feel the caress of untamed wildness within the clouds. The promised evening storms remained a few hours away.... The thought stopped. Just for an instant, I caught a wisp of... something else. Something *other* than the distant rumble of thunder and lightning. A presence that spoke of humanity.

It was gone before I could clearly define or even pin it, but it had definitely felt female.

Not Harold Gould then, though it was yet possible he could give us her name given there were supposedly only five ice witches within the UK—unless of course, there'd been an influx of talents in recent years, or she'd been lured in from overseas. I guess it would be one way of avoiding the guilds here tracking your magical markers.

Sgott returned his attention to us. "Okay, the area is clear and all yours."

"Thanks." I retrieved my knives then handed the purse to Darby. "You two might want to retreat to the tree line. If the explosion has the same force, that should offer enough distance."

"If the explosion has the same force," Sgott said, "that'll put you right in the eye of danger. This is a far bigger building, remember, and you barely got away in time at Kaitlyn's."

And only because he'd run in and saved my ass. Still, I wasn't about to admit that I was every bit as worried as him about survival, if only because that would make him worry even more.

"I've a hot date tonight, so you can be sure I'm not about to let any damn explosion make me miss it."

Though even as I said that, I couldn't help but wish that it was Cynwrig I was meeting. Cynwrig I'd be falling into bed with. Cynwrig's arms that would wrap around me as we fell into blissful slumber.

Of course, it *was* possible that I *could* have all that if I dared to take what the bracelet offered, but was I just...

Scared, I guess. Scared of risking a possible long-term relationship for short-term gratification.

Darby touched my arm lightly, perhaps sensing the inner turmoil. I smiled, and though she no doubt saw the tension running through it, she didn't say anything. She just turned and followed Sgott back to the trees. I drew in a deeper breath to fortify my nerves, then, after tightening my grip on the knives just a fraction, strode determinately toward the black blot of a building.

As tempting as it was to head for one of the windows, where the ice was much thinner, the true heart of the attack seemed to be the vast ice sheet covering the main entrance into the building. Though it was impossible to see doorways or glass through the thick bluish gleam of the ice, fat icicle fingers spread out from this main clump, moving across the portico's internal roofline far faster than they were on the rest of the building.

I stopped at the bottom of the three steps that led up into the portico, my gaze sweeping the gleaming black stone floor. Though ice clawed across it, a clear path remained. I had no desire for any of it to touch me—if it could freeze and utterly demolish a building, then it likely could do the same to flesh if given half the chance. Just because Kaitlyn's condition had been caused more by the chill that came with the ice rather than it actually capturing and encasing her didn't mean they wouldn't attempt such a maneuver with me—especially now he or she knew exactly what I could do.

I raised my gaze to the bluish wall directly ahead, then gathered several strings of the gently stirring wind and spun them all around me, resulting in a whirling barrier few would see, but one that would hopefully afford some protection if I stuck my knives into the ice and exploded the whole damn building again.

I forced my feet up the steps and across the black stone, carefully skirting around the few icy fingers that crossed my path. They didn't chase after me, but I had this weird feeling the person behind this attack was suddenly aware of my presence.

A feeling that was all but confirmed when the activity of the ice above jumped into another gear, and the fat fingers running across the roofline motored over the concealed gutters and disappeared up onto the roof. I had no idea what the witch intended, but I suspected I had better act now, before all the fingers reaching up the sides of the building met with those on the roof.

The chill radiating off the thick block of ice was nowhere near as strong as it had been at Kaitlyn's, but it was still cold enough for my nose and fingers to tingle. I scanned the width of the wall, looking for the best spot to attack, but there didn't appear to be any obvious weak spots. With a half shrug, I raised both knives, drove them into the ice, then released them and stepped back.

As at Kaitlyn's, nothing happened for several seconds. Then the knives pulsed, and thunder rumbled in response, despite the fact the storm remained a good few hours away. These knives were definitely drawing on my connection with the weather to enhance their own power. Beira *had* said that no one truly understood how my genetics would combine with the triune and what might come of it, so was this recent ability of the knives to connect with the storms— seemingly without any input from me—an example of that? They'd always been basically autonomous when it came to protecting me from spells, but I'd always presumed it was a protection that extended to all the women in my line who'd used them. I actually had no idea if that were true because, like so many other things, Mom never mentioned it.

The knives pulsed again, and the sky responded, the sharp crack of thunder loud enough to make me wince. A second crack followed a heartbeat later, one that came from the ice rather than the sky. A fissure had formed in the ice directly above me and quickly became a spider web of cracks that spread rapidly across the ice covering the portico's roof. Large slabs began to fall, shattering as they hit the black stone, sending deadly spears of gleaming ice spinning in all directions. I hastily ramped up the vortex surrounding me, and not a moment too soon; the gleaming spears aimed at my heart were neatly spun back into the portico's vastness.

More chunks of ice slammed down, thick enough to kill. The stone under my feet vibrated with each blow and the heat radiating from the blades increased. The roof above me quickly cleared of ice, and though I couldn't physically see the rest of the building, both the rumbling thunder overhead and the wind that spun around and over it told me it was now also free. Which just left this wall.

As the burning power focused solely on it, the ice witch attacked.

It was something I felt more than saw—a sudden chill in the stone under my boots—but through it, I could feel her power and presence. My second sight flared to life, and a vision rose—a woman huddled in front of a laptop that showed what looked to be multiple street views. Her hair was short and spiky, glittering silver in the pale shafts of light streaming in from the window behind her, her skin pale and wrinkled, and her long face drawn. Emaciated almost. Around her neck was a simple leather cord attached to a drinking horn—one that she gripped with her left hand, from which a constant stream of icy particles dripped. They never hit the floor; instead, they spun away into the ether, no doubt heading for this building.

I frowned and tried widening the scope of the vision fractionally. There was movement around her, voices and conversations, a continuous wave that suggested she was somewhere public. If she *was*, then there had to be some sort of protective or concealment magic happening alongside the main spell, because surely someone would have noticed the relic if not the ice. As the vision began to fade, I caught sight of a familiar sign.

She was sitting at my favorite burger joint down at the river, not far from the boat hire place, no doubt using their free WIFI.

The vision slipped away completely, and awareness returned. Frost now crept over the toes of my boots and up the heel. I couldn't allow it to touch my skin. Dared not.

I swore and spun myself away from the portico, using the air surrounding me like an overly large if unseen beachball. I bounced down the steps and rolled across the grass, the world spinning around me. It was so disorientating that I briefly lost control and crashed into the branches of a lovely young oak. As the air bubble began to dissipate, I slithered gently down to the ground, the tree's song filled with confusion over the brief but thankfully harmless impact. As the remaining slivers of wind slipped away, I scrambled upright, my gaze on the black building. Ice continued to fall in chunks, but there was only one section remaining now, and it was off to the right of the entrance. I could no longer feel the witch's presence; perhaps she'd simply given up the fight once I'd bounced away from her attack. Or perhaps that attack had taken the last of her strength.

"Bethany? You okay?" Sgott asked, his voice sharp with concern.

My gaze snapped around. He and Darby were running toward me. "Yeah, fine, but I know where the witch is—she's at Two Chicks and a Patty near the boat hire dock. She's tall, thin, mid-fifties at a guess, and has short, spiky silver hair."

Sgott immediately got onto his phone, though I had serious doubts even a bird shifter would get there in time to stop her escape. Darby stopped a couple of feet in front of me, her narrowed gaze sweeping me critically. Then she caught my hand, holding it firm as her healer energy flooded through me, scanning for any internal damage.

After a few seconds, she let me go, her expression relieved. "You've little more than a few scratches and some impending bruising, which is pretty close to a miracle given the speed you came tumbling away from that building. Damn near gave me a heart attack."

I smiled. "I had a bubble of air around me. I wasn't in any danger of being hurt."

"The bruising threatening to develop down your spine counters that comment to some extent. I did take care of them, by the way. Can't have an achy back getting in the way of good sex now, can we?"

"We definitely cannot."

"Okay," Sgott said as he stopped beside Darby. "We've two teams, a witch, and a shifter on the way to Two Chicks. If she's still in there, we'll get her. But at least now we have a description to work with."

Which wouldn't do much good if she wasn't the brains behind these attacks, but simply another employee. To be honest, if Keeryn was anywhere near as proficient at creating concealment spells as Maran had been, how could I even be sure that what I'd seen in the vision was the witch's real form and not a concealment? Especially given my second sight had already proven unable to see past such spells?

I crossed my arms. "You want me in to do a facial composite?"

"I'll send Jenny around to the tavern tomorrow. I'm thinking you need to be getting home and resting up for your big night."

I laughed. "Yeah, I don't think Eljin will appreciate me faceplanting into the middle of my fancy appetizer."

"Never a good thing," Sgott agreed sagely, then motioned to a nearby officer. "Mandy will escort you both back to the mini. Please obey the speed limits on the way back."

Darby laughed. "I think the cobwebs have been well and truly shaken from her engines today."

"No doubt, but the warning still applies, given the number of speeding tickets you have on record." He stepped back and motioned us forward.

As we fell in step behind Mandy and moved away from him, Darby said, "So where's Eljin taking you tonight?"

"Viridis."

Darby sucked in a breath. "Is he aware that was one of the first places Cynwrig took you to, and that it's likely to raise unwanted comparisons, no matter how much you try to avoid it?"

"No, and I won't be mentioning it either. Besides, we'll likely be in a completely different area, given Cynwrig appeared to have a permanent table there."

"Well, he does like treating his harem well."

Indeed, he did. And I did not want to think about how much I missed that. Missed him.

And I was seriously becoming something of a lost cause who really needed to move on.

Would I though?

Probably not, I thought, a smile tugging at my lips. At least, not until I'd decided whether it was worth the risk of donning the bracelet and tasting the delights of sex on the dreaming plane.

Darby dropped me off close to Eastgate Street and as I walked down to the tavern, I sent the two names to Mathi, asking if he could chase up some contact details and telling him why I needed them. The tavern wasn't busy, and, after checking in with Ingrid again, I headed upstairs. Eljin wasn't picking me up until eight, so that gave me a good four hours to sleep before I had to start getting ready. After opening the old sash window just enough to allow a slither of wind entry, I connected to the frame's fibers to lightly lock it in place, ensuring that no one else—not even a damn rat—could get in. Then I stripped off and fell into bed. I was asleep before my head hit the pillow.

Eljin opened the umbrella, then offered me a hand and helped me out of the Uber. The night was positively shitty, the storm I'd sensed earlier having hit about an hour ago. I'd been briefly tempted to just wear dress pants and a warm sweater, but this place—and this man—deserved something better. After much indecision, I'd gone with a form-fitting emerald-green sheath dress, long, soft leather boots, and a thick woolen coat. Eljin hadn't seen the dress yet, and I was definitely anticipating a heated reaction.

The room we entered wasn't particularly large, but filled with Victorian splendor. The tables were well spaced, the lighting muted, and while there was no evidence of a bar, there was one here and it served some seriously good —and seriously expensive—alcohol.

A dapper-looking older woman approached, took care of our coats and the umbrella, and then, after checking our booking, said, "Please, this way, Mr. Lavigne."

Eljin didn't answer. He could barely even nod. The dress and the boots, it seemed, had the desired effect.

We were led through the stylish and beautiful room to a staircase near the back. I once again ran my fingers across the worn and obviously original volute at the base of the stairs and let them drift along the curved oak handrail as we moved up. Its song danced through me, and I couldn't help smiling. This building had been a long and happy resting place for the wood in this staircase, and there weren't many left in Deva of this age that could make such a boast.

Last time I'd been here, we'd been escorted to the more intimate loft space, but this time, we stepped off at the first floor and were led across to a cute table located between the lovely old Victorian fireplace and the sash windows dominating the front of the building. There were three tables here, all occupied by couples. This was not a place where you brought kids.

The older woman—whose name was Leanne, according to her badge—seated us, then handed us a drink menu. "Would you like to order a drink now, or would you prefer a few minutes to scan the menu?"

I placed my purse under the table, then said, "I might try the Glenlivet Nadurra, please."

"And you, sir?" Leanne asked.

He pursed his lips, then said, "I'll have the Royal Salute Old Snow."

"Both excellent choices. I shall return with your drinks and to take your meal order presently."

As she walked away, he leaned forward and crossed his arms on the table, his gaze sliding slowly from my lips to my neck to my breasts. My nipples puckered, despite how warm the small room was, and a smile tugged at the corners of his lips.

"That dress leaves little to the imagination and I have to admit, I'm somewhat torn."

I raised an eyebrow, amusement lurking. "Over what?"

"Over the fact that I was not the only man in this room or the other who was admiring your luscious curves."

"I have no problems with other men looking."

"So it would seem." His gaze rose to my neck. "You're not wearing your mother's seeking stone."

"I took your fears about being burned at the wrong moment to heart and decided to wear a simple gold chain instead." I still had it with me, because instinct kept insisting I needed to keep it close, but it was currently tucked in a side pocket of my purse. My knives remained safely hidden at home, however.

"And the possibility of deflation recedes, for which I am grateful."

I laughed. "So am I, trust me."

Once Leanne returned with our drinks and took our order, Eljin pulled several sheets of folded paper from his pocket and handed them to me. "Lugh said you were after these notes on Borrhás's Horn. He apparently translated some of Nialle's worst scrawls for you."

I smiled and accepted the paper. "When he was on an information roll, he used to resort to a mix of scribble and shorthand. Lugh could always read it, but not many others."

"My writing tends to do the same; problem is, I often can't read it afterward, which is why I now use speech-to-text programs. I take it the horn is your latest search subject?"

I nodded. "First official one for the council."

"Nice of them to start with something easy."

I tucked the papers into my purse without looking at them. "Why would you say that?"

"Well, you're a storm witch, and the horn controls the weather, does it not?"

"Not the weather, per se. More the ice within a storm."

"Which, as a storm witch, you should be able to sense."

"If I was trained, maybe, but I'm not." I half shrugged—hoping he'd take it as a sign I really didn't want to talk about it—then picked up the Glenlivet and drew in its scent. It smelled of apple and pears, with hints of nutmeg and oak, vanilla cream, and white pepper, and was fresh and lively on the tongue. Absolutely lovely, but perhaps a little bit too fruity for my palate. Not that I was going to waste a single drop.

He took the hint, and the conversation moved on, flowing easily between the two of us over the three courses of the meal.

Leanne came back once the dessert plates had been cleared and asked if we'd like a coffee or perhaps a brandy. Eljin met my gaze, eyebrows raised in question.

I smiled and said, "I think we'll just have the check, thank you, Leanne."

"I do so love a woman who understands silent communication," Eljin commented as Leanne walked away.

"More like a woman desperate to get her man into bed."

He laughed, and, once we'd paid, we headed back downstairs. Eljin helped me into my coat, his fingers brushing across my nape, leaving a heated trail. I shivered, and he laughed again, pressing a hand against my spine as he opened the door, and we stepped outside, keeping to one side of the building's awning, out of the rain, as we waited for the Uber. As thunder rumbled a promise of more violence to come, Eljin wrapped an arm around my waist and pulled me close, pressing my length hard against his. The heat and anticipation surged, then his lips came down on mine, and any awareness of anything and anyone else momentarily slipped away. The kiss was wanton, filled with intensity and passion, and it left me breathless and needy.

It was nothing like *any* other kiss we'd ever shared.

I shivered again when he released me. He didn't say anything, but his eyes gleamed knowingly as he helped me into the back of the Uber. His apartment was the penthouse suite of a lovely old red-brick church that had retained all its beams and original windows when it had been converted into five apartments a few years ago. It was located within walking distance of the river and the museum, and also happened to be close to the tavern.

He opened the door and ushered me inside as the internal fires continued to rage. I wanted this man as I'd never wanted before, and I couldn't help but wonder if maybe I'd had too much wine. Attraction and desire was one thing, but this was something else entirely. Hell, it was close to Cynwrig levels of wanting.

I swallowed heavily and tried—without any real success—to regain control over my hormones as I handed him my coat and walked into the main room. It was a large, double-height expanse, with the lovely old oak trusses painted white to give the room an even airier feeling. Their song, though muted, was rich and warm, a consequence of being one of the few churches that had undergone major renovations without major destruction. On the street side of the building there were two beautifully simple stained windows, and at the other end of the room, a compact but well-equipped kitchen. Beside this was a chrome-and-glass staircase that wound up to the loft bedroom.

His hand slid around my waist again, and I went up in flames. It was a ferocity that was obviously shared, because he wrapped a hand around the back of my neck, holding me still as his lips came down on mine, hard and desperate. For several minutes there was nothing but this kiss, this man, and the wanton hunger that surged between us. His fingers found and undid the zip at the back of my dress, then he hooked his fingers under the garment's shoulders and slid it down my body, taking my knickers with it. His gaze swept my nakedness, and he swore softly in French. I smiled and, with shaking, desperate hands, helped him undress; his pants, shirt, and shoes quickly joined my dress on the floor.

"The boots can stay," he growled, then lifted me up, pressed me back against the nearest wall, and sheathed himself deep within me. A low moan of utter pleasure escaped my lips, and I leaned my head backward, eyes closed, simply enjoying this most basic of moments.

Then he began to move, and I wrapped my arms around him, moving with him, increasing our rhythm, riding him hard, desperate for completion. When it came, it was glorious.

For several minutes, we were still, our foreheads touching and our rapid breaths mingling. Then he laughed and brushed his lips lightly across mine. "Well, the intended slow seduction certainly did *not* happen, though I am not inclined to apologize."

I grinned. "There's nothing wrong with fast and furious."

"No, there certainly isn't, but I am a man who generally likes to take his time and fully explore his partner and her needs."

I grinned. "You've done that before and can certainly do it again. As many times as you wish, as often as you wish, in fact."

"And what of the competition?"

"Currently out of the picture." Which wasn't a lie even if it felt like one. Until I put the bracelet on my wrist, Cynwrig was not in my life.

"Suggesting I need to do all in my power to ensure he remains that way." He shifted his grip on my butt, and I couldn't help but notice the man remained erect. Perhaps someone had spiced our foods with an aphrodisiac, because he certainly wasn't the only one primed for another session. Our sex life had never been lacking, but this... this was another level of intensity. "Shall we continue this upstairs?"

"If we *don't* continue *somewhere*, I'll be most disappointed."

He laughed and, despite our intimate lock, carried me up the stairs with surprising ease, where we did indeed continue on long and hard into the night. When I finally slept, no dreams hit, which was the first time that had happened since I'd been staying overnight at Eljin's. A good omen, I couldn't help but think.

But when I checked the Eye in the morning, lightning flashed furiously in its dark heart. It did *not* approve of being pushed aside, even if only for the night.

That, however, turned out to be the least of my problems. The mother of all headaches hit, and neither copious amounts of tea nor the strongest painkillers Eljin had were cutting it. And I wasn't the only one suffering, which suggested maybe it was something we'd consumed last night.

He eventually bundled me into an Uber with the promise to ring me on his lunch break. I closed my eyes as the driver swept into peak hour traffic, which meant it took longer to arrive back home than it usually did. By the time I climbed out of the car, I was feeling nauseous. The cause simply *couldn't* be having too much to drink—unlike elves, we pixies had a high tolerance for the stuff—but I also hated to think the problem lay with Viridis.

I ran upstairs, stripped off, and headed into the bathroom for another shower. The hot water helped the ache in my head but not so much my stomach, and a few minutes later, I was hunkered over the loo, dripping water all over the floor as I vomited my heart out.

When I'd finally finished, I stepped back into the shower to clean up, then dried off and stumbled into my bedroom, where I fell into bed and a deep sleep comforted by the gentle song of the old building.

The phone ringing woke me who knew how many hours later. I groggily groped for it on the bedside table, then remembered it was still in my purse, which remained in the living area. I swore, flicked off the bedding, and padded out naked to retrieve it.

It was close to three in the afternoon, and it was Mathi rather than Eljin.

"What's up, Mathi?" I scrubbed a hand across my face. While I felt decidedly better after the sleep, a dull ache remained in the back of my head.

"You sound like shit—everything okay?"

"I think I just ate something last night that disagreed with me. I'm fine."

"I'm not convinced. What say I collect coffee and a bacon butty from the shop just down the road from you, and we do some research while you eat and recover. We do have a relic to find, and the council will be wanting a prelim report in the next twenty-four hours."

"Sounds like a plan." And there was nothing quite like a thick bacon butty to chase away a lingering headache, no matter what the cause.

"I'll see you in about twenty, then."

Meaning he was already on his way here. I hung up, then checked for missed calls. There were several from Eljin, so I sent a text back explaining what had happened, then added that while I felt better, I might stay home tonight. Alone, I was tempted to add, but held off.

Sounds like a good idea, he wrote back. *Call if you do want some company. Happy to just sit and watch TV with you.*

A vague sense of relief stirred, which probably had more to do with the lingering headache than any desire not to see him tonight. *You've been here how many times now, and you've never noticed how very rarely I watch TV?*

Several shocked emojis came back. *Then what the hell do you do to relax?*

Read. Eat. Drink. Have sex.

Well, if you feel like company doing any or all of those, you know my number.

I sent him a smiley face blowing a kiss, went down the stairs to unlock the door, then hustled back into the bedroom to get dressed. Mathi would definitely take naked-ness as an invitation, and I wasn't in the mood to deal with all that right now.

The building's song announced his arrival as he entered via the main door. I got out plates and cutlery, putting them down on the table as he headed up. The delicious smell of bacon preceded his arrival, and my stomach rumbled in appreciation. Obviously, it had finally gotten over whatever had caused this morning's upchucking episode.

His gaze scanned me quickly and critically, and came up relieved. "You look far better than you sounded on the phone."

"That's because your call woke me up from a very deep sleep."

"Sorry about that."

"You brought me a butty and coffee, so you're forgiven."

He laughed. "If I'd only known bacon was the path to forgiveness, I might have tried it earlier."

"There are some problems even a butty cannot resolve, and that's when you bring chocolate." I reached for one of the paper bags, slid out the toasted sandwich, then reached for a knife to slice it in two.

"Well," he said, bedevilment dancing through his expression, "the butty has at least gotten me back up here. Now I just need to get—"

I balled up the paper bag and tossed it at him. "Do not finish that sentence."

He batted it away with another laugh. "I can but try."

"And you're certainly very trying. Eat your sandwich. As you noted, we've work to do."

Once we'd finished our meal, I retrieved the papers Lugh had given me and spread them out on the coffee table. He edged forward on the sofa, his arms crossed over his knees as he studied the three bits of paper.

"You know," he said after a few minutes, "none of these

make a whole lot of sense, even with Lugh transcribing them."

"It's just random bits of information Nialle found while searching for the Claws. According to Lugh, he often jotted stuff he found on other relics he thought the museum might want to chase up at a later date."

"Meaning these"—he paused and motioned to the papers—"fifteen random bits of musings all concern the horn?"

I nodded and pointed to two words sitting on its own page—Ballynastaig Souterrain. "That sounds like a location to me."

"Could be." He retrieved his phone from his pocket and googled it. "Okay, it's an ancient underground structure that's part of a larger Iron Age fort, and is located within the Ballynastaig Stone Fort, near Gort in Galway. Might be worth checking it out, because the old gods do have a liking for hiding things underground."

I had no idea where Gort was, but I was familiar enough with Galway, given that's where my aunt had moved to when she'd had the falling out with Mom. "I saw the witch using the horn, Mathi, so even if it had been kept there, it's not there now."

"Perhaps not, but by investigating its former resting place, we might uncover some useful information about it."

He gave me his phone so I could look at the images. What remained of the fort's stone walls and earthen ramparts were overgrown and dotted with trees, and the souterrain in its center was rather small and wild-looking. The thick slabs of stone it had been constructed with did at least appear to be in good shape, despite their lean.

I handed the phone back. He tucked it into his pocket,

then said, "I'm not seeing anything remotely useful in any of the other notes though—"

"Which might be because they're partial rather than whole sentences that make little sense overall. They will mean something, even if we don't understand it."

He grunted. "What about the codex librarian—did it give you any information about the horn?"

"It said the horn was designed as a gift to a queen who wished to bring winter down on all her enemies and that it had been cleaved in two so that it could not be used in such a manner ever again."

"Well, someone has obviously found a way to make it whole again." He tapped the word *revenge* on the second page that had been circled several times. "This suggests we were right—whoever is wielding this thing is out for revenge."

"Seems like." I swept my gaze over the three pages again, then tapped another half sentence. "'Destroy via gods' fire' could mean the forge of the gods we discovered. Nialle wouldn't have known about it when he was doing this."

"Why would he note a means of destruction if he was researching for the museum, though?"

I shrugged. "Because it never pays to overlook any information, however unlikely it is to be useable. Or so Lugh once said."

He briefly pursed his lips. "The quickest and easiest way to check the souterrain would be to take a private jet over to Shannon Airport and have a car waiting."

"And you can do all that at short notice?"

He smiled somewhat wryly. "I will never be outdone by a Lùtair when it comes to this sort of stuff, especially when

I have the advantage of being able to charge the costs back to the council."

"Which makes me suspect the jet you will be hiring may well belong to Dhār-Val Enterprises."

"And they will of course be billed at a competitive market rate."

I laughed. "So generous of you."

"They are abusing my position on the council and my friendship with you to use me as a liaison, just as they used Cynwrig's attraction to you. They pay neither of us a stipend, so it's only fair they are charged in other ways."

Which made me wonder what Cynwrig had been charging back to them. "You could quit the council."

"And lose an advantage over my competitors by knowing what changes the council intends to implement to rules and regs before they come into being? Do not be so naïve."

I laughed. "Isn't that called insider trading and illegal?"

"Technically, no, given the legal definition of insider trading is the buying or selling of a publicly traded company's stock by someone with non-public material information about that company. I am neither buying nor selling stock. I merely use it for my own company's benefit. As do, I may point out, most there."

"Still sounds shady to me."

"You run a tavern, not a multimillion-dollar company."

"Oh, knifed through the heart."

"A comment that would have more impact if you weren't smiling so broadly."

I laughed again and motioned to the papers. "So, we head there tomorrow and investigate?"

He nodded. "If we leave by seven, it should give us plenty of time to investigate the site and get back home.

Unless, of course, you'd like to stay overnight. Galway is a lovely place."

I couldn't help smiling. "I'd rather sleep in my own bed."

"Or Eljin's?"

My smile grew. "I tend to get more sleep in mine."

"Undoubtedly. A wise man never lets a luscious woman go to waste when she's in his bed." He rose and dragged a slip of paper from his pants pocket. "Before I forget, here's the address and phone number for Harper Jones. Couldn't find any details for Harold Gould, so maybe he died or simply moved out of the area."

"Thanks." I reached out and accepted the paper. Harper also lived in Hoole. Perhaps it was a favorite area for guild members. "Male or female?"

"Female, about thirty years old."

I glanced up. "What database did you have to break into to get this information?"

"None. She's listed with IIT, and though her file was sealed, they're still tracking her movements."

"Meaning whatever she did as a juvie was pretty damn bad—should I be worried?"

"Aside from the occasional speeding and parking fines, she's been clean since she turned eighteen, so I wouldn't think so."

"Good. I'll go have a chat while you make the arrangements for tomorrow."

"Do you want company?"

"It's less intimidating if there's only me."

"I can do unintimidating."

"No, you can't. Not with people you don't know, anyway."

Mathi could certainly turn on the charm when he

wanted to, but like most light elves, the face he presented to the world in general was cold and unemotional.

He didn't disagree. I listened to the vibration of his movements as he moved down the stairs, then picked up my phone and brought up the souterrain images. At first glance, it didn't appear to be all that deep or large, but if there's one thing I'd learned over the last few weeks it was things weren't always as they seemed. And they very definitely weren't as *safe* as they sometimes appeared.

In any other situation, I would have instantly called Cynwrig and asked him to come with us. Lùtairs were, among other things, manipulators of stone, which would definitely come in handy if the souterrain decided to collapse three seconds after we'd entered.

But this *wasn't* any other situation. I sighed and, after grabbing a couple of painkillers to take care of the lingering remnants of my headache, shoved on a pair of boots, swept up my purse, phone, and the piece of paper holding the address, then headed down to the back lane, grabbing one of my waterproof coats on the way. It wasn't raining—in fact, for a winter's evening, it was quite pleasant—but I wasn't about to risk the distant rumblings becoming a full-fledged storm.

I was lucky enough to catch a passing cab on St. Werburgh Street and, despite the traffic, it didn't take us all that long to get over to Hoole. Harper lived in a two-story, red-brick, semi-detached house on a tiny side street opposite a kids' small soccer field. It wasn't a particularly large or attractive place, with a black door situated in the middle of the building and three weirdly placed windows that formed an odd V-shape up the front. There was a white Ford parked to the right of the building, just in front of an untidy-looking picket fence that divided both the front yard from the back and her property from the next-door neigh-bors. A proper wooden fence sat at the rear of the yard. The whole area was obviously very close to the A41 because the constant rumble of traffic was very audible.

As the cab drove away, I walked up to the front door, rang the bell, and then stepped back to scan the upper window. A curtain twitched, and though I didn't see anything more than a brief flash of pale skin, it did tell me there was someone home. Whether it was Harper or not was another matter entirely, as I hadn't thought to ask Mathi to get a description as well.

No one bothered to answer the door, however, so I rang the bell again, then pressed my fingers against the thickly painted door and slipped inside the faint music of the old building.

There was indeed someone home.

Trouble was, at that very moment she was heading out the back door, running like hell for the back fence.

CHAPTER

EIGHT

I SWORE AND RACED AROUND THE SIDE OF THE BUILDING JUST AS A thin, gray-haired woman leapt for the back fence and flung one leg over the top of it. I caught the air and snapped it toward her, looping the leash around her waist, then yanking her back. She squawked and fell, landing heavily in a thick patch of lavender. It at least broke her fall. The air certainly didn't.

I extended the leash to both legs to prevent her climbing back up, and she instantly attacked it, using her own storm skills to try and dismantle it. Interestingly, despite the fact the wash of her energy across my leash suggested she was powerful enough in her own right, she had no luck. Her gaze jagged to me, and I felt her energy switch. I raised a hand in warning. "Don't. Anything you hit me with, I'll rebound double-strength."

I wasn't sure I had enough knowledge to actually follow through with the threat, but she wasn't to know that.

She scowled up at me, steely eyes flashing with anger. "You're a fucking storm witch? No one told me that."

"That seems to be a common theme when it comes to

felons hiring others to go up against me, though it generally refers to me being a pixie." I squatted in front of her but kept well out of fist reach. "Who told you about me?"

"I can't say."

"Why did they hire you, then?"

"I wasn't hired."

"Then why did you run when I turned up at the door?"

She sniffed, disbelieving. "I was told not to trust you."

I studied her for a second. "If you weren't hired, were you paid to provide information? The name of an ice witch, perhaps?"

"Can't say."

I sighed. "Look, we can do this the easy way or the hard. Your choice."

"No, it ain't, because another goddamn pixie beat you to it. I literally cannot give anyone *anything* in the way of information as to who I spoke to. Not you, not the IIT, not nobody."

Well, that was fucking inconvenient, especially when it was generally impossible for one pixie to undo the mental commands of another. I'd heard the pixie council *could*, if pushed, but they only ever did so under extenuating circumstances. Apparently, unpicking a truly in-depth enforcement risked destroying the mind. Which was why they used the red knife for deep control crimes; controlling other pixies was considered the second-worst crime you could commit—murder being the worst, naturally enough —especially when it involved family. Though I might hate it, I was well aware I was damn lucky to be serving out my sentence with the council.

When it came to controlling everyone else, however, it was basically anything goes, unless, of course, you were foolish enough to magic someone famous. This woman wasn't famous, but if she'd been so broadly restricted I wasn't going to get past it.

I nevertheless reached out and touched the visible bit of leg between her jeans and her shoes. She swore and slapped at me. I flicked a sliver of air around her hands, trapping them, and told her to behave or I'd gag her. To be honest, I was surprised she hadn't started screaming the minute I'd pulled her from the fence, but maybe she didn't want to attract neighborly attention any more than I did.

I didn't have to deepen the touch to feel the caress of another in her mind, and the sheer breadth of it was astonishing. Someone had made very sure this woman really couldn't talk about a wide range of subjects.

I released her and sat back on my heels again. There had to be some way around the restrictions. There always was —Vincentia had certainly proven that. I just had to find the right question.

I pursed my lips for a second. "Did this other pixie contact you through the guild?"

"No. Privately."

"How, when all hiring is supposed to go through the guild to keep things upfront and avoid backlash?"

"It was a recommendation from a now retired client, and the guild turns a blind eye to private contracts all the time."

"What is the retired client's name?"

She hesitated. "Will she be in trouble?"

That she asked meant the restrictions hadn't covered the recommender. A careless but understandable mistake. "No. I just need to know the name of the person who magicked you."

"Then the recommender was Alys Tew."

Tews were the smallest of the pixie lines and had the

ability to communicate and control bees and insects. They often worked in conjunction with storm witches on farms, parks, and gardens. "She live in Deva?"

"No, Galway. She has a cottage in a little place called Menlo."

Tension slithered through me. Aside from the fact all roads seemed to be leading to Galway right now, Menlo just happened to be where my aunt had lived. Coincidence? Possibly. Possibly not. Just because my aunt was presumed dead didn't mean any relatives she had on her former husband's side of the family hadn't hired someone to enact a little revenge. Given how little contact I'd had with my aunt and her family over the years, it wasn't like I knew how close any of them were to Riayn or Vincentia.

"Address?" She gave it to me, and I quickly added it to my phone. "And the pixie who placed the controls on your mind—what coloring did she have?"

As I'd said to Mathi earlier, other pixie lines did have the skill, though it generally came via marriage with an Aodhán or Tàileach pixie, and often resulted in a diluted version of the skill running through the next few generations.

"Can't say because she was using a morphing charm. Saw it shimmering in and out of focus when she touched my neck."

Given Keeryn Gordon had been part of the trap waiting in that graveyard for me and Mathi, it was highly likely she'd been the supplier. If, that was, these events were all connected. Just because I suspected they were didn't mean I was right.

"Did this other pixie tell you to ring her when or if I appeared?"

"Can't answer that."

In other words, yes. I held out a hand. "Phone?"

"You've no right—"

I rolled my eyes but really couldn't be bothered arguing. Not when I had to ring the IIT anyway. "You're right. I don't. But I know someone who does."

While she frowned at me, I got out my phone and rang Sgott. He answered after a few seconds with a resigned, "And what is it this time?"

"Sorry, but I have a suspect related to the two ice attacks—"

"I didn't attack anyone with ice," she snapped. "That's not my talent."

I ignored her. "She ran the minute I appeared at her door, but she's been pixie-restricted so can't tell me anything. She does have the contact details of that pixie in her phone."

"It's likely to belong to a burner phone, but I'll send a team straight over to collect her. Address?"

I gave it to him, then asked, "How long can you legally hold her?"

"Hold me? What the fuck?"

"Seventy-two hours with permission from a court," he replied. "Up to fourteen days without permission if they're a terrorist suspect, and it can be argued these attacks fall into that category."

"I ain't no fucking terrorist!"

Maybe not, but she did have damn good hearing. "It might be an idea to contact the pixie council, then. They might be able to clear at least some of the restrictions so we can get some information out of her."

"You know, if you ever get tired of running the tavern, you'd make a damn fine consultant for the IIT."

I grinned. "Well, I did grow up with one of their best officers as my dad."

He made a gruff noise I couldn't quite make out but knew from past experience was an indication he was heavily controlling his emotions.

"Talk later," I said, and hung up.

"Now listen here," Harper growled, "you can't do this. I've done nothing wrong."

"You're right, I can't, but the IIT certainly can." I studied her for a second. "The recommendation you gave to the other pixie—was that woman from Deva?"

"No, Whitlow."

All paths were definitely leading back to Ireland right now. "Address?"

"Can't say."

I swore and scrubbed my hand across my face. "Is the ice witch registered with the guild?"

"No, she is not, so good luck locating her."

It was rather maliciously said. I shook my head and rose. "If you walk away from this episode without spending a good portion of your remaining life in jail, can I suggest you go through the guild from now on rather than taking personal commissions?"

In response, she muttered something decidedly unpleasant about my heritage, which only made me grin.

As the sound of sirens grew closer, I wound the wind up the rest of her torso, just to ensure she didn't attempt to crawl anywhere—not that she'd get very far if she did— then returned to the front of the building.

A black vehicle pulled up a few seconds later, and two women climbed out. I didn't know either of them. The taller of the two flashed her badge and then said, "Bethany Aodhán?"

I nodded. "My captive is around the back, currently leashed by air."

"You've leashed a storm witch, and she hasn't escaped yet?" the other woman said. "Interesting."

"My power is stronger than hers, fortunately." Even if my skill level probably wasn't.

I followed them down the lane and, once they'd cuffed the suspect, unleashed the wind.

As the taller of the women led her back to the car, the other said, "You done a search of her house?"

I raised an eyebrow. "I legally can't."

She smiled. "The boss said you sometimes ignore legalities."

"That could be true, but not in this particular case."

She laughed. "And when we leave?"

"I'm calling an Uber and heading over to the cemetery. I've a ghul I need to speak to. Oh, and tell Sgott that our ice witch apparently comes from Wicklow but isn't registered with the guild."

She nodded and climbed into the driver's side of the vehicle. As they took off, I rang an Uber, then walked down to the end of the small court to wait for it.

Night had fallen by the time I reached the cemetery. I once again followed the path around to the right until I was standing in the bowl-shaped seating area surrounded by the old oaks. For several minutes I simply stood there, my eyes closed and my mind deeply immersed in the incandescent pathways of power that flowed all around me; it was beautiful and powerful, and it went a long way to easing the background niggle of utter weariness.

Maybe I needed to come to this spot more often. While the tavern's song was familiar and comforting, this was probably the closest thing I would get to an ancient forest, even in a city as old as Deva.

"Do you come to revive your senses, or do you have another question for me?"

I opened my eyes. The ghul's filmy presence hovered near one of the seats to my left. "A bit of both, really. This place is truly magical."

"Why do you think I call it home? Aside from the practicalities it offers one such as I, that is."

Those practicalities being her dining habits. "Does that mean you're affected by the energy that wells here?"

"It does not revitalize me as it does you and your kind. But places of peace such as this are a draw to those sensitive to the energy here, whether they are aware of it or not, be they human, fae, or shifter. It provides a wide range of conversations and people to follow and has been an invaluable source of information over the years."

"I'm surprised more people haven't come here to tap that information."

Her scratchy laugh echoed across the silence, but this time, unlike last time, nothing stirred in the distant shadows. "Not even your mother did, though she knew of my existence."

"You knew Mom?"

"I followed her on a few occasions. She acknowledged my presence, which was gratifying, but she never asked any questions."

"And that offends you?"

"Perplexes. I am aware she used others."

Suggesting the ghuls, while they tended to be solitary beings, did have some means of communicating with each other when necessary. "Perhaps she believed you would have no knowledge of the information she was seeking."

"If one does not ask, one cannot be certain."

"Then I shall ensure to ask, even if I know you can't or won't answer."

Her amusement swam sharply around me. "And the question you are here to ask tonight falls into the latter?"

"Kinda." I hesitated. "The woman who came to see you last week, was she a pixie?"

"Yes."

"What kind?"

"Aodhán, like yourself."

Instinct stirred uneasily. "Can you describe her?"

"Aside from what I have already said, she had green eyes, but was older, taller, and less bosomy than you. Though she was wearing a hood, the few strands of hair that escaped were red, streaked with silver."

Which was a pretty damn close description of my aunt. But then, it was also a pretty damn close description of any older pixie from the Aodhán line. We might be one of the more human-looking pixies, but certain characteristics—like the red hair and frost-green eyes—did run through the lot of us.

Even so...

"You said she limped—do you think that was real?"

Once again the ghul's sharp amusement swam around me. "It was real. I followed her."

"How far did you follow?"

"She went into an inn opposite the old Roman gardens. I could not follow her in, of course, but I did not see her come out, though I remained near listening to the conversations of those within."

I knew the gardens and, as far as I was aware, there weren't that many inns or hotels in the area.

"Thank you." I paused. "Would you like payment for the information?"

"I appreciate the offer, but not this time. Perhaps when I have something related to the horn or those who wield it, I will."

I nodded, bid her good night, then left. As I walked back to the gates, I dragged out my phone and rang Mathi. Technically, I should have called Sgott, but he'd probably heard enough from me for one day. Besides, if it was my aunt—and seriously, I couldn't see how it could be given the only way she could have avoided the restrictions of the red knife was via death, and if she'd died, she simply *couldn't* be here—I wanted to be the one to confront her. She was family, even if she'd denounced any connection. I at least owed it to Mom's memory, if not my aunt, to give her time to explain what the hell was going on before I called Sgott and the pixie council on her.

I couldn't avoid doing the latter for very long. Dare not, in fact. I was in trouble enough with them; I didn't want to risk them extending my time working for the council.

"Hey, Mathi," I said, the moment he picked up. "Are you busy?"

"Your timing," he replied, "is as impeccable as ever."

His tone was dry but edged with frustration. I couldn't help but laugh. "Gods—don't tell me I've caught you mid-coitus again?"

"Thankfully, it's more the seduction phase this time."

"I take it she's not in close proximity?"

"No. You're now listed as 'The Council Project' and have your very own ringtone. I told her I had to take the call and moved into another room."

"I'm not sure I like being listed as a project."

"And yet, a project you are and will remain until I once

again get you into my bed. And yes, I am aware that will likely never happen. What is it you wish?"

"I thought I'd let you know I have several possible leads, but we can discuss them tomorrow. I take it everything is arranged?"

"Yes indeed, and I did send the details. One of these days, you will stop ignoring my messages."

"Force of habit, sorry. I'll let you get back to proceedings."

"Thank you." He paused. "You're not following a lead alone tonight, are you?"

"No, because right now, I'm leaving the cemetery, having just had a nice chat with the ghul."

"That doesn't answer my question."

"I'm just scouting, nothing more."

"I am not convinced. Give me a few minutes and I'll come—"

"If you come in a few minutes, your partner isn't going to be pleased," I cut in with another laugh. "I'm fine, Mathi, and I'm not stupid."

"No, but you can sometimes act rashly. You and Lugh are very much alike that way."

And so was Mom. He didn't say that, but he didn't really need to. "Stop talking to me and get back to your seduction. I'll ring before I do anything too rash."

"Promise?"

I sighed. "Yes."

"Good. I will see you in the morning."

He hung up, and I checked my messages. There was a text confirming he was picking me up at seven. I tucked my phone into my purse, then shoved my hands into my pockets and followed the lane to the nearest bridge crossing. There was a surprising number of people out and about considering the bite in the air, but maybe they were all enjoying the momentary break in the weather. And it was only momentary—the threat of more rain ran heavily through the gathering wind.

As I reached the other side of the river, an odd prickle ran across the back of my neck. I carefully glanced around but couldn't see anyone in the nearby area overtly watching me. Which didn't mean anything, given we were dealing with someone who had the use of a concealment charm of some kind. This area was fairly well lit, but there were still patches of darkness remaining in which someone could hide.

I walked under the old Roman gateway and headed toward Duke Street; the sensation of being watched faded but didn't entirely go away. I did my best to ignore it—it was either that, or investigate the area another day, and I was here now—so I followed Duke Street until I reached the old city walls dividing the street from the old Roman gardens. According to Google, there were a couple of hotels scattered over several nearby blocks, but the first one happened to be called The Old Roman Inn. It was described as a two-story, old-fashioned pub with a couple of B&B rooms upstairs, and both the name and the location were just too perfect not to check out first.

It turned out to be a Victorian rather than Roman building situated on the corner of two streets. Lights burned brightly from the three windows on each side of the ground floor, but there were no lights shining through the windows on the floor above. But they obviously had a good crowd in if the babble of conversation was anything to go by.

I opened the lovely old door and stepped inside. I might as well have stepped back in time. The walls were adorned with lots of World War One memorabilia and old tin adver-tising plaques, the wallpaper underneath old-fashioned and faded. Wainscoting covered the lower half of the walls, the dark wood matching the small but ornate bar. There was also a small fire, the large green tiles forming the surround holding images of white trees. Seating was a mix of old-fashioned booths and time-worn tables and chairs. I spotted a booth for two in the back corner and made my way through the tables and claimed it.

A middle-aged woman bustled over a few seconds later, her cheeks red and her smile warm. "You here for a meal or just a drink?"

"Both, I think."

"Excellent." She handed me a menu. "Special tonight is beef cottage pie with a cheese, potato, and leek topping, accompanied by steamed veg."

"That sounds perfect. I'll have a double whiskey, too."

"Any preference?"

"Glenfiddich?"

She nodded. "I'll be back with your drink in a few minutes. Dinner will take about twenty."

"That's fine."

She collected the menus and hurried away. I crossed my arms on the table and looked around the room, studying the customers and listening to the various snippets of conversation. Once my drink arrived, I picked it up with one hand and let my other drop under the table, running my fingers over the darkly stained wood. The building's inner song was strong and sweet, and I slipped into her network easily, following the weblike lines of energy up to the next floor. There were two ensuite bedrooms up there from the feel of things, the weight of furniture in each almost identical. There was a small additional bit of weight in the bedroom to the rear of the building, but it was too light to be human. A suitcase or bag of some sort, I suspected. Neither room was currently occupied, so I followed the network of energy around to the door frame of the room that contained the suitcase. A trick that I—and most other pixies with the ability to manipulate wood— often used to give forewarning of an intruder was to lightly weave the frame to the door. Even if said intruder was another pixie, there was usually some lingering evidence of their presence in the song of the wood. The door here remained unaltered. I continued on, following the glowing golden rivers to the outside of the building and the room's window frame. It also showed no sign of alteration.

Did that mean the ghul had been wrong and the pixie she'd followed wasn't staying here? Possibly, but I doubted it. That other pixie had snared the ghul's interest, and I rather suspected she'd kept watch on the *entire* premises for much longer than she'd made out. If that pixie had slipped out another entrance, the ghul would have noticed.

I pulled out of the network and sipped my drink, debating what I should do next. Questioning the owners about whoever was staying up there was out, if only because I didn't want them warning their guest someone was asking after them. And I couldn't use the pixie obedience magic on them because it would leave a tell for the other to sense. I checked the terrain images on Google Maps, which told me there was a sturdy metal staircase along the side of the building that led onto a small walkway and a gate. That was obviously what guests used to come and go when the pub was closed. There also appeared to be rear cameras, though whether they worked or not was another matter entirely. Still, I wasn't about to risk a little external breaking and entering until I knew for sure whether the room's occupant was my aunt. I certainly did *not* want to barge in on some innocent pixie.

A younger waitress arrived with my meal and cutlery. I thanked her and hungrily tucked in. It was the best damn pie I'd eaten in ages.

As I sat back with a satisfied smile, the older woman approached. "Can I get you something else, dear? A dessert, perhaps? I can recommend the apple pie and homemade ice cream."

I hesitated, and then nodded. To hell with the waistline. "And a pot of English Breakfast would be good, too. Tell me, have you rooms to rent here?"

"Aye, two, although one is booked for the next week. You looking for accommodation?"

I nodded. "We just need the one night, if that's possible."

"We can do that, no problems. We'll sort it out when you're paying up before you leave."

"Perfect. Thank you."

Once she left, I dragged out my phone and rang Eljin.

He answered immediately. "I hope this call means you've changed your mind about tonight?"

"Sadly, I'm flying out early tomorrow with Mathi—"

"Council business, I take it?" he cut in.

"We got a lead on the horn, and another on a woman who may know the name of the person behind this whole mess. They're in the same area, so we're combining searches."

"Then to what do I owe the honor of this call?"

"I was wondering if you might be available tomorrow evening?"

"Always, though I take it you have something more than a mere date planned?"

"I need company for a cover story."

He laughed. "More than happy to help out."

"Excellent. I'll send you the details when I book the room."

"Room? I like the sound of that."

"There's no guarantee of sex, I'm afraid. It's a watch-and-wait operation."

"Understood, but I will point out that sex isn't the be-all and end-all of a relationship."

"You would be the first man in history who thinks that."

"You obviously hang around the wrong sort of men."

Given my terrible luck with men, that was undoubtedly true. "I need to go. I'll talk to you tomorrow."

"I look forward to it."

He hung up, and I spent the next couple of hours having a few more drinks and enjoying the atmosphere while listening to the old building's song, waiting to see if the other pixie arrived upstairs. She didn't, so once it neared closing time, I paid the bill and arranged to stay tomorrow night, using Eljin's name. At least that way, if the innkeeper happened to mention the presence of another pixie to their other guest, they'd get his details, not mine.

The storm I'd sensed earlier had hit full force by the time I stepped outside. I tugged up my hood, shoved my hands in my pockets, and headed home. I'd never minded walking in the rain, and honestly, by the time an Uber arrived I could have been almost home anyway. Which didn't mean I wasn't soaked by the time I got there—I certainly was. I shucked off my coat, dripped upstairs and, once I'd cranked up the fire, quickly stripped off and jumped in the shower to warm up. But as I was tugging on my thickest, fluffiest dressing gown, my fingers brushed the

Eye, and it flared to life, spinning dark lightning through the firelit shadows.

There were visions to be had.

I sucked in a breath and released it slowly, and made myself a mug of tea first, using one with a lid to keep it hot while I used the Eye. Then, after grabbing a block of peanut caramel crisps to refuel after, I tucked my knives into the gown's other pocket and headed for the loft. Once comfortable on the sofa, I crossed the knives on my lap, placed one hand on them, and wrapped the other around the Eye. Maybe it was the growing connection between me and the triune, or maybe I was simply becoming accustomed to using my second sight, but my mind's eye was swept away so damn fast it was briefly disorientating.

The shadows faded enough to reveal stone steps leading down into a shadow-filled chamber that was surprisingly large, with a roof made of stone beams that fit tightly together. The entire thing was partially flooded and the air thick and damp. The vision moved toward the back of the chamber, where a step and an arch seemed to indicate a doorway. It highlighted a symbol carved into the center section—that of lightning—then swept on, through the stone, into a deeper darkness that went down, way down, into the ground and a smaller chamber. Under a single beam of improbable moonlight sat a horn whose metal rim was frosted and icy.

The vision shifted fractionally, revealing the horn had been neatly sliced in two lengthwise.

This was Borrhás's Horn. Or at least, one part of it.

Underneath it, carved into the stone and written in a language I didn't understand, were three long sentences.

Then that vision faded, and I was spun into another location entirely. One that provided no images, only sound.

Which meant I was about to "see" Carla and whoever her damn boss was.

I swore softly, but it wasn't like I could alter anything. Not until I found some way of getting past whatever shield they were using and forced these visions into sound *and* sight mode.

What news from the council? the man asked, his cold voice once again tinny-sounding. He was definitely using some sort of voice modulator along with the damn shield.

The Harpē remains low priority. Carla's voice was clipped and somewhat annoyed. *They have sent the pixie witch on a quest for the ice horn.*

Mathi remains her control?

Yes. You have not spoken to him?

I have no reason to, especially on a matter such as this. That is not our way.

A comment that very much suggested this man knew Mathi, if only peripherally. Interesting.

What of the potion Linette created? Did it have the desired effect?

Linette was a new name. Shame they didn't mention a surname, but Sgott had the group's secretary in custody, so a quick Q&A session might be in order.

It did not. It was far too strong and all-consuming.

Unease slithered through me. All-consuming was definitely what I'd felt with Eljin last night, but it *had* to be a coincidence. Didn't it? The museum had thoroughly vetted his past before he'd been offered the position there, so if there'd been any shady or unsavory connections, they would have been found. Besides, why would he have mentioned a past altercation with the Ninkilim if he was one of them? Even if it had been meant to make me less suspicious, it was too easily checked and ran the risk of raising suspicions if not true.

No, these two *had* to be talking about the council members. Carla definitely had her claws into at least a couple of them, and she'd likely be aware of the new testing measures implemented after it was discovered Gilda had been drugging Mathi. That they were now attempting to find another drug to use that would not be picked up in the screening was a totally logical step.

All-consuming is not a bad thing when the aim is to lower inherent barriers.

It is when control is lost by both parties. One cannot question if one cannot control one's own actions. I have asked for it to be watered down.

The man sniffed. It was an unimpressed sound. *The longer this all takes, the higher the probability of discovery. They are all too alert to our presence now.*

The old gods dare not move directly against us. Not yet.

No, but they are becoming more active. We need to find a reason to have the Harpē moved further up the council's list.

I am working on it.

Work harder.

Even I have a limit as to how many lovers I can take on without raising suspicions.

Given your history, I find that hard to believe.

That history has benefited yourself just as much as our master over the centuries. Her tone was amused rather than annoyed.

It was a rather illuminating comment, because if Carla *had* been active for centuries, she had to be something other than just a face shifter. Shifters did have a longer lifespan than humans, but the longest living shifter on record had been just under two hundred years old. From what these two were implying, Carla was far older than that.

Which suggested she was either part elf or part pixie. Knowing our luck, it would be the former rather than the latter, which would give her immunity from pixie truth magic.

And I would hope they will continue to be of benefit in centuries to come, the man replied coolly.

And is that why you have chosen this location? The amusement in her reply was stronger. *Because you wish to partake in an aforementioned benefit?*

I do find myself in need of your tender administrations.

She laughed, a surprisingly saucy sound, but thankfully, the vision faded on what was the beginnings of a sexual encounter.

I released the Eye and closed my eyes, breathing slow and deep to ease the erratic pounding of my pulse. I was beginning to suspect the cost of using the Eye was the one thing that would never change, no matter how proficient at using it I became.

After a few minutes, I grabbed the chocolate, opened it up, and broke off a couple of rows to munch on while I sipped my tea. I felt a little better once I'd finished both, but tiredness nevertheless hit. I really didn't feel like moving, so I simply stretched out on the old sofa, tugged a blanket over my body, and went to sleep to the sound of the old building's song and warm memories of Mom's presence.

Mathi's chauffeur picked me up at the appointed time and drove me over to the company's private airfield. A flight attendant in a dark green suit greeted me and ushered me into the cabin, seating me in a luxurious lounge seat before offering me a cup of tea. Mathi—who was seated opposite—was on the phone but gave me a nod and a quick, tense smile before getting back to his conversation. From what I could gather, the contract his company had missed out on might just be up for negotiations again.

Given what he'd said about his dislike of losing, I did not want to think about how *that* might have come about.

Once the plane had taken off, I was offered a delicious selection of pastries along with a selection of hot foods, all of which were sublime. The Dhār-Vals did not skimp when it came to providing the finest hospitality on their planes.

Mathi didn't eat and didn't end the call until the plane had landed at Shannon and was taxiing to its assigned position.

"Sorry about that," he said. "Got notification of a contract breach by an opposition company and had to jump on the opportunity while it existed."

So, *not* the contract they'd recently lost. "When did it all go down?"

"Got the call at one last night. Been dealing with it since." Something almost animalistic gleamed briefly in his eyes. Like most light elves, Mathi considered the hunt and securement of a deal one of the great pleasures in life.

"Meaning you haven't slept?"

"No, but that is of no matter. A good deal sealed is something I find very invigorating."

"Yeah, I know," I said, smiling in memory. "But you'll have to wait until we get back to Deva and your latest prospect before you unleash said vigor."

"Ah, you're a cruel woman, Bethany Aodhán."

"And you, dear Mathi, would take a mile if given an inch."

He laughed and, with a hand pressed lightly against my spine, guided me down the stairs and across to the waiting silver Mercedes.

Once we were underway, he said, "Any updates since I saw you last?"

I quickly told him about the pixie and what I'd seen in the vision. He frowned. "The 'that is not our way' comment suggests we are dealing with a highborn Ljósálfar elf, but there are very few I'm on good enough terms with to talk about the family's business, let alone council. I don't even talk to my father about the latter."

"Whoever this person is, they're a rat god acolyte, and surely that's a rarity amongst the Ljósálfar population, highborn or not."

"Yes, but how does one search for inclinations like that? Given how despised Ninkilim are, even today, it is unlikely they would be vocal about it."

"Could you talk to your father?"

"Possibly, but remember, it is extremely likely rat followers have infiltrated both the IIT and other government bodies. We'd run the risk of alerting them."

"Can your father keep the search off books?"

"Again, possibly." He paused. "We might have better luck searching for Carla Wilson, given the IIT has issued warrants for her arrest."

I raised my eyebrows. "They have? When?"

"She became a person of interest after the deaths of those men in custody. I should have no problems pulling up her records or doing a search through the archives."

"She has multiple identities though."

"Yes, but if she was a prostitute picked up by the IIT at some point and given the option of becoming an informant, there will be some record of her somewhere. All we have to do is find it."

"Worth a shot, I guess." After all, what was the worst that could happen? They already knew we were looking for Carla, and even if there *were* records to be found, it wasn't like they'd list all her other identities. Fingerprint and DNA records of her *original* identity might be a possibility, though, depending on whether such things were recorded back when she was initially arrested.

We continued on toward Gort, then cut across to Cloonteen and headed up a narrow bitumen road that went through several small but pretty villages until we reached our destination.

Mathi pulled over and parked next to an old iron farm gate. "The fort is on private land, but I've arranged for us to enter. There's a couple of flashlights in the back—can you grab them while I ring the owners to let them know we're here?"

I slung my purse over my shoulder, then climbed out and moved around to the back of the car to get the flashlights. The fort lay in the field directly ahead, and looked like little more than a sweeping, grass-covered mound dotted with lovely old trees. From what I'd read online, the walls that couldn't be seen from where I stood were two meters high in some parts but missing or collapsed in others.

Mathi climbed out of the car, then locked it. I handed him a flashlight, and we headed into the field, closing the gate behind us to ensure no stock could get out. The ground was wet and muddy underfoot, and the trees barren, their limbs reaching for skies that held little light thanks to the thick blanket of clouds. There was no rain in them, thank-

fully, but the day remained cold, and the wind held a definite bite.

As we made our way up the earthen rampart, the stone
wall appeared, though it remained well camouflaged by long
grasses and thick stands of youngish trees. We walked
around the top for a few seconds until we found a gap, then
half slid down the other side into the enclosure. Google had
said the area was about fifty meters in diameter, but it was so
badly overgrown it looked much smaller. Various remnants
of stone buildings poked through the long grass, and yet
more saplings filled the area, their joyous song bright in the
air. We found a faint path coming in from the right and
followed it left into a narrow alleyway. The souterrain
revealed itself slowly, the entrance support stones possessing
the same lean I'd seen in my vision and almost concealed by
the saplings growing in front of it. The roof slab—which had
to be at least a foot thick—was covered by vines that draped
over the entrance, and while it was little more than a bare
brown curtain now, that would change come spring.

I flicked on my flashlight, then bent and shone it into
the darkness. The light danced across the five moss-covered
steps and the dark still water shimmering beyond.

"Do we know how deep that is?" Mathi asked.

"Nope, but if you can get me one of those dead sticks off
to your right, I'll test it."

He did so. I carefully moved down the steps, keeping
one hand on a sturdier sapling just in case I slipped. Once
I'd brushed away the brown ivy curtain, I leaned forward
and pressed the stick into the water. It went down about a
foot before hitting something solid.

"Should have brought gumboots," Mathi commented.

"Yeah, sorry, should have mentioned that." I had seen

the water in the vision, after all. "I blame the early start and the lack of food until we got onto the plane."

"There was nothing or no one stopping you from getting up a little earlier—"

"Don't you dare swear at me, Mathi Dhār-Val."

He laughed, a warm sound that slid uneasily across the dark water. Trepidation stirred through me, though the knives remained silent and I had no sense of magic or spells within the chamber.

Which didn't mean we wouldn't trigger something once we stepped into it, of course.

Mathi joined me on the fifth step and skimmed his light across the chamber's width. "Google says this place stretches back seven meters, but I'm not seeing any end walls."

"They're there, if the vision is to be believed." I placed my free hand on the stone lintel to my left and carefully stepped down. Water seeped into my shoes and soaked my jeans, making them cling to my calves. It was also goddamn icy. I had woolen socks on, so my toes weren't in any immediate danger of frostbite, but it was still uncomfortable.

I used the stick to test the ground ahead before I stepped onto it, and we slowly made our way across the chamber. The ripples of our movement fanned out slowly, and an odd sense of... expectation?... began to stir in the deeper shadows.

My knives remained inert.

I flexed my free hand and resisted the urge to reach for one of the blades. I might feel better with the weight of it in my hand, but it wasn't as if I had to be holding them for them to work against anything that might be forming.

We waded on for what seemed like forever, but eventually, a damp stone wall thickly decorated with moss and lichen came into sight. I swept the light across its length, looking for the arch I'd seen in the vision, and spotted it slightly to the left of the wall's middle. There was no sign of the step, but given the water was deeper now than what I'd seen, perhaps it lay underneath. It wasn't until we got closer that I saw the carved symbol.

"That," Mathi said, as my light pinned it, "looks like a very crude drawing of a lightning bolt."

I nodded and carefully edged forward until I'd found the edge of the single step, then stepped up. A faint flicker of energy ran down the sheathed knives, something I felt rather than saw. There was magic here, but it wasn't threatening.

I scanned the arch for a second and then, not sure what else to do, pressed a hand over the worn image. For several seconds, nothing happened. Then the knives pulsed, and the carved image came to life. Light shot across the old stone, tiny bolts of bluish-white that fled to the very edges of the arch. With a groan not unlike that of an old man rising, the stone pushed back several inches, then slowly slid to one side.

"Loving those sound effects." Mathi shone his light on the newly revealed steps. Water from the cavern spilled over the sill, making the black stone shimmer wetly, and the air was icy cold and extremely foul. "But I'm not loving that scent."

"No." I drew a knife and warily stepped through the archway. Lightning briefly danced down the blade's fuller, but it was more in response to my touch than any threat coming from below.

The stone steps were narrow and a little crumbly, and the trickling water didn't make them any easier to traverse. I went down sideways, watching where I placed my feet, relying on the knives to warn me of any sort of magical danger, though the air's foulness and how damn difficult it made breathing without giving in to the urge to puke seemed to be the main threat right now.

Below us, just beyond the reach of our flashlights, a tiny beam of light appeared, hitting the plinth, the golden stand that had once cradled one half of a god's horn, and the body that lay in a crumpled heap at its base.

"Ah, fuck," I muttered. It was obviously a woman, but her position made it hard to discern anything else.

"A crude but apt statement in this sort of situation," Mathi commented.

I stopped on the last step and swung the light around. The chamber was small and round, and unlike the one above, absolutely dry. I swung the light up to the ceiling, looking for the source of the light beam, but it seemed to be emerging out of solid rock. Magic? Given this was a chamber that had once held a godly relic, that was more than a little likely.

I swept the light around one more time, but whatever protections had been here had obviously been dismantled when the horn had been stolen.

"Are we going closer, or are we just going to stand here?" Mathi asked, amusement evident.

"Personally, I'd be voting for the latter, given the stench, if not for the need to know who our dead person is."

And breathing through my mouth rather than my nose was *not* helping. This close to the body, the stench of putrefaction was so bad, it coated my throat and made my stomach churn all the more fiercely. The iciness in the cavern might have delayed the inevitable decay, but it hadn't stopped it.

In the flashlight's bright beam, the concave nature of the back of her head was very evident.

"Hit from behind," Mathi said.

"Yeah." I scanned the shrunken figure for a second, then got out my phone and handed it to Mathi. "Record the body position and me moving it. Sgott and whatever team he calls in from down this way will still be pissed at us, but at least we'll have a record of our interference for them."

He immediately recorded not only her position, but also added the immediate area and the plinth for good measure. When he was done, I tugged my sleeve over my hand, then bent, gripped her bony shoulder, and lightly pulled her onto her side.

Her face was skeletal, the skin little more than white parchment stretched over bones, which somehow made the rose tattoo running down the left side of her face stand out even more starkly.

Shock ran through me, and I couldn't help the gasp that escaped.

"What?" Mathi immediately said.

"I know her." My gaze rose to his. "It's Peregrine Stace—the woman who'd been staying with my aunt when we delivered the red knife."

CHAPTER
NINE

Mathi's eyebrows rose. "The woman spying on your aunt for the Looisearch?"

"Yes. The last I'd heard, she was still at my aunt's." Mainly because I'd used my magic on her and had then totally forgotten about her.

"She couldn't have been part of the red knife restrictions, though, because she's not a pixie."

"No, but I'd ordered her not to leave a defined area of my aunt's house. Given the IIT haven't contacted me to release her, she should still be there."

"Unless the IIT reached out to the pixie council to undo your orders."

I wrinkled my nose. "Possible, but I wouldn't think they'd consider Stace a big enough threat to risk the danger of undoing my control over her."

"Then how did she get here?"

"I have no fucking idea."

He stopped recording and handed the phone back to me. "If death can break the red knife restrictions, could it also break another pixie's orders?"

I shrugged and released her shoulder. Her body sluggishly resumed its original position, a stomach-churning sight that was oddly worse than the smell itself.

"Given she's here," he continued, "doesn't it all but confirm that your aunt found a way to escape the red knife restrictions?"

"Just because Stace escaped doesn't mean my aunt did."

"You no more believe that than I do."

"The only way to escape the red knife is death. If you're dead, you're dead; there's no cheating it, it's final." It was almost stubbornly said. Despite all the evidence to the contrary, despite my instincts agreeing with said evidence, there was a part deep within that really did *not* want to believe my aunt was behind the attacks. That she really *wasn't* on a quest for vengeance against all those who did Vincentia wrong.

"That would depend on the definition of final, would it not?" Mathi replied. "Perhaps once upon a time there was no cheating it, but these days, there are dozens of people who technically die on operating tables, at home, or in the middle of some sort of activity, and a good ninety percent of them are successfully revived. The success rate when elven healers are used is even higher."

"Yeah, but something like that would take a bit of organizing, and there just wasn't enough time between her being handed the red knife and her disappearance. Besides, she couldn't receive any visits without permission from the pixie council—with the exception of those supplying vital goods or services."

"Medical services would come under the latter, and if I remember correctly, they never did find her body, did they?"

"No, but there was evidence of a fight and plenty of blood."

"All of which can be staged easily enough—believe me on that." He crossed his arms and stared down at Stace. "Did they test the blood and any DNA found at the scene to see if it was hers?"

"I would presume so." I thrust a hand through my hair. "If my aunt is alive, then why hasn't she come after me? She blames me for Vincentia's death, even if she never came out and said it."

"Perhaps she saves the juiciest morsel for last."

I cast him an annoyed look. "I'm being serious."

"So am I. I would also remind you of the ghul's comment—revenge is a dish best served cold. I do not think it a coincidence she said that to both you and the other pixie."

"If that other pixie was my aunt, she's paid a heavy price for her escape from the red knife."

"Undoing powerful magic often does exact a high toll." He shone his light onto the plinth beyond Stace. The words etching the stone were clearer in person than they had been in the dream. "That looks like old Brythonic, or old Brittonic, as it's also often called."

"And that is?" I asked.

"It's commonly acknowledged as the oldest human language in Britain, and generally used by the Celtic people known as the Britons. Somewhere in the sixth century it split into what we now know as Welsh, Cumbric, Cornish, and Breton."

"Can you read it?"

He glanced at me, amusement evident. "I am not that old."

"Yet. And you didn't answer the question."

"I know enough Welsh and Gaelic to guess, but it'll be by no means perfect."

"We can take a photo and get perfect later."

He nodded and studied the inscription for several minutes. "Okay, the first line says something about *what was once... gifted... is now...*"

He stopped, frowning.

"Cursed?" I suggested.

"Possibly. There's a few letters I don't recognize." He frowned. "*Those who reunite and raise in... hatred... not love will end entombed.* The third line says something about joining the queen in endless sleep within the palace that never melts."

"Borrhás apparently gave the horn as a lover's gift to a queen who wanted to rain winter down on her enemies," I said. "When she won the battle, she forsook Borrhás, and he in turn locked her in an icy sleep from which she will not wake until the earth itself no longer exists."

"Which is why you never double-cross an old god. They get nasty."

I dragged out my phone and took several shots of the inscription and the empty cradle on top, then swung the light around to see if there was anything else here. In one corner, almost invisible against the shadows that hunkered there, was a somewhat grimy-looking brown backpack.

Mathi walked over, picked it up, then opened it. "Purse, phone, keys, that sort of stuff from the look of it." He paused and pulled out a small, almost empty vial of brown liquid. "There's also this. The label says it's Dearil."

I googled it. "Apparently, it's produced by distilling several psychoactive plants. When a minor amount is applied to the skin, it gives a long-term high without long-term effects. When injected, or large amounts are applied, it initially has a hallucinatory effect, but within twenty-four hours will shut down all bodily systems and kill."

"Perhaps that's how the two escaped," he said. "They arranged medical help to be on hand, took enough of this stuff to die and break the magic, and then left after staging a fight."

"If medical help was called in, there'd be some record of it."

He returned the vial and put the pack down. "Not if it was unregistered medical, brought in out-of-hours and out of the sight of whoever was keeping a watch on the place."

It made as much sense as anything else right now. "We should head back up top and ring Sgott. He can organize the local officers to come down and take over."

"And also warn them not to detain us. We still have to check out Menlo, remember, and get back in time for our evening activities."

"I daresay yours will be more pleasurable than mine, given mine is a stake-out."

"Pleasure can still be had in a working environment." He led the way back to the narrow stairs. "One just has to proceed a little more... cautiously."

"Speaking from experience, are we?"

"I never mix business and pleasure in my office."

"Which does not actually answer the question."

He laughed. "I will not deny there have been occasions where mutual desires both contractually and physically were combined to the benefit of all."

I rolled my eyes. "Only a light elf would describe hot monkey sex in such bland terms."

Once we were out of the souterrain, I rang Sgott while Mathi contacted the owners to warn them their property was about to be invaded by the IIT. It took the local division half an hour to reach us, and it was another hour by the time they took our statements and photographed our footwear to account for our prints in the cavern. They were pleased we'd at least had the foresight to record our interference with the body, even if we both got a lecture about doing so. Once we were finally allowed to leave, we walked back to the car and jumped in. As Mathi did a U-turn, I punched the address into the GPS.

We stopped in Gort to grab hot drinks and a couple of pastries—the latter for me, not Mathi, who turned his nose up at the look of them—then continued on, arriving in Menlo just over an hour later. It couldn't actually be described as a village, as it was little more than a collection of single-story, modern-looking bungalows with pretty gardens fronted by waist-height stone fences. The actual village—Menlough—lay a few klicks farther along the main road.

Alys Tew lived in the second on the left. Mathi stopped a few houses farther down. "How do you want to play this?"

"Harper said Alys had retired, so she's probably elderly. It's better if I talk to her alone."

He nodded and "I'll wait here, then, but leave your phone on and open so I can hear the conversation."

"An old woman is not going to overwhelm me."

"No, but she might well set a swarm of bees on you if you piss her off badly enough—and let's face it, you do have a proclivity for doing that."

I laughed, grabbed my phone, and called his. Once he'd picked it up, I locked the screen on mine so I didn't accidentally hang up on him then tucked it into my pocket. Then I climbed out, walked back to Alys's, and followed the path through a row of neatly trimmed roses to a set of stairs and a glassed-in entrance. I rang the bell to the right of the door then stepped back, listening to the building's song. It was a newer house, so its music was greener than what I was used to back in Deva, but it nevertheless spoke of a building well cared for.

The inner door opened, revealing a small woman with golden skin, silver-shot green hair that was tucked into a neat bun on top of her head, and earth-brown eyes. She squinted up at me for several seconds, then said, in a somewhat frail voice that did not match the robustness of her body, "Do I know you?"

"No, ma'am. My name is Bethany Aodhán and—"

"You're Riayn's niece?"

I raised my eyebrows. "Yes, ma'am."

"Well, this is a surprise. She used to speak about you when she dropped in for a cup of tea."

"Not fondly, I would imagine."

Alys cackled. "Not always, I'll grant you that. Would you like to come in for a cuppa? I take it you're here to ask some questions?"

"Did Riayn warn you that I might be?"

"Not specifically." She pressed a button near the door, and the glass door in front of me swung open. "Come along then."

She turned and walked back inside without waiting for me, her movements sure and steady despite the quiver in her voice. I closed both doors behind me and followed her to the right, into the kitchen. She motioned me toward the table then grabbed the kettle and moved over to the sink to fill it. I tugged out the chair and sat down, feeling a little awkward because it, like the counters and stove, had been designed for someone her size not mine. Once she'd filled up the kettle and put it on, she pulled out a drawer to collect the teapot and a couple of cups and saucers.

"What is it you're wishing to know?" she asked when she finally turned to face me.

Movement caught my eye, and after a moment, I realized it was a bee. In her hair. Several of them, in fact. Mathi's comment was not far off the mark after all.

"When did you last see her?"

She pursed her lips. "It would depend on your definition of 'see,' wouldn't it?"

"As in come here, share tea, and have a good old chat."

"Ah, well, that would have been a good three or four months ago." She placed the tray on the table then pulled out her chair. "I did see her in the street a few weeks before the knife, though, and let me tell you, she was furious with you."

Given it would have been around the time Vincentia had made the unwise decision to work with the Looisearch and Rogan, that was no surprise. "Let me guess, she claimed I'd stolen Vincentia's heritage?"

She raised an eyebrow, briefly disturbing the bee crawling through her fringe. "And did you?"

I smiled. "Technically, no. I simply stole back what they took from my mother."

"Well, technicalities aside, I've never seen her so angry. You should watch your back, young woman, because that sort of anger can twist a mind."

That sort of anger *had* twisted a mind. "And the time she came here—was it simply a social visit?"

She wavered a hand. "Mix of business and pleasure."

"Can I ask what she wanted, then?"

She studied me for several long seconds, the bees in her hair buzzing around a little more energetically. "Why are you asking me all these things? Why not just ask your aunt? Surely the council will give her niece special dispensation."

"No, they won't, given Vincentia's attacks on me are part of the reason she was given the red knife." I motioned toward the teapot. "Shall I?"

When she nodded, I poured two cups, adding, "Besides that, there'd be no point, as she's not there. She's gone missing."

Alys frowned. "How? The only way to escape the knife is death."

"Yeah, I know. The IIT are looking into it." I slid her cup across and poured milk into mine. "I take it there's been no rumors floating about?"

"No, but then, it was pretty widely advertised that her place was off-limits except under certain circumstances." She took a sip of her tea, her expression thoughtful. "As to your question, she was looking for storm witch recommendations, and came here because she knew I'd worked with a number over the years."

"Did she say why?"

"Said they had a wealthy client who was looking for some sort of god's horn for his collection." She shrugged. "I told her no good would ever come from messing with godly artifacts, but I doubt she listened."

Meaning she *had* known about Borrhás's Horn, and well before the hoard, which it had supposedly been a part of, had gone missing. Then the old woman's choice of words hit. "*They* had a client?"

Her eyes gleamed. "You didn't think Vincentia was the only hunter in that little unit, did you?"

"Well, yes."

Alys cackled. "Your aunt saw, Vincentia hunted. They were a good team, from what Riayn said over the years."

Meaning it hadn't only been the codex that had aided Vincentia in her hunts, and I guess that made sense given the codex had never been blood-bonded to her.

I took a sip of tea. "I don't suppose Riayn mentioned the client's name?"

"No, but it could no doubt be found in that study of hers. She was meticulous when it came to her records."

"The IIT likely took her computer when they were investigating her disappearance."

"No doubt, but it won't do them any good, because she never listed their private commissions on the computer. Riayn always declared she never trusted the things, and did things the old-fashioned way, as the gods intended. Of course, it helped that they didn't have to pay tax on payments they didn't declare."

The latter certainly sounded like something my aunt would say, even if the former didn't. But then, it wasn't like I'd ever really known her all that well, and time did change people.

Time, bitterness, and greed.

"I might head over there and check it out, then." Whether I actually could get onto the property, let alone into the house, would very much depend on whether the red knife restrictions remained. But it would be one sure way to uncover whether she'd faked her own death—if actually dying and then being brought back to life could be called faking it—or not.

"So, tell me," Alys said, "do you still run that old tavern in Deva? Riayn was a little annoyed that your mother got the place in its entirety."

"Given Riayn got just about every other investment in Gran's will, I daresay that was her greed showing."

Alys cackled in agreement, and the conversation moved

on. I flicked off the phone about halfway through so as to not bore Mathi, and left an hour later with the promise to visit if I was ever up this way again.

"Well," Mathi said as I climbed into the passenger seat. "I have spent more boring hours in my lifetime, but not by much."

"Yeah, sorry about that."

"No, you absolutely are not."

I laughed. "Let's head over to Aunt Riayn's and see if we can get in."

"Wouldn't the IIT have a watch on the place?"

"From the little Sgott said, it was the local coppers who were tasked with keeping an eye on the place, and they were generally contacted before any approved visitation so they could be on hand to check IDs and ensure the person entering was who they're supposed to be."

"I thought the red knife's magic had entry restrictions built in?"

"It does, but no magic is one hundred percent insurmountable—and if my aunt really is alive, then that's certainly solid proof."

I guided him across to my aunt's, which was only a couple of minutes away. Mathi stopped the car yards short of the gate, and we both climbed out. I caught the wind and spun her off to the left and right, trying to get some sense of what might await within the property's boundaries, but she came back with little more than the happy song of the leaves she had danced across.

"The wind says we're alone out here," I said.

"Makes sense, given crime scenes are very rarely preserved more than a couple of days." He studied me for a second. "You okay?"

"For the moment, yes."

"I am unconvinced by that, but I shall pretend other-wise. Are we driving in or walking?"

"I think we need to first discover if we can actually enter."

"That's a given, isn't it? The IIT and crime scene bods got in here, remember?"

"They might well have been part of red knife inclusions—the IIT would no doubt have ensured they could inter-view her if the need arose in the future."

"Sgott is nothing if not thorough," he agreed, and motioned me to proceed.

I took a deep breath to calm the sudden rise of nerves and walked around the open car door toward the front gate. I paused just a fraction before stepping over its boundary and continuing on for several yards. There was no response. No thrust of magic forcing me back. No barrier slowing my feet and making it impossible to continue.

"Well, that's definitely confirmation the red knife has been voided," Mathi said. "To repeat, are we walking or driving in?"

I hesitated. "Let's drive, just in case we need to leave in a hurry."

He nodded, and we jumped back into the car and drove in. The driveway was long and narrow, winding its way through a forest of lovely old trees. They were a random mix of pine, rowan, and ash, and their chorus was so strong I could hear it over the engine.

Before too long, the house came into view. It was a long, stone-built gable-ended farmhouse centered in a small clearing, with chimneys either end, a whitewashed front, and a bold red door. There were two windows on either side of the door on the ground floor and five above. Wisteria covered the front of the building, and though it was bare now, it'd be postcard-perfect in spring.

My gaze went to the open-fronted shed sitting to the right of the house. There was no car sitting there now; had Stace taken it, my aunt, or someone else perhaps? Given the knife's restrictions no longer held, it was perfectly possible the car had been stolen and the house ransacked. It wouldn't be the first time we'd walked into that sort of mess.

Once Mathi had stopped the vehicle, I dug my knives out of my purse and strapped them on. The wind stirred forlornly around the building, and an odd sense of... not foulness, not darkness, but something in between filled the air. It might have been a result of the red knife, but something within doubted it. My gaze rose to the first floor; Stace's window was open several inches, the curtains fluttering through the gap almost happily, the material's ends wet and a little raggedy. That window had been open for quite a while, because those curtains had been pristine the last time I'd seen them.

I walked around the front of the car and up the steps to the front door. From within the building came the song of wood, but it was a forlorn, lonely note that held just a hint of darkness.

That darkness, I realized, came from the blood that still stained the kitchen floor.

The red knife remained where Lugh had rammed it, hilt deep in the doorstep.

I wasn't getting any hint of magic, not from the red knife and not from the building overall. I nevertheless drew one of my knives and pressed its tip against the door handle. No light flickered down the fuller. Nothing ill clung to the metal.

I sheathed the knife, then carefully turned the handle, pushing the door all the way open without entering.

The hallway beyond was spacious and airy, with stairs that led up to the next floor directly ahead, and doors to the left and the right. Wainscoting lined the walls and ran up the stairs, the wood painted but its song so strong and vibrant despite the wisps of dark loneliness that ran through it. I glanced to the left, where the coat hooks were. The two coats that had hung there the first time I'd come here remained, though they were lightly covered in dust, the same as everything else. At first glance, at least, it didn't appear as if anyone had been in here recently, let alone ransacked the place.

I glanced around to Mathi. "You check the living area to the left; I'll head into the kitchen."

Where she'd supposedly been murdered.

He nodded, and I moved forward cautiously. Other than the dark stains of blood and the fingerprint dust that just about covered every surface, little in the kitchen had changed. It was a typical farmhouse style and ran the full width of the building. An old green AGA on which there was a dark spray of what I suspected was blood sat in the brick fireplace directly opposite, and kitchen cabinets ran to the left and the right of this. More cabinets and an old butler sink lay to the left, against the rear wall. The long, well-used oak table sat in the middle of the room, surrounded by a cheerful variety of mismatched wooden chairs, three of them upturned, and one broken.

I carefully made my way around all the stains, then tugged my sleeve over my fingers and began opening the drawers. Alys might have said the details of the buyer would be in the study, but it always paid to be thorough.

Thorough in this case revealed absolutely nothing other than the usual shit that collected in kitchen drawers.

I returned to the hall and glanced in at Mathi. "Anything?"

He closed the bottom drawer of the exquisite Victorian cabinet he'd been inspecting. "Nothing more than old birthday and Christmas cards. Why do people collect that sort of stuff?"

"Sentimentality," I said dryly. "And that is definitely something you would know nothing about. Let's head upstairs."

I led the way, running my fingers along the wainscoting like I had previously, though this time I was using the network's song to settle my increasing nervousness rather than slipping into its golden stream to trap Stace in her room.

At the top of the stairs, I paused and motioned to the room on our right. "Why don't you start checking the study, while I head down to the B&B guest room and see if there's any clue as to when Stace got out."

He nodded, and once he'd moved past I walked down the far end of the hall. The room was surprisingly large, and unlike the kitchen, hadn't been dusted for fingerprints. Did that mean Stace had still been locked in here when Riayn had been attacked? Or had she gone by then?

Hell, it was even possible she'd been my aunt's attacker. Whether that attack had been staged or not was something we might never know.

The room itself held a queen bed, a dresser, and a table on which sat all necessary tea-making paraphernalia. To my left, between the door and the window, was a small, two-door wardrobe. A bright red suitcase sat against this end.

I walked over and checked the tag—it was Peregrine's —then lifted it up. It felt empty, but I nevertheless laid it down flat and opened it up. All that was inside was a luggage strap. I stood the case up again and tried the wardrobe next. A good assortment of sweaters and T-shirts sat neatly folded on the shelves, and several pairs of jeans and an assortment of shirts hung on the rail above.

If Stace had found a way to escape my restrictions, why would she leave her clothes here? I looked around, spotting other personal bits on the bedside table—medicine and a couple of charger cords—and several pairs of shoes under the nearest end of the bed.

Frowning, I walked over to the dresser and checked the drawers, finding knickers and bras, but little else, then moved over to check the drawers in the bedside tables. The bed had been neatly made, but I tugged off the pillows and pulled down the blankets. And about midway down the bed, I found an iPad. It was deader than a doornail, so I grabbed its charger and headed out to the study. Bookcases lined the wall behind the lovely old mahogany desk to the left, and four filing cabinets sat against the wall to the right of the door. The front wall had a large window that looked out into the yard and gave a good view of anyone entering, and on the wall directly opposite the door were multiple photos in mismatched frames. Most of them featured Vincentia and the son my aunt had lost, but there were a number of Mom and Riayn together in happier times, as well as a few with them and Gran, and even a couple of me and Lugh.

"Anything?" Mathi asked without looking up.

I jumped a little and dragged my attention back to the task at hand. "An iPad that might just provide a clue or two once we charge the thing and look at her messages."

"It's probably locked."

"When has a lock ever stopped you?"

He laughed. "The lock on this top drawer has, but only because it's been pixie molded to the frame and you wouldn't approve of me simply ripping the thing open."

"Indeed, I would not."

I walked around and pressed my fingers against the wood. The desk's song was faint, but nevertheless told me where its wood fibers had been twined into the drawer's. I carefully unthreaded them, then tugged the drawer open.

It was empty.

"Well, that's damnably disappointing," I said. "Why would she lock a drawer with nothing in it?"

"The devious part of my soul believes all is not as it seems." He lightly tapped the drawer's base, then shifted and compared the inside depth to the outside. "The base is false."

"Really?"

He nodded. "An old but good trick, especially in the age of everything electronic." He reached in, felt around, then made a small sound of satisfaction. There was a soft click, and a heartbeat later, he was sliding the base free.

Underneath it were a number of leatherbound accounting books, one that said Contacts, and another that said Record of Contracts.

"Jackpot," I said.

"Presuming they do hold what we are actually seeking." He handed me the Record of Contracts. "You search that; I'll go through the account records."

I moved around to the front of the desk and sat down on the chair there, placing the iPad on the desk before opening the book. The book had been divided into months and didn't appear to hold any actual contracts;

instead, a name and three numbers. Presuming my aunt filed things in a similar manner to my mom, one was the year, and the second a month, and the last was a date. I quickly shuffled through the pages until I hit May last year. Alys might have said the commission had come in only three or four months ago, but it was doubtful that was when the initial approach had been made. There would have been at least a few weeks—if not months—of research beforehand to ensure it was both viable and profitable.

"According to these accounts," Mathi commented, "they were making good money relic hunting—though the most profitable part of their business appears to have been selling off found relics to the highest bidder."

"Yeah, it was something that pissed Lugh off no end, especially when Vincentia beat him to one."

Mathi looked up. "Did that happen often? Surely not."

I smiled. "Only a couple of times, but once would have been more than enough for Lugh."

There was nothing that mentioned the horn in either May or June, though they did get a couple of good commissions for nongodly artifacts.

"There's a record here for a partial deposit on service to be rendered," Mathi said. "July eighth, which, if we're presuming she went to Alys *after* she'd found the horn, fits in with the timeframe."

I flipped through the book and found it. Like the other records, there was no name listed, just the numbers and an addendum that said, "private collection."

I rose, walked over to the filing cabinets, and scanned the drawers until I found the right one. Unsurprisingly, it was locked. "Mathi, I don't suppose you have your lock-picking thingies on you, do you?"

"I never leave home without them." He rose and moved around the desk.

I stepped back, watching as he removed a small leather pouch from his wallet and then removed a thin metal pick. After a few minutes of intense concentration, there was a click and the cabinet drawer opened.

"What are we looking for?"

"Record number 8-3-C."

He flicked through the files, found the folder, then placed it on top of the cabinet and opened it. "Okay, according to this, they were commissioned to find the two parts of Borrhás's Horn by one Reginald Cowley, a collector of Viking artifacts. Lives in Alderley Edge."

Which just happened to be one of the most affluent and expensive areas in Cheshire. I pointed at the bottom line. "Says here they found one half of it five weeks later and the full commission was paid." Which, when it came to missing artifacts, was a pretty damn quick turnaround. "Wonder why he paid in full if he didn't get both halves?"

"Maybe they all believed half of the horn was all that remained."

Hardly, given my aunt obviously had both. "You know, if we ever do retrieve the whole hoard, it might pay for the council to keep a closer eye on things. Or, at the very least, order the Ljósálfar to do more regular audits."

"The council hasn't that power, and the Ljósálfar are unlikely to agree."

"Why not—they are the keepers after all, and surely it is part of the job to do that sort of thing."

"Audits *are* done, but you have to remember, we have a rep for somewhat shady business dealings and the love of a good profit. And, as has been proven by the hoard's theft, not even the bibliothecary, who are possibly the most dedicated law-abiding members of the Ljósálfar society, are immune to a worthwhile bribe."

"But what of Liadon? She is the keeper of all records, so surely she'd be aware of unaccounted differences between one audit and another."

"That's presuming the bibliothecary actually made a note of the missing items. If they are being paid by outside sources to steal smaller relics—and I would guess that is what happened to the horn, and even that singing bowl that mysteriously appeared at the museum—then they are unlikely to implicate themselves by noting their absence during an audit."

"Did they ever interview the other bibliothecaries about the theft and the missing man?"

"I would presume so, as the council did request it."

"And did the council ever get an answer?"

"Said bibliothecaries were all memory 'adjusted' and had no recollection of events leading up to the theft or indeed their dead counterpart."

"Convenient."

"But a sensible course of action if you wish to avoid blame."

My eyebrows rose. "You think they intentionally had their memories erased?"

"I think there's no one—beyond our small circle, that is —above suspicion when it comes to the hoard."

I wrinkled my nose. There was a part of me tempted to say, "There were plenty of people we could trust," but it was becoming ever clearer that Fate had woven threads of deceit and deception through the fabric surrounding us. I also suspected the whole trust issue would become even murkier in the future.

"That doesn't explain why, if Vincentia and Riayn found

half of the horn for their client months ago, Stace's body was in that souterrain. She didn't appear on the scene until much later."

"You're presuming the half they found *was* in the souterrain. It could well have been the missing half."

"True." I got out my phone and took a pic of the page. "I guess the easiest way to clear the timeline up is to get back home then head out to Alderley Edge and speak to the man."

Mathi glanced at his watch. "It's an hour's drive from the airport—we might be cutting it fine for our hot dates."

"I'm sure Eljin will happily sit in the pub if I'm back late, but if your date is the impatient type, I'm happy to head out alone."

"Oh, and wouldn't Sgott be pleased about me abandoning you like that."

"How would he even know?"

"He would, trust me, but it is irrelevant because we are a team and one does not abandon a teammate mid-quest, even if the prospect of hot sex looms on the horizon."

"Then we had best get going." I paused. "Should we keep the accounts and contracts books with us, do you think?"

He nodded and tucked the file back into place. "It might also be worth asking Sgott to authorize the removal of these records to the council's premises. It's possible your aunt and Vincentia found other minor hoard artifacts that could be of use to the council's quest to curb the black-market trade in relics."

"A trade the Myrkálfar and no doubt many others on that council profit from."

My tone was dry, and he smiled. "The sensible do not

trade in godly relics, and even the Myrkálfar tread warily around them."

"I think that's the nicest thing I've ever heard you say about them."

He rolled his eyes. "Get moving, woman, or we will never get home in a timely matter."

I laughed, picked up the iPad, and got moving.

Reginald's address led us to the outskirts of Alderley Edge, though it remained within walking distance of the village. It was a huge, white-rendered, double-fronted modern-looking building with lovely arched windows and slate roofing. Positioned to one side of the house was a large, open-fronted garage housing two Ferraris and three Porsches.

Mathi pulled to a halt in front of the arched entranceway and undid his seat belt. "The antique collecting business obviously does well."

"If you can afford to park your expensive cars in sheds that have no doors, then you can afford a hobby as expensive as collecting godly relics."

I shoved my knives into my purse, then climbed out and glanced up at the sky. While the flight back from Ireland had been without problems, we'd hit peak-hour traffic on the way here and, as a consequence, it was now close to five and dusk was staining the clouds a pretty shade of pastel pink.

"I'm betting that shed," Mathi said, studying the house rather than the shed, "houses all sorts of security measures that make doors surplus to requirements. There's certainly a good range of measures on the house."

"Not unexpected if he's a collector."

I walked around the front of the car and up the marble steps. Cameras tracked our movements, and the large intercom to the right of the double oak door came to life.

"How may we help you?"

What I presumed was a small circular camera positioned at the top edge of the intercom had lit up, so whoever that voice belonged to was obviously viewing us.

"We're here to speak to Reginald Cowley on a matter of some urgency."

"Do you have an appointment?"

"No, but as I said, the matter is urgent."

"Then I'm afraid it is not poss—"

"It's about Borrhás's Horn," I cut in, "an item he commissioned Riayn and Vincentia—"

I didn't get a chance to finish. The oak doors crashed open, revealing not only a man-mountain, but the biggest fucking shotgun I'd ever seen in my life.

And it was aimed straight at my face.

CHAPTER

TEN

"I SUGGEST YOU DO NOT GIVE IN TO THE TEMPTATION TO PULL THAT trigger," Mathi said in a calm, somewhat dry tone, even as he edged slightly in front of me. "Because this woman is Sgott Bruhn's adopted daughter, and I am the only son of Ruadhán Dhār-Val, and both those men could bring a whole world of IIT hurt down on you, your family, and whatever businesses you run if you decide to kill us."

The big man studied us for several extremely long seconds, then took his finger off the trigger. He didn't immediately lower the gun, however. "Prove it."

I could almost hear Mathi's eyes rolling. I dug my purse out of my handbag and showed the big man my driver's license. Once Mathi had shown his, our stranger broke the gun open to make it safe, and took out the shotgun cartridges for good measure.

I didn't relax. The anger remained in him, and while the gun was no longer loaded, it would still make a damn fine club.

"I'm Reginald Cowley. Why are you here?" His voice

219

vibrated with anger and seemed to come from the depths of his boots. "What do you want?"

"What I'd like is an explanation as to why we were greeted with a shotgun," Mathi said before I could say anything. "What we are actually here for are the details of your transaction with Riayn, and to ask whether you still have the horn in your possession."

"That is a private contract between me and her. You have no right, and no authority—"

"You're right," I cut in curtly. I was getting rather sick of people telling me that. "We don't, even if we're working with the IIT on a case involving the horn right now. So why don't I just call Sgott Bruhn, and he can send a team out to do a thorough and complete search of your house, business, and acquisition records."

Alarm flicked through his expression. Obviously, not all of his collection was legal. "Now, now, let's not be hasty—"

"Then start fucking cooperating, because people are dead and the horn is the reason."

"You can't think that I—"

"Given you greeted us at the door with a loaded shot-gun," Mathi said in that same dry tone, "I certainly think we can."

Reginald's face lost more of its ruddiness. He muttered something under his breath, then stood to one side and motioned us in. "Second door on the left."

I warily stepped past him, my gaze sweeping the hall-way's opulence, looking for anything in the way of magic and possible problems. There was no sign of magic, but there were a couple of security cams situated in strategic spots. He also wasn't alone here, as there were several voices coming from the rear part of the house—a woman and a couple of kids, from the sound of it. Which, more than anything, had the tension within relaxing a little. Reginald might have a temper, but now that it had cooled, I doubted he'd cold-bloodedly murder us. Not with his family within earshot.

The second door on the left led into a study. There was a teak desk the size of a boat in the middle of the room, behind which were a plush leather chair and several glass-fronted antique bookcases that held a variety of leather-bound books, various old mugs, and other antique what-nots. There were no Viking items that I could see, and certainly nothing resembling a drinking horn.

Reginald locked the gun in a cabinet, then motioned us to sit in the chairs fronting the desk. I did. Mathi remained standing behind me.

Reginald steepled his fingers on the desk and said, "I apologize for greeting you in the manner I did, but I'm afraid when I saw your face in the camera, young woman, I saw red."

"Why? I look nothing like Riayn or Vincentia."

"After a more thorough look, I agree, but at first glance, through a tiny screen, there's definitely a resemblance. Are you related?"

"Riayn is my aunt."

"Then why are you here asking about the horn?"

"Because her records show you commissioned her some nine months ago to find it for your collection, and that the transaction was completed five weeks later, after she handed over one half of the horn."

"All of which is true. I also commissioned her to continue searching for the remaining piece."

"Then you still have your half of the horn?"

"I do not."

"What happened to it?" I asked.

"What do you think happened? The bitch came here under false pretenses and stole it back."

"Under what pretense?"

"She said she'd found the horn's remaining piece, but needed mine to enter the underground chamber in which it was held. When I didn't believe her and refused to hand it over, she pixied me."

Is that why Stace had been in that chamber? Had she gone in with my aunt to dismantle the magic within the chamber so that Riayn could retrieve the other bit of horn? If she *had*, then why had my aunt killed her?

Even more interesting was the fact that, while she'd forced him to hand over the horn, she hadn't taken that extra step and forbidden him to speak about either it or her. Did that mean she simply didn't care anymore? Or was it more the knowledge she likely wasn't going to get out of this mess alive, so it didn't really matter?

"Do you know where she found your section of the horn?"

He shrugged. "Some private collection."

"And she stole it from said collection?"

A smile briefly touched his lips. "I commission. I do not question methods. Why?"

I took out my phone, brought up the pic I'd taken of the plinth, and showed it to him. "It means she wasn't actually lying about the other half of the horn, even if she used it as a ruse to get your half back."

He sucked in a breath, staring at the image on the phone with more than a hint of avarice. "May I?"

I handed over the phone, and he spent several minutes examining the photo. "Solid gold, by the look of it. The plinth is also an unusual-looking stone, and the inscription not a language I'm familiar with."

"It's old Brythonic," Mathi commented.

"Ah, that explains it." He handed the phone back. "I take it the plinth remains where you found it?"

I raised an eyebrow. "If you're thinking to acquire, I would not. Borrhás remains active in this world, and he would not be pleased with the desecration of his relic's tomb."

He stared at me for a second. "You're serious."

"I am. And the last person who abused Borrhás's trust ended up entombed in ice."

"But that's just a legend—"

"No," I cut in. "It is not. When was my aunt here?"

He went back to scowling. "A good three weeks ago now."

"And you did not think to report her theft?"

"I can hardly report the theft of what the police would consider stolen goods. Besides, for all intents and purposes, I gave the thing to her—and she has a recording to prove it."

"I'm surprised you haven't got this place lined with a multitude of charms and magic preventing such a thing from happening," Mathi said.

"I have, but the woman who accompanied her obviously disarmed them."

Was that woman Stace? Or someone else? Someone like Keeryn Gordan perhaps. "Did you get the other woman's name?"

"No."

"What about the house's security system? Did it record the two of them approaching the house, or were you ordered to erase it?"

"The latter." He smiled. "But there is a smaller, unconnected system within the vault. I was not ordered to delete that."

"Do you still have the files? Are you able to bring up their images?"

"Indeed, I have them right here on the computer."

"How convenient," Mathi said, in a dry sort of tone. "I take it you've been canvassing revenge possibilities?"

"I merely wish a return of what I paid for."

I daresay the collector Riayn had stolen it from was saying the exact same thing.

He turned the laptop around. The first image was definitely my aunt, but she looked older, more time-worn and ragged than when I'd last seen her. The woman standing to one side of her was the spitting image of Maran Gordan.

"Well, well," Mathi said. "At least we now have confirmation that Keeryn is working with your aunt."

"But not who the damn ice witch is."

"Does that mean the ice events in Deva are related to the horn?" Reginald asked. "It does actually work?"

My gaze returned to his. "Yes, it does."

"And it is for that reason you are unlikely to ever get it back," Mathi said. "I would advise you to put in a compensation claim with the fae council."

His demeanor instantly brightened. "Is that possible?"

"Presuming you have a full record of the transaction with Riayn, and the record of them forcing you to enter the vault and hand over the horn, it should provide plenty of justification for compensation. It would not be the first time the council has paid out to secure a dangerous relic from a so-called 'legitimate' owner."

I motioned to the image on the screen. "Are you able to send that photo to my phone?"

When he nodded, I gave the number and, a few seconds later, my phone pinged several times.

"I included the shots of their number plate I got from the gate cam. That system is also separate."

"Canny," Mathi murmured.

"Careful," Reginald replied. "Who do I have to contact regarding the compensation claim?"

Mathi gave him the details, then added, "Is there anything else you can tell us about the two women?"

"Riayn had acquired a limp, but other than that, no."

Which confirmed my guess that the woman who'd spoken to our ghul the week before me was indeed my aunt. I rose from the chair. "If you do think of anything else, you have my number."

He nodded. "Sorry about the gun. No hard feelings, I hope?"

Which was code for "please don't report the incident to your adopted father," I suspected. I smiled, said goodbye, and headed out.

Once we were back in the car and heading toward Deva, I sent a text to Eljin to let him know how far out we were, then another to Sgott detailing everything Reginald had said and adding the images. He replied, *Seriously, you need to become a consultant once your relic hunting days are over*, to which I responded, *No thanks, I plan to settle down, run the tavern, and produce babies.*

The latter of course being a long-term goal given, aside from the fact there wasn't a man in my life I wanted to have babies with, I was barely even on the cusp of fertility. Both pixies and elves aged fairly normally until we hit our twenties, which was when the whole process came to a screaming halt—something scientists had spent forever trying to understand with no success. Pixies didn't actually get periods or become fertile until we were at least one hundred, and for elves, with even their longer lifespans, it was a couple of hundred years later. We were, of course, as physically capable of having sex at the same age as any human—and thank fuck for that. Having to wait one hundred years before I could legally indulge would have killed me.

Darkness had set in by the time we arrived back at Deva. Mathi dropped me at the top of the lane with the promise to contact me tomorrow, then sped off. I jogged down to the back door, then quickly made my way upstairs, grabbing a shower, then stuffing a change of clothes and some toiletries into a small wheely suitcase to match the cover story we'd given. I also grabbed a couple of silicone gloves out of the kitchen to use if we happened to do a little breaking and entering.

It still wasn't raining, despite the scent in the air, so I walked down to the small inn. Once again, it was packed. I scanned the crowd and found Eljin in a booth not far from where I'd sat last night.

"Hey," I said, dropping a kiss on his cheek before sliding onto the bench seat opposite, "How was your day?"

"Slow and boring."

"Slow and boring is a big part of an antiquarian's job, is it not?" I picked up the menu and scanned it. It hadn't changed in the twenty-four hours between visits, and I rather suspected that if I came back here in a year or so, they'd have the same items listed.

"Apparently, but that doesn't mean I have to like it." He raised a hand, motioning for the waitress moving through the room. "How did your day go?"

"Found another dead body."

He blinked. "Should I be worried about your propensity to find such things?"

I grinned. "Only if you turn out to be a bad guy."

He laughed but didn't reply as the waitress stopped and said, "Ready to order?"

I nodded and asked for the pork sausages, which came with applesauce, creamed potatoes, and steamed veg, while Eljin went for cottage pie.

"And drinks?" she added.

I hesitated, then ordered a large pot of tea. I would have liked a double whisky, but I was tired enough as it was. Alcohol was likely to send me over the edge.

As the waitress bustled away, Eljin leaned forward and caught my hands in his. "You look beat."

I shrugged. "It was an early start and a long, somewhat unsuccessful day, and I really don't want to go into all that right now."

He smiled, though there was a flick of something—concern?—briefly in his eyes. "I managed to grab a look at the register when I was checking in."

"And?"

"The woman in the next room is a Mrs. Rhonny Brown."

I frowned. "Could be a false ID. It wasn't like the owner asked me for ID when I booked."

"No, and it's also possible Mrs. Brown paid by cash. They did ask if I was paying cash or card."

Surprise ran through me. "It's rare for places to take cash these days."

We did, but only because some of our elderly patrons still preferred hard currency over credit or debit cards.

"Depends, I guess," Eljin said. "For small places like this, the credit fees could be the difference between profit and not."

"Not when they have a pub attached that seems to attract a good nightly crowd. What are you working on at the moment?"

"Still cataloging Nialle's bits and pieces. The man really seemed to prefer chaos over order, at least at the museum."

I grinned. "Harder to steal what can't be found."

Our conversation moved on from there, and our meals eventually arrived. It was once again damn delicious, but the tiredness hit halfway through, and suddenly I couldn't stop yawning.

"Sorry," I said, covering my mouth for the umpteenth time.

"I think we need to get you upstairs and into bed."

"We have a job to do tonight, remember?"

"Yes, and you're not going to do anything in your current state. I'll keep watch while you sleep, and we can swap over around four."

Which would only give me five hours, given it was already close to eleven now, but it was hardly fair to let him do the entire shift when this was my idea in the first place.

"As long as you do wake me to take my turn."

"Scout's honor."

Amusement lurked around my lips. "Somehow, I'm not really envisaging you as a Boy Scout."

"In that, you're definitely right."

I signaled for the bill, and once paid, he picked up my suitcase and led me up the stairs to our room. It was low-key and quaint, with old-fashioned but pretty wallpaper, a comfortable-looking double bed, and a dressing table that also held coffee-and-tea-making facilities. The ensuite, while small, was perfectly formed and quite modern by comparison.

Eljin placed my bag on the floor next to his. "I actually

have a couple of tricks up my sleeve to make things a little easier tonight."

"Do tell."

"First off, we break and enter. As far as I can tell, she's not interwoven the building fibers to prevent entry, so we should be able to get in without her being any the wiser."

"Just as well I brought some silicone gloves, then. I gather you've also checked for any security measures the building owners might have in place?"

"Indeed. And before you ask, yes, I'm quite capable of getting into that room without a key. We relic hunters have by necessity a wide range of skills."

I smiled. Lugh had often spoken of said "wide range" of skills coming in handy on multiple occasions. "What if she's got magical measures in place?"

"Your knives should give us warning of that, shouldn't they?" When I nodded, he added, "If there *are* such measures, we still have option two in play."

"Which is?"

"Good old-fashioned motion sensors. We lay one at the external exit and another at the top of the stairs, with the signals sent to my phone."

"Won't she see—or at the very least, feel—the weight of them through the wood song?"

"Not these ones. They're miniaturized and have the weight and look of a freckle. They won't affect the song."

Meaning they likely used the same sort of technology as the bio trackers I'd run afoul of a couple of times, though bio trackers used the body's natural electromagnetic field to fuel a constant, low-level signal that allowed tracking. It was doubtful a sensor could plug in to the wood song. "Will they last the entire night?"

"Guaranteed six hours before needing recharging."

And using them would also give us backup if either of us fell asleep during our shift. "Let's get this done, then, while there's still people downstairs to cover any noise we might make."

He pulled what looked like an Apple AirPods case—only slightly smaller—from his bag, then headed out, leaving our door open as he moved to the old staircase. After opening the little pod, he carefully picked up what did indeed look to be a largish freckle and placed it at hip height on a spindle a third of the way down from the top of the stairs.

"Okay, let's test this thing." He dug out his phone. "Head past the freckle, then come back up when I give the word."

I did so and, when he nodded, clattered back up. As I passed the freckle, his phone rang softly.

"Perfect," he said. "Let's hit the rear door."

He headed there while I went back into our room to retrieve a knife and the gloves. Once the second sensor had been placed and checked, I pressed the knife against the other room's door. There wasn't even the slightest flicker of light down the fuller.

I handed him a pair of gloves, then stepped back and motioned him to do his thing. He donned the gloves then pulled a lockpick out of his wallet—seriously, did all men carry one, just in case it was needed? Or was it just the men I knew?—and got to work on the door. He was a little slower than Mathi, but still pretty proficient.

After he tucked the pick back into his wallet, he dropped a kiss on my cheek and said, "I'll keep an eye on the stairs while you check the room."

As he walked back, I pulled a glove over my free hand and pressed the door open with my fingertips, watching the knife to ensure there was no magical reaction, then scanned the room to see if physical security measures had been installed. Again, there was nothing obvious. I tucked my knife into the back of my belt, took a picture of the room to ensure I left it as I found it, then moved in, putting on the other glove as I did.

There wasn't much here—a smallish suitcase, a smattering of cords, an iPad on the bedside table, and a used coffee cup with a lip imprint sitting next to the kettle on the dresser. I walked over and bent fractionally to study it. Maybe it was my imagination, but it looked to be the same shade of red that both my mom and my aunt wore... along with thousands, if not millions, of others.

I carefully opened the dresser's two drawers, but they were empty, as was the one underneath the bedside table. I walked over to the suitcase sitting on the far side of the dresser. The damn thing was heavy—unsurprising if she hadn't unpacked—and hadn't been locked. I took a photo of the inside of the case to ensure I could place everything back in its original position, then rifled through the layers, finding one of those travel jewelry organizers between her jeans and sweaters, and right down at the bottom, a phone. Given few people these days went anywhere without their phone, I suspected this was either a burner or had a specific usage, such as a direct connection to one person—the ice witch, perhaps.

I picked it up, but just as I did, it rang, the abrupt noise making me jump and drop the thing. Caller ID briefly flashed up on the screen and I managed to grab a photo before it faded. I pressed the home button to see if I could get in and see if a message had been left, but the phone, unlike everything else, was locked. I tucked it back under the clothes, closed the case and put it back into position, then rose and headed into the bathroom. There was a toothbrush and toothpaste, but little else. She was obviously using the provided soap, shampoo, and conditioner.

I brought up the photo I'd taken before I'd entered to ensure everything looked the same, then headed out and locked the door.

Eljin pushed away from the wall he'd been leaning against and followed me into our room, closing and locking the door behind us. "Anything?"

"Found a phone at the bottom of her suitcase and took a pic of the caller ID when it rang, but other than that, nothing."

"You didn't recognize the phone number or the ID?"

"No, but I'll get Mathi to trace it tomorrow."

He frowned. "Why not ask Sgott tonight?"

"Because then I'll have to explain why I was breaking and entering, and I just haven't got the energy for that conversation right now."

"Then get yourself to bed and get some sleep."

Amusement tugged at my lips. "You don't want to join me? We do have the phone alarm, after all."

"Oh, I would love to join you, but if I did, sleeping would be the last thing on my mind.

"Maybe it's the last thing on my mind."

"She says through another large yawn."

His tone was dry, and I laughed, dropping a quick kiss on his lips before turning away.

"Oh, my dear girl, do not think you're going to escape *that* easily."

He wrapped a hand around the back of my neck, his fingers oh-so warm against my skin as he turned me around and pulled me into him. His lips claimed mine, the kiss fierce, demanding, and so very thorough.

Neither of us were breathing very steadily by the time he released me. "That probably wasn't wise, but I do not for an instant regret."

My gaze skimmed his length. "There are parts of your body disagreeing with that statement."

"Luckily, the bigger head remains in control over the little."

I laughed again and headed into the bathroom to use the facilities and do my teeth. I kicked off my boots, then stripped off to my knickers, tank top, and bra, and climbed into bed. I was asleep almost instantly.

To be woken by the soft ringing of a phone who knew how many hours later.

I jerked upright, my heart racing inside my chest and the knives and Eye ablaze. Eljin was sitting at the end of the bed, tugging on his boots.

"Did someone just walk through one of the sensors?" I whispered.

"Back door."

I threw off the comforter and shivered my way into my jeans and sweater. I left the boots where they were and followed him across to the room in my socks, grabbing my phone, the keycard, and a knife on the way through. Hopefully I wouldn't need the latter, but I still felt better with its weight in my hand.

Eljin gripped the handle but didn't immediately open the door; instead, he pressed his ear closer and listened for a few seconds.

Then he swore, flung it open, and raced out.

I was right behind him. The door into the other room was open, as was the exit door, the metal stairs vibrating softly as someone raced down them. Eljin flew out after her, vaulted over the railing, and dropped to the ground below. I swore, caught the wind funneling in from outside, and ran out after him, reaching the top metal landing just as he pinned the woman front first against the exit gate and growled, "Don't move."

She didn't, but magic rose in the air, sharp and dangerous. Dark purple light instantly boiled down the knife's fullers and spread out into the night, reaching with lightning speed toward the spell being cast, cindering it before it could fully form.

The woman swore and cast a look over her shoulder.

It wasn't some unknown woman called Rhonny Brown.

It was Keeryn Gordon herself.

And I couldn't help the faint sliver of relief that ran through me. I wasn't sure how I would have reacted had it actually been my aunt.

I walked down the rest of the stairs, doing my best to avoid the puddles. As I approached the two of them, her magic began to rise again.

I raised the knife and said conversationally, "I'm not sure what my aunt has told you about these things, but they are designed to protect me and kill magic. I've a theory that the latter also means it could kill the magic within a spellcaster if I stuck the knife into his or her flesh, and I really would love the opportunity to test that theory out."

The spell died. She obviously wasn't willing to give me that opportunity.

"I can't tell you anything," she growled.

"You don't have to. I know who you are, and I know you're working with my aunt. What I don't know is why."

"You killed my sister. Why would I not?"

"I didn't kill your sister, greed did. She tried to claim a relic she wasn't powerful enough to control, and it consumed her."

Which was the truth, even if, in the end, it was me who'd sliced her in two.

"You lie."

"No, but hey, you're free to believe whatever you want, even the lies spouted by my aunt, who never actually witnessed what went on with the Claws or her daughter's deep involvement with the people who eventually murdered her." I drove the knife into the wooden door leading out into the street—silently but profusely apologizing to the fibers as I did so—then rang Sgott.

"I've just caught Keeryn Gordon," I said the minute he picked up. "You want to come and collect her?"

He snorted softly. "Seriously, are you after my job or something? Where are you?"

I smiled and gave him the address. "We actually owe the ghul for this one—she gave the heads-up. In truth, I had thought it was Riayn staying here, not Keeryn."

"Which is why you didn't give *me* the heads-up," he said, in a tone that was a mix of annoyance and resignation.

"I wasn't on watch alone—I'm not that silly."

"I guess I should be thankful for small mercies, then. We'll be there in ten."

He hung up and I tucked my phone back into my jean's pocket. Eljin glanced from me to Keeryn and back again, then raised his eyebrows in silent question. When I nodded, he released her and stepped back. Keeryn rotated her shoulders, took a quick glance toward the still-glimmering knife, and obviously decided not to do anything untoward.

"Why did you run?" I asked. "You barely even walked into that room."

"I knew someone had been in searching the room."

"How? There were no active warding spells, and I certainly didn't see any motion cameras."

If there *had* been the latter, why would she even have bothered to come back here?

"I used an old but simple trick—cotton thread lightly attached to a couple of drawers and along the base of the bathroom door."

"I'll definitely look out for that one next time I break and enter. Thanks."

She didn't look amused. "I'm not sure what you think you're achieving by handing me over to the IIT. They've no proof I have, in any way, been involved in recent events—"

"Actually, they do." I gave her a not-so-sweet smile. "Remember that attack at the cemetery, the one where you and your team tried to kill Mathi and me, and you then killed said team?"

"*I* did not. You can't pin that on me."

"Well, technically no, because we're aware they were pixied into shooting themselves and that's not a skill you possess. Thing is, we found several strands of hair hanging from a tree branch, and I'd bet a million that the DNA will be a match for yours. That puts you at the scene of the crime and, at the very least, makes you an accessory."

She scowled at me but made no comment. Sirens swept down the street toward us, then cut out abruptly. I pulled my knife from the door, quickly brushed my fingers across the wood to heal the wound so the song could continue on unhindered, then swiped my keycard across the reader and opened the gate.

Sgott and Frankie strode toward us, while two others I didn't recognize were taping off the street.

"Hey," Frankie said, tone amused. "The boss tells me you're joining the force as a consultant."

"The boss knows that's impossible."

"The boss knows no such thing," he commented.

"You're too much your mother's daughter, my girl. Once this gig with the council is over, you'll be looking for something to replace it."

"Not on your Nelly."

He raised an eyebrow in obvious disbelief, but simply stepped past me and pulled rather odd-looking handcuffs from his jacket pocket. The cuff on these weren't the standard double-strand metal, but were instead a good inch thick and emitted a soft aura of magic—one that increased the moment he snapped them around Keeryn's wrists. They were obviously inlaid with some sort of inhibiting spell.

Once she was secured, he stood back and motioned Frankie to take her away. Then his gaze returned to mine. "I take it you're staying here, and that you've been in her room?"

"Yes to both, though I wore gloves, so I didn't leave prints." I raised my hands and wiggled my fingers, even though my hands were actually bare. "She's got a locked phone buried under the clothes in her suitcase that might throw up some leads. There's also an iPad. Which reminds me, I've also got Stace's iPad—we searched Riayn's home after we found Stace in that cavern." I paused. "I suppose it's too early yet for an autopsy report?"

"Yes, although I am expecting it will come through in the next twenty-four hours." He glanced around as one of his men approached. "Rick will take your statements, and I'll drop by sometime tomorrow to pick up Stace's iPad. Keeryn's room is where?"

"Up the stairs, first door on the left."

He nodded and headed up the stairs. Once Rick had taken both our statements, we headed back to our room, closed the door, then stripped off and climbed into bed. With all the noise next door, I didn't expect to sleep, and I certainly wasn't about to have sex—maybe I was being a little prudish, but I just didn't feel comfortable when the man who was basically my father was working next door and the walls were paper thin.

Eljin seemed to understand without me saying anything, and simply cradled me in his arms until sleep claimed us both.

I got back to the tavern at ten and headed straight to the office to do the accounts and make sure everyone would be paid on time. Thankfully, Ingrid was now taking care of the stock orders, so that was one less thing I had to worry about. One of Sgott's men came in at about one to pick up Stace's iPad, by which time the headache that had been with me since waking had definitely worsened. I walked down to the staff break area to grab a couple of painkillers out of the medical kit, then went into the kitchen to make myself a sandwich and a cup of tea before returning to finish the accounts.

It was close to four by the time I was done, and the headache was finally beginning to abate. But as I headed upstairs, an odd sense of... awareness?.. surged. I slowed, put my overnight bag down, then reached into my purse for a knife. The blade was inert, but that prickly sense of awareness was growing. I warily continued, my back pressed against the wall, my gaze searching the shadows above. I couldn't immediately see anyone, but something or someone was definitely up there.

A fact confirmed by the soft green glow coming from the center of the living room.

As I neared the landing, I realized what it was.

Liadon's orb.

It spun rapidly around the moment I appeared, but Liadon didn't speak through it, as she had in her underground system. Maybe she couldn't thanks to the distance. I opened my mouth to say something, but the orb disappeared before I could.

Obviously, I had to go to *her*.

I swore softly. I really didn't feel like going out again, but I suspected ignoring Liadon's summoning would not, in any way, help my long-term goals. I dumped the overnight bag in my room, made myself a cup of tea, then put it in a travel mug and clattered back down the steps, grabbing my warmest coat from the hook on the way out the back door. The air was icy and filled with the promise of an oncoming storm, but there was a whisper of something —or *someone*—else within it. It definitely wasn't Beira, if only because the presence within the wind felt too normal, and very definitely not angry enough.

I scanned the rooftops but couldn't spot anything out of place. While the presence within the wind suggested whoever watched me had some control over the weather, that didn't eliminate the possibility of a regular human watcher. Hell, it could also be shifter; they'd certainly been the go-to choice for many in the past. But if there was one thing I'd learned over the last few months, it was to take at least *some* precautions if instincts started warning of trouble stirring ahead.

I caught the wind and spun it lightly around my body, forming a gentle but continuous shield of air that would spin away a prelim attack of air or ice. It wouldn't— couldn't—deter a full-scale attack, but it would at least give me warning and some time to either protect or retaliate.

I continued on, senses alert as I sipped my tea. Nothing happened, but the awareness of being tracked continued to loom large, and the wind still had little in the way of details when it came to who or what was out there. Which probably meant it was a storm witch with far better control over the wind than me.

Our ice witch perhaps? It would make sense, given I was on both Keeryn's and my aunt's revenge lists. Whether my recent actions and the sensation of being watched meant I'd jumped to the top of my aunt's list, I couldn't say. Maybe they simply were keeping an eye on me while they worked on whoever the next target might be.

I guess I'd find out soon enough.

I reached the council building just as the first few drops of rain started. The security guard opened the door and gave me a polite nod as I walked past. The council might have given me twenty-four-hour access, but the guard not asking for ID did surprise me.

But maybe they'd issued security with a photo. Or maybe there was some sort of bio scan in play that I didn't know about. He was wearing an earpiece, so it was possible the control room gave him the all-clear as I strode up.

I clattered up the stairs to the second floor, then made my way around to the old staircase leading up to Liadon's door. Once at the top, I tucked the now-empty travel mug into my purse then pressed my hand against the oily wood. The unseen symbols flared to life and, a heartbeat later, the door slid silently open.

This time, the orb was waiting.

"I do appreciate your promptness," Liadon said. "Please, come in."

I stepped over the threshold and followed her orb into the winding darkness, its light once again giving the sheer black walls an odd luminosity. The shadows that had been vague last time seemed stronger now, and it was very evident that the vast majority of them held a form that was not humanoid.

I shivered and decided it was probably better if I didn't, in any way, dwell on what else might live in this world between worlds.

The orb led me into the chamber and once again hovered over the chair. I sat and crossed my legs, my gaze scanning the room, looking for the presence I could feel but not see. She slithered into view a few seconds later, coming in from behind me, her black scales once again possessing a vibrant green and gold sheen under the pale light still hovering above my head. She was, in many respects, quite beautiful—something I'd never thought I'd say about such a being.

"I take it you've found some information about Borrhás's Horn?"

She stopped in front of me, her golden gaze sweeping me briefly. Critically. "I sense frustration in you."

Said frustration flared a little more at her avoidance of the question, and amusement briefly glinted in her eyes.

"It's been a frustrating search," I replied, somehow managing to keep my tone even.

"It is ever thus when searching for godly relics. If it was easy, all would be doing it."

"If my—admittedly brief—experience with relic hunting is anything to go by, a hell of a lot of people *are* doing it."

She laughed softly. "That goes with the territory when the old gods stir. Chaos is no fun if there are few players."

"Well, I do wish they'd kept their godly game boards in the cupboard for a few more centuries."

"Your father started this round of games. There was never going to be a chance that you would remain uninvolved."

Meaning I should probably be thankful they'd waited for me to grow up before involving me more fully in their schemes. "Then I need to speak to my father, because seriously, I'm not impressed with his efforts so far. Don't suppose you know how he can be contacted, do you?"

She laughed again, her sinuous form rippling with the movement. "When the game is afoot, there should not be too much contact between the players and their footmen."

"There's a vast difference between too much and none," I said dryly, "And I'm glad you didn't call us pawns."

"Pawns have no self-awareness or true control over events. What makes the godly games so intriguing is the fact one can never truly predict how those within any active game will react to whatever stimuli is provided." She crossed her arms across her chest. "Which does lead me to the matter at hand."

"Then you *did* find information on the horn?"

"No more than what you have undoubtedly already gotten from within the codex's library. I did, however, find Borrhás himself. Or rather, he found me when he became aware of my search."

Surprise rippled through me. "Beira had mentioned he was currently in this world, but she was under the impression *he* was behind the horn's appearance."

"An impression many have but one that is not correct according to him. He does, however, wish his now reunited relic returned rather than destroyed, as has been the case with some of the other relics you have come in contact with."

"The only relic I've actually destroyed was the shield.

The other three had been taken into Annwfyn, and who knows what had happened to them after that."

"If they are no longer in play in either this world or the godly realms, they are considered destroyed."

I hoped she was right but feared that she wasn't. While the Annwfyn learning to use the Claws wasn't likely to happen in my lifetime, it remained a distant and dangerous possibility for my children, given how long-lived we Aodhán were.

"So how am I supposed to get the horn to him if I do get a hold of it?"

"You bring it here, to me. I shall ensure it is returned to him. That is not his only demand, however."

"Why am I not surprised?" I muttered, perhaps a little unwisely. There was no saying that Borrhás himself wasn't amongst those ghostly figures I'd viewed in the tunnel or that even now he wasn't standing beyond the cavern's walls, listening to our conversation.

She arched a delicate eyebrow. "One should always expect the unexpected when it comes to the gods, be they old or new."

"Something I'm definitely discovering. What else did he want?"

"He wants the wielder."

To be locked in ice, as the queen who'd betrayed him had been. "I'm not sure our law enforcement will allow—"

"Your laws do not apply here, and he will brook no argument on this. If you do not do as he wishes, he will punish the city in which you live."

"*What?*"

"Your city—Deva. He will encase it in ice if you do not acquiesce to his wishes."

"But—" I stopped and tried to come to grips with the

casual cruelty of the threat. I had no doubt he could do it given one of his so-called names was the devouring one, but still... "Why punish the whole fucking city rather than me?"

"Because, as I have already mentioned, you are the queen of an ongoing game, and the gods would not be pleased if you fell so soon."

I didn't want to think about the implications of *that* statement, especially given some of the dreams I'd had in the past involved the sacrifice of a figure with red hair—a figure that had no face but was obviously an Aodhán.

Instead, I asked, "I don't suppose you know who my king is then, do you? Because that would be really handy knowledge right now."

"That is a question only Fate can answer."

"Sadly, she's declined to talk to me." I drew in a breath and released it slowly. It didn't help the tension, the fear or the frustration. It never did. "Okay, I'll try—"

"Do not try. Do."

Despite everything, I couldn't help the slight smile. "That sounded like something Beira would say."

"She is a wise woman. Cantankerous, but wise."

"On that, we agree." I pushed up from the seat. "If that's all—"

"It is not."

I frowned at her, even as a deep sense of dread bloomed. "What else could there be?"

She smiled. It was not a pleasant thing to behold. "He not only wants the wielder, but the mastermind *behind* the abuse of his relic. He wants your aunt."

CHAPTER
ELEVEN

"No, that's not—" I stopped and gulped. "Damn it, she's family. Whatever she's done, whatever she might do, we share a bloodline, and I can't forsake that connection completely."

"I admire your willingness to risk all Deva for one who is unworthy of such consideration. But again, in this you have no choice."

"Even so—" I stopped again and scraped a hand through my hair. "What happens if, for some reason beyond my control, she dies? Not at my hand, but someone else's?"

"You bring us her body. Her spirit will not move on; she has touched the horn with ill intent, and her spirit will remain frozen in her flesh."

I frowned. "How is something like that even possible?"

"She is an Aodhán, and both your line and the Tàileach were enhanced by the gods at the dawn of time. What the gods enhance, they can also alter. It is the way of such things."

"Meaning if I piss off some god or goddess going

forward—and I'll have you know that seems to be a major talent of mine—I might find myself being altered in some way?"

Her smile flashed. "You are no mere Aodhán. You are a godling, and as such, cannot be otherwise adjusted."

"Well, that's a relief."

"I would imagine so." Her body uncoiled as she moved to one side. "You may go. My orb will once again lead the way."

I nodded a goodbye and followed the bobbing green light back through the tunnels. As much as I wanted to ask about Mom and her interactions with the council, now was not the time. Once through the oily feeling door, I leaned my head against the wall and swore, long and hard. Then I grabbed my phone and rang my brother.

"We need to talk," I said the minute he picked up. "Where are you?"

"Just about to head home." Which in brother-speak meant he was probably another half hour away from leaving. "You want to come for dinner?"

I glanced at the time and saw with surprise it was close to seven. Liadon's underground world definitely stretched the boundaries of time and place. "That would be great."

"I'll give Darby a heads-up then." He paused. "You okay?"

"Yeah, but we've got a big problem. I'll explain when I get there."

"I shall hurry myself up then."

As I made my way down the stairs, I called for an Uber. By the time I got down to street level, it was absolutely chucking it down, but the worst of the peak hour traffic had at least passed, so it didn't take us long to get across to Lugh's.

As I hastily punched in the code to open the door and then dripped inside, Darby shouted out, "Wine or tea?"

"Both!"

She laughed, but I heard the tap running as she filled the kettle. I hung up my coat, then shucked off my boots and padded into the living area. The air was rich and warm, filled with the delightful scent of roast chicken.

"God, that smells divine." I perched on the stool and accepted the white wine she handed me. "My brother is never going to let you go if you keep this up."

"That is, of course, my wicked plan."

I smiled and took a sip of the wine. It was a chardonnay that was rich, buttery, and quite lovely. "How's the week off going?"

"Great—been spending time with Talein, Rossita, and Ruairí."

Talein was Darby's older brother and Ruairí his son, the first-born male in their generation, meaning the family had an heir to carry the name forward and all the pressure on Darby to marry and produce said heir had dissipated, allowing her to marry whoever she chose, whenever she chose. Of course, given the fertility differences between elves and pixies, Lugh would be well into his middle years by the time Darby reached her fertile period. Not that I thought either of them actually cared. I knew for certain Darby didn't, as she and I had discussed that very thing many times over the years. I might have gently pushed my brother toward her, but only because I was certain she'd considered all the realities.

"Is he still impressing everyone with the power of his lungs?"

"Believe me, when that boy wants to be fed, the entire encampment knows about it." She made a mug of tea then pushed it across the counter toward me. "Oh, before I forget, Win called me. He's got some names for you, and wants to meet for morning tea tomorrow, if you're free."

And was no doubt anticipating more sticky buns. "I gather he talked to Harold then?"

"No, Marjorlaine."

My eyebrows rose. "I thought he quit because he didn't see eye to eye with her?"

"He did, but as he noted, an ice witch running around Deva causing havoc does the guild no good at all. I also suspect he might have put a rocket up the woman's butt— he might have retired but he still has a lot of respect and pull within the guild."

"Which makes it all the more shameful that he's basically been forgotten by the guild."

"He has a pension with them, but he's philosophical about the lack of contact otherwise. Says it's natural for friendships to fade with time."

"Our fucking friendship had better not," I growled, in mock anger.

She laughed. "Not a chance in hell. Besides, I'm going to be your sister-in-law, so there will be no escaping me."

I lightly clicked my wine glass against hers. "Are you coming to Win's too?"

"No, I'm babysitting for my sister to give her a break."

"Then do you think he'll mind if I bring Mathi along?"

She shook her head. "From what he's said, he's done some work for the Dhār-Vals in the past. Could be a meeting of old friends."

"Let's all hope it was a good working relationship rather than a bad one," I said, amused.

"If it was a bad one," she said dryly, "I'm thinking he wouldn't be here to talk about it."

"I can't imagine Win double-crossing anyone, let alone a Dhār-Val. He strikes me as the wily, common-sense type."

Darby took a drink, a speculative light flaring in her eyes. "So, have you done it yet?"

I frowned. "Done what?"

She rolled her eyes. "Put on the Bruadar bracelet and had amazing dream sex?"

"I have not."

"Why not?"

"I don't know, I just—" I paused and shrugged. "There's a part of me that believes I should use the next three months to sort out where my relationship with Eljin is going. And it's not like my relationship with Cynwrig is end game anyway."

"That makes total and utter sense, so why the hesitancy? Aside from the fact Myrkálfar elves are as addictive as hell when it comes to sex."

"I honestly don't know."

She took a sip of her wine, her expression thoughtful. "Is instinct twitching?"

"No. Not really." I wrinkled my nose. "Maybe I'm just afraid to open my heart because I don't want it stomped on."

"A perfectly legitimate fear, given your shitty record with men, but one you're going to have to confront if you ever want what your mom had with Sgott—because that *is* your ideal, isn't it?"

She knew well enough it was, having heard me talk about it over the years. "I know, but—"

"Look," she cut in, her tone and expression serious. "Has Eljin stopped going out with other women? Has he mentioned wanting to take the next logical step—moving in together, forsaking all others, that sort of thing?"

I raised my eyebrows. "Has Lugh?"

"Not yet, but he will. I do have an advantage over you though—I've known the man for a very long time now and have watched his relationships with other women from afar. I can practically see his moves before he makes them. And you avoided the question."

I smiled and drank some tea. If I had too much wine before my meal, it'd go straight to my head—and I'd already had more than enough headaches recently. "He did say he'd have to ensure the competition remained in the wings over the next three months, but I don't think he was serious."

"Then put on the bracelet and have some fun, no harm done."

"Except, maybe, for a deepening of that addiction you mentioned a second ago."

She laughed, but the seriousness remained in her gaze. "I believe the Myrkálfar crown has the same rules and restrictions as the Ljósálfar, which means he will have to take a wife at the coronation. Your time with him is likely limited anyway."

Perhaps that was why the lovely Orlah was now part of his harem. Perhaps, given what little he'd said about their previous relationship, he was well aware they were compatible in the bedroom and out. It also explained their sudden urgency in finding Geitha's Tears—perhaps it would be bequeathed to the woman who'd be the next king's wife.

An image of Orlah—tall, dark-skinned, with long, curly black hair and a to-die-for figure wearing the gorgeous necklace I'd been commissioned to find—flashed up in my mind. I picked up my wine and took an indecently large gulp. It made my head buzz, but it also shoved the image from the forefront of my mind.

"I thought Myrkálfar only married for love?"

"The royal line comes with certain responsibilities, and marriage is treated very differently. When one generation is crowned, the next must be born to ensure succession."

"I knew succession was a priority for highborn Ljósálfar but had no idea it also applied to the Myrkálfar."

"*Only* to the royal line."

Which was of course why Fate decided to throw one of the heirs my way, because why not twist the knife a little deeper?

The door opened, and Lugh came in with a cheery, "And how are the two most important people in my life this fine evening?"

I raised my eyebrows, my gaze meeting Darby's. Happiness shone from hers, and with good reason—she'd definitely had a major boost up my brother's emotional rankings.

"We're good," we both echoed together, before she added, "I take it you found a new relic for the museum?"

He laughed as he walked around the bench, then kissed her soundly. "And outbid several other museums in the process."

"Congrats, brother," I said, raising my glass. "Are we allowed to know this relic's name?"

"Arion's Flute."

I frowned. "Where have I heard that name before?"

"It was one of the relics Vincentia sold off to a private collector. I believe I might have ranted about it for a day or so."

Because he'd always believed selling important relics—be they godly or not—to private collectors was utterly wrong. The fact that Vincentia had been behind the sale only made his acquisition all that much sweeter.

He accepted the wine Darby poured him with a nod then returned his attention to me. "So, what is this problem you mentioned on the phone?"

"No business discussions over dinner," Darby said. "Food first. Go set the table while I pull everything out of the oven."

"She's becoming very bossy," he commented, amusement tugging at his lips even as he obeyed.

"She's always been bossy," I said dryly. "You've just never been the focus of it until now."

"And hey," she said breezily. "At least you're getting to see all my faults before things get too serious."

"Hmmm" was all he said to that.

We ate dinner, chatting about everything and everything except Eljin and the reason I was here. It wasn't until dessert was eaten—sticky date pud with caramel sauce—and we'd retired to the sofa that I told Lugh about Borrhás's demands.

"Look, she's kin, and under normal circumstances, I would say we simply can't comply, but she escaped the red knife and is now hunting everyone she believes killed Vincentia, including you." He scraped a hand across his chin. "And given Borrhás's threat, what choice do we really have?"

"You don't," Darby said, voice flat. "The only real choice either of you have is whether you hand her over alive or dead. Aside from the fact that doing anything else would risk the lives of all in Deva, would not disobeying Borrhás's order and allowing destruction bring the blood curse down on you both?"

I wrinkled my nose. "I don't think there's ever been a

situation that's tested the rules that way, but I just can't stomach the thought of handing her over alive. And yet, I also can't just kill her, thanks to the curse."

"Nor I," Lugh admitted softly.

"Then you need to make sure she attacks you, and you need to ensure you don't pull your punches. Either of you." Her gaze ran from me to Lugh and back again. "I'm a healer. I fix life rather than take it, but I'm also an Ljósálfar elf, and I see no gray here. It comes down to a simple choice—one death, or many."

I took a deep breath and released it slowly. She was right, but knowing that didn't make me feel any better.

"It's also a decision we don't have to make straight away," Lugh said. "We've got to find her first. It may well be that she'll come to her senses and retreat."

"Which is not going to help us or our decision at all, because there was no ifs or buts. It was 'bring her to Borrhás or else.'" I rose. "On that somber note, I'd better get back home."

"Call an Uber," Lugh said immediately, "or let me drive you."

"I'm fine—"

"And she's still out there," he growled. "I know we'd all feel better if she took the decision from us and attacked, but let's not make it too easy for her."

"I wasn't intending to, brother mine."

I immediately called said Uber, then, once the app said it was close, hugged them both goodbye, grabbed my coat, and headed out. The rain had cleared, but thunder still rumbled overhead, and the night remained bitterly cold.

That unseen presence in the wind remained.

I shivered and cautiously reached out, trying to find his or her location. The minute I did, the presence retreated.

I swore in frustration and climbed into the Uber as it halted in front of me. It didn't take all that long to get home, as it was almost midnight and the streets basically empty. Once back in the tavern, I dumped my purse on the coffee table then lit the fire—as usual saying a small thank-you prayer over the wood for its sacrifice—then walked over to the kitchenette to make myself a hot chocolate. It might be late, and I should have been tired, but an uneasy energy ran through me, and I had no idea if its source was the still rumbling sky or the prickling knowledge that I was still being watched.

I made my hot chocolate, then retreated to my chair, tucking my legs underneath me as I pulled out my phone and sent a text to Mathi, detailing everything Liadon had said.

His reply was almost instant. *Not a hard decision, Bethany.*

An opinion Darby shares.

And why would you expect her to say anything else, when the man she loves and her best friend are in the firing line? If you're looking for someone to talk you out of what you know you must do, you'd be better discussing the matter with Sgott rather than any of us elves.

I knew that. I also knew there was no way I was going to burden him with that sort of decision. *Listen, I've a morning tea-date with Win Frost, who's a retired storm witch. You want to come along?*

I take it this storm witch might have some names for us?

According to Darby, yes. We can go talk to them straight after, if you'd like.

Sounds like a plan. What time? I've got to update the council at nine, but I can delay if necessary.

He said ten, so plenty of time.

Perfect. Shall I pick you up at the end of the lane?

Please.

See you then.

I sent him back a smile, then tucked the phone away and sipped my chocolate, watching the flames dance as the storm continued to threaten overhead. Its energy ran across my skin and made the tiny hairs at the back of my neck rise.

The presence was back.

I could hear the vibration of it in the storm, feel it in the wind stirring through my bedroom's open window. The energy felt more male than female, which meant that, given I'd sent the wind on a mission to find the witch using the horn, whoever it was, they weren't the horn's wielder. They also felt some distance away and oddly uncoupled—which made absolutely no sense. The wind also spoke of height, of steep sandstone cliffs overlooking a meandering river. Which was decidedly more information than Beira had suggested was possible.

But if this witch was working with my aunt, then why wasn't she attacking? Why was she simply keeping tabs on me? Was Mathi right, and she was saving me for last? If that were the case, then who else was on her list? She'd already hit Kaitlyn and the Myrkálfars' building, and really, the only other person she could go after was Rogan, and I knew for certain he was dead, having witnessed his bones being burned to ashes.

I had a bad feeling we'd soon discover the answer to that particular question.

I shoved the worry that insight raised aside, grabbed my purse from the coffee table, and tugged the bracelet's box from its depths. The midnight stone bracelet reacted the minute I opened the lid, the tiny stars seeming to shine with anticipation. I once again ran a finger across its surface and the pulsing energy that caressed my fingers felt stronger, sharper. It was tempting, so tempting, to put it on and see what happened, but uncertainty held me back.

I needed more than assumptions and theories before I donned anything that held this much magic.

I snapped the lid back on and shoved the box back to the bottom of my purse. Then, before I could really think about it, I sent a text to Treasa. I had no idea if she knew about Cynwrig's gift, but given I couldn't talk to him about it without actually using it, she was my next best option. After telling her what he'd done, I added that I would not accept the gift until I knew more about it and the consequences of wearing it.

Then I drained the rest of my hot chocolate, placed the fire screen over the fire to catch any embers, and went to bed.

And once again dreamed of deception.

Mathi's driver ushered me into the car and nodded without comment when I mentioned we needed to go to Panna's first to pick up an order. As he smoothly headed back into the traffic, Mathi looked me up and down and then said, "Bad night?"

"Is that a polite way of saying I look like shit?"

He smiled but there was concern in his eyes. "You've rather large bags under your eyes. It is not a good look."

I wrinkled my nose. "I keep having these dreams of deception, but they come with no goddamn details, and it's annoying."

"Interesting, given said dreams didn't warn you about Rogan."

"Exactly." And really, they should have, given Rogan had tried to toss me into that Annwfyn's gate in Pynwffynnon.

"Perhaps the dreams will become clearer as your talent grows stronger."

"Yeah, but what do I do in the meantime? Look suspiciously at everyone?"

He laughed. "Maybe just be cautious about letting anyone new into your life."

"I have more than enough men in my life, if that's what you're referring to."

"I wasn't."

"Like hell."

He laughed again and, as his driver drew to a stop, leaned forward and said, "Henrick, can you collect Miss Aodhán's order and bring me the receipt?"

"Mathi, you can't pay—"

"I can charge the council for expenses. You cannot."

Which was absolutely true, so I didn't argue any further. Henrick came back a few minutes later, handed us the coffees and the buns, then smoothly drove off to the address I gave him. We arrived right on ten, and Win was waiting at the door.

His bushy gray eyebrows rose when he spotted Mathi. "You wouldn't be Amir Dhār-Val's boy, would you?"

"His nephew." Mathi held out his hand. "Pleasure to meet you, Mr. Frost."

He laughed. "Not sure your uncle would agree with that. We've had some words over the years."

"As have I," Mathi said dryly.

Win laughed again and ushered us inside. I led the way into the kitchen, and Win shuffled after us. This time, the table had already been set.

I put the coffees down, then used the tongs to place three buns on the serving platter and handed him the remainder. His cheeks dimpled. "You're definitely spoiling me."

I sat down with a smile. "According to Darby, you're chattier when you're well fed, and I need to pick your brain."

His grin flashed, but he nevertheless tucked the extra buns into the bread bin before sitting back down and reaching for the butter. "And what would you be needing to pick my brains about? More than just the names of the ice witches you came here for, I take it?"

I nodded. "There's a storm witch following me via the wind, and he seems to be operating from a position of height—some place that has sandstone cliffs overlooking a meandering river. I don't suppose there's a special place you lot gather to muster storms is there?"

"No, there is not, though that might have changed since my day." He took a sip of coffee and made an appreciative noise. "There's really only one hill around these parts that fits that description—Helsby Hill."

Which wasn't a place I'd ever been to, but I could vaguely remember seeing it on various motorway signs I'd passed over the years. "He also felt disconnected. Unanchored, if you will."

"It's a rare talent to be feeling such a thing," Win commented.

"'Rare' and 'Bethany' have become synonymous with each other," Mathi said dryly. "It makes interesting times even more so."

Win's gaze ran between us. "You two together?"

"Sadly, no," Mathi said before I could.

"Why not? What's wrong with you, lad?"

"Bethany deserves more than I could ever offer her, though that doesn't mean I do not want her back in my bed, and she is well aware of this."

"She is," I replied dryly. "Just as he's aware *why* that will not happen. Now, can we please get this conversation back on track?"

Win laughed. "I'd apologize, but it would be a lie. I've always been a bit of a nosy parker—it's part of the reason Marjorlaine dislikes me so much. Anyways, if this witch feels unanchored, then he likely is. It means his ties to the guild have been severed."

"He must have done something pretty nasty for the guild to take such an action," Mathi commented. "They're renowned for looking the other way in their desperation to keep members and, even more importantly, their tithes."

"Aye," Win said. "Once you're in, it's usually hard to get out unless you retire or die."

Which was another point in the favor of *not* asking the guild for help. "This guy feels young, so the severance must have happened recently. You heard gossip along those lines?"

"A severance is a dire event and cannot be described as mere gossip, young lady." His voice was severe, but amusement twinkled in his eyes. "If he's young, then it likely means he is—was—attending the training academy and living in. There's only been one severance from there and it happened some three years ago—a young witch ignored the rules and ended up destroying part of the damn accommodation wing."

"I take it he killed some students?" I asked.

"Worse," Win grumbled. "He took out two house cats."

"That says a lot about the value the guild puts on their trainees' lives," Mathi commented dryly. "Even we Ljósálfar elves do not value a feline's life over that of humans, and everyone knows just how little we value humans."

Win chuckled. "One reason why I remain surprised that I didn't end up fertilizer for some tree in one of your plantations. Amir did threaten it more than once."

"He must have rated your services more than he indicated," Mathi said. "He is not one for recanting threats."

I suspected there was more than a little of that in Mathi, even if he rarely showed that side to me. I munched on more bun, then picked up my coffee and leaned back in the chair. "Do you happen the know the name of the young man whose tenancy was severed?"

Win frowned. "Ascott, I think. Tony Ascott."

"As in, Ascott Weather Services?" Mathi asked.

The older man nodded. "You know them?"

"I've had dealings with them."

I glanced at him. "Enough that you could contact them and perhaps get them to bring their son in? Because the minute I go anywhere near his location, he'll feel it and run."

Mathi smiled. It was not a pleasant smile. "They'll cooperate. In fact, I'll give them a call now. The sooner we sort him out, the better."

As he rose and headed out to the hall to make the call, Win said, "And that, right there, is pure Amir."

"I would have said it was more his father than his uncle, but same thing, I guess." I paused. "How dangerous is this kid likely to be?"

"He's quick to temper and has something of a superiority complex, according to what I heard."

Meaning the likelihood of him being *very* dangerous was high. "Is his belief justified?"

"Both his parents are competent storm witches, but his

abilities are stronger than either. The temper, however, is his downfall." His gaze narrowed. "I'm thinking that you, however untrained you might be, could take him."

I smiled. "Except for the fact the minute he feels my presence in the wind, he retreats."

"Then don't let him feel you."

"Easily said, not so easily done when you haven't a clue as to how to disguise your presence."

"Ah, well, that is a problem." His expression became thoughtful. "If you're not willing to go to the guild for training, then perhaps you need to seek private tutoring. It's not my field, but I've a friend who might be able to help, if you don't mind paying a fee."

"More than happy to."

"Then I'll contact her and see what she says. She's semi-retired these days, but she does still do some outsource tutoring for those who aren't skilled enough to enter the academy."

"That would be brilliant, thanks."

He nodded. "Now, I'd better give you those names I promised, because it's likely our young Dhār-Val will have set up the meeting and be wanting to leave the minute he gets off the phone."

I smiled. "Probably."

"There's two—Martha Gale and Amara Li. Harold's opinion is that, of the two, Martha is your more likely candidate. There was an incident at the guild's Whitlow branch, and she was held accountable. She wasn't severed but did 'retire' shortly after. According to Harold, she was extremely unhappy with the guild's handling of the whole affair."

"I don't suppose he gave you a description of either woman?"

"Amara's allegiance lies with the Japanese guild, though she is currently working in the UK as a private tutor, so he wasn't able to access much information about her. He did access Whitlow's archives, however, and he sent me Martha's profile picture."

He reached into his pocket for his phone, then brought up the image and showed it to me. The woman on the screen had a thin, wrinkled face, silvery blue eyes, and short spiky hair that glittered silver.

It was the same woman that I'd seen in my vision.

"That's her," I said. "That's our ice witch."

Win raised his eyebrows. "You sound very certain."

I grimaced. "I've second sight and had a vision of her when she was attacking the Myrkálfar building. Can you send me the image? I'll forward it on to the IIT and they can put out a warrant."

He did so. "I take it you're also working with the IIT on this matter?"

I nodded. "Sgott Bruin also happens to be my stepdad."

Win blinked. "You're Meabh's little girl? Well, I'll be damned."

This time it was my eyebrows that shot up. "You knew Mom?"

He nodded. "Met her a couple of times in the course of guild business. Lovely woman. How's she doing these days?"

"She died, I'm afraid."

"Ah, so sorry to hear that."

Mathi strode back into the room, saving me from saying anything else. Exactly as Win had predicted, he said, "I've a meeting with the Ascotts at eleven-thirty. They'll ensure Tony is there, so once I go in to ensure the kid is in check, you can come in and question him."

I glanced at my phone. It was close to eleven now. "Where are we meeting them?"

"Helsby."

Which was a good twenty minutes away. I drained my coffee and pushed to my feet. "We'd better be leaving then."

"Yes." Mathi glanced at Win. "I apologize for cutting our visit so abruptly."

Win waved a hand. "Council business takes priority over visiting old men, lad."

I swung my purse over my shoulder and picked up the remains of my bun. "I'll make up for our sudden exit with a visit next week."

"I should have an answer from Kitty about the tutoring by then."

Mathi's car was already waiting out the front. Once we'd climbed in and were on our way, I said, "If this kid is as volatile as Win says, he might well attack you before his parents can restrain him."

"That is entirely possible," Mathi agreed, "but a good twenty percent of their livelihood comes from contracts we have with them. I believe they will do as they promised."

"I hope you're right."

Lazy amusement played around his lips. "But fear I'm not?"

"Things have been falling into place a little too easily for my liking."

"Maybe Fate has decided to be gentle on us for a change."

"And maybe tomorrow you'll fall madly in love."

He laughed. "Such perfection does not exist."

"I thought you were looking for compatibility rather than perfection?"

"I am, but if we're talking about love, then elven perfection is perhaps the only thing that could draw it from my cold, unemotional heart."

I rolled my eyes. "How are we going to play this? Me waiting in the car is unlikely to work. He'll be wary and will sense my presence the minute you open the door."

"If you're not in the front or the back seat, then he can't possibly 'see' you through the open car door and has no reason to be suspicious."

I stared at him for a second. "You want me to hide in the trunk?"

"Only for a few minutes."

"Large pixies and car trunks are not compatible." At least, they weren't with this large pixie.

He patted my knee. "You'll be fine. I've had larger bodies than you in there."

I continued to stare at him, uncertain as to whether he was kidding or not. He merely raised his eyebrows, as if daring me to ask. I didn't. As he'd noted before, there were some things I was better off not knowing.

Once we were close to our destination, Henrick pulled the car over. I retrieved my knives and phone from my purse, then climbed—grumbling all the way—into the trunk.

"It'll take two minutes to get there. Henrick will release the catch three minutes after I head in," Mathi said, not quite able to control his amusement. "That should give me enough time to ensure Tony is present and that his parents do have him under control."

I didn't reply, but I did glare. He laughed and slammed the trunk lid back down, enclosing me in darkness. A few seconds later, we were back underway. The following five minutes were probably the longest of my life. I wasn't claustrophobic, but my heart was beating as loudly as any drum, and sweat trickled down the side of my face. Fear, no doubt due to watching too many movies where bad things happened to women stuck in trunks.

The hum of tires on bitumen was soon replaced by the crunch of gravel. A few seconds later, we stopped. I gripped the Eye in an attempt to remain distant from the wind, and wished, with everything I had, there was some way I could shield from the force that hunted around the car. That thought had no more crossed my mind when energy stirred across my fingers and the knives pulsed in response. A heartbeat later, a faint curtain of purplish light fell around my body. Surprise stirred; while the knives had always protected me from magic, I had no idea they could also form other sorts of shields. But then, until this moment, I'd never actually *wished* for such a thing while gripping the Eye. Perhaps that was—

I cut the rest of that thought off as the car door opened and Mathi stepped out. The rattling wind whipped inside; thick fingers of air slipped into the boot, sliding over the shield without seeming to recognize anything was there or that I hid underneath it. As the fingers pulled back, the fierce, suspicious pulse running through the air eased, though it didn't entirely go away. Tony remained on edge, primed and ready to explode.

I'd have to move fast when I got out, because I had a really bad feeling Tony's parents had overstated their ability to control their son.

Footsteps crunched across the gravel, then a door opened. After a brief conversation, they moved inside and the door closed. I waited, my heart beating so loudly it seemed to echo in the shadowed confines of the trunk. The seconds ticked by slowly, and just as I was ready to scream for Henrick to open the damn thing, he did so. I released the Eye, letting the soft shield fade as I pushed upright and swung my feet over the edge.

In that instant, the wind roared back to life. It swept underneath the car, lifted it with dizzying speed high into the air, then flung it violently away. I yelped and braced, but before I could even think, let alone retaliate, the wind whipped in, wrapped violent arms around my body, and ripped me free.

Then, with all the fury of an unsound mind, it flung me with deadly force back toward the ground.

CHAPTER

TWELVE

The speed at which I was now traveling meant I only had seconds, if that, to save myself. With fear thick in my throat and my heart racing as fast as I was falling, I reached for the wind, only to hit a thick bubble of violent air. *His* air, his shield, stopping me from reaching the forces that might save me. If I had time, I might be able to break his barrier, but I didn't, and the ground was approaching fast, and if I didn't do something soon, I'd fucking die.

Panic surged but I did my best to shove it away. Did my best to *think*.

Thunder rumbled overhead, a sound that seemed to echo my desperation. I might not be able to call the wind, but could I call the lightning?

Dare I?

Dare I *not*?

The knives slapped into my hands without me really ordering it. I quickly raised one and called to the incandescent fury that lurked within the storm. I wasn't anchored so this was dangerous, but no more so than hitting the ground at my current velocity.

Lightning flashed around and then through me, making me one with the storm, a being without flesh and substance. I pointed the second knife toward the cottage, directing all that fierceness at the section that *didn't* hold the source of the furious whirlwind surrounding me. Bright light flashed out from the blade's tip, three fierce forks that hit the building sequentially. As deadly missiles of bricks, slate, and wood flew in all directions, the whirlwind surrounding me fell apart. I immediately caught the wind, ordering one thick finger after the car to cushion its tumbling fall and another to halt my speed.

And not a moment too soon.

I still hit with enough force to jar every bone in my body and stumbled forward for several feet before dropping to my knees and plunging the other knife point into the ground. The dangerous energy that still burned through muscle, fiber, and flesh channeled out into the earth, leaving me shaking and weak.

I sucked in several deep breaths that didn't really help the inner quivering, then pushed to my feet. My legs shook and my knees wanted nothing more than to buckle and hit the ground again, but I locked them tight, determined to remain upright. When I felt secure enough to move, I stumbled forward, my grip on the knives so fierce my knuckles were white. Tiny wisps of jagged light still played around the tips of both blades, a warning the power I'd invited in hadn't completely dissipated. Thankfully, I didn't feel in immediate danger of being boiled alive by it.

Which might be famous last words, but still...

I staggered up the steps, stepped through the remains of the front door, and followed the soft sounds of groans to the rear of the remaining portion of the house—a kitchen diner,

I discovered as I entered. Dust danced through the air and both the walls and the ceiling were cracked, but the song of the wood in this section was strong, even if distressed.

I swept my gaze around the room, quickly spotting Mathi. He had a cut across his cheek but was pushing into a sitting position and otherwise looked okay. An older man and woman were unconscious under the breakfast counter, while my target lay in an ungainly heap to my right and showing signs of stirring. He was also the one making all the noise.

I hurried over, touched his neck, and said, "You will not use your storm-held gifts in any way from this point on unless I say otherwise, nor will you attack me or anyone else physically. You will also answer every single question Mathi and I ask."

As my power washed through him, surprise ran through me. Given my aunt's propensity to use pixie compelling magic on those she employed, I'd expected to find at least *some* sign of it within the kid. But there was none. Maybe she simply didn't think he'd be found, or she'd reached the point where she didn't really care.

He made a low, growly sound of frustration and opened his eyes. They were silver and filled with the violence he could no longer unleash. The whites of his eyes were also very red, suggesting he'd pushed his limits to raise then fling the car and entrap me.

I told him to sit upright but not move anywhere else, then left him to stew in his own insignificance and went over to check his parents. His mom had a nasty cut on the back of her head that was going to need attention, and his father had broken his wrist if its odd position was anything to go by, but other than the dust covering him, seemed fine.

I quickly checked their pulses—both were strong, even if a little fast.

I dragged out my phone, called an ambulance and the IIT, then staggered over to Mathi and sat beside him. After driving a knife blade into the slate in the vague hope it would earth me enough to allow the remaining few flickers of inner lightning to dissipate, I said, "Well, that didn't exactly go to plan, did it?"

He laughed softly. Ruefully. "It would seem that I did indeed tempt Fate a little too much. What did you do to the building?"

"Blew it apart."

"Obviously, but how?"

"I called down lightning."

"Which explains the little flickers of energy still dancing around you." He lightly poked my shoulder with a stiffened finger. "It somewhat reminds me of the effect you get with one of those plasma lightning balls."

"An effect I hope is fading, because if it doesn't, I might be in big trouble." It *felt* like the heat was retreating, and the blade slammed into the slate continued to pulse, but it might also be a reaction to contained fury sitting across the other side of the room.

"It is." He paused. "What happened to Henrick?"

"Our angry and rather stupid witch over there picked up the car and flung it. I sent the wind after him, so hopefully I was in time to break the smash back down."

I'd barely finished when Mathi's phone dinged. He dug it out from inside his coat pocket and glanced at the screen. "Seems you were. He's shaken, but fine, apparently. Two tires were punctured when the car landed, so he's called the RAC."

"He might want to head to the hospital to get checked out once that's done. We can catch a cab back."

"No need. I'll just call for the company chauffeur."

As Mathi sent his two messages, I continued to study our captive. To say he radiated fury would be the understatement of the year, but there was no fear in him. Not yet, anyway. Maybe it was bravado, maybe it was simply a matter of not realizing the depths of trouble he was truly in.

Mathi tucked his phone away, then glanced at me. "Shall I do the honors and start the questions?"

I waved a hand towards our felon. "Feel free."

Mathi gave Tony his best seriously unpleasant smile. "Now, young man, kindly explain to us why you were so eager to attack when all we wished to do was talk."

Any sensible person would have answered immediately and honestly, even without my magic blanketing him, but Tony and sensible obviously weren't bosom buddies. He fought answering for several seconds, but in the end had no real option.

"I was warned she was deadly. That she would kill me the minute she realized what I was doing."

The "she" was accompanied by a chin pointed my way and a bit of a sneer.

"And who told you that?" Mathi asked.

"I only know her first name—Riayn."

It wasn't unexpected, but regret nevertheless twinged through me. There'd been a bit of me—a very *tiny* bit, granted —that had hoped we were wrong, that my closest living relative aside from Lugh wasn't now hunting me down.

"What were you ordered to do?" I asked.

The sneer appeared again. "Keep an eye on your movements and report back to her."

"Did she say why?" Mathi asked.

"She said she needed to know your location on an hourly basis, in case her plans had to change in a hurry."

Did that mean her plans *hadn't* yet changed? It certainly seemed to be the implication.

"Which means you must have her phone number," I said. "Give it to me."

He did so, though not at all happily. As I tapped it into my phone, Mathi asked, "Did you meet her at any point?"

"No."

"You have no idea where she's staying?"

"Not in Deva. I had some friends checking for me."

"Why? Didn't you trust your employer?" I said dryly.

"I don't trust no one." He sent a dark look his parents' way. "Even those closest to me can apparently be bought out."

"More threatened than bought out," Mathi said. "And no doubt a good portion of the income they get from my company supports their somewhat useless only son."

"And so they should. That's what parents do."

What his parents should have done was slap him upside the head a few times. Maybe that would have shaken some of the attitude loose.

"What else can you tell us about her or her plans?" I asked.

"Nothing." It was sullenly said.

The lad didn't like not being fully clued in as to what was going down.

The knife stopped pulsing, so I pulled it free of the stone. From outside came the sound of approaching sirens, and the noise seemed to impinge on the old man's consciousness. His eyes flickered open, and his gaze swept around the room until it hit me.

Confusion ran through his expression. "Who are you?"

"Mathi's friend. You should stay still, because I think you've broken your wrist."

"Where did you come from?" He ignored me and struggled into a sitting position, his breath hissing through thin lips. "What happened to my house?"

"She did it," Tony growled. "She's the fucking storm witch I warned you about. Did you listen? Fuck no, so here we are."

The old man's eyes widened. "Why would you do such a thing? We did nothing—"

"Which is blatantly obvious where your son is concerned," I couldn't help snapping. "He lifted Mathi's car and flung it a good half kilometer away, almost killing his chauffeur, then he wrapped me in air and tried to slam me into the ground."

"He wouldn't—"

"He did, just as he destroyed the guild's accommodation wing. Or didn't he tell you about that, either?"

"Tony?" Bewilderment danced through the old man's expression. "Is that true?"

"Yeah, what of it?"

The old man simply stared at his son. Said son didn't seem to care. *You reap what you teach*, I couldn't help but think.

Or in this case, *didn't* teach.

The sirens stopped out the front of the house. Or what remained of it, anyway. Two medics soon appeared, followed by two IIT officers I didn't recognize. They'd obviously been briefed by Sgott, though, because they walked immediately over to me and Mathi, took our statements, then told us we could go.

"Hey," Tony said. "What about me?"

The taller of the two IIT officers cast a wry look his way. "We'll get to you in a second, lad, never fear."

"I wasn't talking to you. I was talking to *her*. She magicked me. She needs to release me before she leaves."

The IIT officer's gaze met mine, eyebrow raised in query. I smiled and pushed upright, wobbling a little as a wave of weariness washed over me. Mathi caught my elbow, steadying me, then released me. I walked over to Tony and touched his shoulder lightly. "I release you from the restriction of remaining still, but you will follow all directions given by the IIT and answer all their questions."

"I didn't mean that. I meant restoring my powers."

"Oh, those restrictions can stay, as can the orders to not physically attack me or indeed anyone else. Good luck finding a new profession, young man. With your attitude, you're going to need it."

I turned and left. It took a few seconds for him to realize I was serious, and for his thick curses to follow me.

"That," Mathi said as he caught up with me, "was very well done."

"At least his fucking temper can't hurt anyone else now. Might also have the side effect of making him a better human."

"I would think the superior attitude is too ingrained now to be muted. Ah, there's the car now."

Said car was almost a carbon copy of his own; the only difference was the color of the chauffeur's uniform. Once we were seated and on the way back to Deva, I said, "Will you be able to use your access to the IIT's files to run a search on Martha?"

"As soon as we drop you home. I take it you'll be resting the rest of the day?"

I gave him a mock scowl. "Are you saying I look like shit again?"

"Totally."

"Thanks."

"Welcome." He paused. "Would something to eat help refuel the well?"

"When have I ever refused food?"

He laughed. "Never, granted, though I'm thinking that, in this case, you're after something fast rather than decent."

"There is nothing wrong with a Big Mac and fries."

"There is everything wrong, but I will concede that I'll never convince you of this fact." He leaned forward and added, "Marc, please stop at the nearest McDonald's."

A few minutes later, he did so, and I happily refueled while Mathi drank his coffee and did his best to hide his horror. We were on the outskirts of Deva when my phone rang sharply, the tone telling me it was Lugh.

I hit the answer button and said, "Hey, brother, what's up?"

"Ice, up to our windowsills, that's what."

Fear leapt into my heart. "The witch is attacking your *home*?"

"No, the fucking museum."

Mathi immediately leaned forward and ordered the driver to head there ASAP.

"But why—" I stopped.

Rogan was why. The website still had him listed as the head of the department, as they hadn't yet gotten around to employing someone else or even updating the page.

"Are you okay?" I asked.

"Yes—I ordered the entire wing evacuated the minute I realized what was happening. Where are you?"

I glanced at Mathi, my eyebrows raised in silent query.

"About eight minutes out if the traffic's bad," he replied.

"Heard that," Lugh said. "I'm with Sgott—he's set up shop in the Queen Vic parking area. A number of witches from the guild are also here, though they're not having much success stopping the ice."

"That's because they aren't ice witches."

"True, but they are managing to at least slow its progress. Got something to do with the freezing point of water and keeping the air temp above it. Marjorlaine did say that the slowing could also be partially due to the witch attempting to ice such a large portion of the building and overextending her skills and strength."

If Marjorlaine was there, the guild had to be worried about unwarranted publicity and the possibility of being held accountable. "I'd vote for the overextending, given it's unlikely she knows where, exactly, Rogan's office is."

"Why would they be going after Rogan? He's dead. If anything, it's more likely to be me they're after."

"That's a possibility, but it could also be they're not aware Rogan is dead—his death hasn't been officially announced, has it? Aren't they still waiting for the IIT's official report?"

"Yes, so maybe our crazy aunt is attempting a two-for-one deal."

We swept into Deva's outskirts and continued to drive through the narrower streets with unwise speed.

"Tell Sgott we're coming in fast," I said, and gave him the registration number. If he could get a quick warning out, it would at least give us a better chance of avoiding the cops pulling us over before we got to the parking area.

As he hung up, Mathi said, "Are you going to be able to stop the attack?"

I scrubbed my forehead wearily. "I don't know, but I have to try."

"You're not going to be of any use to anyone if you fry your brain out."

"I'm not going to call on the lightning, just the storm."

"Because that is *so* much easier on your body," he said dryly.

I half smiled. "Actually, the knives do the majority of the work."

"I no more believe that than you believe I'll marry for love."

I snorted but didn't reply as we neared the museum. The chauffeur slowed down and, once our names were taken, we were ushered through the road barriers the police had set up. A few seconds later, we stopped close to what looked like chaos HQ. I tugged on my coat, then grabbed my knives and climbed out, leaving my purse in the car.

We walked over to where Sgott and Lugh were, the heat in the air increasing with every step. With them was a well-dressed woman in her mid-forties; she had spiky silver hair, dark brown skin, and was surrounded by a thick veil of energy that, while it didn't fizz with lightning, still felt electric.

Marjorlaine. Had to be.

Sgott introduced us all then said, "Do you think you'll be able to halt the progress of the ice, Beth?"

"Maybe." I narrowed my gaze and studied the building critically. "It's not as thick as it was on the Myrkálfar building."

"There's a bigger area though, and after your adventures in Helsby, I'm thinking you'll not be at full strength."

"What the hell happened at Helsby?" Lugh asked, his gaze jumping from me to Sgott and back again.

"Just a little destruction via lightning," Mathi said, somewhat drolly.

Lugh sucked in a breath. "Weren't you warned—"

"Yes, unless I was grounded. And I was. Kinda."

"As statements go, that one is not at all comforting."

I smiled but returned my attention to the building. There were at least a dozen witches kneeling on the ground, each with one hand thrust into the earth and the other raised. The air around the latter rippled fiercely, a haze that washed over the building in waves.

They were drawing the heat from the earth, not the air as I'd half expected.

"You might want to push your people back, Marjorlaine," I said. "If events follow the same path as previously, they're in danger of being hit by slabs of ice."

"You cannot possibly draw enough power to shatter that much ice."

"I'm not. The knives are."

Her gaze dropped to the knives I was holding. "Silver knives cannot dissipate the power at play here."

"Silver knives can't, but these are goddess-blessed and part of a triune of power."

"Indeed? I look forward to seeing them in action, then."

She didn't bother controlling her skepticism, and I found myself suddenly understanding why Win disliked her.

I flexed my fingers against the hilts of my weapons, then strode forward with a confidence I didn't really feel. The closer I got to the building, the warmer the air became. Sweat dribbled down the back of my neck and the side of my face, but I ignored both, concentrating on the building, looking for the launching point. At the Lùtair Enterprises building it seemed to have begun at the main entrance, but here, the ice appeared to be fractionally thicker at the employees' entrance. I walked around to it and stopped several feet away. The chill coming off the ice crawled across my skin, despite the heat that otherwise pressed around me. Through it, I once again felt the witch.

Felt her fury.

This time, though, she didn't attack me. She simply withdrew. *Totally* withdrew.

The ice coating the door and the lower portions of the building instantly started to melt, the thick slabs quickly forming rivers of blue that raced down the wall and flooded the concrete.

Unease stirred through me. Her fury, and her sudden retreat, just didn't gel.

Something else was going on.

I rubbed my arms uneasily and turned, walking back to Sgott and the others.

"Well," Mathi said. "That was anticlimactic, especially after this morning."

"She fled the second she felt my presence."

Sgott frowned. "That makes no sense, even after what you did at the Lùtair building and at Kaitlyn's."

"Perhaps this was merely a diversion." My gaze shot to Lugh's. "Darby's not at your place at the moment, is she?"

"I don't think so, but I'll check."

"Might be wise for you both to stay somewhere else tonight, just in case."

He nodded and moved away to make the call. I returned my gaze to Sgott. "She might well come back once she thinks I'm gone. It looked as though she'd hacked into street cameras when she attacked the Lùtair building, so it's possible she's doing the same here."

"Even if she has," Marjorlaine commented. "It's unlikely

she'll have the strength for a second attack so soon. Not given the energy output she must have employed encasing this building and battling my people."

And I was betting that Marjorlaine, who hadn't really witnessed what this witch was capable of with the horn in her hand, was seriously underestimating her.

"Are you able to leave a team of witches here, just in case she recovers quicker than normal?" Sgott asked.

The older woman nodded. "I had a secondary team ready to step in should the battle go on much longer, so they can stay."

"Good—thank you." His gaze came back to me. "You and Mathi should go rest. We'll call you if anything unto-ward happens here."

I nodded. While a part of me wanted to remain here and monitor the situation, I was well aware that unless I got some sleep, I wouldn't be able to battle a gnat let alone this witch *or* my aunt.

Mathi touched my elbow, but as I turned to follow him back to his car, Lugh got off the phone. I stopped and said, "She okay?"

He nodded. "She's with her sister-in-law at the compound."

"Which means she's safe from any form of reprisal your aunt might be planning, but you are not," Mathi said. "I would offer you one of our company's apartments, but given your aunt appears to have done her homework and might well be planning retribution on every single person involved in the Claws quest, that might not be any safer."

I glanced at him sharply. "If your company's apart-ments aren't safe, then your private residence won't be either."

"Indeed, which is why, after I do the requested research

on Martha, I'll be spending the rest of the evening in the encampment."

Relief stirred, but so too did wisps of amusement. "That wouldn't happen to be where last night's hot date is located, would it?"

"Indeed." His gaze met mine. "I suggest *you* spend the evening somewhere other than the tavern, preferably with company."

"I'm quite able to spend a night alone."

"Yeah, but *I'd* feel better if you had company," Lugh said.

"I could fling that right back at you, brother."

"Then stay with me at Talein's. He's meeting me in half an hour with the keys to Rossita's old apartment. It's apparently undergoing renovations but remains livable."

"It's doubtful your aunt has done such a deep dive into either Lugh's contacts or Darby's that she'd know who her brother's wife is, or where she lived before she moved back to the encampment," Mathi commented. "It should be a fairly safe option."

"*Should* is not a word I'm about to rely on right now," I replied. "Besides, by bunking in together, we risk presenting her the irresistible—two targets in the one place."

"We don't know for sure she's coming after me," Lugh commented.

"We don't know she's not, either, especially after that little display at the museum. And remember, she disavowed us both when we presented her with the red knife." I half shrugged. "I think right now it might be best for me to rent a hotel room for a couple of days."

If nothing else, with Tony out of action and the guild fully aware of what was going on, she'd find it harder to employ another storm witch at such short notice, even one that was off their books. It should at least give us a day or so free to find and stop both her and Martha.

"Fine, have it your way, but if you get kidnapped or dead, I will *not* be pleased." He glanced at his watch. "I'd better go. Make sure you keep me updated on your movements."

I nodded and kissed his cheek. And, as he strode away, I found myself hoping Riayn's plans didn't include kidnapping him to bring me to heel. Because she, more than anyone, knew I would do anything to save him.

Even walk into a trap.

I shivered and rubbed my arms. Fear, not second sight. Or so I hoped.

We returned to Mathi's car, and he dropped me off at the top of the tavern's lane after first making me promise to text him once I knew where I was staying. I once again checked in with Ingrid to ensure there were no problems needing my attention, but everything was running smoothly, just as I'd expected. When she finished her update, she added, "Oh, there's a woman waiting for you in the upper bar. Been there for a good half hour, at least. Told her you might not be back for hours, but she said she wasn't in any hurry."

"Not Beira, then?" I said, in amusement.

Ingrid shook her head. "Myrkálfar, by the look of her."

My stomach dropped. Treasa. Had to be. No other Myrkálfar had a reason to come and see me.

I thanked her and headed up. Treasa was seated in a booth at the far end of the room, close to the doors that led out onto the upper row. After ordering a whisky for myself and a second drink for her—a Veuve Clicquot, I discovered, and one of my favorite champagnes—I headed over and slid into the seat opposite.

"Well, this is a surprise," I said.

She raised an eyebrow, the movement eloquent and somehow amused, though little of the latter showed in her expression. "I cannot see why given you all but demanded answers before you would even consider the gift so willingly given."

"I was expecting a text or a phone call, not another personal visit."

She took a drink then shrugged eloquently. "There are some things best said in person, and you certainly deserve your fears to be allayed in such a manner, given the lengths you went to in saving the Lùtair building."

"Given it's my aunt behind these attacks, it behooves me to go that extra length."

Surprise flickered briefly through her expression. "We were not informed of that connection."

"Sgott plays his cards close to his chest when it comes to family."

She nodded. "Meaning revenge is behind these attacks? Cynwrig theorized as much, although Sgott, again, has not confirmed them one way or the other."

"Given how well he knows Sgott, that should not surprise him. But please, warn your brother to remain safe within the Myrkálfar compound until we can sort this out."

A wry smile touched her lips and briefly flared in her eyes. "And *you* surely know Cynwrig well enough by now to understand he is not one for taking orders or following protocol he does not agree with."

And yet he was following protocol when it came to me. At least at surface level, anyway. "Which brings us neatly back to his gift. Powerful magic lies within it, and we both know it's designed to do far more than allow non-physical communication."

She nodded. "It does indeed allow sexual interactions, although the latter is rare, and only available to those who are compatible and/or committed."

"Well, he and I are not—and never will be—committed, so that leaves us with compatible. Which, given the Myrkálfar can be sexually compatible with just about everyone on the planet if they so wish, kinda makes a mockery of the rarity thing."

She laughed lightly. "It is certainly true that when we concentrate the full force of our magnetism on someone, there is little problem with compatibility. But it is a weapon as much as a delight, and again, rarely used at full capacity."

That they used sex as a weapon wasn't really news, as sex had always been used as a means of information-gathering "Is this bracelet another means of ensuring attraction?"

"Gods, no, Cynwrig would never do something like that. Not to you."

I glanced up as Zoe brought over our drinks and nodded my thanks. "Why? While there is no denying the attraction between us, our relationship started as an information resource—him using me to keep an eye on the hunt for the Claws, while I needed a source close to the council and what your lot were doing."

"That may well be true, but I doubt it is why he gifted the bracelet."

"Well, with the severing of all non-Myrkálfar personal relationships for the next three months, it would be one way of ensuring he kept up to date with what we were doing."

"Do you really think so little of my brother?"

I couldn't help a wry smile. "I may know the man extremely well sexually, but in many other ways, he remains a mystery. And he's a mystery that is keeping some serious secrets."

She took another drink and studied me for several seconds. She seemed to be considering what to say next, which only made me curious as to what she might be hiding. Because she, like he, *was* hiding something, of that I was suddenly sure.

"Is it not true that relationships starting in less-than-ideal grounds are often the strongest and deepest?"

I raised my eyebrows. "That might well be, but how deep can *our* relationship ever be when, come coronation, he's expected to pick a bride? I don't ever intend to be the other woman, Treasa."

Surprise flitted through her eyes again. She hadn't expected me to know that. "He wouldn't want you to be."

"Then what the hell *does* he want? What good can come of using the bracelet to extend a relationship that has such a limited time left anyway?"

She hesitated. "Perhaps he merely wishes to enjoy what time he *does* have left."

"And how is that fair to me? He is not the only man in my life, and perhaps I should use this break to give that other man *and* our fledgling relationship a chance to become something more."

Even if it was the last thing my heart really wanted.

Of course, my heart had already proven to be decidedly stupid.

It wasn't like I was in love with Cynwrig, even if I did fear it might become a consequence of spending too much more time with him.

"That is of course your decision to make," Treasa said softly.

I took an overly large gulp of my whisky. "Then perhaps I should return the gift—"

"You should not. It was designed for you, and solely for you. Wear it or not, that is your choice, but returning it is pointless."

"Almost as pointless as having a bracelet I cannot risk wearing, no matter how beautiful it is."

"He will be pleased to hear you think that." She paused. "If you wish to erase the magic within the bracelet, you can do so. You simply press four fingers against the surface, wait for the stars to spiral around them, and then simply say, *end this dalliance.* The magic will flee, and the bracelet will become nothing more than stars encased in stone."

I nodded, though the thought of doing so broke something deep inside. "Thank you for that."

She nodded and finished her drink. "I don't suppose you've had any time to consider Geitha's Tears?"

"I've done a little research but haven't yet discovered anything more than what you've already told me. Once this mess with my aunt is over, I'll try a little scrying."

She hesitated, then simply nodded, and rose. "Stay wary, Bethany. Deceptions abound in this world right now, and some of them wear a pleasant face."

And with those ominous words hanging between us, she left.

The urge to run after her and ask her to explain hit hard but I suspected it would be of little use. Like Cynwrig, she would only tell me what she wanted me to know, when she thought I needed to know it, especially when it involved family.

Though why I thought that might be the case here, I couldn't say.

I sighed, finished my drink, then went upstairs to pack some bags. After a quick ring around various hotels, I found a suite in the Abode Hotel, which was a modern glass-and-black-steel semicircular building a country mile away from anything I'd generally choose to stay in. It also wasn't that far away from the museum, which meant I could keep an eye out for any resumption of attack there.

I sent a message to both my brother and Mathi to let them know where I was headed, then picked up my bags and headed out of my bedroom. I'd barely reached the stairs when the wind whisked in from the still-open bedroom window and whispered her secrets.

The witch might have retreated from the museum, but she hadn't gone very far.

Right now, she was kneeling on the roof of the lovely old neoclassical bank building on the corner of Eastgate and St Werburgh Street, preparing to ice us over.

I dropped my bags, ran down the stairs, and found Ingrid. After explaining what was happening, I told her to get everyone out of the building via the rear lane.

She didn't argue. Aside from the fact she'd worked with both Mom and Gran, and had witnessed some pretty strange things over the years, she was aware of the attacks on both the tavern and me over the last few weeks. And, no doubt, also knew about the three recent ice attacks. I might not watch the news, but I knew she did.

As she started ushering the customers out and organizing the staff to quickly secure their various sections before heading out themselves, I ran back upstairs, hauled down the loft ladder, and scrambled up it.

The minute my fingers touched the upper floor, I could

feel the chill in the old wood, though it wasn't yet cold enough to form ice or kill its song. The witch had obviously flipped her method of attack again, this time going top to bottom, just as she had at Kaitlyn's.

I made no attempt to halt the steadily increasing chill. I didn't reach for my knives or drive them into the fabric of the building to break her hold on it. Doing so risked her simply retreating again. My best bet was to attack *her* rather than her ice, and my best way of doing that was via a storm.

More specifically, via lightning.

Whether I had enough strength left to do that, I honestly couldn't say. But I had to try.

After sending Mathi a quick text to tell him what was happening and what I was about to do, I grabbed the ottoman footstool in front of Mom's chair and carried it down to the skylight at the end of the room. I still hadn't gotten around to getting it fixed, so it remained locked in place by a long but sturdy piece of wire. I undid that, then leaped onto the footstool and pushed the skylight all the way open. Stars twinkled high above, but I could feel the distant caress of thunder and hoped like hell there was enough power within it to stop the witch hiding further down the street. After a quick plea to any gods that might be listening to give me a damn break for a change, I grabbed the sides of the skylight and half jumped, half wiggled, my ass onto the roof. The slates were slick with moss, forcing me to concentrate and proceed cautiously when all I wanted to do was damn well run. Even so, I slipped more than once, but each time managed to catch my balance before sliding right over the edge. I reached my neighbor's rooftop without killing myself and sighed in relief, but it was likely a little too early given there remained a good half dozen buildings between me and the witch.

A quick glance behind me revealed the tiles now had a silver sheen. If I didn't stop her soon, the building's song would start dying.

I swore and moved on. Thankfully, the newer rear sections of the next couple of buildings weren't as steep as mine, allowing me to go faster. Two buildings from the end of the street and the bank building, however, I struck a large problem—an additional floor that had been tacked on top of the old building. I scanned it crossly—partially because the heritage council had given us shit for raising the tavern's roof and yet had allowed this monstrosity to be built—looking for a way up. There was no ladder and nothing I could stand on. Nothing that wouldn't buckle under my weight, anyway.

Which meant *this* roof would have to do. She wouldn't at least see me from here, and it was doubtful she'd sense me. All her concentration and strength were probably being channeled into icing over the tavern, so it was unlikely she'd notice the gathering force of electricity in the air until it was too late.

I recalled the finger of wind that had warned me of her presence and sent it skittering forward again to get a clearer indication of her location; it returned with news she was near the front corner of the bank building, a position that would give her good views of both streets.

Meaning she likely planned to run again the minute she either sensed my presence in her ice or saw the IIT swarming the area.

I took a long deep breath that did little to ease the trembling weariness that remained deep within, then drew my knives and reached for the distant clouds. Technically, I should be on the ground and grounded, but there were too many people out on the streets and, if things went wrong, too many people that could be hurt. But shoving a blade into the slate flooring in the kitchen at Tony's had certainly succeeded in ridding my body of the lingering remnants of lightning, so it should work equally as well here. And, at the very least, this building had a long expanse of slate, and that hopefully meant it would more easily disperse the force I was about to call down.

If I could call it down.

I closed my eyes, pictured the witch's position, then raised a knife and reached for the electricity that gently rolled through that distant storm. Pain knifed through my brain, and a gasp escaped. It was just as well I was already sitting because I definitely would have fallen. Moisture squeezed past closed eyelids, but I bit my lip, using one pain to counter the other as I continued to call to the storm. After a moment, thunder cracked, a distant but powerful force, then light shot across the dark sky, momentarily blotting out the stars as it streaked toward me—a fierceness I could not only feel but see through closed eyelids.

The lightning hit the raised blade, and pain exploded through me. While the storm's electricity was nowhere near as powerful as the tempest I'd called down earlier, my insides now felt like they were being boiled alive. Doing this twice in one day without giving my body a decent chance to rest was obviously *not* a good thing.

I quickly fixed the witch's position in my mind, then pointed my second knife in her direction and unleashed the power, doing my best to force all the inner electricity through the blade and back into the air. My lungs burned, and I couldn't seem to get enough air into my body—a body that was on fire figuratively if not yet literally—and my vision was clouding over.

If I didn't get rid of the heat very quickly, I could die, just as Beira had warned.

I thrust the knife point into a slate tile, somehow managing not to slice all the way through and hit the framework underneath. The slate itself was fire resistant, but the wooden fabric of the building was not, and the last thing I wanted was to set it on fire or fry all their electrics.

The blade began to pulse and the tiles underneath me became heated. My body continued to shake, and my vision became tunnel-like as I zoomed toward unconsciousness. I dropped one knife, dragged my phone from my pocket, and used voice command to send Mathi another text that simply said, *Drained. Hurry.*

It took the last of my strength.

When I came to, he was squatting beside me, a bottle of water in one hand and a block of chocolate in the other. I was somehow still gripping the knife, though I'd fallen sideways heavily enough to crack nearby tiles. How I managed not to skewer myself with the knife's hilt I'll never know.

"You brought me chocolate," I croaked. "And here I was thinking you didn't care."

"I will always care, just not in the way you deserve." He put them both down, then gently helped me sit upright. My breath hissed through clenched teeth, and muscles from top to bottom protested. Even my damn hair seemed to hurt. He handed me the bottle of water, then opened the chocolate for me. "I take it our witch got away again?"

"I actually don't know. She was on the bank building's rooftop." I sheathed the knives, took a long drink, then accepted the row of chocolate he handed me, demolishing it in seconds. "What time is it?"

There was still a lot of noise coming from the streets below, and the moon hadn't appeared to have risen too much more, so I doubted hours had passed. But we had a witch to deal with, and if she wasn't dead, then we needed to get her—and the horn—back to Borrhás.

Before he decided we'd had enough time and started a little destruction of his own.

"It's just gone eight," Mathi replied. "And please, do not ever send me a text stating that you're drained again. Had I a heart, it would have had an attack."

"Idiot." But at least I'd been out for less than five minutes. I held out my right hand. "Help me up."

"I don't think that's wise. Your hair looks kinda fried and your eyes are as red as Tony's were."

"Neither of which alters the fact we need to check whether I managed to stop the witch or not, and if I *did*, we can't let the IIT know. Not when we have a god demanding her soul."

He hesitated, then nodded and took my hand; he was nothing if not practical. Though he was as gentle as possible, the movement still had a dozen different parts of my body protesting, and another hiss escaped.

It was apparently too much for him to handle, because he scowled and said, "Seriously, you need to let me go take care of the witch while you—"

"You can't take her to Borrhás, Mathi. You can't even get into Liadon's domain."

"I'm well aware of that, but if she's not dead, I can keep her under sedation until you're capable—"

"We're running out of time. We need to do it now."

Why I was suddenly sure of that, I couldn't say. Maybe

second sight was subtly prodding; maybe it was simply fear. Either way, we dare not waste precious minutes, let alone hours.

"Fine," he said, voice flat. A sure sign he was seriously annoyed.

I took several deep breaths in an attempt to ease the latest wave of dizziness hitting my brain, then ate some more chocolate and put it and the water into my coat pocket before cautiously moving forward. Mathi kept close, catching me when my steps wavered, or feet slipped. Thankfully, we made it back to my rooftop and the skylight in one piece. Mathi went down first and steadied me as I followed.

After he released the skylight and had leashed it in place again, I said, "How did you get here so quickly?"

"I'd just left the IIT building when the lightning streaked across the sky. I guessed that meant you were either in trouble or battling the witch, so I asked to be driven here. *That* was when I received your first text. Knowing your propensity for tackling problems alone, I do believe we broke the local speed limits getting here."

I smiled, though it felt a somewhat pale imitation of its usual self. "But how did you get in? Ingrid would have locked up when she left, and I can't see her giving you the code without clearing it with me first."

"She didn't have to, because I know the rear code."

I glanced up as I cautiously went down the loft ladder. "You do? How?"

"I pay attention, that's how."

His voice was wry, and I couldn't help smiling. "I guess, given the current situation with the council, that's probably wise anyway."

I stepped away from the ladder, drank more water, then

tucked it back into my pocket and pulled out the chocolate again. I was starting to feel a little more "human" even if the aching weariness was probably three times worse than it had been.

I followed him down the stairs, and we headed out the back of the building where Ingrid, the staff, and most of our customers waited.

"Clear?" she asked.

I nodded. "Give everyone a free drink for the inconvenience."

A cheer went up at that bit of news. I smiled and continued down the lane. Mathi's car waited in a no-standing zone, but he motioned the driver to remain and turned right, hurrying down to the next lane.

"There's no rear or rooftop entry to the bank building from here," I said, a little confused. Which wasn't surprising given my brain was still spinning out every now and again, forcing me to run my fingers against the side of a building to regain my center.

"Not directly. But there's an old fire escape up ahead, and we can use that to get up to its roof then make our way across."

I had no idea there was a fire escape in this lane and I'd certainly traversed it plenty of times over the decades. As it turned out, there was a good reason why—it was one of those ones where the ladder retracted back up to the first landing if it wasn't in use. If you didn't look up, you wouldn't see it.

He lightly leapt high, pulled the ladder down, and then climbed up. I followed at a slower pace, not trusting the rather rusted-looking framework. It held my weight even if it creaked ominously. Once he'd retracted the ladder again, we continued up the rest of the fire escape until we reached the roof and then carefully made our way across to the bank building next door.

There was no sign of our witch on this side of the roof, so I caught the wind and spun it lightly forward. Even that had tears stinging my eyes. I blinked them away and, after a few seconds, the wind came back with the news she remained. It couldn't tell me if she was alive or dead, of course, but the fact she wasn't moving did point to her being seriously injured. But then, I *had* aimed two bolts of lightning at her. At the very least, her respiratory system would have been momentarily paralyzed, and she might have even suffered secondary burns as her hair or clothes cindered.

"She's still there," I told Mathi.

"Good. Let's keep moving, before someone reports us."

"Like you're actually worried about that," I said dryly.

"I'm not, but it is the sort of thing you tend to get overly concerned about."

Given I couldn't actually argue that point, I simply motioned him to continue. We cautiously climbed to the roof ridge, then paused again, keeping low as we scanned the other side. She was lying right where the wind had said, near the old chimney, and had one arm stretched out above her head and a pool of water surrounding her fingers—the melted remnants of her ice attack, perhaps? A strangely pale circle of what looked like ash surrounded the rest of her body. I suspected it was a result of my lightning, and if it could do that to slate then there was very little chance she'd survived.

Which was in truth a relief.

I might not have any choice about handing over this woman or my aunt, but I just couldn't stomach the thought of doing so when they were alive.

Of course, that also led to another major problem—killing my aunt. That was something I still didn't want to contemplate, even in self-defense.

"I'm not seeing the horn," Mathi commented. "So it's either under her body or Riayn has beaten us here."

"I can't see my aunt physically coming up here, but I certainly wouldn't put it past her to have hired a shifter to keep an eye on Martha's movements. She's obviously developed serious trust issues—"

"And just as obviously leapt off sanity's edge."

"—and is wealthy enough to be able to afford a twenty-four-hour watch."

"The IIT would have frozen her accounts when she was supposedly killed, but that does not mean she has no access to money. Not these days." Mathi glanced skyward. "I'm not seeing any indication we've a winged watcher."

"The wind agrees, but maybe that's because they've already taken the horn to my aunt."

"Possibly."

He carefully slipped down the other side. I followed him over to our witch and stopped close to her feet. The soles of her shoes, I noted, had been burned out and her feet blackened. I gulped, not really sure I wanted to see anything more, but we needed to know whether the horn was here or not, and to do that, we needed to turn her over.

"If the horn *is* underneath her," I said. "You can't touch it with bare skin. Borrhás might have said it's only when you use the horn with hatred or revenge in your heart that your fate is sealed to ice, but let's not take any chances."

He nodded. "She looks as stiff as a board, and it's too soon for rigor mortis to have set in."

"Perhaps when he mentioned being wrapped in ice, he

meant *immediately* upon death." I rubbed my arms. "They're not going to get her into a body bag like that."

"They'll probably use a shroud."

He squatted beside her then carefully rolled her onto her back. I couldn't help but gasp. One side of her face was completely covered by a network of tiny red welts that resembled a river and its tributaries. They extended down her neck and across one breast, which was visible thanks to her sweater and a portion of her bra being burned away. There were other patches of burning dotted across the rest of her clothing, and I really didn't dare look closer to see if the revealed skin bore the same sort of scarring.

The horn—which was indeed whole—remained clenched in her left hand, but her fingers were seemingly welded to it by bands of ice. Given they hadn't existed when second sight had shown me her location in the café, it must have happened when death had claimed her. Perhaps it was a means of not being parted from the person who'd abused its power—a way of ensuring the abuser's body and soul could be claimed by Borrhás. Godly relics often had minds of their own, so it was entirely possible.

"It looks like she'll have to be moved as is," Mathi said. "And that's not going to be easy."

"The whole carrying her across several rooftops and then getting her down that fire escape aside, someone is bound to report us carrying a dead person through the streets."

"Indeed, which is why our best bet is to not walk across the roof or through the streets at all."

"But how—' I stopped. "Company helicopter? Isn't this area out of bounds for all air traffic except for emergency air evacs?"

"I can get special dispensation from the council if necessary, but it might—"

"Special dispensation could take days, and to repeat, we haven't got that long."

"You forget we've been tasked with returning—"

"To Borrhás, not the council."

He rolled his eyes. "Seriously, can you just let me finish a sentence?"

I couldn't help the smile that tugged briefly at my lips. "I could; not sure that I will."

Amusement briefly echoed in his eyes. "The minute they hear Liadon has been tasked by the god himself to retrieve his artifact, they'll work with inhuman speed to get us all that we need. Which, in this case, is a fire ladder to get us all off this roof, and either an ambulance or a morgue van to transport us and the body over to the council's building."

"And while you arrange all that, I will drink water and eat the rest of this block of chocolate."

"The *whole* block?"

"You should have seen how many blocks I went through when we broke up."

He shook his head, got out his phone, and started making calls. I retreated to the other side of the roof and sat down to eat, drink, and rest. By the time the fire brigade had arrived, I'd completed my self-assigned tasks but didn't really feel any better. Only a good ten hours—or more—of sleep would do that.

But actual sleep wasn't something I was going to get all that much of... unconsciousness was another matter entirely.

I frowned at the thought but didn't have the chance to chase it down as Mathi walked over. "They're raising the ladder now. Once we're down and Martha has been removed, a morgue vehicle will transfer us all over to the council's headquarters. Dhruv Eadevane will meet us in the foyer to witness and document the horn's return."

"I'm sure Liadon would make a note of it."

"No doubt, but they nevertheless want to make their own record of it in case anything is said in the future."

I personally thought it was a little too late for them to be worrying about future records, but I wasn't about to say that to any of them. Eadevane seemed friendly enough now that I'd spoken to him outside the confines of the council chambers, and I needed all the friends I could get there, especially if, after the coronation, Cynwrig stepped away from it.

I really hoped he didn't. Even if our relationship was doomed, it would still be nice to see him—talk to him—occasionally.

"Come on, up you get." Mathi held out a hand. "The sooner we get this task done, the sooner you can get to your hotel and get some rest."

I put my hand in his and once again he hauled me up easily. "I need to return home first—I left my overnight bags there."

"That might not be safe."

"The tavern is full of people. If my aunt intended to send anyone after me, she'd only do so when the place was closed and there were no possible witnesses. As long as I'm gone well before that happens, it'll be fine."

"Famous last words," he growled, but didn't actually argue.

We were roped up, then sent down the ladder and escorted over to the morgue truck, which was nothing more than a basic white van in appearance. A stretcher and a shroud were sent up to the roof, and a few minutes later she was brought back down and carried over to the van. Once they'd placed her on a trolley and closed the rear door, we climbed into the front and were soon underway. The driver didn't speak—perhaps he'd been told not to—but he did make record time getting over to the council building, despite the traffic.

Once there, he opened the rear door, pulled out the trolley, and motioned Mathi to take over. He did so, quickly wheeling over to the main doors, which the guard was already holding open.

Eadevane waited between the stairs and the elevators, his gaze scanning us critically before sweeping across the covered trolley. "And the horn?"

Mathi stopped, undid the straps, then flipped away the shroud. Martha lay on her side, and the chill radiating from her body was now sharp enough that I could feel it from several feet away. The horn might not currently be in use, but it remained dangerous.

Eadevane moved around taking photos, then nodded and motioned Mathi to cover her up again. "There is no elevator to Liadon's door, and I suspect it would also be nigh on impossible to get the stretcher up the stairs."

"I'll use the air to get her body up there," I said.

Mathi frowned. "Unwise, given your current state. We can simply carry her—"

"No," I cut in, "we can't. She'll be just as hard to maneuver in her current state as the stretcher and besides, we can't risk touching the horn."

"The shroud should—"

"She may be dead, but that horn is still active. Look at the trolley's legs, Mathi."

His gaze darted down. The visible metal sections now held the slightest silver sheen.

"We can't risk the chill leaching across to us via contact, no matter how brief or protected we may be."

He didn't look happy but didn't argue any further, either. The plain fact of the matter was, I was the only one who could get into Liadon's domain and would probably end up having to use the air anyway.

"You head up while I release the remaining straps."

I nodded and walked around the two men to the elevator. There might be only two flights between me and Liadon's stairs, but the less I had to climb, the better for my energy levels.

Even so, by the time I reached her door, my breath was a harsh rasp and my body shaking. I pressed a hand against the unnatural-feeling wood and waited for it to do its scanner thing. Once it had opened, I stepped back, leaned over the metal railing, and shouted, "Okay, I'm here. She clear?"

"Yes," Mathi said. "I'll come up and wait for you."

"You don't—"

"I do, and I am."

His tone said "don't bother arguing" so for once, I didn't. I sucked in a deeper breath, then created a rope of air and flung it down to Martha. Pain exploded through my brain, and I hissed, fighting tears as I hauled the older woman's body off the trolley and up through the atrium. A red mist began to fall across my vision, but I ignored the warning and dragged Martha's body over the railing, then thrust her into Liadon's tunnel. I staggered in after her but had barely taken half a dozen steps when my strength gave out, and both Martha and I crashed to the shiny black stone.

For several minutes, I didn't move. Couldn't move. I just knelt there, my arms huddled around my body as I rocked back and forth, fighting the dark unconsciousness that threatened to overwhelm me. While I doubted Liadon meant me any harm, there was probably a very good reason the sheer black walls separated me from the other beings that inhabited this place.

And walls, no matter what kind, could always be breached if the attack was determined enough.

After a few more minutes, a greenish light began to press past closed eyelids. I forced them open and glanced up. The orb hovered several feet in front of me. Martha was nowhere to be seen. She'd obviously been silently swept away while I'd been wrapped in misery.

"Borrhás wishes to thank you for the return of his horn" came Liadon's soft comment. "And for the soul and the flesh of the one who wielded it so unjustly."

I nodded. I really couldn't do anything else.

The orb drifted closer, its light washing waves of oddly warm air across my face and down my length. Strength trickled back into my system, and the immediate desire to simply collapse retreated a fraction.

I sucked in a breath, then whispered, my voice still tremulous, "Thank you."

"I wish I could do more, but I am considered neutral in these games of theirs and will not risk that position being altered. What I protect is too valuable."

And what she protected was what I was hoping to use to find my mom's killers, so I wasn't about to argue.

"He did also wish me to remind you that he wants the woman behind this scheme captured as soon as possible. He does, however, understand that even a godling needs rest."

"That's good of him," I muttered.

Her amusement swam around me, even though she wasn't physically present. "You have no idea how true a statement that is. You should go and recover. Darkness still hunts you, and you will need the strength to survive what comes."

"I don't suppose you want to expand on what comes?"

"Again, that would be a risk too far."

And with that, her presence withdrew, though her orb remained. I sighed, pushed wearily to my feet, and staggered back to the door. Mathi was waiting on the other side.

He gripped my arm with one hand to keep me upright, then gave me a large reusable mug filled with hot tea. I took a sip and sighed in happiness. "Where the hell did you get this? The council chambers?"

"Good grief, no, that muck is undrinkable. I had Grant go fetch some."

"What happened to Marc?"

"He's the company driver and now off duty. Grant is a recent hire and will fill in for Henrick when he has time off or is otherwise unavailable."

"Ah." I took another sip, and though the tiredness remained, strength was definitely returning. While it was probably due more to Liadon's gift of healing than the tea, I wasn't about to give said tea up.

"You up to walking down, or shall we wait a few more minutes?" he asked.

"As long as we don't rush, I'll be fine."

He raised his eyebrows but didn't say anything. Instead, he turned and headed down in front of me, keeping close enough that should I slip or falter, he could easily catch me.

I didn't slip, though by the time we reached street level,

the temporary strength Liadon had gifted me was disappearing fast. I made it to the car, dropped the now empty reusable mug into a holder, then closed my eyes and leaned back against the headrest, listening to the gentle thrum of the engine as Grant whisked us away into the traffic.

"Right," Mathi said, after what seemed only a few minutes. "I'll go get your bags, then we'll escort you over to the hotel."

I nodded. I should have argued, really, because not doing so would only confirm his suspicions that I wasn't in a great state, but in all honesty, I just didn't have the strength. He returned what seemed to be only a couple of minutes later, tossed my bags into the trunk, then climbed back in and gave Grant the address of the hotel.

When we arrived, he collected my bags, then collected me and escorted me inside, checking me in and then taking me up to the room—and made me wait in the hall while he checked it was empty and safe.

"Really," I said, caught between amusement and annoyance, "isn't this all a little over the top?"

"No. And Lugh would expect nothing less." He glanced at me. "Would you be protesting if it was Cynwrig being overcautious?"

"Yes."

"You lie, Bethany Aodhán." He waved me inside. "Now, make sure you lock this door—using both the supplied locks and your own wood weaving—and get some rest. I'll be here tomorrow—"

"Come for breakfast," I said. "Apparently they do a fantastic full English downstairs. My treat."

"Did I not mention me being able to claim all expenses?"

"Yes, so I'll give you the docket."

He laughed, kissed my cheek, and left. I locked the door behind him, then gently pressed my fingers against the frame and wove the two together. No one was getting into this room—not without making a whole lot of noise, anyway. Well, my aunt could, but I doubted she'd show her face so readily. It was more likely she'd send more lackeys.

I staggered into the bathroom to grab a quick shower, then tugged on a T-shirt and some knickers and climbed into bed. After sending a quick text to Lugh to tell him where I was, I fell, long and hard, into sleep.

I wasn't sure what woke me gods knew how many hours later. I lay there for several minutes with my eyes closed, listening to the gentle song of the building, though it seemed much more distant than it should have been. It spoke of movement, but I wasn't sure if it was in this room, in the hall beyond, or even several floors away. Confusion swirled through me, and I tried to shift, tried to throw off the blankets, but my limbs felt as heavy as my mind, and I just couldn't.

Alarm stirred even as the song of the wood briefly sharpened in warning.

Then a cloth clamped over my nose and mouth while hands held me down. I struggled, but every breath was filled with the slightly sweet-smelling scent that soaked the cloth, and it made my head spin. Darkness rushed in.

The last thing I clearly remembered was a voice. A familiar voice.

My aunt's voice.

CHAPTER
THIRTEEN

WAKING WAS A SLOW AND PAINFUL PROCESS. MY HEAD WAS ON fire, my lungs burned, and my limbs were achy and bruised. It really felt like someone had spent the last few hours using me as a football and, given who now held me captive, I wouldn't be at all surprised if that was a reality rather than a perception.

I didn't bother moving. Didn't bother opening my eyes. Right now, neither was wise, not until I had a full grasp of the situation, anyway. Nor did I immediately reach for the wind; instead, I just listened. To the building, to the air, to the very distant storm that raged beyond the walls of where I lay. Even making that vaguest connection to the storm hurt, though not as fiercely as it had who knew how many hours earlier. It was nevertheless a warning I wasn't yet at full strength.

I had no sense of anyone in the room with me, and the building's wood song, while present, was as distant as the storm. This place, this room, was made of stone, and the bed on which I lay metal—something I knew because the slats were digging into my spine. Sunlight caressed my face, its warmth muted, suggesting it was late afternoon. My hands and feet weren't tied, which surprised me a little until I remembered who had me.

Fuck... had she done to me what I'd done to Vincentia?

I tried to move, but other than an answering twitch in my fingers and toes, I couldn't. And this time, it had nothing to do with overextending my strength. The bitch had deep-magicked me.

I swore, long and loud, and from somewhere in the room to my left came a tinny laugh.

"The betrayer learns of her predicament" came the comment. "How delicious."

I opened my eyes and looked around. As I'd sensed, the room was bare stone and held little in the way of furniture aside from this bed. The window to my left was grimy and barred, and what little I could see of the floor from my supine position suggested it was stone. I couldn't see any cameras from my current, somewhat limited, field of vision, but what I did spot was a small metal speaker perched on the window's stone sill.

"Why are you doing this, Riayn? I didn't kill Vincentia, and I didn't betray either you or her. In fact—"

"You possess what should have always been hers by virtue of greater suitability and skills. You stole what had been given—"

"That is a bald-faced lie," I cut in brusquely. "The codex was never yours, and you had no right to gift it to her."

She didn't tell me to shut up, which surprised me, but simply continued on, as if I hadn't spoken. "The knives and the Eye are now mine, but the codex is missing. Where is it, Bethany?"

I tried not to answer. Fought the words that pressed

against my lips with all the strength I had, but, like so many of those I'd forced to comply, it was impossible.

I ground the answer out and then swore at her again.

"The tavern upbringing has certainly gifted you with colorful vocabulary," she said with a laugh.

"The tavern wench will have the *last* laugh, Aunt. The god who made the horn is displeased with your use of it, and he hunts you."

"The old gods disappeared from this world eons ago. I have no fear of what does not exist."

"Tell that to Martha. She now lies wrapped in ice, her soul forever bound to her body."

"Using godly relics always comes at a cost." Her reply was dismissive. "It sounds like she simply raised more than she could humanly control."

"No, she raised that force in anger and revenge, just as you directed. It is for that reason Borrhás comes for you."

"I think the chloroform has addled your brains, my dear niece. And I, well, I'll worry about this god of yours no more than I'll worry about Lugh finding you in time."

"The wise never would underestimate my brother."

"Perhaps that is true, but I am not located in your section of the complex, and he will come for you first, giving me time to escape. And then, of course, there is the toxin that even now flows through your veins. You have no more than ten hours, my dear niece, to find help, and even if you do, survival is not guaranteed."

My heart began to beat a whole lot faster—never a good thing if I'd been injected with something deadly. "Toxin? What fucking toxin?"

"It's just a little natural something Stace had in her bag of tricks before I forced her on."

Was that bag of tricks the same one we'd found in the

chamber under the souterrain? The one that had held the near-empty vial of Dearil?

"Goddamn it, you've magicked, so why inject me? And if you intend to kill me, why not do so now?"

I'm pretty sure I knew why—she wanted me to suffer before I died. Wanted me to know I'd lost everything I held dear, just as she had. Which probably meant she had a trap waiting for Lugh here, too.

As Mathi had said, she'd well and truly leapt off sanity's ledge.

"Because there's always a chance you have somehow been less than honest about the codex's location. Wouldn't want you to die before I have that in my hands, now would I?"

"Meaning you're retrieving it yourself?"

"Oh, I am not that foolish."

Which was a damn shame, because Sgott would have placed the tavern under tight scrutiny the minute he and everyone else realized I was missing—and they should have by now, given that I'd missed my breakfast meeting with Mathi. "What did you inject me with?"

I might suspect, but it never hurt to have it confirmed. Besides, she would think it odd if I didn't ask.

"What does it matter to you? You'll be dead."

"If you're so certain of that, what does it hurt to tell me? Besides, you wouldn't really want to be responsible for my death, would you, and risk the curse when you're on the cusp of achieving all that you wanted?"

She laughed—a soft sound that reminded me of Mom's and just made the inner anger surge all that much more. My fingers twitched again, the movement stronger this time. Was anger the key to breaking her orders? Surely not, because if it had been that simple to break pixie magic, then all the pissed-off people I'd used it on over the last few weeks would have surely broken free.

"Oh, I think I'm way past worrying about the curse, given how many lives I have now taken," she drawled. "As for death, been there, done that. It no longer holds any fear for me."

Meaning we were right—she had been killed and revived. "Did Peregrine Stace aid you in that bit of trickery?"

"Indeed. Shame she got a little too demanding—she'd been useful up until that point."

"Where are my knives and the Eye, Aunt?"

"The Eye adorns my neck—such a charming cage you've made for it, I must say—and the knives are safely tucked away, never to be found by you and your brother. They will fetch a pretty price on the black market, I'm sure."

"They were goddess gifted to our family, Riayn. You can't sell them—"

"Oh, you're in no position to be telling me what to do. Now, be still and be quiet, dear Bethany, until I say otherwise. I have a retrieval mission to organize."

My mouth snapped shut, and anger surged anew. I clenched my hands and then wondered why that was happening. I had no charm or other form of magical interference on me, and while the knives... I blinked. The knives countered any and all magic that attacked me. Was it possible that protection extended to a pixie's personal magic?

It was more than possible, given the twitching that had been barely negligible when I'd first woken was increasing in intensity as the minutes ticked by. To date, the knives' protection had only worked when I was awake and aware, so it would make sense that it hadn't started countermanding my aunt's magic until I'd regained consciousness.

Of course, at the current speed of disentanglement, I'd be dead before I could fully move, but maybe I could speed the process up if the knives were physically in my hands. It was worth a try and, given Riayn had said they were tucked away securely, maybe she wouldn't even notice they were missing until the blades were at her throat and it was all too damn late to say sorry.

I closed my eyes and silently called to them. For several seconds, nothing happened, and I couldn't help but wonder if being compelled by my aunt was somehow running interference with the signal. Then the air shimmered and the two of them thudded into my waiting hands. I gripped as tightly as I could, relief so fierce tears stung my eyes. With these weapons in my possession, I had a real chance of surviving.

The minutes continued to tick by as the knives pulsed and burned, sending a spray of purple light spiraling through the gathering shadows. Gradually, ever so gradually, the feeling of life and strength seeped back into my limbs. I carefully turned my head and examined the room more fully. It was narrow and rectangular and reminded me of a prison cell. An old, abandoned cell—something bad guys had thrown me in once before. It also explained the metal nature of the bed and the cobwebs and dust that adorned its frame and every corner of the room. The nearby window was small; the glass was cracked and grimy and the bars thick. The distance between bars was narrow; I'd barely get an arm through that gap, let alone my head or ass.

The door lay to my right and was a mix of metal and wood. No wood song emanated from it, though even if it *had*, I wouldn't have been able to use it. My aunt would feel it the minute I tried to connect to or use the song's power.

The air, my knives, and my wits were my only weapons, and there was a bit of me that couldn't help thinking, *Gods help me.*

After a few more minutes, I carefully tested my limbs for movement, then slowly swung my legs over the edge of the bed and sat up. The effort had my head spinning, and I had no idea if it was the toxin or the lingering remnants of overexertion.

I drew in several deep but silent breaths, then carefully pushed upright. Another repeat of spinning, but it didn't last quite so long this time. I studied the speaker for a second, waiting for it to squawk to life, then slowly, carefully walked over to the door. There was no lock on this side, which made sense if this had once been a jail cell. I bent slightly but couldn't see anything through the slight crack between the frame and the door—not even a bolt.

I raised a knife and lightly pressed it against the frame. The blade pulsed, and there was the softest fizzle of energy, accompanied by a sharp, almost metallic scent. The door silently cracked open.

I swallowed heavily to ease the sudden dryness in my throat, then gathered the air and pushed her through the gap. Minutes passed, and tension had sweat trickling down my spine. I shifted from one bare foot to the other, and it was only then that I realized I was still wearing nothing more than knickers and a T-shirt.

Great. Just great.

The wind returned, her whispers clear and sharp in my ears. The building was a two-story stone construction with a central heart and two wings. I was on the first floor of the right wing, with two men stationed down the hall and several others roaming the floor below. All of them were armed.

My aunt was located in the other wing, in an office close to an external exit.

All of which meant I'd have to be damn fast when I took out the two closest men, otherwise I risked them getting a warning out to Riayn and any others who patrolled this place.

After sending another silent prayer to gods likely more intent on enjoying the situation I was in rather than helping, I thrust the door open and sent the air spinning toward the two men at the far end of the hall. I chased after it, my steps echoing on the cold stone and my heart beating so loud it was a drum that filled the silence.

The two men turned and raised their guns, but before either of them could fire, my air-based battering ram sent them flying. One smashed back against the wall with a loud crack and dropped unconscious to the floor. The other hit the metal bars that divided this section of cells from the next and bounced back onto his feet. I swore, drew back my arm, and threw a knife... just as he fired his weapon.

I threw myself sideways. Felt metal thud into my shoulder and the explosion of pain. Hit the ground hard but somehow rolled onto my knees, the other knife gripped fiercely in my left hand while blood soaked through the T-shirt and ran down my right.

My throw might not have been fast enough, but it had been true. The man lay on his back, the knife hilt deep in his forehead.

The wind swirled around me again. The men on the floor below had heard the shot and were running toward the nearby stairs. I swallowed heavily and pushed upright, staggering sideways slightly as the stone under my feet briefly rolled and shuddered. I flung out my right hand to steady myself, only realizing the mistake when my fingers hit the wall. Waves of pain reverberated up my arm and through the mess that was my shoulder, swiftly followed by thick waves of nausea. Sweat broke out heavily across my forehead, and I breathed deep in an effort to battle the looming threat of unconsciousness.

But I was running out of time, and I didn't need the wind to tell me that.

I pushed away from the wall and ran like a drunkard toward the metal gate and the stranger I'd killed. I pulled my knife from his head, doing my best to ignore the bits of flesh and bone and gods knows what else clinging to the blade, and then stepped over him and opened the gate.

The vibrations of movement were drawing closer, and it wasn't just the air's warning now; the stone under my feet echoed with the same urgent ferocity.

I shook my head, wondering whether the combination of drugs and blood loss was affecting my senses, then followed the tug of the wind to the right, away from the thunder of approaching steps. The hall was long and straight, my steps less so, but I made it to a second, smaller set of stairs before the other men appeared behind me.

I staggered down, but I was leaving a trail behind me now, bloody breadcrumbs that would lead the men who'd just reached my guards straight to me. There was nothing I could do about it. The increasingly ferocious movement of the stone under my feet and my growing lack of strength simply made it impossible to go any faster.

I hit the bottom step and staggered down the hall, following the wind's whispers toward my aunt. She was probably aware of my escape by now, but hopefully, she'd count on her people recapturing me rather than simply running.

Movement, to my left. I raised a knife defensively, felt

more than saw my attacker leap back. I didn't dare follow up with another blow; aside from the fact I simply didn't have the strength, I'd more than likely fall. I did the next best thing and raised a thick barrier of air between us. He hit it and bounced back hard, landing on his butt, his gun slithering away from his grip. I flipped the knife in my left hand, caught it by the blade, and smashed the hilt with all the strength I had across his face. As he fell back, my air barrier disintegrated. I didn't bother regathering it. Doing so would take what little strength I had left.

It was a mistake. A *big* mistake.

I'd barely taken two steps when I was hit from behind and sent sprawling onto the floor, skinning my knees and knuckles, the knives falling from my grip as pain exploded through my shoulder and on through the rest of me. A bloody mist filled my eyes and blurred my vision, but I didn't need to see to know what was coming straight at me.

I called to a knife, felt it thud into my left hand, then swept it back viciously. Heard him leap out of reach, heard the thick, confident chuckle that followed. He thought me easy prey.

He thought wrong.

I flung the air at him, swept him off his feet, and smashed him hard against the ceiling. Bones cracked, a sickening sound, but I was beyond caring. As he thudded lifelessly back to the now convulsing floor, I pushed upright yet again and staggered on.

But that red mist was increasing, and my strength fading as fast as the blood flowing down my arm.

If I didn't get to my aunt soon, I wouldn't get to her at all.

From up ahead came a soft *whoomp* and the sound of fighting. The violence underneath my feet increased, making it nigh on impossible to walk in anything resembling a straight line. Or maybe the floor wasn't moving at all; maybe it, like the sound of distant fighting, was nothing more than a hallucination caused by the Dearil's increasing grip on my system.

I didn't know and didn't have the time or energy to contemplate it.

I staggered on, down to the end of the hall and into a foyer that was wide and high, and, once upon a time, undoubtedly grand. But trees now riddled its expanse, reaching for skies visible through the collapsed roof, and the air held the hint of rot.

My aunt was standing on the far side, close to an exit sign. "Stop, dear Bethany."

I didn't.

"Stop, or you will be killed."

I continued to ignore her. I had no idea what she saw in my expression, but fear flicked briefly through hers. She took a step back, and it was only then that I saw she was holding a gun.

"I haven't used one of these all too often, but I figure that with the sixteen bullets at my disposal, at least one of them will prove fatal."

I stopped. That was when I saw the limbs of trees that stood at her back, between her and the exit, were extending sharp, woody fingers toward her. I blinked, but the movement continued. Real or imaginary? I had no goddamn idea.

I shifted the bloody knife from my right hand to my left, then slowly wove the air around my fingers. My head was a mess of agony and confusion, my arm becoming number by the moment, and my knees threatening to buckle, but sheer force of will—or sheer fucking stubbornness—kept me upright and focused, at least as much as possible given the amount of blood I was losing and the drug wreaking havoc in my system.

"Give me the Eye, Aunt."

"You are not the one giving orders—"

"In case it's escaped your notice, neither are you."

A warning whispered past my ear. I half turned, saw a man attempting to creep up on me, and with a flick of air, sent him tumbling backward. Then I whipped the leash at my aunt, ripped the Eye from her neck, and brought it back to me, lightly wrapping its chain around the hilt of one of the knives. As the caged Eye touched the blade, purple lightning exploded around me, a force that was fierce, threatening, and protective.

Fear stepped fully into her expression, and her grip on the gun barrel tightened. "I have no idea what the fuck is going on or how the fuck you are doing what you are doing, but you will die in this place, right here, right now, and I will dance on your bones with bloody glee."

And with that, she raised her gun and fired.

As she did, two things happened.

The thick wooden fingers of the trees whipped around her, pinning her arm and the gun close to her body, preventing her from getting more than one shot off.

At the same time, the floor between me and her erupted upwards and caught the bullet in its stony maw, preventing it from getting anywhere near me.

For several seconds, I simply stared, unable to believe what I'd just witnessed. It had to be an illusion, didn't it? Perhaps these were nothing more than my dying dreams, formed in a drug-addled mind that refused to accept either defeat or death.

Then someone leapt out of the crater that had formed behind the maw, and shock ran through me.

Cynwrig. It was *Cynwrig.*

No, I thought hazily, it couldn't be.

My knees gave way, and I started to topple. He caught me and swept me into his arms, holding me close to his big, warm body.

I pressed a bloody hand against his chest. Felt the furious thunder of his heart under my fingertips.

"You're real," I murmured. "You're actually here."

"That I am, my dearest Bethany."

His voice rolled over me as sweetly as any kiss, deep, warm, and familiar. It held a touch of amusement, but there were deeper emotions running in the background that had my foolish heart dancing.

I licked my lips, fighting the blackness and the rising urge to just let go and slip into unconsciousness. "But... how? Why?"

"The how doesn't matter right now. As for the why, well, did I not once vow that no one would ever take you away from me?"

"Eljin has."

"Not in any way that matters."

"But—"

"No buts. No more questions. You need to conserve your strength, and we need to get you to the hospital."

"We?" I said, my voice fading fast.

"Mathi is with me."

"The trees," I realized. "He moved the trees."

"Accelerated their growth more than moved, but yes."

"Tell him—" I stopped, struggling for the strength to finish, knowing I could die if I didn't. "Dearil. Tell him she gave me the Dearil."

And with that, unconsciousness claimed me, and I knew no more.

~

I woke to a soft, rhythmic beating. I listened for a very long time, comforted by its presence and the fact that it meant I remained alive, despite my aunt's best efforts. Beyond the small room in which I lay came the everyday noise of a hospital, though it was muted, suggesting some sort of noise shield was in place.

If there was, it had failed to counter the loud, somewhat guttural racket coming from my right. It was a sound that had haunted my nights back in the days when we were kids and shared the same room. I smiled and opened my eyes. Lugh was asleep in a chair, his big feet propped on the end of the bed, his arms crossed, and his head tilted back. A vague sense of déjà vu rolled through me, and I couldn't help but wonder how long he'd maintained his bedside vigil this time.

"And she wakes," a soft voice to my left said.

Mathi, sitting in the other chair, looked relaxed even if his features were rather drawn.

"She does," I replied with a smile. "How long was I out?"

"Three days."

"Three?" I said, surprised. "The bullet wound wasn't that bad."

"Oh, it was, but specialists were able to knit it together without too many complications. It was Dearil that caused the problems—they had to keep you under while the healers chased it through your system and repaired its effects. Apparently, had you spent a few more hours in that place without treatment, they would not have succeeded."

Meaning I really *had* been lucky. Or was it not so much

luck as the gods being unwilling to let their major player leave the game so soon?

"How did you find me?"

"I didn't. Cynwrig did."

"But... how?"

He shrugged, a small but elegant motion. "Something to do with being in tune to your unique resonance on earth and stone."

"I had no idea something like that was even possible."

"Nor I," he said dryly. "And I've known dark elves, and Cynwrig, for more years than you've been alive. I suspect there is more to the skill than what he mentioned, but he stonewalled any further questions."

"I take it he's back at the compound now?"

"Once it was certain you would survive, yes."

That he'd stayed here even that long was surprising, given the edict of no fraternization with non-elf lovers. "And my aunt? What happened to her?"

"I might have squeezed a little too hard when I wrapped her in tree limbs."

"She's dead?"

He nodded. "And currently on ice in a morgue, waiting for your recovery so that she can be taken to Borrhás."

"Thank you," I said softly.

He raised a pale eyebrow in query. "For what?"

"For saving me from the task."

"Ah."

He didn't say anything else. He didn't need to. We both knew that *that* was exactly why she'd died in the arms of those trees, though not because he feared I wouldn't do it. He knew that guilt would have haunted my dreams for years to come.

He pushed upright. "I should go ring Cynwrig. He asked to be informed the minute you woke."

My silly heart did its usual dance, and I did my best to ignore it. After all, while he'd literally moved earth, if not heaven or hell, to find me, nothing had really changed. Not his restrictions, not the danger to my heart.

"And Eljin?"

"Lugh rang him yesterday. I daresay he'd appreciate a more personal update."

I smiled. "I would, except I'm not seeing my bags or even my phone in the vicinity."

"That's because they're in IIT hands. Sgott had forensics going over them to glean clues—"

"What about my knives and the Eye?"

"Lugh's secured them. You want me to fetch a cup of tea while I'm out making the call?"

"That," Lugh said gravely as he opened his eyes, "has to be the stupidest question ever."

I laughed. "No, the stupidest question ever would be asking me if I wanted chocolate."

"Which," Mathi drawled, "you're not allowed to have until the docs do their rounds and clear you."

I glanced hopefully at my brother as Mathi left. "Meaning I can get out of here today?"

"No, because they want to keep you under observation for another twenty-four hours. But all things being equal, you should be out of here tomorrow."

"Well, good, because we've still got shit to do and an impatient old god to deal with."

He nodded. "Sgott has decided we need to attach a tracker to you, because you seem determined to keep getting yourself kidnapped."

I grinned. "It's only happened twice."

"Neither of us wish a third time."

"I don't either, I can assure you of that. But I'm not having a bug in my body that allows anyone to know my location at a moment's notice. I have a private life, and I wish it to remain that way."

He sniffed—an indication there would be discussion on this matter at a later point.

I moved said discussion onto safer subjects, and time slipped by slowly. The healers came through late afternoon, and after a thorough examination, declared me fit to leave in the morning. Which was annoying, but there was no arguing with them.

Mathi brought me in a bag of newly purchased clothes to change into, then his driver whisked all of us back to Deva, dropping Lugh home first before continuing on to the council chambers. A white van waited out the front of the building, and Dhruv Eadevane inside.

The van's driver wheeled her in this time, presented a clipboard to Eadevane to sign, and then cheerfully went back outside, not to his van but rather across to the smokers' section, no doubt to wait for the return of his trolley. As he lit up a smoke, Mathi undid the bindings and then glanced at me. "Ready?"

I crossed my arms and nodded. He flipped off the shroud, revealing the fact my aunt remained wrapped in wicked wooden fingers. He hadn't taken any chances, even after he'd crushed her.

But what I noticed, more than anything, was the fact that she looked every bit as frozen as Martha, despite the fact she would have been stored in a cool room rather than a freezer.

Borrhás had already claimed her, even if she wasn't yet physically in his possession.

I rubbed my arms and said a silent goodbye to the woman my mother had once loved so much. While her actions had betrayed me, they'd also betrayed my mom—and it had all started with Riayn's theft of the codex and the insane belief that her daughter deserved everything I had.

Mom, had she lived, would have grieved her sibling's downfall but not the manner of her death. I felt that within every inch of my being.

Once Eadevane had made a record of Riayn's receipt, Mathi tugged the shroud back over her body and secured it in place.

"Same procedure as before?"

I nodded. In truth, we could have carried her easily enough, but I just didn't want to physically touch her. "At least this time I'm not on the cusp of collapse."

"No, but I'll still have a mug of tea waiting for when you come back out."

"You really are the best friend."

"I believe that I am, though I remain determined that it once more shall become a 'friends with benefits' situation."

I laughed, kissed his cheek, then headed up in the elevator to the second floor. Once I'd reached Liadon's door, I once again opened the door, shouted down to warn them, and then leashed my aunt with air and brought her back up. Then I sent her through the open door and followed her in. The door closed behind me, and darkness briefly dominated.

Liadon's orb appeared. "Please follow us, Bethany."

Us? I scanned the area but had no sense of anyone or anything being present other than the orb through which she spoke. Did that mean the orb itself had sentience? I guess anything was possible in this world between worlds.

The orb's green light washed over my aunt's body,

easing her from my grip then guiding deeper into the tunnel. I followed and, as my eyes became more used to the darkness, realized we were on a different path, one that appeared to curve flatly around rather than dive deeper into the earth or air or whatever this place truly was. We were obviously going somewhere other than the cavern and its solitary chair.

We more we walked, the more translucent the black walls became. Once again, shadows examined me from the other side, fantastical creatures that resembled myths of old, and human figures that did not.

Eventually, we reached what looked to be a small antechamber with several doors leading off it.

"Please stop in this room and wait," Liadon said. "There is someone who wishes to speak to you."

"Borrhás?" I said, with more than a little trepidation.

She didn't answer, and her orb guided my aunt's body through the door directly ahead. It closed with a thump that reverberated softly through the room and had my heart rate accelerating. I flexed my fingers in an effort to remain calm, and looked around, though I dared not move. The room was made of the same black stone as the rest of this place, but held none of its smooth luminosity. In fact, the bits of brownish red that streaked its surface rather oddly looked like earth, making me wonder if we were closer to the surface than the journey down here had implied.

The door to my left opened, but for several seconds, nothing else happened and no one stepped through. I frowned, wondering if the door's opening was a rather ominous invitation I was supposed to accept, but as I stepped toward it, a man appeared.

A man who was tall, thickset, and handsome. A man

who had long silver hair and storm-clad eyes. A man whose aura was both powerful and thunderous.

"Who are you?" I whispered, even as instinct stirred.

He smiled. It was my smile, wrapped in male features.

I took a step back. I just couldn't help it.

This wasn't any old storm god.

This was my father.

Also by Keri Arthur

<u>Drakkon Kin Trilogy</u>

Of Steel & Scale (Nov 2024)

Of Scale & Blood (May, 2025)

Of Blood & Fire (Sept, 2025)

<u>Relic Hunters Series</u>

Crown of Shadows (Feb 2022)

Sword of Darkness (Oct 2022)

Ring of Ruin (June 2023)

Shield of Fire (March 2024)

Horn of Winter (Jan 2025)

Bia's Blade (Jan 2026)

Geitha's Tears (TBA 2026)

<u>Lizzie Grace Series</u>

Blood Kissed (May 2017)

Hell's Bell (Feb 2018)

Hunter Hunted (Aug 2018)

Demon's Dance (Feb 2019)

Wicked Wings (Oct 2019)

Deadly Vows (Jun 2020)

Magic Misled (Feb 2021)

Broken Bonds (Oct 2021)

Sorrows Song (June 2022)

Wraith's Revenge (Feb 2023)

Killer's Kiss (Oct 2023)

Shadow's End (July 2024)

.

<u>The Witch King's Crown Trilogy</u>

Blackbird Rising (Feb 2020)

Blackbird Broken (Oct 2020)

Blackbird Crowned (June 2021)

<u>Kingdoms of Earth & Air</u>

Unlit (May 2018)

Cursed (Nov 2018)

Burn (June 2019)

<u>The Outcast series</u>

City of Light (Jan 2016)

Winter Halo (Nov 2016)

The Black Tide (Dec 2017)

<u>Souls of Fire series</u>

Fireborn (July 2014)

Wicked Embers (July 2015)

Flameout (July 2016)

Ashes Reborn (Sept 2017)

<u>Dark Angels series</u>

Darkness Unbound (Sept 27th 2011)

Darkness Rising (Oct 26th 2011)

Darkness Devours (July 5th 2012)

Darkness Hunts (Nov 6th 2012)

Darkness Unmasked (June 4 2013)

Darkness Splintered (Nov 2013)

Darkness Falls (Dec 2014)

<u>Riley Jenson Guardian Series</u>

Full Moon Rising (Dec 2006)

Kissing Sin (Jan 2007)

Tempting Evil (Feb 2007)

Dangerous Games (March 2007)

Embraced by Darkness (July 2007)

The Darkest Kiss (April 2008)

Deadly Desire (March 2009)

Bound to Shadows (Oct 2009)

Moon Sworn (May 2010)

<u>Myth and Magic series</u>

Destiny Kills (Oct 2008)

Mercy Burns (March 2011)

<u>Nikki & Micheal series</u>

Dancing with the Devil (March 2001 / Aug 2013)

Hearts in Darkness Dec (2001/ Sept 2013)

Chasing the Shadows Nov (2002/Oct 2013)

Kiss the Night Goodbye (March 2004/Nov 2013)

<u>Damask Circle series</u>

Circle of Fire (Aug 2010 / Feb 2014)

Circle of Death (July 2002/March 2014)

Circle of Desire (July 2003/April 2014)

Ripple Creek series

Beneath a Rising Moon (June 2003/July 2012)

Beneath a Darkening Moon (Dec 2004/Oct 2012)

Spook Squad series

Memory Zero (June 2004/26 Aug 2014)

Generation 18 (Sept 2004/30 Sept 2014)

Penumbra (Nov 2005/29 Oct 2014)

Stand Alone Novels

Who Needs Enemies (E-book only, Sept 1 2013)

Novella

Lifemate Connections (March 2007)

Anthology Short Stories

The Mammoth Book of Vampire Romance (2008)

Wolfbane and Mistletoe--2008

Hotter than Hell--2008

About the Author

Keri Arthur, the author of the New York Times bestselling *Riley Jenson Guardian series*, has written sixty novels–35 of them with traditional publishers Random House/Penguin/Piatkus—and is now fully self-published. She's won seven Australian Romance Readers Awards for Favourite Sci-Fi, Fantasy, or Futuristic Romance & the Romance Writers of Australia RBY Award for Speculative Fiction. Her Lizzie Grace series won ARRA's Fav Continuing Romance Series in 2022 and she has in the past won The Romantic Times Career Achievement Award for Urban Fantasy. When she's not at her computer writing the next book, she can be found somewhere in the Australian countryside taking photos.

for more information:
www.keriarthur.com
keriarthurauthor@gmail.com
Buy eBooks & Audiobooks directly from Keri & save:
www.payhip.com/KeriArthur

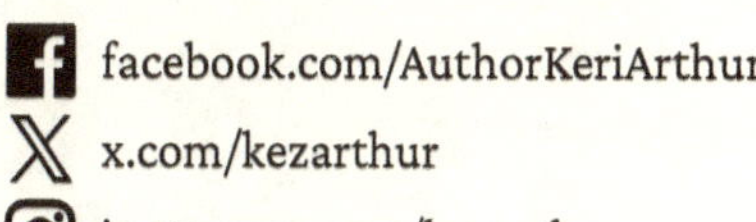

facebook.com/AuthorKeriArthur
x.com/kezarthur
instagram.com/kezarthur